PLAY DEAD

Harlan Coben

WINDSOR
PARAGON

First published 2010
by Orion
This Large Print edition published 2012
by AudioGO Ltd
by arrangement with
The Orion Publishing Group Ltd

Hardcover ISBN: 978 1 445 85958 3
Softcover ISBN: 978 1 445 85959 0

British Library Cataloguing in Publication Data available

39145031

Printed and bound in Great Britain by
MPG Books Group Limited

In memory of my father,
Carl Gerald Coben,
The best dad in the whole world

INTRODUCTION

Okay, if this is the first book of mine you're going to try, stop now. Return it. Grab another. It's okay. I'll wait.

If you're still here, please know that I haven't read *Play Dead* in at least twenty years. I didn't want to rewrite it and pass it off as a new book. I hate when authors do that. So this is, for better or worse, the exact book I wrote when I was in my early twenties, just a naïve lad working in the travel industry and wondering if I should follow my father and brother and go to (shudder) law school.

I'm hard on it, but aren't we all hard on our early stuff? Remember that essay you wrote when you were in school, the one that got you an A-plus, the one your teacher called 'inspired'—and one day you're going through your drawer and you find it and you read it and your heart sinks and you say, 'Man, what was I thinking?' That's how it is with early novels sometimes.

Over the years, I've borrowed a bit from this book—names, places, even a character or two. Close readers may recognize that and will hopefully smile.

Finally, flawed and all, I love this book. There is an energy and risk-taking in *Play Dead* that I wonder if I still have. Youth, as they say, is wasted on the young. I'm not this guy anymore, but that's okay. None of us are stagnant with our passion and our work. That's a good thing.

Enjoy
Harlan Coben

PROLOGUE

May 29, 1960

It would be a mistake to look directly at her when she spoke. Her words, he knew, could not affect him; her face and body could.

Sinclair turned and gazed out the window as she closed the door. It was a warm day, and outside he could see many of the students lazing in the sun. A few played touch football, but most just lay on blankets, couples cuddling close to one another; opened text books sprawled near them, ignored, giving the illusion at least that they had actually planned to study.

A flash of golden highlights drew his vision toward a head of blonde hair. He turned and recognized the pretty sophomore heartthrob from his two p.m. class. Half a dozen boys surrounded her, all battling for her attention, all hoping to draw her brightest smile. A stereo from one of the rooms blasted Buddy Holly's final single across the commons. Once again, he looked at the attractive blonde who was not one-tenth as striking as the brunette standing behind him.

'Well?' he asked.

From across the room, the stunning beauty nodded and then realized he was still not facing her. 'Yes.'

He sighed heavily. Below his window, a few of the boys moved away from the blonde with dejected faces, as though they had been eliminated from a competition which, he guessed, they were.

'You're sure?'

'Of course I'm sure.'

Sinclair nodded, though he could not say why he did so. 'What are you going to do?'

She stared at him in disbelief. 'Correct me if I'm wrong,' she began with blatant annoyance, 'but I think you might be involved in this, too.'

Again he nodded for no reason. On the commons, another boy had been thrown from the ring, leaving only two to battle for the blonde's potential favors. He turned his attention to the touch football game and watched a pass float slowly through the humid air. A bare-chested boy extended his hands. The ball spiraled toward him, bounced off his fingertips, and landed on the ground.

Sinclair concentrated on the game, feeling the boy's disappointment, trying his best to ignore the power she wielded over his mind. His eyes inadvertently shifted back to the blonde. A winner had been chosen. With down-turned eyes, the runner-up stood and sulked off.

'Will you please turn around and face me?'

A smile played on his lips, but he was not foolish enough to turn around, to expose himself to her devastating weapons, to allow her to cast her sensual spell over him. He looked down at the young man who had captured the blonde. Even from his window on the second floor, he could see the hunger in the boy's wide eyes as he moved in to claim his hard-sought prey. The boy kissed her. His hands began to wander.

To the victor goes the spoils.

He diverted his attention toward the library, feeling as though he were invading the young couple's privacy now that their relationship was getting somewhat physical. He put a cigarette in his mouth. 'Get out.'

'What?'

'Get out. Do whatever you please but I don't want you here anymore.'

'You can't mean that.'

'I can.' He lit the cigarette. 'I do.'

'But I was going to tell—'

'Don't tell anybody anything. It's already gone far enough.'

There was silence for a moment. When she spoke again, her voice was pleading, the tone strumming at his nerves. 'But I thought . . .'

He inhaled deeply on the cigarette as though he wanted to finish it in one puff. From the commons, he heard a sharp slap. The blonde had halted the young man's hormones as he tried to slip past the innocent groping stage. 'Obviously, you thought wrong. Now get out.'

Her voice was a whisper, 'Bastard.'

He nodded yet again, but this time he was in full agreement with what had been said. 'Just get the hell out of my office.'

'Bastard,' she repeated.

He heard her slam the door. Her high heels echoed against the wooden floor as the most beautiful woman he had ever known headed out of the ivy-covered building.

He stared out the window at nothing in particular. His vision unfocused, and his world became a blurry mass of green grass and brick buildings, his mind racing with a series of what-ifs.

Her face swam in front of his eyes. He closed his eyes, but the image did not fade.

I did the right thing. I did the right thing. I did

the—

His eyes flew open. Panic filled him. He had to find her, had to tell her he did not mean any of it. He was about to swivel his chair, turn, and run for her when he felt something metallic push against the back of his head.

A coldness rippled through him.

'Bastard.'

The gunshot shattered the still air.

CHAPTER ONE

June 17, 1989

Laura opened the window and felt the gentle tropical breeze refresh her naked body. She closed her eyes as the palm trees' cool wind made her skin tingle. The muscles in her legs still quaked. She turned back toward the bed and smiled at David, the man who had put her legs in this precarious position.

'Good morning, Mr Baskin.'

'Morning?' David repeated. He glanced at the clock on the night-table, the day silent except for the crashing of the waves outside the window. 'It's well into the afternoon, Mrs Baskin. We've spent almost the entire day in bed.'

'Are you complaining?'

'Certainly not, Mrs B.'

'Then you won't mind a little more exercise.'

'What have you got in mind?'

'How about a swim?'

'I'm spent,' he said, sprawling back against the pillows. 'I couldn't move if the bed was on fire.'

Laura smiled seductively. 'Good.'

David's eyes widened with awe as she slowly strode back toward the bed, remembering the first time he had seen that body, indeed the first time the world had seen that body. It was almost a decade ago and a full eight years before they met. Laura had debuted as a seventeen-year-old cover girl on *Cosmopolitan* wearing a—ah, who the hell saw the dress? He had been a junior at the University of Michigan at the time and he could

1

still recall the way the mouths of every member of the basketball team dropped when they saw the issue on a newsstand in Indiana before their Final Four game.

He feigned panic. 'Where are you going?'

Her smile grew. 'Back to bed.'

'Please, no.' He held up his hand to ward her off. 'You're going to put me in the hospital.'

She kept walking.

'Vitamin E,' David pleaded. 'Please.'

She did not stop.

'I'm going to scream rape.'

'Scream.'

His voice was barely audible. 'Help.'

'Relax, Baskin. I'm not going to attack you.'

His face registered disappointment. 'You're not?'

She shook her head, turned, and began to walk away.

'Wait,' he called after her. 'Where are you going?'

'To the Jacuzzi. I'd invite you to join me but I know how tired you are.'

'I feel a second wind coming on.'

'Your powers of recuperation are truly incredible.'

'Thank you, Mrs B.'

'But you're still out of shape.'

'Out of shape?' David repeated. 'Playing against the Lakers isn't this exhausting.'

'You need to work out.'

'I'll try harder, Coach, really I will. You just tell me what to do.'

'To the Jacuzzi,' Laura commanded.

She threw a silk robe over her shoulders,

partially covering the gorgeous figure that had made her the world's highest paid fashion model up until her early retirement four years ago at the tender age of twenty-three. David slid out from under the satin sheets. He was tall, a shade under six-five, which was on the short side for a pro basketball player.

Laura eyed his naked physique admiringly. 'No wonder they say you've revolutionized the game.'

'Meaning?'

'Your ass, White Lightning. Women come to the game just to watch it wiggle down court.'

'You make me feel so cheap.'

David filled the circular tub with hot water and turned on the jet streams. He uncorked a bottle of champagne and lowered his muscular frame into the water. Laura loosened her robe and began to take it off. Talk about paradise. Everything was perfect. The phone rang.

Laura rolled her eyes. 'I better get it,' she said reluctantly, retying the silk cord and heading back into the bedroom. David leaned back, his legs floating in the water. He felt the warm streams massage his aching body. His muscles were still sore from the rugged play-offs even though they had ended almost a month ago. He smiled. The Celtics had won so it was a good ache.

'Who was it?' he asked when she came back in.

'Nobody.'

'Nobody called us in Australia?'

'It was just the Peterson Group.'

'The Peterson Group?' David repeated. 'Aren't they the company you've been trying to get to carry the Svengali line in the South Pacific?'

'The same.'

'The company that you've been trying like hell to set up a meeting with for the past six months?'

'You got it.'

'So?'

'So they want to meet with me today.'

'When are you going?'

'I'm not.'

'What?'

'I told them I couldn't meet with them while I was on my honeymoon. My husband is very possessive, you know.'

David sighed out loud. 'If you blow this opportunity, your husband is going to kick your ass. Besides, how are you going to support him in the style to which he's become accustomed if you blow big opportunities?'

Laura's robe fell to the floor and, though he had seen her body so many times since they fell in love two years ago, he still found himself gaping. She joined him in the tub, her eyes closing as she released a long breath. David watched the water surround her breasts. Her black hair cascaded down her shoulders, framing that incredible European-exotic face.

'Don't worry,' she said, opening her sparkling blue eyes with flecks of silvery gray. She gave him a look that could slice through solid steel. 'I promise you'll be well taken care of.'

He shook his head. 'What happened to that business-first bitch I fell in love with?'

She placed her foot between his legs, probing. 'She loves it when you talk dirty.'

'But—'

'Forget it, Baskin. I'm not leaving my husband for even a moment.'

He groaned. 'Look, we have three weeks together. If I spend twenty-four hours a day with you for three weeks, you'll drive me nuts. For my sake, go. Go to the meeting. You're already getting to be a pest.'

'Smooth talker. No wonder I fell for you.' She leaned forward and massaged his powerful legs. 'Did I ever tell you that you have great legs?'

'Frequently. And what's with all the compliments? You trying to give me a swollen head?'

Her foot circled and then rested against him. 'Feels to me like I already have.'

He looked properly shocked. 'That kind of language from last year's businesswoman of the year? I'm stunned, ashamed . . . and aroused. Mostly aroused.'

She moved closer to him, her full firm bosoms pressing against his chest. 'Why don't we do something about that?'

'Only if you promise to meet with the Peterson Group afterwards.'

Her lips found his ear. 'Sometimes I don't understand you,' she whispered. 'Men are supposed to feel threatened by a woman with a career.'

'A very successful career,' he corrected proudly. 'And if I was one of those men, you would have dumped me long ago.'

'Never,' she said softly, 'but if I do go, how will you keep yourself occupied while I'm gone?'

He cupped her buttocks in his strong hands and lifted her on top of him, his lips inches from her nipple. 'I'll shoot some hoops,' he said. 'Like you said before, I'm out of shape. Do you promise or not?'

She felt his breath on her skin. 'Men, They're always using their bodies to get their way.'

'Promise?'

His hardness was just below her. She ached for him, her body quivering. She was barely able to nod.

He lowered her onto him. She gasped and then cried out, wrapping her arms around his head. Her body rocked back and forth, her fingers digging into his hair, clutching his face into her breasts.

*   *   *

Laura rose from the bed, gently kissed a sleeping David, and showered. She dried off her long, supple legs and began to get dressed. She wore very little make-up, just light touches around the eyes. Her olive complexion did not need cosmetics to enhance its God-given glow. Laura put on a gray professional suit bearing her Svengali label and buttoned her white blouse.

Laura was full-breasted—not what most would consider huge but when she first began modeling ten years ago, she was considered almost too large for conventional modeling, except bathing suits and face shots. Her agency wanted her to strap down her chest during runway events, which Laura would not do, comparing it to asking a man to tie his testicles against his inner thigh. But once she appeared on *Cosmo*, nothing could stop her career. Laura was the face and body you could not see enough and along with some of her colleagues like Paulina Porizkova and Elle Macpherson, she helped bring cleavage back into style—if indeed it had ever really been out.

David stirred, sat up, looked at his wife of four days. 'The transformation is complete.'

'Transformation?'

'From nymphomaniac to business barracuda. I feel sorry for this Peterson fellow.'

Laura laughed. 'I shouldn't be more than an hour or two.' She put on her earrings and walked over to kiss David. 'Will you miss me?'

'Not even a little.'

'Bastard.'

David threw back the blankets and stood. 'You kiss your mother with that mouth?'

She glanced over his rugged build, shaking her head. 'Incredible,' she muttered. 'You expect me to leave that body for even a little while?'

'Uh-oh.'

'What?'

'Problem in the transformation, Captain. I still sense a few molecules of the nymph hidden under the business facade.'

'You sense right.'

'Laura?'

'Yes?'

David took her hand. 'I love you,' he began, his eyes misting over. 'You've made me the happiest man in the world.'

She hugged him, her eyes closing. 'I love you too, David. I couldn't live without you.'

'Grow old with me, Laura, and I promise I'll always make you happy.'

'You've got a deal,' she said gently, 'and you better stick to it.'

'Forever,' he said.

Laura kissed him then, not realizing that the honeymoon was over.

*   *   *

'G'day, ma'am.'

'Good morning,' Laura answered the receptionist with a smile. They were staying at the Reef Resort Hotel in Palm's Cove, about twenty miles from Cairns, Australia. The private resort was a quiet slice of Eden, a secluded paradise overlooking the Pacific. They were hidden within the century-old palm trees and lush bush of tropical northern Australia. Take a boat out in any direction and you would be mesmerized by the rainbow colors of Australia's Great Barrier Reef, nature's most exquisite masterpiece of jagged coral and exotic marine life, an underground park that man both explored and preserved. Travel in any other direction and you would be wandering through green rain forests with cascading waterfalls, or the beginning of Australia's famed outback region. It was like no other place in the world.

The receptionist's voice was heavy with an Australian accent. 'Your taxi should be here in a few minutes, ma'am. You and your husband enjoying your stay?'

'Very much so.'

'Lovely here, ain't it?' he said proudly. Like most locals, his skin had a bronze-to-red tone from the constant exposure to the sun.

'Yes, it is.'

He began to tap his pencil on the desk, his eyes darting around the sun-drenched room. 'Do you mind if I ask you a sort of personal question, ma'am?'

'I guess so.'

8

He hesitated. 'Your husband I recognized right away from the telly. Even in these sticks we get some of your important basketball games—especially the Boston Celtics. But, ma'am, you also look a might familiar. You used to be on magazine covers or something, right?'

'Used to be,' Laura responded, amazed at both how widespread certain publications were and how far the average person's memory stretched. Four years had passed since Laura had been on any magazine covers, with the exception of last November's *Business Weekly*.

'I knew I'd seen you before. But don't worry, ma'am. I won't let on. No way I'm going to allow anyone to disturb you and Mr Baskin.'

'Thank you.'

A horn honked. 'That'll be your taxi. Have a good one.'

'I'll try.' She left the lobby, greeted the driver, and sat in the backseat. The air-conditioning was at full blast, making the car almost too cold, but against the outside sun, it was a most welcome change.

Laura settled back and watched the tropical foliage merge into a wall of green as the taxi sped toward town. Every once in a while a small building would pop out of the natural habitat but for the first ten minutes of the ride, they were only a few hidden bungalows, a post office and a grocery store. She gripped the briefcase that contained the catalogues of all the latest Svengali products. Her right leg bounced up and down restlessly.

Laura began modeling when she was only seventeen. Her *Cosmo* debut was followed by *Mademoiselle* and *Glamour* covers in the same

9

month, and then *Sports Illustrated*'s annual swimsuit issue made her name somewhat household. The cover photo was taken during a sunset on Australia's Gold Coast about 500 miles from Palm's Cove. In the photograph, Laura was wading knee-deep in the water, her eyes staring into the camera as she pulled back her wet hair. She wore a black, strapless one-piece that molded to her curves, her shoulders bare. It ended up being the best-selling issue *Sports Illustrated* ever had.

From there, the amount of covers and layouts grew along with Laura's bank account. Sometimes she appeared on the cover of the same magazine for four or five months in a row, but unlike other models, there was never a backlash to too much exposure, never an overkill. The demand did not let up.

It was all very odd. As a child, Laura had been fat and unattractive. Her classmates had teased her mercilessly about her weight, about her stringy hair, about her thick glasses, about her lack of make-up, about the way she dressed. They called her names and taunted her with the painful insults of cruel children. Their oral barrages never slackened or let up. In the cafeteria, in the hallways, in the schoolyard, in gym class, Laura's classmates were relentless in their savage attacks upon their defenseless victim.

They made her childhood a living hell.

Sometimes, a group of the really popular girls would beat her up in the woods behind the schoolyard. But physical abuse never hurt little Laura as much as the cruel words. The pain of a kick or a punch went away. The cruel words stayed with her always.

In those days, Laura would come home from school crying to a mother who had to be the most beautiful woman in the world, a woman who could not understand why her baby was not the most well-liked girl in her class. Mary Simmons Ayars had always been unusually gorgeous, had always been popular amongst her peers. Girls had always wanted to be her friend; boys had always wanted to carry her books and maybe hold her hand.

Laura's father, her dear, sweet father, would be heartbroken over the situation. It tore at Dr James Ayars's stomach to see his daughter spend every night crying alone in a corner of her darkened bedroom. He too tried to help, but what could a father do in a situation like this?

Once, when she was in seventh grade, Dr Ayars bought his daughter an expensive white dress with a designer's label on it. Laura loved the dress. She was sure that it was going to change her whole life. She looked pretty in it. Her father had said so. And Laura was going to wear it to school and all the popular girls were going to think she was pretty too. They would all like her—even Lisa Sommers, the prettiest girl in the class. They would ask her to sit with them during lunch instead of by herself in the back of the room. They would ask her to play hopscotch with them during recess instead of making her stand away from them where no one would talk to her. And who knows? Maybe Lisa Sommers would invite her to go over her house after school.

Laura was so excited she could hardly sleep. She got out of bed very early the next morning, showered, and put on her new dress. Her older sister Gloria, who was really popular with the boys, helped her get ready. Gloria brushed Laura's hair out, curled it, and even added light touches of make-up. When Gloria was finished, she stepped back and let Laura look at herself in the mirror. Laura tried to be critical but she could not help it. She looked pretty.

'Do I really look okay?' she asked her sister hopefully.

Gloria hugged her and stroked her hair. 'Just perfect.'

When she came down to breakfast, her father smiled. 'Well, well, just take a look at my little princess.'

Laura giggled happily.

'You look lovely,' her mother added.

'The boys will be fighting in the playground today,' her father chipped in.

'Do you want me to walk you to school?' Gloria asked.

'That would be great!'

Laura beamed with joy as she headed to school with Gloria. When they reached the edge of the playground, Gloria turned to her little sister and gave her another big hug. Laura felt warm and secure in her sister's arms. 'I have cheerleading practice after school,' Gloria said. 'I'll see you at home later tonight, okay?'

'Okay.'

'You can tell me all about your day then.'

Laura watched her sister start walking down the hill toward the high school. Then she turned and faced her own schoolyard. Laura could not wait to hear the comments of her peers when they saw the new Laura. Finally, it was going to be her day. With a deep breath she crossed over to where her schoolmates were playing.

The first comments came before the bell. 'Hey, look! Tubby Laura is wearing a new *tent!*' Cruel voices came from everywhere. 'She looks like a great white whale!' 'Hey, Four-Eyes Fatso, since you're wearing white, we can use you as a movie screen!'

Lisa Sommers walked up to her, looked her up and down, and then held her nose. 'You're disgusting!' she shouted with glee.

And the cruel laughter. The cruel laughter that scraped at Laura's young heart with a jagged piece of glass.

She ran home with tears streaming down her face. She put on a brave face and tried to hide the rip that Lisa Sommers had made in her new dress during recess. But parents are very sensitive to the pain of their children. When her father found the torn dress, he was furious. He burst into the principal's office to report what had happened. The girls responsible were punished.

And of course, that only made the popular girls hate her even more.

During her anguished childhood, Laura studied as hard as she could. If she could not be popular or even liked, at least she was going to be smart.

And she had Gloria. Laura often wondered if she could have survived those long years without her only two friends: her school books and her older sister Gloria. Physically, Gloria was the buxom bombshell all the high-school boys lusted after. But she was also big-hearted and kind to a fault. When Laura felt the world was coming to an end, Gloria would comfort her with warm words and warm hugs. Gloria would tell her that everything was going to be okay and for a little while, everything was. Sometimes, Gloria even canceled dates with boys just to stay home and console Laura. She took Laura to the movies or to the big department stores or the park or the roller rink or wherever. Laura knew that she had the greatest sister in the whole world. She loved Gloria very much.

That was why Laura had been devastated when Gloria ran away from home and came very close to committing suicide.

Laura's physical metamorphosis took place in the summer before her junior year of high school. Yes, she exercised. Yes, she started to wear contact lenses. Yes, she dieted (stopped eating actually). But that would not have been enough to explain the change. Those things may have accelerated the process, but the transformation would have occurred anyway. It was simply her time. She suddenly blossomed and no one in her school could believe their eyes. A little while later, a modeling agency spotted her and she was on her way.

At first, Laura could not believe she was beautiful enough to be a fashion model. Fat, ugly Laura Ayars a fashion model? Uh, uh. No way.

But Laura was neither blind nor stupid. She could look in a mirror and see for herself what everyone else was talking about. She soon got used to the whole idea of being attractive. By some queer twist of fate, the homely child had turned into a high-paid supermodel. Suddenly, people wanted to be with her, to dress like her, to be her friend. Just because she was now physically appealing, those who had wanted to spit on her and tease her thought she was something special. Laura became more than a little suspicious of people's motives.

Modeling was easy money for Laura. She made over half a million dollars when she was just eighteen. But modeling was not an occupation she particularly enjoyed. While the hours were at times grueling and tedious, the work was never what she would call demanding. There was little challenge to be found in posing for a series of snapshots. It was downright boring actually. She wanted to do something more but the world seemed to have forgotten she had a brain. It was all so ridiculous. When she was ugly with glasses, everybody thought she was a bookworm. Now that she was beautiful, everybody assumed she was an airhead.

Laura did not do many location shootings in those days—just the one in Australia and two on the French Riviera—because unlike many of her colleagues, she did not leave school. It was no simple task but she managed to finish high school and graduate from Tufts University four years later. Once Laura received her degree, she was ready to take on the fashion and cosmetics industries. The industries, however, were ill prepared for her onslaught. June 1983 marked her last cover appearance on a women's magazine as Laura retired from modeling at the ripe old age of twenty-three. She invested her substantial earnings to develop her own concept, Svengali, a company for the woman-on-the-move, blending practical, intelligent and sophisticated looks with the feminine and sensual.

The slogan: Be your own Svengali.

To say the concept caught on would be the fashion understatement of the eighties. At first, critics scoffed at the model-playing-business-tycoon's success, claiming it was just another in a series of fads that would disappear in a matter of months. Two years after promoting women's clothes and cosmetics, Laura expanded into casual shoes and fragrances. By the time she was twenty-six, Svengali had gone public with Laura the majority stockholder and Chief Executive Officer of a multi-million-dollar conglomerate.

The taxi made a sharp right turn. 'Peterson's office on the Esplanade, right, missy?'

Laura chuckled. 'Missy?'

'It's just an expression,' the cabbie explained. 'No offense meant.'

'None taken. Yes, they're on the Esplanade.'

Copycat corporations began to crop up like so many weeds beside her thriving flower. They were all vying for a slice of the profitable Svengali business, all searching for the secret of Laura's success. But like so many other bothersome weeds, they were pulled out of the corporate world before they could truly take root. Laura's close administrators knew the secret that competitors sought, the aspect that made Svengali unique: Laura. Her hard work, determination, brains, style and even warmth steered every phase of the organization. Corny, yes, but also true. The woman was the company.

Everything had gone according to plan—until she met David Baskin.

The taxi slowed to a stop. 'We're here, luv.'

*   *   *

The Pacific International Hotel in Cairns was not far from the Peterson office. It was near the center of town and across the street from the Marlin Jetty

16

where most of the sightseeing and diving boats set sail. The hotel was a popular vacation spot, ideal for those who wanted the tropics of Australia but did not crave absolute seclusion.

But the occupant of room 607 was not here to vacation.

The occupant looked out the window but did not notice or care about the breathtaking beauty. There were more important things to worry about. Awful things. Things that had to be taken care of no matter how tragic the consequence. Things so horrible that even the occupant of room 607 had no idea of their full scope.

And they had to be taken care of now.

The occupant turned away from the breathtaking view that past visitors had gazed upon for countless hours and walked toward the phone. There had been very little time to plan. Now, as the occupant lifted the receiver, there was a moment to wonder if there was another option left open.

No. There was no other option.

The occupant lifted the phone and dialed.

'Reef Resort. Can I help you?'

The occupant swallowed away the terror. 'David Baskin please.'

*   *   *

The meeting droned on steadily. The first two hours had moved smoothly enough and the deal was nearly set. But now they were getting down to details and, as usual, a few snags tangled up the works. Laura eyed her watch and realized she was going to be back later than she originally anticipated. She asked if she could use a phone, excused herself and dialed

17

the hotel. When there was no answer in their room, she asked to be transferred to the front desk. The same receptionist was on duty.

'Your husband went out a few minutes ago,' he informed her. 'He left a note for me to give you.'

'Could you read it to me?'

'Of course. Would you hold on a second?'

She heard the phone being dropped heavily to the wooden desk and then the sounds of somebody stumbling around echoed into the receiver. 'Here it is.' Paper was unfolded. Hesitation. 'It's . . . it's rather personal, Mrs Baskin.'

'That's okay.'

'You still want me to read it?'

'You already have,' Laura replied.

'True enough.' He paused and then, reluctantly, he read David's words. 'Stepped out for moment. Should be right back.' The receptionist cleared his throat before continuing. 'Black garter belt and stockings are on bed. Put them on and wait for me . . . my, uh, my little sex kitten.'

Laura stifled a laugh. 'Thank you very much. Would you mind giving my husband a message when he gets back?'

'I'd rather not, ma'am. He's rather large, you know.'

This time she did laugh. 'No, nothing like that. Just tell him I'll be back a little later than originally planned.'

His voice was relieved. 'I can do that,' he said. 'Yeah, sure, no worries.'

Laura replaced the receiver, took a deep breath, and returned to the negotiating table.

* * *

Two hours later, the deal was set. The few minor obstacles had been removed and soon, department stores throughout Australia and New Zealand would be inundated with Svengali products, maybe even before the Christmas season. Laura sat back in the taxi's plush cushion and smiled.

So much for business.

By the time the taxi dropped her in front of the hotel, night was beginning to settle in, snatching the spare rays of the sun that still lighted Palm's Cove. But Laura was not tired. Business rejuvenated her—business and the thought that David was only a few feet from where she now stood, waiting for her . . .

'Mrs Baskin?'

It was the receptionist. She walked toward the desk with a bright smile.

'Another note from your husband.'

'Would you like to read this one to me too?' she asked.

He laughed and handed her an envelope. 'I think you can handle this one all by yourself, thanks anyway.'

'Thank you.' She opened the sealed envelope and read.

LAURA,
BE BACK SOON. WENT FOR A SWIM
IN THE OCEAN. I WILL LOVE YOU
FOREVER. ALWAYS REMEMBER THAT.
DAVID

Puzzled, Laura folded the note and went to the room.

*　　　*　　　*

19

The black stockings were on the bed.

Laura slid them over her ankles and then slowly rolled them up her slender legs. She unbuttoned her blouse and removed it. Her hands reached behind her back and unclasped her lace brassiere. It fell forward and slipped down her arms.

She strapped on the garter belt and attached the stockings. She stood and looked in the mirror. Then she did what few people who beheld such a magnificent sight would do.

She laughed.

That man has made me completely loony, she thought with a shake of her head, remembering what a different person she had been before David entered her life two years ago. Thinking back, Laura recalled that she and David did not hit it off right away—to be more precise, their first meeting had been about as romantic as a two-car accident.

They had met on a humid Boston night in July of 1986 at a gala black-tie party for the Boston Pops. The place was packed. Everyone who was anyone in Boston society was there.

Laura hated such events. She especially hated the reason she attended them (she felt she had to) and she hated the phony smiles and the phony lines everyone handed out. Even worse were the men who showed up for such functions—cocky, persistent and overbearing neo-playboys with egos that were nearly as vast as their insecurities. She had been hit on so many times at these things she felt like a stubborn nail jutting out of a piece of plywood. Over the years, her manner of dealing with such approaches began to border on the rude. But at times, only a cutting phrase could slow down

20

a charging bull.

Laura had built a wall around herself—more like a fortress with a shark-infested moat. She also knew that she was developing a reputation of being a 'cold bitch,' a woman who 'knew she was hot and thought her shit didn't stink.' This reputation was well-known and also, in her mind, untrue. But Laura did little to discourage it since it helped keep some of the animals at bay.

At this particular party, she had been standing a few yards away from the buffet table, watching with disbelief as the well-dressed patrons attacked the food like the poor in Bangladesh. That was when she turned away and bumped into David.

'Excuse me,' she said without looking at the man.

'Grim sight,' David replied, motioning toward the ravenous savages at the buffet table. 'Welcome to Day of the Locust.'

She nodded and began to walk away.

'Wait a minute,' David called after. 'I don't mean to sound like a groupie but aren't you Laura Ayars?'

'Yes, I am.'

'Allow me to introduce myself. My name is David Baskin.'

'The basketball player?'

'The same. Are you a basketball fan, Miss Ayars?'

'Not in the least bit, but it would be impossible to live in Boston and not hear your name mentioned.'

'I blush in modesty.'

'I'm sure you do. If you'll excuse me . . .'

'The brush-off already? Before you go, Miss Ayars, may I just say that you look enchanting this evening.'

21

Her voice was tainted with sarcasm. 'Original line, Mr Baskin.'

'David,' he replied calmly. 'And for the record, I'm not handing out lines.' He paused. 'May I ask why you don't like basketball?'

Typical jock, Laura thought. He thinks that the planet Earth could not possibly spin without grown men grunting and sweating while running back and forth in a meaningless wave. This guy shouldn't take long to get rid of. He's probably not used to carrying on a conversation that involves complete sentences.

'It's inconceivable, isn't it?' she began. 'I mean, it must be impossible for you to imagine a thinking person who doesn't enjoy watching illiterate men whose brain capacity is in adverse proportion to their height try to jam a spherical object through a metallic circle.'

His expression did not change. 'Aren't we a little cranky today?' he replied. 'And all those big words. Very impressive. Have you ever been to the Boston Garden to watch the Celtics?'

Laura shook her head in mock self-pity. 'I guess I haven't really lived yet.' She looked at her watch but did not even see the time. 'My, my, time does fly. I have enjoyed this little chat, but I really must be go—'

'We don't have to talk about basketball, you know.'

The sarcasm was still there. 'We don't?'

His smile remained unfazed. 'No, we don't. Believe it or not, I'm capable of discussing matters of greater substance: economics, politics, peace in the Middle East—you name it.' He snapped his fingers and his smile grew. 'I have an idea. Why don't we talk about something really intellectual—like modeling! But no. I mean, it would be impossible for you to imagine a thinking person who doesn't enjoy watching people whose brain size is in direct proportion to their body-fat level try to look as much like a mannequin as humanly possible.'

For a moment their eyes met, and then Laura lowered her head. When she looked up again, David was smiling in such a way as to soften his words.

'Lighten up, Laura,' he said gently, an expression she would hear so many times in the future. 'I wasn't trying to do anything but talk to you. I've read a lot about you and Svengali—yes, some basketball players can indeed read—and I thought you would be an interesting person to meet. I wasn't looking for anything else but with your looks, I'm sure you think this is just another line. And I don't blame you. Maybe it is.'

He bowed slightly and began to turn. 'I won't bother you anymore. Enjoy the party.'

Laura watched him walk away, hating herself for being so defensive, for not trusting the motives of even one man. He had spoken her mind as though her forehead was a window in which he could see her thoughts. But even so, this man would be all wrong for her. A jock? Forget it. She decided simply to push David Baskin from her mind. Strangely, she couldn't do it.

Back in Australia, a near-naked Laura leaned over and reached for the clock.

10:15 p.m.

The sound of the bush penetrated through the darkness that had blanketed her window. If it were anybody else but David, she would be seriously worried. But David was a superb swimmer, a near-Olympic participant, and more to the point, he was masterfully unpredictable, always throwing a surprise at those who knew him, always tossing an unexpected curve into life. And this was one of the reasons the sports media loved him so. He was the player whose locker the reporters rushed to after a game, the man with the perfect quote for the morning edition. He was the polite-yet-cocky superstar who always managed to live up to his off-color predictions.

Laura threw a blanket over her body. The night air was cool, tingling her nerves as it gently caressed her skin. Hours came and left, taking with them the excuses that had staved off Laura's panic and dread.

*   *   *

She got dressed at half past midnight and headed down to the lobby. The same receptionist was still on duty and Laura wondered if he ever slept.

'Excuse me,' she began, 'have you seen my husband?'

'Mr Baskin? No, ma'am. Haven't seen the mate since he went swimming.'

'Did he say anything to you before he left?'

'Not a peep, ma'am. He just handed me the key and that note I gave you. He didn't even look up.' The receptionist saw the worried look on her face. 'Has he not shown up yet?'

'No, he hasn't.'

'Well, now, I wouldn't worry too much about that. Your mate has got quite a reputation in the

24

papers of being a bit of a wild one. He'll be back by morning.'

'I'm sure you're right,' she said, unconvinced. She considered looking for him but realized it would serve no real purpose except to satisfy her need to—in her mind at least—do something beside sit in their suite. But the reality was that a lone American strolling through the Australian bush in complete darkness hardly constituted a competent rescue party. More likely, David would come home while she was busy getting lost in the wilds.

Laura went back to her room, firm in the decision that she would not panic until morning.

*   *   *

When the room's digital clock read 7:00 a.m., Laura officially began to panic.

CHAPTER TWO

'The call will be put through in a moment, ma'am.'

'Thank you.'

Laura sat back and stared at the telephone. With the time difference, it was nearly nine p.m. yesterday in Boston and she wondered if T.C. was going to be home yet. His shift normally ended at a little past eight and she knew that he often stayed a lot later.

Laura's hands trembled, her face and eyes harried and swollen from the torment of the seemingly endless night she had just endured. She

25

glanced out the window and saw the sun shining. The bright rays and the clock beside her bed were the only clear signs that last night had turned into today, that the night had indeed given way to morning. But for Laura, the night continued, her heart squeezed in a nightmare that would not move on.

She closed her eyes for a moment and remembered the second time David Baskin had entered her life. It was three weeks after their initial encounter at the Boston Pops, three weeks in which their short conversation constantly jabbed at the back of her mind like a dull ache, never all-consuming but still bothersome enough to make its presence felt whenever she tried to forget about it.

Subconsciously (or so she would claim), Laura began to skim through a few of the many articles about him. Though the press could not shovel enough praise about David's talent, sportsmanship and positive influence on the game, Laura was more fascinated (well, not fascinated, she told herself; more like interested) by the few sprinkles of information about his upbringing, his academic prowess at the University of Michigan, his time spent in Europe as a Rhodes Scholar and his selfless work with the handicapped. She found herself feeling oddly guilty about the way she had treated him, as though she had somehow to even the score or stay forever in his debt. It might be nice to see him again, she told herself, and maybe just apologize so he would see that she wasn't really a cold person.

That was when she began to accept invitations to functions and gala parties that he was likely to attend. She, of course, would never admit that David Baskin had anything to do with her social calendar. It was just coincidence, she would claim. Svengali needed her exposure at these events and if David Baskin happened to be there, well, life sometimes works that way.

But to her inward dismay, David only made token appearances, smiling broadly as people gathered around him to shake his hand and slap his back. Laura thought she noted a wince or small look of repulsion on his face as these phonies reached out to touch him, but it may just have been her imagination.

David never approached her, never so much as glanced her way. Finally, Laura decided to do something truly childish. Spotting him by the bar at one such event, she took what has been termed by teenage girls as a 'strategic walk'—i.e., a casual stroll where she would 'accidentally' bump into him. It worked. He spotted her. He smiled cordially at her (or was there something else in the smile? like mockery?) and then moved on without a word. Her heart sank.

Laura returned to her office, fuming. She felt embarrassed at her behavior, upset she was acting like a high-school girl with a crush on the football captain. She could not understand why she felt this need to confront him again. Was it simply because he had bested her, made her reconsider her normal behavior and defense mechanisms? Or was there an attraction—albeit dormant—causing this static electricity in her brain? True, he was not bad-looking, rather handsome in a non-conventional way. His face and body were dark and strong like a lumberjack on a lite beer commercial.

His green eyes were warm and friendly, his thick hair groomed short. Actually, he was quite attractive, more natural and real-looking than the supposedly gorgeous male models she used to work with.

But even if Baskin wasn't a typical, self-centered, immature jock, he was nonetheless a jock, hero-worshipped by adolescents of all ages, a man who played a child's game as a career. Undoubtedly, he was playboy-athlete, surrounded by airy bimbos who sought the spotlight and wanted to get on television with the other wives in the stands. And Laura wanted nothing less than to be considered another bimbo, another conquest by the immortal Celtic great. Clearly, David Baskin was the very antithesis of what she would want in a man, if indeed she had been interested in a relationship at all. Right now, there was no room for a man. Svengali was her ambition, her life-long dream and partner.

Laura tilted her chair back and put her feet on her desk. Her right leg shook as it always did when she was somehow uptight or in deep thought. Her father had the same annoying habit. They both drove people crazy because the movement was no mere quiver—it was a full-fledged shake. When she or her dad really got that right leg going, the chair, the desk, the very room would vibrate under the leg's tenacious assault. For those in the area, it was an unnerving spectacle, one that Laura had tried unsuccessfully to stop herself from doing.

The vibrations her leg caused eventually knocked her pencil-holder off the desk, but she did not stop to pick it up. After a few more minutes of leg shaking, Laura managed to dismiss the basketball

28

player from her mind as Marty Tribble, her Director of Marketing, entered her office with a large smile.

Marty Tribble was not a man who smiled all that often during working hours. Laura watched him confidently stroll into her office, his hand pushing away the few strands of gray hair that had lasted the five decades of his life, his face beaming like a Little Leaguer after his first homerun.

'We've just made the advertising coup of the year,' Marty exclaimed.

Laura had never seen him act like this before. Marty Tribble had worked with Laura from Svengali's conception. He was a serious-faced executive, a down-to-earth conservative in a rather liberal, flighty business. His sense of humor was famous around the office only because no one believed he had one. Crack a joke in front of ol' Marty and you'd see the same reaction if you tickled a file cabinet. He was the office rock, not a man who became excited over trivialities.

'Which product?' she asked.

'Our new line.'

'The casual walking shoes and sport sneakers?'

'The same.'

Her eyes met his and she smiled. 'Sit down and start talking.'

The plodding Marty (he wanted to be called Martin but everyone called him Marty for that very reason) practically leaped into the chair, his legs showing a spryness not yet seen in the downtown Svengali headquarters.

'We're going to run a national advertising campaign on television starting this fall. We'll introduce the entire line to the public.'

29

Laura waited for him to say more, but he didn't. He just continued to smile, looking like a game-show host who was trying to build suspense by not revealing the answer until after the last commercial. 'Marty, that's hardly an earth-shattering announcement.'

He leaned forward and spoke slowly. 'It is when your spokesman is the sport's idol of the decade. It becomes even more earth-shattering when that sport's idol has never endorsed a product before.'

'Who?'

'David Baskin, alias White Lightning, the Boston Celtics superstar and three-time league MVP.'

His name struck her like a sharp slap. 'Baskin?'

'You heard of him?'

'Of course, but you say he's never done any endorsing before?'

'Only those ads for handicapped children.'

'Then why us?'

Marty Tribble shrugged. 'Beats the hell out of me, but Laura, all we have to do is throw a good advertising blitz during basketball games in the fall and David Baskin's broad shoulders will carry Svengali's sneakers to the top of the sporting world. He'll give us instant recognition and legitimacy in the market. It can't miss. I'm telling you the public loves him.'

'So what's our next step?'

He reached into his breast pocket where he neatly kept his matching Cross gold pen and pencil. His fingers plucked out two tickets.

'You and I are going to the Boston Garden tonight.'

'What?'

'We're going to watch the Celtics play the

30

Nuggets. The contracts are to be signed afterwards.'

'So why do we have to go to the game?'

Again he shrugged. 'I don't know. For some strange reason, Baskin himself insisted on it. He said it would be good for your soul or something.'

'You're kidding.'

He shook his head. 'It's part of the deal.'

'Wait a minute. Are you trying to tell me that if I don't go to this game—'

'Then the deal is off. Right.'

Laura tilted her chair back again, her fingers interlocked, her elbows resting against the arm-rests. Her right leg started doing its gyrating dance of annoyance again. Slowly, a smile formed on her lips. She began to nod her head, quietly chuckling to herself.

Marty eyed her worriedly. 'So, Laura, what do you say?'

For a moment, the room was still. Then Laura turned her eyes toward her Director of Marketing.

'It's game time.'

*   *   *

The Boston Garden experience had been nothing short of shocking. When Laura first entered the old eyesore in North Station, she was skeptical. The Garden? This decrepit old building was the Boston Garden? It looked more like the Boston Penitentiary. Most arenas in the country were modern glass and chrome towers, shining and sleek with air-conditioning and cushioned seats. But not the Garden. The Celtics' home was a run-down, seedy hunk of cement with a beer-stale odor and an oppressive heat all its own. The splintered

31

seats were hard, broken, uncomfortable. Glancing around her, Laura was reminded more of a Dickens novel than a sporting event.

But then she watched the thousands of anxious fans fill the Garden like parishioners on Christmas morning. To them, the climate was utopian, the aroma was that of roses, the seating arrangements plush and luxurious. It was as if these people thrived on escaping the niceties of the day to delve into the more perfect dwelling of their Celtics. Here was the Boston Garden, the zenith of the world's millions of college, high-school, backyard and driveway basketball courts, the place that countless children had imagined hitting the winning jump shot, grabbing the winning rebound. She looked up at the rusted rafters and saw the championship banners and retired numbers standing proudly like medals on a general's chest. Silly as it sounded, this place was history, as much a part of Boston as the Bunker Hill Monument and Paul Revere's house, but there was one big difference: the Celtics were living history, constantly changing, consistently unpredictable, always coddled and loved by their fair city.

The frenzied crowd cheered when the players took the floor for warm-ups. Laura spotted David immediately. From her seat in the third row, she tried to catch his eye but it was as if he were alone on the parquet floor, completely oblivious to the thousands who surrounded him. His eyes were those of a man possessed, of a man on a mission from which he could not be diverted. But Laura thought she also noted a peacefulness in the bright green, the calmness of a man who was where he wanted to be.

Next: the opening tap.

Laura's skepticism dissolved away slowly, like acid eating through a steel chain. By the end of the first quarter, she found herself smiling. Then laughing. Then cheering. Finally awestruck. When she turned around and gave the man behind her a 'high five,' she had officially been converted. The basketball game reminded her of the first time she had been to the New York Ballet at Lincoln Center as a wide-eyed five-year-old girl. There was a similar artistry to the basketball players' movements, like a complicated, well-choreographed dance interrupted by unpredictable obstacles that only made the spectacle all the more fantastic to the eye.

And David was the principal dancer.

She immediately understood the sweeping praise. David was poetry in motion, diving, leaping, swooping, spinning, twisting, chasing, ducking, pirouetting. There was a tenacious, aggressive gracefulness to his movements. One moment he was the cool floor leader, the next a daredevil trying the impossible like some comic-book hero. He would drive toward the basket only to have a man cut him off and then, like a true artist, he created, often in mid-air. When he shot, his eyes would focus on the rim with a concentration so strong she was sure the backboard would shatter. He had a sixth sense on the court, never looking where he passed, never glancing at the ball on his fingertips. When he dribbled, it was like the ball was part of him, just an extension of his arm that had been there since birth.

And then the finale.

Scant seconds remained, the outcome very

much in doubt. The beloved boys from Beantown were down by one point. A man wearing the familiar Celtics green and white passed the ball to David. Two men from the enemy camp covered him like a blanket. One second remained. David turned and launched his unique, high-arching, fade-away jumpshot. The shot lofted the orange sphere impossibly high, heading for its target from an impossible angle. The crowd stood in unison. Laura's pulse raced as she watched the ball begin its descent, the game and hearts of the crowd riding on its slow movement toward the basket. A buzzer sounded. The ball gently kissed the top of the glass backboard, and then the bottom of the net danced as the ball went through for two points. The crowd screamed. Laura screamed.

The Celtics had won another game.

'Telephone is ringing, Mrs Baskin,' the Australian accent said.

'Thank you.'

Laura rolled over on her stomach, the phone gripped tightly in her hand. She wondered if it had been during that fade-away jumpshot that she first had begun to fall in love with David. She heard a click and the ring that originated in Boston traveled halfway around the planet to the small town of Palm's Cove.

On the third ring, the receiver on the other end was lifted. A voice came through the static-filled wire.

'Hello?'

'T.C.?'

'Laura? Is that you? How's the honeymoon?'

'Listen, T.C., I need to talk to you.'

'What's up?'

34

She quickly recounted the past day's events. T.C. listened without interrupting and, like Laura knew he would, he immediately took control.

'Have you called the local police?' T.C. asked her.

'Yes.'

'Good. I'll catch the next plane out of here. Captain said I'm due for a vacation anyhow.'

'Thanks, T.C.'

'One more thing: stress to the police the importance of keeping this quiet. The last thing you need is a plane-load of reporters pounding on your door.'

'Okay.'

'Laura?'

'Yes?'

He heard the strain in her voice. 'He'll be all right.'

She hesitated, almost afraid to speak her mind. 'I'm not so sure. Suppose he has one of his . . .' The words stayed in her throat, the thought too unpleasant to be spoken. But T.C. was one of the few people David trusted. He would understand what she was talking about.

'T.C. is my closest friend,' David had said to her last year. 'I know he's rough around the edges and I know you don't easily trust, but when there's real trouble, T.C. is the one to call.'

'What about your family?' Laura had asked him.

David shrugged. 'I only have my older brother.'

'What about him? You never mention him.'

'We don't talk.'

'But he's your brother.'

'I know.'

'So why don't you two talk?'

'It's a long story,' David said. 'We had a problem. It's all in the past now.'

'So why don't you call him?'

'I will. But not yet. It's not time.'

Not time? Laura had not understood. She still didn't.

'Just get here fast, T.C.,' she said now, her voice quivering. 'Please.'

'I'm on my way.'

In Boston, Massachusetts, home of the beloved Celtics, T.C. placed the phone receiver back in its cradle. He glanced down at his dinner—a Burger King Whopper and fries he had picked up on the drive home—and decided he was no longer hungry. He reached for a cigar and lit it with a Bic lighter. Then he picked up the phone again and dialed. When the receiver was lifted on the other end, he spoke three words:

'She just called.'

*   *   *

Twenty-seven hours passed. Terry Conroy, known to his friends as T.C., a nickname given to him by David Baskin, fastened his seat belt as Qantas flight 008 made its final approach before landing in Cairns, Australia. It had been a long journey, beginning with an American Airlines flight from Logan to LAX then from Los Angeles to Honolulu with Qantas, and finally, the flight from Honolulu to Cairns. Almost twenty hours in the air.

T.C. pushed open his shade and looked down. The water of the southern Pacific was unlike any other he had ever beheld. The color was not merely blue. Describing it as blue would be like describing

Michelangelo's *Pietà* as a piece of marble. It was so much more than simply blue, too blue really, gleaming in its purity. T.C. was sure he could see straight through the miles-deep water right to the bottom. Small islands dotted the ocean's canvas, beautiful landscapes formed from the rainbow corals of the Great Barrier Reef.

He loosened his seat belt because his newly formed gut was getting crunched. Too much junk food. He looked down at his rolls of flesh and shook his head. He was starting to get fat. Ah, face facts. For a guy under thirty he was already too flabby. Maybe he would start an exercise program when he got back to Boston.

Sure, right. And maybe he'd meet an honest politician.

He threw his back against his seat.

How did you know, David? How did you know for sure?

T.C. had turned twenty-nine last week, the same age as David. They had been roommates at the University of Michigan for four years, best friends, amigos, partners, equals; and yet David had always awed him. It wasn't his basketball ability—awesome as it was—that set him apart. It was the man, the man who seemed to let problems and unhappiness run over him like small ripples of water. Most felt David was carefree because he had everything going for him, that he had never known real hardship or conflict, but T.C. knew that was bullshit, that David had survived the early wallops to end up on top, that he still had his moments of private hell that fame and fortune could not counter.

'It's not real, T.C.,' David had told him during

37

his rookie season with the Celtics.

'What's not?'

'The fame. The girls. The groupies. The adulation. The people who hang around you because you're famous. You can't let it mean anything.'

'Well, then what is?'

'The game,' he replied, his eyes lighting up. 'The feeling on the court. The competition. The moment when the game is on the line. A perfect pass. A fade-away jumpshot. A dunk. A clean block. That's what's it's all about, T.C.'

And years later, T.C. thought now, Laura was put on the top of that list.

The Boeing 747 landed with a thump and began to coast towards the small terminal building. David. T.C. shook his head, thinking he'd seen just about everything in the last few years but this . . . Hell, it wasn't his place to ask a lot of questions. It was his place to help. Explanations would come later.

He filled out the quarantine form, grabbed his suitcase off the rotating carousel, passed through customs and walked to the waiting area where Laura said she would meet him. The electronic doors slid open and T.C. found himself in front of a wall of faces. To his right, chauffeurs held up signs with names printed in capital letters. On the left, local guides wore shorts and T-shirts, their signs stating the name of a hotel or tour group. T.C.'s eyes searched for Laura.

A minute later, he spotted her.

T.C. felt something sharp slice through his stomach. Laura was still the most beautiful woman he had ever seen, still ravishing enough to knock any man to his knees, but David's disappearance had crawled all over her and attacked with a vengeance. She was practically unrecognizable. Her high cheekbones were sunken. Her eyes were dark circles staring out with bewilderment and fear, their bright blue color terrifyingly dim.

She ran to him and he hugged her reassuringly.

'Anything new?' he asked, but the answer was all over her face.

She shook her head. 'It's been two days, T.C. Where could he be?'

'We'll find him,' he said, wishing he was as confident as he sounded. He took her hand. There was no reason to stall the investigation. He might as well dive right in. 'But let me ask you something, Laura. Before David vanished, did he have—?'

'No,' she interrupted quickly, not wanting to hear that word. 'Not in more than eight months.'

'Good. Now where can I find the officer in charge of the investigation?'

'Palm's Cove only has two officers. The sheriff is waiting for you at his office.'

Forty minutes later, the taxi pulled up in front of a wooden building marked 'Town Hall' and 'General Store.' There were no other buildings on the street. The lone structure looked like something out of Petticoat Junction, except for the surrounding lush tropics.

'Listen, Laura, I think it might be best if I speak to the sheriff alone.'

'Why?'

'Look at this place,' he said. 'It looks like something out of *Bonanza*, for chrissake. I doubt the sheriff here is much of a progressive thinker. Out here, women's lib is probably a concept for the distant future. He may be more willing to talk if I speak to him alone, cop-to-cop sort of thing.'

'But—'

'I'll let you know the moment I learn anything.'

She hesitated. 'If you think it's best . . .'

'I do. Just wait out here, okay?'

She nodded mechanically, her eyes wet and glassy. T.C. got out of the car and walked down the path. His head was down, his eyes finding the weeds popping through the cracks in the worn cement. He raised his line of vision and stared at the building. It was old, the paint chipped, the structure looking as if a good push would topple it over. T.C. wondered if it was age or the climate of the tropics that made the wood look so weathered. Probably both.

The front door was open. T.C. leaned his head through the frame.

'May I come in?' he asked.

The Australian accent was the first he had heard since landing. 'You Inspector Conroy?'

'That's right.'

'Graham Rowe,' the man said, standing. 'I'm sheriff of this town.'

While his words were those of a sheriff in a cheap Western, his accent and size were not. Graham Rowe was huge, a mountain of a man who looked like Grizzly Adams or some professional wrestler. A gray-blonde beard captured his entire face, his hazel eyes serious and piercing. His green uniform with shorts made him resemble an overgrown Boy Scout, but T.C. wasn't suicidal so he kept that thought to himself. A bushwhacker hat with its right side tilted up rested on his head. A rather large gun and an equally large knife adorned his belt. His skin was leathery and lined but not aged. T.C. guessed him to be in his mid-forties.

'Call me Graham,' he said, extending a giant hand/paw. T.C. shook it. It was like shaking hands with a catcher's mitt.

'They call me T.C.'

'You must be tired after that long flight, T.C.'

'I slept on the plane,' he said. 'What can you tell me about your investigation?'

'Kind of anxious, huh?'

'He's my best friend.'

Graham moved back behind his desk and beckoned T.C. to take a seat. The room was bare except for a twirling fan and the many rifles hung on the walls. A small holding cell was in the left-hand corner.

'Not much really,' the sheriff began. 'David Baskin left a note for his wife saying he was going swimming, and he hasn't been seen since. I questioned the lifeguard at the hotel. He remembers seeing Baskin shooting baskets by himself at around three in the afternoon. Two hours later, he saw Baskin walking up the beach heading north.'

'Then David didn't go for a swim?'

Graham shrugged. 'He might have. There are swimming areas all over the place but there's no supervision where he was walking and the current is mighty powerful.'

'David's a great swimmer.'

'So his missus tells me, but I've lived here all my life and I can tell you when one of those damn currents wants to drag you down, there's not much a man can do but drown.'

'Have you begun a search for the body?'

Graham nodded his head. 'Sure have, but not a trace of the lad so far.'

41

'If he had drowned, should the body have shown up by now?'

'Normally, yes, but mate, this is northern Australia. More things could happen to a man in that ocean than on your subways. He could have washed up on one of the small unmanned islands or gotten snared on jagged coral in the Barrier Reef or been eaten by Lord-knows-what. Any one of a million things could have happened to him.'

'What's your theory, Graham?'

The large Aussie stood and crossed the room. 'Coffee?'

'No, thanks.'

'In this heat, I don't blame you. How about a Coke?'

'Sounds good.'

Graham reached into a small refrigerator behind his desk and took out two bottles, handing one to T.C.

'You say you're mates with this Baskin, right?'

'For many years.'

'Do you think you can be objective?'

'I think so.'

The sheriff sat back down with a long sigh. 'T.C., I'm just a sheriff of a small, friendly community. That's the way I like it. Nice, quiet, peaceful. You know what I mean?'

T.C. nodded.

'I'm not looking to be a big hero. I don't want no glory and I don't like complicated cases like you mates in Boston handle. You know what I'm saying?'

'Sure.'

'Now, being a simple man, let me tell you how I see it. I don't think Baskin drowned.'

'You don't?'

Graham shook his head. 'I may have made a nice speech about all the possibilities for a corpse in the Pacific but the truth is almost always much simpler. If he had drowned, his body should have been here by now. Not one hundred percent of the time, mind you, but almost.'

'What then?'

The large man took a swig of Coke. 'Could he have developed a classic case of cold feet? It wouldn't be the first time a mate has run away on his honeymoon. Almost did it myself once.'

T.C.'s answer was a grin. 'Have you taken a good look at his wife?'

Graham whistled his appreciation. 'Never seen anything like that in my life, mate. My eyes almost popped out of the sockets.' He took another sip of his Coke, lowered the bottle, wiped his mouth with a forearm the size of an oak tree. 'I guess we can assume he's not on the run. But let me ask you something else, T.C. I've been doing some research on this Baskin—part of the job, you know—and he seems to be quite the joker. Any chance he's just out for a last kick or something?'

'And worry her like this? It wouldn't be like him, Graham.'

'Well, I've radioed all the nearby towns and the coast guard. None of them wants a lot of press around either so they'll keep mum. Other than that, I'm not sure there's much we can do.'

'I'd like to ask a favor, Graham.'

'Name it.'

'I know I'm out of my jurisdiction, but I'd like to help out with the investigation if I can. David Baskin is my best friend and I know him better—'

43

'Whoa, whoa, slow down there,' Graham interrupted. The sheriff stood. His gaze traveled north to south, from T.C.'s face to his scuffed-up Thom McCann loafers. He took out a handkerchief and dabbed the sweat on his forehead. 'I'm undermanned as it is,' he continued slowly, 'and I guess it wouldn't hurt any to deputize you for this case.' He pulled out a sheet of paper and handed it to T.C. 'Here's a list of places I want you to call. Report back to me if you hear anything.'

'Thanks. I really appreciate this.'

'No worries. But let me ask you one last question: is there anything wrong with Baskin?'

T.C. felt his pulse begin to pound in his throat. Memories flashed across his brain. 'Wrong?'

'Yeah, you know, does he have any injuries, a bad heart or something?'

'Not that I know of,' T.C. lied.

'And who would know better?' Graham grinned. 'After all, you're his best mate.'

T.C.'s eyes met the big sheriff's for a brief moment. They revealed nothing.

*   *   *

Laura and T.C. remained silent during the short ride back to the hotel. T.C. checked in, left his bags at the front desk, and followed Laura to the honeymoon suite.

'So what do we do now, T.C.?'

He drew in a deep breath. He scratched his head, his fingertips wading through the thinness of the strands as they made their way to his scalp. No gray hairs yet, he thought, though he hoped his hair would last long enough to develop some. He

44

doubted it. The light brown strands were quickly losing ground, his forehead taking over his scalp like Sherman through Atlanta.

T.C. looked out the window of the suite and felt in his pocket for a cigar. None were there.

'Call around. Search the area.'

Laura's voice was surprisingly steady and matter-of-fact. 'By calling around, you mean the morgues.'

'Morgues, hospitals—that kind of thing.'

'And by searching the area, you mean the ocean and beaches to see if David's body has washed up.'

He nodded.

Laura walked over to the telephone. 'Do you want to change or rest up before we get started? You look like hell.'

He turned and smiled. 'I just got off a long flight. What's your excuse?'

'I'm not exactly ready for a cover shot, huh?'

'You'd still put the competition to shame.'

'Thanks. Now do me a favor.'

'Name it.'

'Go down to the lobby and buy a couple of boxes of their finest cheap cigars.'

'Huh?'

She lifted the receiver. 'Stack up your supplies. We might be here a while.'

*　　　*　　　*

First, she called the morgues.

Laura had purposely wanted to call them first, to get them out of the way as fast as possible. Better to dash madly through the valley of the shadow of death than to take a casual stroll. Her head sat on a guillotine from the moment the coroner said, 'Hold

45

on a moment, luv,' until a hellish decade later—or so it seemed—when he came back on to say, 'No one fitting that description here.' Then relief would flood her veins for a few seconds before T.C. gave her the next number to dial.

The room reeked of cigar stench like a poker table on the boy's night to play, but Laura did not notice. She felt trapped, suffocated—not by the smoke but by each ring of the phone, her body constantly crossing between hope and dread as she now began to call the hospitals. She wanted so much to know—needed to know—while at the same time, she was afraid to find out. It was like living in a nightmare, one where you are terrified to wake up because then the nightmare might become reality.

An hour later, the calls were completed.

'Now what?'

T.C. flicked an ash onto the table-top. He had smoked many cigars in his day but this Australian stogy was like smoking duck manure. One puff from this baby would have done to Fidel what Kennedy and the Bay of Pigs could not. He decided this would be his last one.

'I'm going to run downstairs and get you a few more numbers to call from the phone book,' he said. 'Then I'm going to start questioning the staff. No reason for both of us to sit by a phone.'

He stood, walked to the door, sighed, turned slowly back around. He reached back and grabbed his Australian cigars. What the hell. His taste buds were dead already.

*　　　*　　　*

A little while later, as Laura sat alone in her room waiting for T.C. (or better yet, David) to return, she decided to call home. Glancing at the clock, she realized that it was around eleven p.m. in Boston.

Her father, Dr James Ayars, would be sitting in his immaculate study at his immaculate desk. Medical files for tomorrow morning's rounds would be neatly stacked, the right side for those already reviewed, the left for the ones not yet read. He would be wearing his gray silk robe over neatly buttoned pajamas, his reading glasses gripping the end of his nose tightly so they would not slide off during one of his frequent sighs.

Her mother, the lovely socialite Mary Ayars, would probably be upstairs waiting for her husband's nocturnal voyage to their bedroom. She would be propped up in bed, reading the latest provocative novel assigned for her reading group, a clan really, containing some of Boston's most influential pseudo-intellectuals. They enjoyed spending each Thursday evening dissecting the 'in' books and attributing meanings that even the most creative of authors could not have imagined on the loftiest of drug trips. Laura had gone to one session (they were sessions, her mother had told her, not meetings), and decided that *Webster's Dictionary* should have a picture of this group next to the word 'bullshit'. But this was merely her mother's latest in a long series of Thursday-night attempts at female bonding, running the gambit from bridge games to sexual-awareness encounter groups.

'Hello?'

For the first time since David's disappearance, tears suddenly came to her eyes. Her father's voice was like a time machine. She fell back over the

47

years, wanting to wrap herself in the past, wanting to wrap herself in her father's strong and confident voice where she had always been safe and warm.

'Hello, Dad.'

'Laura? How's everything going over there? How's Australia?'

She did not know how to start. 'It's beautiful. The sun shines all the time.'

'Well, that's great, honey.' His tone grew businesslike. 'Now why don't we cut through all the red tape, okay? What's up?'

That was her father. Enough haggling and small talk. He wanted to get to the bottom line. 'Something's happened to David.'

His voice was as authoritative as always. 'What, Laura? Is he okay?'

She was very close to crying now. 'I don't know.'

'What do you mean you don't know?'

'He's missing.'

There was a long silence that frightened Laura.

'Missing?'

His voice was more full of dread than real surprise, like when you hear your friend who smokes three packs a day has developed lung cancer. Tragic and yet obvious. She waited for him to say more, to request all the details like he usually did, but he remained quiet. Finally she spoke.

'He left me a note that he had gone swimming. That was two days ago.'

'Oh God,' he mumbled. His words formed into a sharp needle that punctured Laura's skin. Gone was the confident voice that was her father's trademark. She could feel him struggling to regain his normal tone, but the sound was hollow, distant. 'Why didn't you call sooner? Have you contacted the police?'

'They're looking for him now. I called T.C. He arrived a few hours ago.'

'I'll catch the next flight. I'll be there—'

'No, that's okay. There's nothing you can do here.'

'But—'

'Really, Dad, I'm okay. But please don't tell Mom.'

'What could I tell her? She doesn't even know you're in Australia. Everybody's wondering where you and David are.'

'Just keep the elopement a secret for a little while longer. Is Mom there?'

Dr Ayars froze. 'No.'

'Where is she?'

'She's in Los Angeles for the week,' he lied. 'Laura, are you sure you don't want me to fly out there?'

'No, really, I'll be fine. I'm sure we'll find him soon. He's probably just pulling another stunt.'

Again, there was silence. Laura waited for him to agree with her, to say of course he'll be back, to tell her to stop worrying like a typical wife. But he didn't. Where was his comforting voice of reason? Where was the man who was supposed to be strong for everyone else? Her father, the man who was always calm, always in control, the man who had seen death and suffering on both a professional and personal level for his entire life and had never let it affect his cool exterior, was strangely without words.

'I'll call you as soon as I know something,' she said while a small voice in her head told her that her father didn't need to be informed, that he already knew what the outcome was going to be. But that was silly. She was just overtired and frightened. This whole episode was turning her brain into mush.

'Okay,' Dr James Ayars replied, defeated, crushed.

'Is there something else, Dad?'

'No,' Dr Ayars said mechanically. 'I'm sure everything will work out for the best.'

Laura listened to his words, puzzled. The best? She suddenly felt very cold.

'Is Gloria around?'

'No, your sister's working late again. You should be very proud of her.'

'I am,' Laura replied. 'When's Mom going to be home?'

'A few days. Are you sure you don't want me to fly over?'

'I'm sure. Goodbye, Dad.'

'Goodbye, Laura. If you need anything . . .'

'I'll let you know.'

Laura heard her father replace the receiver.

*　　　*　　　*

She tried not to let the conversation bother her. After all, there was nothing specific in his words, nothing concrete her father had said or done that she could truly call troublesome. And yet, the feeling that something was wrong—very wrong—lay like a heavy weight in her stomach. She opened her purse, rumbled through its contents, came up empty.

God, why did she ever quit smoking?

Again she glanced out the window, away from

50

the beach and toward the start of the Australian Bush. She remembered once when she and David had decided to slip out of their city-slicker facade and head out into the New England Bush. Growing up in Michigan, David had had some experience with camping out. He enthusiastically billed it as a weekend away from the world. Laura, who had been a content city dweller all of her years, saw it as more of a chance to sleep in the dirt with a lot of bugs.

'You'll love it,' he insisted.

'I'll hate it.'

They drove up to Vermont where they strapped heavy knapsacks onto their backs. They walked through the muggy forest for what seemed like a millennium until, mercifully, they arrived at their secluded camping site. Laura cleaned herself off in the nearby stream, unrolled her sleeping bag, and climbed in.

Then David began to join her.

'What do you think you're doing?' she asked. 'I thought you had your own sleeping bag.'

'I do. But we have to cuddle for warmth.'

'Body heat?'

'Exactly.'

'One problem.'

'Oh?'

'The thermometer reads ninety-five degrees.'

'That warm?'

She nodded.

David thought a moment. 'Then I suggest we sleep au naturel.'

Their lovemaking was fierce, frightening in its intensity, and afterwards, they lay naked in each other's arms.

'Wow!' David managed, finally beginning to catch his breath.

'What?'

'I just love being in touch with nature. I don't know, Laura, these surroundings . . . they make me feel so alive, so one with nature, so . . .'

'Horny?'

'Bingo.'

'I'm becoming a bit of a nature lover myself,' Laura pronounced.

'I noticed. But you have to be more careful.'

'Why?'

'That screaming of yours, woman. You'll scare our furry friends to death.'

'You love it.'

'True.'

'Besides, you were hardly Marcel Marceau.'

'Moi?'

'That was some moose call. I kept waiting for the female to emerge from the bushes.'

'No such luck. I guess you'll have to do.'

'Vicious, David.' She reached into her crumpled jeans and pulled out a pack of cigarettes.

David groaned. 'Are you going to smoke those?'

'No. I'm going to feed the animals.'

'Smoky Bear says people start forest fires.'

'I'll be careful.'

'Listen, Laura, I don't mind when you smoke back home—'

'Bullshit.'

'Okay, bullshit. But out here in the wilds, we have to think of our furry friends.'

'Why do you hate my smoking so much?'

David shrugged. 'Aside from the fact that it's disgusting, terrible for your health and a habit without one redeeming quality, I guess I just don't like french-kissing an ashtray.'

'But I have an oral fixation.'

'I know. It's one of the reasons I love you.'

'Pervert. You should be used to smoke by now. You lived with T.C. for four years. And what about Clip? The two of them are always smoking those stinking cigars.'

'Yeah, but I rarely french-kiss those two. I mean, maybe T.C. every once in a while . . .'

'I suspected as much.'

'Plus T.C. could never survive without his cigars. They're a part of him, a personality appendage, so to speak. And Clip is both seventy years old and my boss. We don't make it a habit of criticizing our boss. Besides, I like it when Clip smokes.'

'Why?'

'The Victory Cigar. It means we're about to win a game.'

She wrapped her arms around him. 'My cigarette is kind of like a Victory Cigarette.'

'Oh?'

'Clip likes to smoke them after a game. I like to smoke them after an especially powerful org—'

'Keep it clean, Ayars.'

'Sorry.'

David sat up. 'Do you want to know the real reason I want you to quit?'

She shook her head.

He held her, his hand gently stroking his hair. 'Because I don't want anything bad to happen to you,' he said softly. 'And because I want to be with you forever.'

She looked at him hopefully. 'Do you mean that?'

'I love you, Laura. I love you more than you can ever know.'

Two months later, she had quit. She had not even thought about smoking since—until now.

A loud knock on the door jarred her back to the present.

'T.C.?'

'Yeah.'

'It's open.'

He came through the doorway, his face drawn. 'Some civilization. No MacDonalds. No Roy Rogers.'

'Anything new?'

Laura watched T.C. shake his head, his movements oddly jittery.

'What is it?' she asked.

'Nothing. I guess I'm just a little tired and hungry.'

'Order some room service.'

'In a little while.'

'Why wait? If you're hungry—'

The phone rang.

T.C. quickly reached over Laura and grabbed the receiver. 'Hello?'

Laura tried to read his expression, but T.C. turned away, his face hunched over the receiver like a bookie at a pay phone. Minutes passed before T.C. finally said, 'Right. I'm on my way.'

'What's going on?'

'I'll be back in a little while, Laura.'

'Where are you going? Who was that on the phone?'

He started toward the door. 'Just a potential lead. I'll call you if it turns into anything.'

'I'm going with you.'

'No, I need you here. Someone else might call.'

She grabbed her purse. 'The receptionist can take a message.'

'Not good enough.'

'What do you mean? I can't do any good here.'

'And you certainly can't do anything but get in my way out there. Look, Laura, I want to get all the facts. I don't want to have to worry about coddling—'

'Coddling?' she interrupted. 'That's a lot of bullshit, T.C., and you know it.'

'Will you let me finish? One of these Crocodile Dundees sees the new bride and clams up or softens his words.'

'Then I'll stay in the car.'

'Just listen to me a second. I'm expecting an important call in a little while and I need you here to answer it. I'll call you as soon as I know something. I promise.'

'But—'

He shook his head and hurried out the door. Laura did not chase him. In Boston, she would never have tolerated such brusque and patronizing treatment by any man or woman. But this was not Boston. T.C. was David's closest, most trusted friend. If anyone could bring him back safely, T.C. was the man.

*   *   *

On the other end of the line, the caller listened to T.C. hang up and then waited. The dial tone blared its monotonous trumpet of noise but still the caller stood mesmerized and did not replace the receiver.

It had been done. T.C. had been notified.

Everything was moving forward. There was no turning back.

When the phone was finally hung up, the caller fell onto the bed and started to cry.

*   *   *

Laura sat alone in the hotel room, her mind hazy and confused. The phone did not ring. No one knocked on the door. Time trudged forward at an uneven, unhurried pace. She began to feel more and more isolated from the world, from reality, from David.

Her eyes skittered around the one-time beautiful suite, finally resting on an object they found soothing, familiar, comfortable. A pair of David's size twelve-and-a-half green hi-top sneakers, extra sturdy in the ankle since he had broken his right one while in college, lay sprawled on the carpet. One was tilted over like a capsized canoe; the other stood upright, perpendicular to its partner.

She could clearly make out the Svengali label on the right sneaker. On the left, the label was blocked by a sweat sock. Her eyes swerved and found the other sock about a yard away, twisted on the carpet like a man sleeping in a fetal position. David was not the neatest man she had ever met. He used chairs and doorknobs for hangers. The carpet made a perfect bureau for sweatshirts and pants, while the bathroom floor tiles served as an underwear, sock and pajama drawers. His personal appearance was compulsively clean, but his apartment looked more like a fire hazard than a human dwelling.

'It's homey,' he would argue.

'It's messy,' she'd insist.

56

Once again, a knock made the images of the past flee from her mind.

Laura glanced at her watch and saw that T.C. had been gone for almost two hours. She could hear the wild birds of the Australia coast cawing outside her window, the sun still potent despite the hour.

'Who is it?' she called out, although she knew it was T.C.

'It's me.'

T.C.'s voice made her stomach churn painfully. She stood and walked mechanically toward the door. She passed a mirror, caught her reflection in the corner of her eye, and realized she was wearing one of David's button-down shirts with her Svengali jeans. She wore his clothes all the time, his Celtics practice sweatshirt on cold Boston nights, his pajama tops as a nightshirt. Odd for a woman who ran a fashion empire. She shook the thought out of her head, puzzled by how her brain could focus on something so inane at a moment like this.

She had another second to wonder if her thoughts were a defense mechanism, blocking out the grim reality, and then she swung open the door.

Her gaze instantly locked onto T.C.'s, but he looked away as if scalded by her eyes. His vision sought the floor to escape her onslaught of hope. T.C.'s face was now completely covered with patches of stubble.

'What is it?' Laura asked.

T.C. did not step forward. He did not speak. He just stood in front of her without movement, trying to sum up some inner strength. With great effort he raised his head, his soulful eyes hesitantly meeting Laura's expectant ones.

Still no words were spoken. Laura stared at him, tears swelling in her eyes.

'T.C.?' she asked, her face bewildered.

T.C. raised his hand into her line of vision. Her look of bewilderment crumbled into one of sheer anguish.

'Oh God, no,' she cried. 'Please no.'

T.C. held David's multicolored swimming trunks and clashing green Celtics shirt.

They were both shredded.

CHAPTER THREE

Gloria Ayars closed her briefcase, turned out the lights, and headed down the empty hallway. The company's other executives had gone home hours ago. But that was okay. They had all paid their dues already. Gloria had not.

She glanced at her watch. The digital numbers read 11:12 p.m.

'Good night, Miss Ayars,' the security guard called to her.

'Good night, Frank.'

'You've really been burning the midnight oil, huh?'

She smiled brightly. 'Sure have.'

Gloria walked toward her car. She shook her head, the smile still toying with the corners of her lips. It was still so hard to believe. Gloria had heard the whispers before Laura left on her trip (honeymoon, actually, but that was a secret). Don't do it, her cohorts had warned her. You'll ruin your business. But Laura had ignored them and taken the risk. A big risk. She had decided to leave Svengali in Gloria's hands during her absence—a move that had stunned even Gloria. Has Laura gone crazy, Gloria had wondered, leaving the controls of a multi-million dollar company in the hands of someone like me?

But now Gloria knew that the answer was no. Laura's confidence had been well placed.

As she continued to stroll down the sidewalk, men in passing cars slowed down to whistle or at the very least, roam her body with their eyes. Gloria was used to the ogles of men. She was by no means as beautiful as her sister, but Gloria was still capable of making any man's blood race. There was an innocence about her looks, a gentleness to a world that had constantly punched and abused her. Worse still, all that sweet innocence lay locked in a body that could only be defined as a Marilyn Monroe-type sexual dynamo, a body that was all voluptuous curves, a body that, no matter what she wore, screamed rather than hinted sensuality.

She hopped into her car, adjusted the rear-view mirror and glanced at her reflection. She smiled again, wondering if she was really looking at the same Gloria Ayars who until very recently had been a heroin addict, a cocaine-snorter, a pothead, and an easy lay for any man who had wanted to exploit her. Hard to believe that it was not so long ago that she was jamming needles into her veins and on the verge of making porno films.

As she drove home, Gloria silently thanked Laura for the millionth time for saving her. If it had not been for her younger sister, Gloria would almost certainly be dead by now. Dead or worse. She pushed the thought from her mind and pulled into the Ayars' driveway. She parked her car next to her father's and took out her house key. A minute later, she was in the front foyer.

Not so long ago, Gloria would not have been welcome here. There was a time when her father's face would turn red with rage at just the mention of her name, a time when she would have been thrown out of the house in which she'd been raised.

And she would have deserved it.

She put down her briefcase in the darkened hallway, took off her coat and put them both in the hall closet.

'Dad?' she called out. There was no answer. She began to walk toward his study. He never went upstairs before midnight; plus, her mother was away in Los Angeles for the week, so lately he had been working even later than normal.

The door to the study was open, the desk lamp illuminating the nearby hallway. She walked into the study and quickly scanned the room. Her father was not there. She turned out the lamp and moved toward the stairs.

'Dad?' she called again, but still no response. His car was in the driveway, so he had to be home. He was probably in bed already. Gloria started up the stairs, moved down the hallway and stopped abruptly.

What the . . .?

The light was on in Laura's old room. Strange. No one had been in that room in years—except Laura during her occasional visits, and the maid. Gloria crept down the hall, reached the doorway and peeked inside.

She suddenly felt very cold.

Her father sat on the edge of Laura's bed, his

back facing the door. His head was slumped into his hands in obvious anguish. The sight shocked Gloria. She had never seen her father look so small, so vulnerable.

'Dad?' she ventured.

She heard a sniffle as he raised his head. He still did not turn and face her. 'Gloria, I'm . . . I'm glad you're home.'

Glad she was home. Those words. There was a time she would imagine Armageddon easier than imagining her father saying those words to her.

'Are you all right?' she asked.

Dr James Ayars did not respond right away, his shoulders raising and lowering with each breath. 'I have some bad news.'

Gloria had known terror in her thirty years, most self-inflicted. Once, when she had dropped some bad LSD at a West Coast party, her mind had conjured up horrors that almost made her jump out of a tenth-floor window. She remembered that fear now, the way her heart had raced in her chest. And then there was another time—

'Mommy! Mommy!'

'Gloria, get out of here! Get out of here now!'

—when she had known terror, but she was so young then. A little girl. She remembered nothing about it, except—

Blood. So much blood.

—what she saw in the dreams.

'What is it?' she asked.

'Laura just called from Australia,' he began slowly, his strength ebbing away with each word. 'David's dead. He got caught up in some powerful current and drowned.'

Despair swept through Gloria. It couldn't be. It

just couldn't be. Not David. Not the only man her sister had ever loved. Not the only man who had ever treated Gloria like a person, the only true friend she had ever had.

She broke then and ran to her father on frail legs, the tears already starting to pour down her face.

It just couldn't be.

*　　*　　*

T.C. sat next to Laura on the plane. She had barely spoken since he had delivered the news, asking only one question:

'When can I see the body?'

T.C. had hoped she would not ask that question. 'There's no need,' he had said gently.

'But I want—'

'No you don't.'

T.C. had taken care of the rest of the details quickly. He knew that David had no real family to contact. His only living relative was Stan, his piece-of-shit brother who none of them had seen for over a decade and who would probably applaud David's death. No need to contact that scumbag. T.C. had also been busy making sure the press did not hassle Laura too much. He knew that once Laura returned to Boston, the press vultures would be all over her, wanting to know the tiniest tidbit of how it felt to have your heart ripped out of your chest. He decided the best thing would be to hide Laura in Serita's apartment for a little while, but T.C. knew from past experience that the press could only be denied for so long.

He turned toward her. He had been searching

his brain, desperately trying to think of a way of easing some of her pain. His eyes watched her, concentrated on her every movement as if they would give him a clue as to what he should do. It was a useless exercise and T.C. knew it.

Damn you for doing this to her, David. Damn you.

He also knew what Laura was thinking under the haze of anguish because he was one of the few people who knew the truth about David and his affliction. He had witnessed its awesome effects firsthand. He had seen it nearly kill his best friend.

But Laura had put that all in the past, thank God. Somehow, she had sought and eventually destroyed the evil spectre that had tormented David Baskin for a good portion of his life. But still, they were haunted by the fear that the spectre would one day return. Was the spectre truly dead, they wondered, or like some Godzilla sequel was he just hiding, regaining his strength, preparing to one day attack with a vengeance that would destroy David once and for all?

And the more immediate question that T.C. knew Laura was asking herself: Had the creature paralyzed David's body in a wave of unbearable agony while he tried to handle the treacherous waters? If she had stayed with him, could she have done something to protect her beloved David from the cruel creature within?

T.C. reached out and patted her hand. He wanted to tell her to stop thinking such thoughts. He wanted to tell her that David had not had another attack. He wanted to tell her that there was nothing Laura could have done to change what had happened.

But of course, he could not tell Laura any of

63

those things. She would never just accept his word. She would demand to know how he knew so much about David's drowning.

And that was something he could never tell her.

*   *   *

Dr James Ayars had seriously considered canceling all his appointments for the day. It was something he had not done in over twenty years, not allowing himself to become ill during that entire time period. He had always prided himself on being punctual. Every Monday through Friday—save his three weeks' vacation each year—began with hospital rounds at seven thirty in the morning, followed by his first office appointment at nine, his last one at four thirty, another quick visit to the patients in the hospital, and then back to his home on the outskirts of Boston. If a day was to be missed for personal reasons, he gave his patients and staff at least two months' notice.

There had been very few deviations from this routine during the last two decades, but the phone call he had received from Laura yesterday was as much a cause for deviation as anything he had experienced during that time. It had left him saddened, confused, so much so that even a man as disciplined as he considered not going in to work. He had just wanted to stay in bed and deal with the harsh blows.

In the end, he had realized that staying at home would serve no purpose. It would only leave him time to brood when what he needed was to keep his mind and soul busy. He had called Gloria's psychiatrist—even with her enormous improvement

Gloria still needed therapy—and told her what had happened. Her psychiatrist had wanted to see Gloria right away.

He pushed his chair away from his desk. There were patients waiting. Mr Campbell was waiting in room five and Mrs Salton was in three.

The phone buzzed.

'Dr Ayars?' the box cawed.

'Yes?'

'Your wife is on line two.'

'Thank you.' He swallowed away his fear, picked up the receiver, and pressed the flashing light. 'Mary?'

'Hello, James.'

'Where the hell are you?' he asked. 'I was trying to reach you all night. I thought you were staying at the Four Seasons.'

'They were having some sort of wild convention. Noise all night long so I moved over to the Hyatt.'

James closed his eyes and rubbed them. He did not mention that there had been no listing under her name at the Hyatt either. 'I have some rather bad news.'

There was a pause. 'Oh?'

'It's about David.'

'What's happened?'

'He's dead.'

'Oh my God! How? Was it . . . was it suicide?'

Predictable enough response, James thought. 'He drowned off the Australian coast.'

'But he was such a good swimmer.'

'I guess he misjudged the current.'

'Or . . .?'

'Or what?'

'How awful,' she continued. 'How's Laura

65

handling it?'

'I don't think it's fully hit her yet. David's friend T.C. is there with her. He's handling all the arrangements.'

'She's going to be devastated, James. We have to help her through this.'

'Of course we will.'

'She'll snap out of it,' Mary said hopefully. 'She's always been a very strong girl.'

'I'm sure you're right,' he replied without much enthusiasm.

'I'll catch a flight back home tomorrow.'

'Do you want me to meet you at the airport?'

'No need, James, I'll grab a cab at Logan.'

'Okay, I'll see you then.'

He hung up the phone, leaned back and took a deep breath. Mary had never been a very good liar. She had not even bothered to ask why Laura and David were in Australia. James Ayars looked down at his hands. With some surprise he realized that they were shaking.

*   *   *

Stan Baskin woke up with a start. He tried to remember the dream that had caused him to wake, couldn't, then gave up. What's-her-name in the bed next to him was still asleep, thank God, her face turned away from him. He tried to remember what she looked like, couldn't, then gave up.

He must have been having a nightmare about last night's Red Sox game. Damn, that had been a sure thing. Stan had studied the match-up carefully and had concluded that there was absolutely no way the Brewers could beat the Sox. Milwaukee could

66

never hit a lefty pitcher with a 7–0 lifetime record against them. Combine that with the way the Sox had been beating up Brewer pitching and then add that they were playing in Fenway Park. It was a sure thing.

The Sox had lost 6–3.

Stan had dropped a thousand bucks on that game. And even worse, the B Man (so named because of his fondness for breaking bones) was after him just because Stan had been late on a few payments. Stan knew that all he needed was one more chance. He knew that today's game between the Houston Astros and the Cards in St Louis was a sure thing. Mike Scott was ready to explode. He may even hurl a no-hitter against St Louis today. And there was a horse in the fifth at Yonkers Stan absolutely loved.

He silently slipped from under the covers, urinated, flushed, then looked at his naked body in the mirror. Not bad for a man in his late (very late) thirties. Everything was still firm this morning (even Mr Happy) and his handsome face still drew the women. Witness last night, his very first in Boston.

He moved back into the bedroom, What's-her-name had not yet stirred. Good. He searched her dresser for some aspirin, found some Tylenol, quickly downed three in the hopes that it would kill his hangover. He turned on the television, flipped the stations until he found what he was looking for, sat on the edge of the bed. What's-her-name finally began to stir from her hibernation as the television warmed up.

The anchorman was talking about his brother again. For chrissake you would have thought the President of the United States had died the way they covered David. He grabbed a cigarette off the floor (how the cigarette had ended up there he had no idea) and lit it as the television droned on:

'The sports world is still shaken and shocked over the tragic drowning death of basketball great David Baskin. Today, our city pays its last respects to Mr Baskin, the Celtics legend who provided us all with so many memorable moments and world championships. A public memorial service will be held today at noon at Faneuil Hall. Thousands are expected to be on hand to say goodbye to David Baskin. Scheduled speakers include Senator Ted Kennedy, Celtics President Clip Arnstein and two of David Baskin's teammates, center Earl Roberts and shooting guard Timmy Daniels.

Stan shook his head. A whole city mourning for that schmuck. Unbelievable. His eyes suddenly grew large when the television flashed a picture of Laura on the screen.

A spokesman for the team said that Baskin's beautiful widow, fashion mogul Laura Ayars-Baskin, will come out of seclusion for today's ceremony and the private burial that will follow. Mrs Ayars-Baskin and her husband were on their secret honeymoon when the tragedy occurred. She has not been seen since returning . . .

Stan was held spellbound by her image. He may not have liked his brother (hated him actually), but oh man, was his bride a different story. Just look at that body! Christ, she had to be a great lay. No question about it. And a girl like that would be crawling up walls soon without a steady fuck. A girl like that would want a real man sharing her bed this time.

And David's dear older brother Stan was just the

68

man for the job.

He stood up.

'Where you going?'

So she was finally awake. Stan tried like hell to remember the name he had used last night, couldn't, then gave up. 'Huh?'

'Did you sleep okay, David?'

He suppressed a laugh. David. He had used the son of a bitch's name. 'Just fine.' He turned and faced her, seeing her for the first time since the night before.

Oh shit.

First the Red Sox lose, and now this beast. He could have sworn she was a whole lot better looking last night.

'What would you like me to make you for breakfast?'

Christ, she was a cow. 'I gotta go.'

'Will you call?'

Moo. 'Sure, sweetheart.'

She lowered her head. 'I mean, if you don't want . . .'

Listen to this cow nag. How had he ended up with her anyway? If Stan didn't know himself better, he would have sworn he was slipping.

He looked at her again. Now he noticed that she had big tits. Real big. Well, that did count for something, but right now, it was time to teach her a lesson, time to teach her who was boss. 'How about if we go out tonight?' he asked.

Her eyes lit up, her face beaming. 'Really?'

'Sure. Dinner, dancing, formal dress, the works. Go out today and buy yourself a new gown. Sound okay?'

She sat up eagerly. 'That sounds wonderful.

69

What time?'

He suppressed another laugh. The cow was buying it. 'How's eight o'clock? I have a business appointment so I may be a few minutes late.'

'Okay.'

He pictured the cow waiting all night in some new dress for a knock that would never come. This time, a chuckle did manage to escape from his lips.

'Anything wrong, David?'

David. He chuckled again. 'Just thought of something funny.' He looked at her again, wondering if he was doing the right thing. Maybe he was being unfair. Maybe he was wrong. Maybe he should reconsider. After all, she did have big tits . . .

Nah.

It would be more fun to stand her up. Besides, he had big plans for tonight. It was time to introduce Stan Baskin to the city of Boston, to the press . . .

. . . and to Laura Ayars.

*   *   *

It made international headlines.

David's death was truly a story no newsman could resist. More than any other athlete, David Baskin had gained international fame through not only his pro basketball excellence, but for his Olympic heroics, his domination of European basketball during his stint as a Rhodes Scholar and, most of all, his tireless work with handicapped children. Add to this the fact that he was married to gorgeous supermodel Laura Ayars, the founder of the Svengali line, and just watch the reporters salivate.

70

What could make the story even more stimulating? Tragedy striking the happy couple. While eloping and secretly honeymooning in Australia, the great White Lightning drowns in a freak accident, leaving behind his beautiful widow to mourn the cruelty of it all.

Newspapers from Warsaw to New York, from Bangkok to Leningrad, gave the story prominence. Every spectrum of the journalism world, from supermarket tabloids to government-run newsletters, covered the sad event.

There were all kinds of clever headlines about how White Lightning would strike no more, how nature was finally able to stop David when no man in a basketball uniform could, but more than any of the others, Laura thought that the *Boston Globe*, the Celtics' hometown newspaper, struck closest to the bone. In simple, huge, sad block letters, the front page screamed in pain:

WHITE LIGHTNING DEAD

Laura laid the newspaper in the bed, leaned back against the pillow and stared at the ceiling. Her eyes blinked spasmodically. Serita had tried to keep the newspapers away from her, but Laura had been insistent and Serita was hardly the type to tell her what she could and could not do. Now, as she lay in the spare bedroom in Serita's apartment for the third straight day, she recalled one particular paragraph she had read claiming that David's body was found 'bloated' and 'mutilated beyond recognition.'

The tears started to come again and yet they did not seem to come from her. She was too numb, too anguished merely to cry. Crying served her no purpose. The pain went far beyond anything tears could help to drown out. She knew the media were searching for her, but very few people knew where she was hiding, and Serita watched over Laura like an Israeli airport security guard.

She also knew that today she would have to rise from this bed, that today she would have to leave the protection of Serita's apartment and face the world for the first time since her David had . . .

He can't be dead. He just can't be. Please tell me it's not true. Please tell me that this is just a stupid joke and when I get a hold of him I'm going to beat the shit out of him for scaring me like this. Please tell him enough is enough, that I know he's okay, that I know his body was not shredded on coral and rocks.

'Laura?'

Laura looked up at her long-time friend. Serita was a devastating beauty, one of the few women in the world who could compete with Laura in the looks category. She was nearly six feet tall, her body thin and very muscular with the most beautiful ebony skin. Serita (she never used a last name) had been the world's top black model since she and Laura had first met six years ago on the modeling circuit. Serita had also become good friends with David over the last two years. In fact, David had liked her so much he had set her up with his closest friend on the Celtics, Earl Roberts, the seven-foot center.

'Yes?'

'Honey, you got to get out of bed now. Gloria called. She and your father are going to pick you up in an hour.'

Laura did not respond.

'And Gloria wants to speak to you first.'

'About what?'

Serita paused. 'Your mother.'

Laura's eyes grew angry. For the first time since David's death, they showed some sort of life. 'What about my mother?'

'She wants to come to the memorial service.'

'Fuck her.'

'That's your answer?'

'That's my answer.'

Serita shrugged. 'I'm but the secretary. Now get your ass out of bed.'

Though Laura had spent the last three days in this bed, sleep never visited her, never gave her an opportunity to escape the nightmare that reality had become. And now she did not want to get out of the bed, did not want to get dressed, did not want to attend a public memorial service at Faneuil Hall.

I love you so much, David. You know I can never love anyone else. Please come back to me. Please come back and hold me gently and tell me all over again how much you love me and how wonderful our life together is going to be. Tell me again about the things we're going to share, about the children we're going to raise.

'They're expecting massive traffic delays,' Serita continued. 'I think everyone in Boston is going to be jammed into Quincy Market for this. I sure hope Earl doesn't screw up his speech.'

Try as she might, Laura felt the tears sliding down her face again.

'Come on, Laura.' Serita gently pulled the covers off her friend and helped her sit up. 'You have to be there.'

'I know.' She wiped her face with her sleeve. 'I'm glad Earl is going to do a eulogy. And I'm glad you two are together.'

'We're not together,' Serita stressed, 'only fucking.'

Laura forced out a chuckle. 'Wonderful.'

Serita was the best friend Laura had with the exception of her sister Gloria, if you wanted to count a sister as a friend, and Laura had befriended very few models during her magazine-cover days. This was not because of the ridiculous stereotype that models are dumb. They're not. Actually, they're a rather crafty and intelligent group. But sometimes their self-image got in the way of uncovering the real them. Plus, with Laura being unquestionably the world's number-one model, many of the other women were somewhat jealous of her. And jealousy was an emotion Laura doubted Serita had ever experienced.

Today, the city of Boston was dedicating a bronze statue to David to be placed in Faneuil Hall, near Clip Arnstein's own likeness. Clip was the Celtics' seventy-year-old president, a man who David had both loved and respected. He, along with the mayor of Boston, Senator Ted Kennedy (a man David had never cared much for), Earl, and Timmy Daniels, another Celtics teammate, were going to eulogize her husband.

The work on the statue had been started months ago but for a whole different purpose. Originally, it was to be placed in a small playground at a school for handicapped children in honor of David's work. Now, it had been speedily completed and moved to Faneuil Hall to stand in memory of his premature death. Laura sighed. She could not help but think that David would have preferred to keep the statue in the small playground.

After the dedication, there would be a private burial. Burial. Funeral. Laura shook her head as Serita led her into the bathroom. She heard Serita turn on the water.

'Go on. Get in there.'

Laura stepped into the shower, the water cascading over her naked body.

Don't make me go to some service, Serita. There's no reason really. You see, David is not dead. It's all a lie. David is just fine. I know he is. He promised he would never leave me. He promised that we would be together forever. And David never broke a promise. You know that. So you see, he can't be dead. He can't be dead. He can't be . . .

Her body slowly slid down the shower's tile wall until she lay huddled in the corner of the stall. Then she placed her hands over her face and cried.

*   *   *

The surgeon looked at the clock on the far wall.

4:45 a.m.

He took a deep breath and continued stitching. A few minutes later, the wounds were all closed.

Six hours of surgery.

The surgeon walked out of the makeshift surgery room, untied his mask and let it fall onto his chest. He approached his friend and business associate. The surgeon noticed that his friend was much more nervous this time than usual.

But that was understandable.

'How did it go?' the man asked the surgeon.

'No complications.'

The man seemed very relieved. 'I owe you one, Hank.'

'Wait until you get my bill.'

The man chuckled nervously at the joke. 'What now?'

'The usual. Don't let him do anything for at least two weeks. I'll check in on him then.'

'Okay.'

'I'll leave a nurse with him.'

'But—'

'She's done this type of thing before. She can be trusted.'

'This is a little different, don't you think?'

The surgeon had to agree. This was most definitely different. 'I assure you she can be trusted. She's been with me for years. Besides, he has to have a nurse.'

The man thought for a moment. 'I guess you're right. Is there anything else?'

A million questions swirled through the surgeon's head but he had been in this business long enough to know that the answers to such questions could be dangerous. Even fatal.

He shook his head. 'I'll see you in two weeks.'

CHAPTER FOUR

Judy Simmons, Laura's aunt, was packing for the trip to Boston when the phone rang.

David is dead, Judy. Pretend all you want but you're to blame . . .

She closed her eyes, struggling to shove the cruel voice away, but the accusations continued to echo across her mind.

You could have stopped it, Judy, but now it's too late. David is dead and it's your fault . . .

She refused to listen anymore. Judy had recently turned forty-nine, lived alone, had always lived alone, had never wanted to live alone. It wasn't her fault. It was just that when it came to men she had the luck of Wiley Coyote chasing the Road Runner. To be more precise, her relationships with the opposite sex ended up being disasters of Hindenberg-like proportions. Though she wasn't any great beauty like her sister Mary, she was attractive enough by most standards. Her face was pretty, if somewhat plain, and she had a very nice figure. Her most noticeable feature was her auburn hair, which she wore at shoulder length. Men had always liked her. The problem was that for some reason she always attracted the wrong kind of men.

That isn't exactly true. I almost had the best. Twice.

But that was a long time ago. Best forgotten. Besides, she was happy enough. She was an English professor at Colgate College and while the winters got cold, she liked the small community lifestyle. She was content, satisfied . . .

Bored.

Maybe. But a little boredom was not always such a bad thing. Right now, she hoped for boredom, begged for it. She wanted no new surprises.

Her poor beautiful niece. Such an awful thing to have happen to Laura. But perhaps it was divine intervention, Judy thought, though it was strange for a woman who was in no way religious, for a woman who had always despised those 'comforting' words that glossed over tragedy as 'God's will,' to have such thoughts.

But maybe that's what it was. God's will. Please let that be what it was. David's death had to be God's will. Or some bizarre, tragic coincidence. Or . . .

The alternative was too horrifying to even consider. She placed her heavy sweater in the Samsonite as the phone rang again. Her hand reached for the receiver.

'Hello?'

'Judy?'

It was her sister. 'Hello, Mary. How are you feeling?'

Tears were her answer. 'Awful,' Mary said. 'Laura still won't talk to me. She hates me, Judy. I don't know what to do.'

'Give her some time.'

'She'll always hate me. I know it.'

'Laura is in a lot of pain right now.'

'I know that,' Mary snapped. 'Don't you think I know that? I'm her mother, for chrissake. She needs me.'

'Of course she does.'

'Judy?'

'Yes?'

There was a pause. 'I didn't tell you everything.'

'What do you mean?'

More weeping came through the telephone line. 'I should have called you earlier. I wanted to. Really. But I know you would have tried to talk me out of it.'

Judy's heart lurched. 'Mary, what happened? You didn't . . .'

Still more tears. 'What would you have done? Don't you see I didn't have any choice? She's my daughter. I couldn't just sit back. And now . . . Oh God, I never wanted this to happen.'

78

Judy's fingers nervously twisted the telephone cord. Her mind jerked back. How long? How many people must pay before it all ends? And why must the innocent have to suffer too? Why must they pay for the sins of others?

Judy fought to keep her voice calm. 'Just tell me what happened.'

*   *   *

Laura's dark sunglasses helped cut down on the warm, summer glare, but that was not the reason she wore them. They served the larger purpose of hiding her puffy eyelids from both the world and cameras that surrounded her. She sat on the dais, T.C. on her right, Serita on her left. Earl was on the other side of Serita. The photographers were pushing to get closer to the pale widow, their cameras clicking at warp speeds. Laura noticed the way T.C. glared at them, his fists clenched in his lap.

They were at Faneuil Hall, one of the most popular leisure spots in Boston. It should have been called Food Hall. Sure, Faneuil Hall had a good variety of stores. There were clothing boutiques, bookstores, even a Sharper Image. But make no mistake: Faneuil Hall was about food, tremendous amounts of food, an abundance of food. The assortment was endless. There was an Indian food stand next to a Chinese, next to an Italian, next to a Greek, next to a Mexican, next to a Japanese, next to a Lebanese, next to . . . name a country and you probably named a restaurant. It was the United Nations of eating.

If you were for some odd reason hungry for something more, you could wash down your foreign feast at a tropical fruit bar or an ice-cream parlor or a frozen-yogurt stand or a cookie bakery or a candy shop. David had once remarked that you could put on weight just walking through it.

There was also inadequate seating in the market (next to none, actually) which helped make the experience all the more fun. Laura recalled how David used to love to watch some poor guy forced to stand, trying to balance a souvlaki in one hand, napkins in the other, a strawberry daiquiri under one elbow, a taco under the other, and lord knows what between the knees.

David used to love . . .

She could not believe she was talking about David when she used that phrase.

Used to . . .

Faneuil Hall attracted many people, but never had Laura seen it this crowded. From her seat on the podium, Laura looked down at thousands, maybe hundreds of thousands, of faces, a sea of people flowing into the distant horizon, a blanket of humanity thrown over the entire area.

Today the restaurants, the bars, the shops, the parlors were all closed and locked. Even the Boston Garden stood sadly in the distance, the weathered building watching over the proceedings like a grieving father over the funeral of a beloved son. Boston's colonial brick buildings and modern glass skyscrapers grieved with heads lowered. It was as if the whole city—the people, the buildings, the streets, the monuments—had stopped momentarily to mourn the death of David Baskin.

From behind her glasses, Laura's eyes darted left and right: David's friends, his fans, his teammates, Faneuil Hall, the tired yellow and blue sign reading

BOSTON GARDEN. It was all too much for Laura, a full-fledged assault on her senses. Her head swam. Her strength ebbed from her body. She could barely make out the eloquent words that were being spoken. Only a sprinkling of the sad passages came through the filter her mind had created. She guessed the filter was a defense mechanism saving her from a complete breakdown, but she really didn't possess the energy to think it through.

'David was fiercely loyal. If a friend had a problem, it was David's problem. I remember a time when . . .'

She turned toward T.C. She had not seen him since he had dropped her off at Serita's, but he looked like he had not slept or shaved since his arrival in Australia almost a week ago. He stared back at her with concern in his bloodshot eyes. She smiled at him as if to say she was all right and turned the other way.

'He was one of the few people I ever knew who did not have to put you down in order to bring himself up. If you congratulated him on a good game, he would talk about the great play of his teammates. If you mentioned his hard work with the handicapped, he would talk about their bravery. But with David, this was no false modesty . . .'

The seat next to Serita was empty now as Timmy Daniels finished speaking and Earl took the podium. She tried hard to tune into Earl's words. The ones she caught were beautiful, moving, straight from the pain in his soul. She noticed that Earl was tearing, his voice choked, his giant seven-foot frame heaving, and she remembered that David had once told her that Earl was the most emotional guy he knew.

But knowing their past, who would ever have

81

imagined that Earl and David would end up being close friends?

Laura did not know anything about basketball back in the days when David had first encountered Earl on the basketball court, but she knew that it had been a shock to everyone when they became best friends—everyone, that is, save Clip Arnstein, who had arranged it all.

David and Earl had always been bitter rivals, starting from their high-school days in Michigan. Newspapers had fueled the rivalry by constantly analyzing the two, theorizing on who was the better college prospect. The media moved out in force for their match-ups, notably the three times they had met in the state championships. Earl had gotten the better of David in those games, his team winning two of the three contests.

Heading into college, both players were the nation's top recruits. David ended up at the University of Michigan. Earl enrolled at Notre Dame. The rivalry became even more intense. Basketball fans debated the merits of both players, claiming their favorite of the two was the better. The media continued to compare the white player who stood six-five with the black seven-footer. All the talk in college basketball rotated around the two superstars.

And the two warriors did not disappoint. The University of Michigan and Notre Dame met in NCAA Final Four competition twice during those years. When they were just freshmen, David was forced to miss the big match-up with a freak broken ankle that occurred the night before the game. But luckily for every basketball fan around the country, their college careers culminated three years later when David met Earl head-on in the championship game.

It was easily the most eagerly anticipated game in the history of college basketball and became the talk of the sports world. Every sports magazine devoted major features on what was being billed the college competition of the decade. The cover of *Sports Illustrated* featured a photograph of David and Earl eyeballing and sneering at one another. The caption read:

WHO'S HUNGRIER FOR THE NCAA CHAMPIONSHIP?

And the game was worth the build-up.

From the opening tap, it was a contest of great genius, both teams moving with the precision of chess masters. But it was the ending that will forever adorn the history books. With twenty seconds left to play, Earl's Notre Dame was up 87–86. David drove toward the basket and hit an off-balance jumpshot to put the University of Michigan up by one point 88–87.

The clock read seventeen seconds.

Notre Dame called their last time out. The coach drew up a play to go to Earl, who was having a brilliant game. Earl had already tossed in thirty-four points. And all he needed was to get his team two more and they would possess college basketball's most coveted prize.

It was a simple play: give Earl the ball on the low post a few feet from the basket. Then just clear out and let him do his thing.

Notre Dame inbounded the ball. They passed around the perimeter, trying like hell to work the ball inside to Earl. But he was being covered closely.

Eight seconds remained.

Notre Dame's point guard finally spotted an opening. He faked left and passed the ball inside. Earl caught it.

Three seconds.

Earl faked, turned, spotted a clearing, took one dribble, prepared to dunk the ball for the easy winning basket . . . and the ball was gone.

Earl quickly spun as the buzzer ended the game. David held the ball. He had stolen it from the big center, preserving the victory for his University of Michigan.

Earl had been devastated. The press could not get enough of the story. They claimed that there was trouble between the two superstars, that their rivalry had taken on nasty overtones, that they genuinely did not like each other. In truth, David and Earl barely knew one another off a basketball court.

Speculation about their dislike of one another began to increase when the media began to concentrate on which player was going to be the first pick in the pro basketball draft. Again, fans broke down into David and Earl camps.

That was when Clip Arnstein, a short, bald senior citizen who looked like he should be working for a deli rather than a pro basketball team, made the deal.

It had cost him. Many questioned the risk of trading three veteran players for two rookie draft picks, but Clip had been making successful deals since the late 1940s and was not about to let the skeptics start bothering him now.

The morning before the draft, the Celtics announced that they had secured the rights to the first two picks in the college draft. When the NBA Commissioner called for the Celtics' senior president to select the first player, Clip Arnstein calmly stood, lit a cigar, reached into his pocket and yelled over to Earl Roberts, 'Call it. Heads or tails.'

'Excuse me, Mr Arnstein?' Earl replied.

'I said call it. Heads or tails.'

Earl shrugged. 'Heads.'

Clip flipped the coin. 'Heads it is. You're the first pick in the draft. Baskin, you're the second.'

The crowd was stunned. Suddenly the long-time rivals were teammates.

Earl was finishing his eulogy now. He concluded by looking over at Laura, smiling, and stating simply, 'I love you, David, I always will.'

He turned the podium over to an ashen-faced Clip Arnstein. A more skeptical person would claim that Clip had lost his most valuable financial commodity and that was the reason for his devastation. But Laura had seen David and Clip together too many times to believe such nonsense.

She watched now as Clip walked over to the roped-off area where his own bronze image sat on a bench, the smile on his bronze face contrasting with the grimace of pain on his real one. He pulled away the sheet next to his likeness and revealed the new bronze statue. Laura and the entire audience gasped. Somehow, the artist had captured David perfectly, his crooked smile, his soaring spirit . . .

Laura wished she was dead, wished she could feel something other than the pain of losing David.

Please, I just don't want to go on. I just want to be with my David, my beautiful David. Please don't be dead. Don't let my David be dead . . .

Mercifully, the ceremony ended. The crowd

slowly drifted off, drifted toward cars that would take them back to the safety of their homes. Laura sat in a murky haze as people walked up to her.

Voices. So many voices.

'I'm so sorry . . .' 'A real tragedy . . .' 'What a waste . . .' 'It's always the good . . .' 'Why him? . . .' 'So sad . . .' Laura just nodded tiredly, their words meshing together in a meaningless wave of sound. Then something was said that truly jarred her.

'I'm David's brother Stan.'

*　　　*　　　*

Somehow, Laura got through the funeral.

Somehow, the endless hours passed, the grim words were spoken, the casket buried in the earth. Somehow, Laura managed to numb her brain enough so that reality could not seep through her haze. If not—if she had truly understood what was going on—she would surely have started screaming, screaming until both her mind and her vocal chords snapped.

Her father helped her out of the car and gently led her into his house. A half-dozen other cars filled the circular driveway while down the street, a roadblock had been set up to keep the press away, but Laura could still hear their zoom-lens cameras snapping away, the constant clacking like buzzing insects in her ears. She felt her knees buckle again, but her father was there to prevent her from crumbling to the ground. He gripped her arm tighter and half carried her into the living room.

Being a private gathering, only those closest to David were in attendance. Laura could see David's teammates, his coaches, Clip, Serita, Gloria, Judy, her father and of course, the surprise show, Stan Baskin. Odd that in this group the only person Laura had never met was David's only living relative. In fact, David had mentioned Stan once, maybe twice, in all the time she had known him. She knew that they had not gotten along, but as of today whatever it was that had separated the brothers was in the past. Stan was family and he was here to mourn the death of his brother. In death, much is forgiven and forgotten, and that at least was a good thing.

After maybe twenty minutes, Laura found herself sitting on the couch alone, her eyes lowered toward her feet. A pair of neatly polished shoes came into view. Laura looked up into the face of David's brother. The two brothers had by no means been identical, but there was no mistaking the family resemblance. Looking at Stan's face twisted her heart until she felt the tears swell once again.

'Won't you sit down?' she said.

'Thank you.'

She paused, swallowed. 'I'm very glad you could make it.'

Stan nodded slowly. 'I'm so sorry. There is so much to say, so many things I should have said a long time ago.'

'There's no need.'

'No, Laura, I really need to get some things off my chest.' He took a deep breath, his handsome face grim and lined. 'David was my baby brother. I can still remember the day he was born. I was ten at the time. David, you see, was the little accident.'

Quiet chuckle.

'Anyway, I loved him like mad and he followed me like I was his hero. Wherever I went, he went with me. A lot of that may have been because our father had passed away, but you should have seen us back then. We were inseparable. We played in the yard, built snowmen, walked to school, collected caterpillars . . . how can two people who shared so much grow apart like that? How can things change so drastically? I never stopped loving him, Laura. No matter what came between us, I never stopped loving him.' His shoulders hitched and then he began to cry.

Laura reached out and gripped his hands. 'I'm sure he understands, Stan. I'm sure he never stopped loving you either.'

*   *   *

Stan continued to cry.

Oh, Stan My Man, you are brilliant. She's buying it all! Now just don't overdo it, my boy, and she'll be crawling into your pants in no time at all.

He glanced up and laughed, but it just sounded like he was bawling more intensely. Her hand gripped his tighter.

How hot is she? She just buried her hubbie and already she's holding my hand!

*   *   *

Laura watched him.

It was so sad. Stan would never be able to forgive himself for not telling David how he felt. And now it was too late. Too much time had been wasted with the petty.

Behind Stan, out in the hallway, a face peeked into the room, a face swollen from tears and torment of sleepless nights. The hair was a mess, the skin sallow and ghost-like. Laura thought about Stan and David's relationship, the time they had wasted in some ridiculous argument with an origin that probably neither one of them could pinpoint. Now, Laura looked at the normally beautiful face of her mother and questioned her own behavior.

Everybody thought that Laura and David had secretly eloped to Australia to avoid the media attention. That was only partially true. The main reason they had run off had just stuck her head through the door. Laura wondered what she should do. She wanted so much to learn from Stan's mistake, to let go of her anger and reach out to her mother but:

'Laura, I want to talk to you.'

'Sure, Mom. What is it?'

'It's about that boy you're seeing.'

'David?'

'I thought I told you I didn't want you to see him anymore.'

'You did. A few times.'

'So why aren't you listening to me?'

'Because I'm not eighteen anymore. I can see who I want to.'

'But I don't like this boy.'

'Good thing you're not dating him then.'

'Don't be such a smart-ass, Laura. I don't want you seeing him.'

'Why don't you like him? You won't even speak to him.'

'I don't have to. I know the type.'

'The type? What the hell does that mean?'

'Playboys with lots of money. That's not for you.'

'You know I wouldn't be with him if he was like

that.'

'You'd be surprised what men could get away with.'

'And what's that supposed to mean?'

'Just what it said.'

'Well, David is not like that.'

'Stop seeing him, Laura. That's the end of the discussion.'

'I'm not going to stop seeing him. I happen to be in love with him.'

Pause. 'Oh no, Laura, please tell me you didn't mean that.'

'Why? I don't underst—'

'Exactly! You don't understand. Just trust me on this. He's not right for you. Look at his family history. His father—'

'He's not his father! And how the hell do you know about that anyway?'

'Please, Laura, I'm begging you. It can only lead to disaster. End it with him now before it's too late.'

Now Laura's eyes locked onto her mother's for a brief moment. Most people remarked on how much Laura looked like Mary and to Laura's way of seeing things, this was quite a compliment. She wanted to stand, to walk over, to throw her arms around her mother, to forgive her. But the pain was still too great, the need to blame someone for what happened—however unfairly—too strong to do any of those things.

Laura lowered her eyes and turned away.

*   *   *

Gloria stood in the corner, her hands fluttering nervously about her face. She looked across the room at her sister. Why does something like this happen to someone like David and Laura? Gloria had spent her life taunting Death, teasing him, dangling her life within his grasp. For some reason, he had never snatched it; she was never worth the effort. It was the good he wanted, those that mattered, those like David. Death did not have time for the insignificant.

She turned toward the bar her father had set up for the mourners. For the first time since Laura had dragged her to the clinic, Gloria really craved a drink, a toke, a snort, anything artificial that would deaden her nerves. Her father realized it. He and Dr Jennifer Harris, Gloria's shrink, had not left her alone, and she was grateful for that.

Gloria was getting stronger. Most were amazed at how far she had come. But she had a long way to go. By now, she was well enough to know that she was far from fully recovered, that her progress and indeed the substance of her life were still fragile.

So she did not mind her father's watchful eye, which was on her even now as he spoke with Timmy Daniels, one of David's teammates. It felt nice. She smiled at him and turned back toward where her sister was sitting.

Gloria's whole body quivered. She bit her lip. One little toke. One little snort. That's all she needed. Then she would be fine. Then she could make it through the rest of the day. Then she would be able to sleep until tomorrow.

And what about tomorrow? Maybe two tokes, two snorts? And then what? She knew. She would start tumbling, tumbling until she didn't care if she woke up in the morning, tumbling until she once again crashed at the bottom. And this time she would never find the strength to climb out.

A finger tapped her shoulder. She quickly spun. The man who had tapped her was very handsome and she recognized the face, if not the man, right away.

His voice was soft. 'Excuse me for intruding. If you want to be alone . . .'

'No, that's okay.'

'You must be Gloria.'

She nodded.

'My name is Stan Baskin. I'm David's brother.'

'I'm so sorry about your brother. I loved him very much. He was a wonderful person.'

Stan lowered his head in a nod. 'I loved him too, Gloria.'

'It's not fair.'

'I . . . I just can't believe my brother is really dead. I keep asking why this happened, if I did something . . .'

'You?'

'The truth is we fought a lot the last few years. You can't imagine how much I regret the past. I wonder if I had been a better brother . . .'

'You shouldn't torture yourself.'

'I never had a chance to say I was sorry,' he continued, 'to tell him how much I loved him.' Stan took her hand then, his wet eyes finding hers. As much as she did not want to think such a thing right now, Gloria couldn't help but be attracted to him. He was very handsome, with looks that were similar to David's. And the way he had opened up to her, the way he had not been afraid to be emotional in front of her . . . just like David.

She could see now that he was on the verge of tears again. She reached out to hold him but he drew away. 'I'm sorry to be troubling you, Gloria.'

'Don't be silly.'

'You're so beautiful and you've been so kind to me. I hope we can see each other again soon.'

'I hope so too.'

'I'm a stranger in Boston, and I feel comfortable with you and your sister. I . . . I hope you don't mind if I call you once in a while.'

Why did her heart leap so when he spoke? 'I'd like that, Stan. I'd like that very much.'

*   *   *

Stan turned away from Gloria and began to walk away.

Did you see that body? I thought ol' Stan My Man was going to pass out! A rollercoaster doesn't have that many curves. And Gloria digs me, no doubt about that. I can always tell—

Bam!

Somebody bumped into Stan with a significant amount of power. The blow knocked Stan out of his daydream. When he focused, he saw a face he had not seen in almost a decade.

T.C. glared at him. 'What the fuck are you doing here?' he hissed.

Stan quickly recovered. 'Why, it's little Terry Conroy. Long time no see. You've put on a few pounds, old buddy.'

'I asked you a question.'

'Can't a man mourn the death of his only brother?'

'A man, yes. A piece of shit like you, no.'

'Big talk from the city cop. You are a policeman now, aren't you, T.C.?'

'What are you doing here?'

'Is this an official interrogation?'

'Call it what you want.'

'How about none of your business?'

'How about I smash your head through a window?'

'Good idea, T.C. Why don't you make a big scene in front of everyone and disturb their mourning? How does that sound?'

'If you dare bother anyone—'

'Please, T.C., would I do something like that?'

'Get the hell out of here.'

'Oh, I'm sorry. I was under the impression this was the Ayars's house. I never realized it was yours. The Boston Police Department must pay very well.'

'What are you doing in Boston anyway?'

'Paying a condolence call to my lovely sister-in-law.'

'Let me warn you, shithead, that if you harm her in any way—'

'T.C., can't you see I've changed? I'm a new man.'

'Shit doesn't change its stink. It only breaks down into nothing.'

'Colorfully put. I must remember that. Anyway, as much as I've enjoyed this conversation, I really must be going now.'

'Back to Michigan?'

'Not yet. I thought I might hang around Boston for a while.'

'I wouldn't advise it, Stan. This city can be awfully tough on strangers.'

'A threat? How nice. If you'll excuse me . . .'

T.C. grabbed his arm. 'I'm warning you, Stan. Don't try to pull any of your shit. I remember what you did to David.'

94

For the first time, Stan's eyes grew angry. 'You know nothing about what happened between David and me.' He pulled away but T.C. hung on. He pulled harder. 'Let go of me now, you tub of shit,' he half whispered, half yelled. 'I happen to be his brother. I'm part of his family. You, on the other hand, are just another in a long line of people who sucked up to my brother for personal gain.'

T.C. let go. 'Get out, Stan. Get out now.'

Stan pulled away, said his goodbyes, and left. As he headed for the door, he wiped away a tear, curious as to why it was so easy for him to get into the role of grieving for a brother he had so hated.

*   *   *

That night, Judy Simmons went back to the hotel by herself. She felt drained, exhausted from the events of the day. She sat on the bed and took her wallet out of her pocketbook. Her fingers reached behind her license and plucked out a thirty-year-old photograph.

Judy lifted the picture into view, her eyes entranced by the black and white images from 1960. She lay back and held the wrinkled photograph in the air above her head. She stared at the picture of the pretty, hopeful college co-ed and the handsome older man.

Why torture yourself?

But the truth was that her past did torture her. It had tortured them all, still tortured them, would continue to torture.

Not necessarily. I could tell the truth.

But what good would it do? Would it stop the torment? Release her guilt? Not really. Better to keep it a secret. Better to hope that all would be okay. Besides, she wasn't sure what had really happened in Australia. It may have been just like they said. It may have been just an accident. A sad, tragic accident.

But it wasn't.

She sat up and put the picture on the night-table. And what if it wasn't an accident? What if . . .? She pushed the thought away. David was dead. Judy's beautiful wonderful niece was crushed. Nothing could change that. It was in the past. The truth could not work as a time machine, allowing her to go back and make everything work out okay. The truth could not bring David back to life.

She glanced at the clock and picked up her suitcase. The truth. The only thing the truth could do now . . .

. . . was kill.

CHAPTER FIVE

Laura finally managed to get out of the bed again.

Three weeks had achingly passed, three torturous weeks where Laura had done little but sulk away the day in Serita's spare bedroom. And God, how she hated to sulk, how she hated lying in bed and feeling sorry for herself.

She pulled back the covers. Her hair was disheveled, her usually dark skin turning gray, her eyes swollen and black. Yes, three weeks had passed but as far as the pain was concerned, it felt like one agonizing second. The pain, the anguish of knowing her David was dead had not lessened, had not loosened its grip for even the briefest of moments.

She had visitors. Gloria was always with her and in many ways, she was the best comfort; not because her words or company were particularly comforting, but because Laura's worrying about her sister was an effective means of escaping from her own torment. The way Gloria's body shook and quaked reminded Laura of the painful days of withdrawal when she first found Gloria's naked body with the needle tracks in her arms.

Stan was also a true support and a sad example of lost opportunity. He visited every day, often at the same time as Gloria. Laura noticed that Gloria had something of a crush on Stan. She wasn't sure how she felt about it, but so far Stan had not done more than be kind to her. That was probably good. At this stage, a bad relationship with a member of the opposite sex would be catastrophic for Gloria.

There were others. Earl was here a lot. So was Clip Arnstein and Timmy Daniels, the backcourt player who had always thought of David as an older brother.

Laura put on a fabulous act when these visitors came to the door. She pretended to be strong and told them all she was doing just fine, that she was taking walks outside every day, that there was no reason to worry. In other words, she lied. She was not sure it was working, but anything was better than allowing people to stare at you with eyes filled with pity. That was something Laura could not handle.

'Whoa, will miracles never cease?'

Laura turned toward Serita. 'Excuse me?'

'The fans are on their feet! Laura is finally out of bed! And oh my, would you look at that? She's

97

actually putting on something besides a nightgown and bathrobe.'

'Funny.'

'Are you going back to work. Say yes.'

'No.'

'Then where are you going?'

'To the house.'

Serita paused. 'Nah, let's do something else. Let's drive down by the Combat Zone and whistle at guys.'

'I'm going to the house.'

'Honey, are you sure?'

'I'm sure.'

'But why?'

'I have to clean up a few things.'

'It can wait.'

'No,' Laura replied, 'I don't think it can.'

'Then I'll go with you. I can be very helpful.'

'With cleaning? Don't make me laugh.'

'I'm very good at supervising.'

'You have to go to work, Serita. You have that big spread for International Health Spas today.'

'It can wait.'

'With the money they're paying you for those TV ads?'

'I said it can wait.'

'Let me be somewhat less subtle,' Laura said. 'I want to go alone.'

'Well, fuck you too.'

Laura chuckled sadly. 'You're a good friend.'

'The best.'

'But I'm taking advantage. I should move out.'

'No way. I need you here. You're my excuse to Earl.'

'You love him, you know.'

98

Serita put her hands on her hips. 'How many times do I have to tell you—'

'I know, I know. He's just a good lay.'

'You got it. But he loves the spa commercials. He says seeing me all sweaty on Nautilus machines makes him hot.'

'I'm happy for you both.'

'Fuck you, too.'

Laura kissed her friend's cheek and left. She got into her car. As she drove, she tried to keep her mind blank, tried to concentrate on the road in front of her. But her mind would not do as she commanded. It kept coming back to David, always back to David, to the way he walked, to the way he held her as they slept, to the feel of his unshaven face against her skin when he kissed her.

David had changed her in so many ways, and yet now that he was gone, she knew that many of those changes would soon dissolve away. She remembered how wonderful it had been to discover each other, to learn of love together. It had taken a while. Love and trust did not come easily to either one of them.

During the second month of their relationship, Laura felt herself finally begin to let down her defenses and open up to him. Before that, she had been afraid of exposing herself to the devastating weapon of love, of being hurt in a way in which she could never recover. But on this cold December night, Laura realized that she and David were destined to be together. True, they had made no commitment to each other, made no pledges. But Laura knew. And now that she did, she wanted to see David, couldn't wait to be with him so that she could at long last tell him how she felt. But would

99

she have the courage? Would she finally be able to say and hear words she had always dreamed about but never allowed herself to hope for? Probably not. Probably she was not ready. But then again, if you don't try . . .

She had been sitting at her desk, her leg shaking as it usually did. A happy, goofy smile, the smile of a woman starting to fall heavily for a man, kept inadvertently leaping upon her face. Laura psyched herself up, working up the nerve to go through with it. Finally, she reached for the phone, called David at the Garden, and invited him over for dinner this Friday.

'Are you cooking?' David asked.

'Of course.'

'Let me see if my Blue Cross is paid up.'

'Stop being a creep.'

He paused. 'I'd love to but . . .'

'But?'

'I can't on Friday. Can I take a raincheck?'

Disappointment gushed through her. 'Sure,' she managed.

'I have to go to this fundraiser.'

Her heart beat wildly in her chest. She mentally chastised herself for her behavior, for hoping that he would invite her to go with him to the fundraiser. It was just that she wanted to see him so much.

'Listen,' he continued, 'I have to get back to practice. I'll speak to you later.'

Laura heard the phone click. She waited for the dial tone to return, and then the annoying noise that tells you that your phone is off the hook followed. After another minute or two passed, she put the receiver back into its cradle.

He had not asked her to go with him.

Sleep became an infrequent visitor for Laura that Friday night. Why hadn't David invited her to the fundraiser? Didn't he need to see her too? Or was she rushing this whole thing too fast? After all, they had only been seeing each other for two months. Maybe he was not ready to make any commitments. Maybe he did not feel the same way she did.

Laura showered and dressed early Saturday morning. Needing something to take her mind off David, she headed into the office and started to wade through last month's financial statements. Earnings were up almost ten percent from the previous year, which was a full four percent better than Laura had anticipated. Content with that, she sat back and grabbed the *Boston Globe*. When she hit the society page, she found a photograph of David at the fundraiser.

With another woman.

Laura felt a hand reach into her chest and grab her heart. The mystery woman was a stunning, older blonde whom the *Globe* identified as Jennifer Van Delft. Ms Van Delft had her arm locked around a tuxedo-clad David, who was smiling like a lottery winner and described by the paper as Jennifer's 'escort.'

Escort. That son of a bitch.

Tears began to work their way into her eyes. She continued to stare at the picture. Why was she crying? What the hell was she getting so upset about? Had she really been stupid enough to think that there was something special between them, that David cared for her more than his other girlfriends?

There was a knock on the door. Laura moved quickly. She folded the newspaper, wiped away her tears, smoothed her Svengali business suit, and regained her composure. 'Come in.'

David came through the door with a smile, not unlike that in the photograph, smeared across his handsome face. 'Good morning, beautiful.'

'Hello,' she said coldly.

David crossed the room to kiss her but she turned away, leaving him only room to buss her cheek. 'Something wrong?' he asked.

'Nothing. I'm just busy that's all. You should have called first.'

'I thought maybe we could grab some lunch together.'

Laura shook her head. 'Too much work.'

Puzzled, David watched her go back to work as though he weren't there. 'You sure nothing is wrong?'

'Positive.'

As he shrugged, David noticed the *Boston Globe* sitting on her desk. A knowing smile came to him. 'Does that upset you?' he asked, pointing at the newspaper.

She looked up at the headline. 'What? The fire in South Boston?'

'I'm talking about the picture of me inside.'

'Why on earth would that upset me?' she asked. 'I don't own you. You're free to do as you please.'

He chuckled lightly. 'I see.'

'But I do think we should mellow out for a while,' she continued.

'You do?'

'Yes.'

'Can I ask why?'

'This relationship is getting way out of hand.'

David sat down in the chair in front of her desk. 'So you want something a little more relaxed—one of those flexible relationships.'

'Flexible relationships?'

'Right. We make no commitments. We see other people—all that kind of stuff.'

Laura's leg would not stop shaking. 'Yes.'

'I see,' he continued. 'So you're not upset that I was at the fundraiser with another woman?'

'Me?' she replied. 'Not at all.'

'But, Laura, suppose I don't like your flexible relationship idea. Suppose I don't want to see other women. Suppose,' David went on, 'I told you that for the first time in my life I am in love.'

Her heart soared and fell at the same time. She swallowed and looked away from his piercing gaze. 'Then I would probably say that you're not ready for that type of relationship.'

'Witness last night?' he asked.

She nodded, her wet eyes still afraid to move toward his.

'Laura?'

She said nothing.

'Look at me, Laura.'

With a struggle, her head rose, her eyes meeting his.

'The woman in the picture was Jennifer Van Delft. Her husband is Mr Nelson Van Delft. Does that name ring a bell to you?'

It did, but Laura could not place it. She shook her head.

'He is the principal owner of the Celtics. Every year, his wife asks me to help her with the muscular dystrophy fundraiser. Her husband was out of town.

103

He asked me to escort her. That was all.'

Laura said nothing.

'But let me go on so I can remove any doubt,' he continued. 'Let me say something I've never said to another woman. I love you. I love you more than anything in the world.'

Surges of emotion ricocheted through her, but she still could not get her mouth to open.

'No response, Laura? Don't you understand what I'm saying? I love you, Laura. I don't want to be away from you.'

Her leg was going like a jack-hammer. It can't be true. It has to be a trick. 'I . . . I'm really busy right now, David. Can't we discuss this later?'

David shook his head. 'I still can't get through to you, can I? I thought I had. I really thought I had. But you're still that fat little girl who can't handle being the awesome beauty. You're still that fat kid who's afraid to lose control of a situation, afraid to let someone else in because maybe you'll get hurt again. But what about now, Laura? Are you still in control?'

She tried to answer. She really wanted to answer . . .

His face reddened, his tone getting louder. 'Nobody can truly love you, isn't that right, Laura? You think your beauty blinds me to the real you, that someone can only love the outside image of you, but that's bullshit. Are you really that insecure, Laura? Do you really think that I don't know what that's all about, that I haven't met a hundred beautiful women who just wanted me because I could stuff a ball through a hoop?'

He stopped. His breathing came in quick spurts. He shook his head, anger seething through him, and headed for the door.

'David?'

His hand moved away from the knob but he did not face her. 'What?'

Again, there was no answer. David turned toward her and saw that she was crying. 'Laura?'

The tears came faster now. 'I'm so scared.'

'Laura . . .'

'I'm scared about how I feel,' she said, her chest heaving from her sobs. 'About how much I love you.'

He quickly moved back toward her and took her in his arms. 'So am I, baby. So am I.'

'Please don't hurt me, David.'

'Never, my love. I promise.'

Never, my love. I promise. The words echoed from the past into the present.

'Please don't hurt me, David.'

'Never, my love. I promise.'

But David had lied. He had left her and that, after all, was what she had always feared most. Laura pushed his face from her mind and continued driving, concentrating as hard as she could on the road in front of her. Fifteen minutes later, she put on her blinker and turned.

The house.

Why had she come here? Why did she do this to herself? She felt tears start to come. Why? It was just a building. A building shouldn't make her cry. It was just a secluded three-bedroom house with two and a half baths. Nothing to cry about unless you thought about all the shattered dreams that lay crumbled on its floors.

She got out of the car and headed to the front door. It was another beautiful summer day, the humidity not as bad as it could sometimes get. She strolled up the path, took out her key . . .

The front door was unlocked.

She knew that David had locked it before they eloped. She turned the knob, walked in, turned off the alarm. Well if the alarm was still set, then how . . .? She dismissed the worry with a weary shrug. If they had been robbed, she really did not care very much. She stepped into the living room. The house was still, the silence swallowing her. The room was bare, but of course that was how it had been before they left.

Two months ago, she and David had purchased the house. There had not been much time to do furniture shopping. Just a few things—enough so that they could move in immediately when they returned from Australia. After all, they were supposed to have a lifetime to do the rest.

She moved toward the stairs. The paint was still unfinished in many spots. She smiled sadly, remembering how David had insisted that they should paint the inside by themselves. The experience had turned into a major fiasco—paint splattered everywhere but where it was supposed to go. Laura's hand gently petted the wall over the area where David had painted. Then she turned away. It would be bad to keep this house, to live here without David. There were not yet too many memories, but worse, there were unfulfilled dreams here, potential memories of the life she and her David would have shared. This was the place where their love would have continued growing, where the children she so wanted would never be born and raised.

'How many children do you want, David?'

106

'Now? Today? Don't you think we should wait?'

'I'm being serious. How many?'

'I don't want children.'

'What?'

'I want to have rabbits.'

'Rabbits?'

'That's right, Laura. Rabbits. Three to be exact. One of each sex. And I think we should raise them Hindu.'

'But I'm Catholic and you're Jewish.'

'Exactly. This way we won't fight.'

'Can't you be serious for one minute? This is important to me.'

'Of course, my love.'

'How many children do you want?'

'How many do you want?'

'I want a lot,' Laura replied. 'Five, ten.'

'You?'

'I want to have children with you, David. I want to have children right away.'

'Not today. I'm tired.'

'Be serious. Think of how much fun it will be—cute little Davids running around the place.'

'Does sound kind of cute,' David admitted.

'And little Lauras too.'

'Yuck. Poor kids.'

'Keep it up, Baskin, and you're going to get slugged.'

He took her in his arms. 'Laura, we are going to have the best family in the whole wide world. You, me, little ones, a couple of disposable goldfish, a family dog, a barbecue in the backyard—the whole Rockwell painting.'

'Mean it?'

'Yeah, I mean it.' He squeezed her tighter. 'I

promise you'll have plenty of little ones running around here.'

Laura continued to walk up the stairs. At the top, she veered into the master bedroom, ignoring the room down the hall which was supposed to one day be their first nursery. She saw the king-size bed they would never again share and an icicle punctured her heart. She glanced to the left. Her eyes opened in pain. Her knees buckled. Near the window, underneath its sill, David had left one of his overturned, ripped sneakers. She walked toward the sneaker that David had once worn, that he would never wear again. He would never see this house again, never smile again, never laugh again. Never. That was always the word that crushed Laura like a helpless insect.

Never.

Oh God, please let David come back to me. Please let him hold me again. I'll do anything you ask. Please
. . .

The morning seemed to laugh cruelly at her prayer. She turned away from the sneaker and that was when she noticed that someone had been in her desk.

The house had indeed been broken into. But that did not worry her. There wasn't much to steal. She and David had bought the bed, the desk, the refrigerator, a kitchen table and some chairs. That was about it. Nothing easy to haul out of here either. And who cared about that stuff now anyway?

The thief had rummaged through their desk.

Everything was in disarray. They must have been searching for money or a checkbook or . . . She hobbled over to the desk and opened the top

108

drawer. Three hundred dollars in cash and David's NCAA Championship ring were right on top. Untouched. Puzzled, Laura spotted David's photo album. Why would that be out? She opened it. Nothing unusual. Everything was in its—

Hold it.

She looked closer. There were several tiny, ripped-up pieces of a photograph caught between the pages. Someone had torn up one of David's photographs. She closed the book and found two more pieces on the floor.

She scanned the rest of the desk. The intruder had also rifled through their schedule diary. But for what? Why would someone look through that? Laura looked at the page left open. David had written the words, 'GETTING MARRIED!' across last week. He had also written down their flight number on Qantas Airlines and the name of the hotel in Palm's Cove.

She did not touch the book. Instead she reached for the phone, thankful that they had ordered it to be turned on so it would be all set when they came home as Mr and Mrs Baskin.

She dialed T.C.'s number. But he was not there. The dispatcher told her he was out for a few hours. She left a message and glanced at the cover of the photograph album. No. She did not yet possess the strength to open the book, to see his image. Laura headed down the stairs and got into her car.

*   *   *

The man stood over the patient. 'Look at all those goddamn bandages. You look like a mummy or that guy in the *Invisible Man* movie.'

No reaction from the patient.

The man wondered if he should tell him about the latest surprise. He decided against it. The patient needed all his strength to recover. It would be a mistake to upset him with something that was beyond his control. 'Are you feeling okay?'

This time, there was a nod.

Progress. 'Those bandages uncomfortable?'

A shake of the head.

The nurse sat in the chair beside the bed. 'That's the way he's been acting all week. He never speaks.'

'Maybe he's not supposed to,' the man replied. 'Maybe it's not good for his vocal chords.'

The nurse shook her head. 'That's where you're wrong. I've watched over millions of these guys. By now, they're all talking like crazy, you know, about their problems and stuff. But this guy? He doesn't say a word. Kinda makes the job boring, you know?'

The man nodded and turned his attention back toward the patient. 'I've got to be heading back otherwise people will wonder. Do you need anything?'

Another shake of the head.

'I'll be back with the doctor in a few days. Take care.'

Underneath a bandage, a tear slid from the patient's eye.

CHAPTER SIX

T.C. turned the knob. 'You left the lock just as it was?'

Laura nodded.

'Who else has a key?'

'Nobody.'

'Was it locked when you left for Australia?'

'Yes.'

They stepped into the foyer. 'And nothing was disturbed down here?'

'Right.'

'Show me the upstairs.'

He followed her up the stairs and into the bedroom.

'Here's the desk,' she said.

'You sure David didn't mess it up?' T.C. asked. 'He was never known for his tidiness.'

'I'm positive,' Laura replied. 'I specifically remember that right before we left I opened the drawer to take out our plane tickets. Everything was neat and in place.'

T.C. examined the desk. Whoever had done this was in a rush. The intruder had rummaged through the top drawer, pulling out papers, books, whatever. But he had left the money and the ring. Why? T.C. studied the few pieces of a photograph that were in the area. Where was the rest of the photograph? Chances are the intruder had destroyed the picture and accidentally left a few pieces behind in his haste. But why? Who?

He pulled out a magnifying glass, feeling like a poor imitation of Sherlock Holmes. He placed it near the small pieces. It was an old photograph, a black and white that had begun to yellow from age.

'Do you know what was in this picture?' he asked.

She shook her head. 'I could go through the photo album and try to figure it out.'

'If you feel up to it.'

'I do,' she lied.

'Then take it with you. We can go over it later.'

T.C. quickly checked the rest of the house. First, he scanned the upstairs, followed by the kitchen and den. Lastly, he went over the basement. There was nothing out of place. No sign of forced entry. When he was finished, he met up with Laura at the front door.

'I don't mean to dwell on this,' he said, 'but this is a rather sophisticated lock and alarm system. How many keys did you make up for this place?'

'Just two. I left this one in my apartment before we left.'

'And the other?'

She swallowed. 'David had the other one with him in Australia.'

*   *   *

Judy contemplated her sister. Despite the years and the recent anguish that had ravaged her face and body, Mary was still gorgeous by any man's standards.

The two sisters sat in Mary's bedroom. It was tastefully decorated in the latest style, whatever that was. Judy noticed that the furniture looked like it had been sculpted out of fiberglass. The bookshelf was jammed with all the latest reading. Mary read all the time, though Judy knew that she did not really enjoy it. Books were props to Mary, her way of telling the world that she was more than a pretty face and gorgeous body. For as long as Judy could remember, Mary had always worried about her image, sure that she had been labeled a 'scatterbrain' because of her physical perfection.

In truth, Mary Ayars was neither an intellectual nor an airheaded stunner. Judy had been told that everyone had a special gift. If that was true, Mary's was beauty and she relied heavily—too heavily—on this asset. True, it had given her much and had always made her the center of attention, but it had also made her somewhat superficial and in the end, her beauty had caused uncontrollable disaster.

Oh, how Judy wished she could start over again. If she could somehow get her hands on a time machine, she would go back to the days when she and Mary were the little Simmons children. She would steal into Mary's room late one night while everyone was asleep. She would approach her sleeping sister and slice up her face with a broken Coke bottle. Or maybe she would use their father's straight razor. Or maybe she would use acid and melt Mary's flawless features into horrible clumps of waxy organisms—something, anything to destroy the evil before it could flourish, before it could make its way out of the womb.

The thought made her blanch.

It was my fault too. My fault as much as anyone's.

She was being hard on herself but that was understandable. Earlier today, Judy had met with Laura. Vivacious Laura, the woman who was everything that Mary wanted to be, was still in shock. Her niece stared dazed, her eyes wondering why the world had suddenly decided to crush her very being.

What have I done to you, Laura? What have I helped cause?

Judy remained silent, letting her sister vent, watching her sister cry uncontrollably as she spoke. Then Judy asked her sister the one important question.

'Does James know?'

The words stopped Mary's hysteria like a sharp smack. 'What?'

'Does your husband know?'

'Of course not. Why should he?'

Judy ignored her sister's question. 'Has he acted any different since you returned?'

'For pete's sake, our daughter has just lost her husband. Of course he's a little uptight.'

'I mean, toward you.'

Mary shrugged uneasily, the tears starting to show again. 'He treats me like I'm not there. Since David's death, he can't even look at me. But he's devastated. James was very fond of David.'

'David was a wonderful man.'

Mary paused. 'He loved Laura very much.'

'I know.'

'What should I do, Judy?'

'Do?' Judy repeated, remembering the last time her sister had asked her for advice. It had led to tragedy and even death. 'This time, don't do anything.'

*   *   *

Laura poured Stan another cup of coffee. 'So when are you heading back to Michigan?'

'Anxious to get rid of me?'

'Of course not. I didn't mean—'

Stan waved her off. 'I'm only kidding, Laura.'

'I'm glad you've been here. Your visits have been very important to me.'

'That's nice to hear,' he replied as he sipped the coffee, 'because I'm seriously considering staying in

Boston.'

'Really?'

Stan shrugged. 'There's not much for me in Michigan. I closed a deal there before I left so I have nothing that ties me there anymore. Plus I'm trying to line something up in Boston. You see, there's a deal I'm hoping to raise some money for. A mall with a basketball theme or something. But more important than that . . .' He stopped and looked up. 'I hope I'm not being too forward.'

'Not at all.'

'Well, to be honest, the most important reason I want to stay is that I have no family in Michigan. And the way you and your family have treated me . . . I don't know, maybe I shouldn't say this, but I feel like I'm part of a family. I feel good when I'm with all of you.'

'You are family, Stan.'

He took her hand. 'Thank you. That's very nice of you to say. It's been so long since I had anybody close to me.'

She smiled sadly. 'I still can't believe David's really gone. I keep expecting Earl and him to burst through that door in their sweat clothes, David spinning a ball on his finger and Earl doing all he can to distract him.'

Stan moved closer to her, his arm snaking around her shoulders. 'You'll get over him, Laura.'

The phone rang.

Laura pulled away and stood.

Shit! I had her. Damn that fuckin' phone.

She picked up the extension in the kitchen. From his seat in the den, Stan could only hear murmurs. Three minutes later, she hung up.

'That was Gloria. She's coming to pick me up in

115

about an hour.'

'She's a wonderful woman.'

'Yes, she is.'

'I like her very much.'

'I'm glad.'

'She seems to be a very interesting person. Had a lot of interesting experiences.'

'And paid for them.'

'Paid?'

'Nothing, Stan. I shouldn't have said anything.'

'She told me she's seeing a psychiatrist. She also told me that you saved her life.'

'That's being a bit dramatic.'

'She's really grateful to you.'

'There's no need for her to be.'

'Was it very bad when she first came back? Oh God, I'm sorry. That's none of my business. Please just forget I asked. I guess all this family talk clouded my judgment.'

Laura sat back on the couch. 'No, Stan, like I said, you're family. From the sound of it, Gloria doesn't want to hide anything from you.' She nervously played with her empty coffee cup. 'It was very tough at first. She needed constant care. We hired full-time help.'

'Was she institutionalized?'

Laura nodded. Despite her earlier words, she felt a pang of discomfort talking about her sister like this. 'More of a dry-out farm.'

Stan understood from the tone of her voice that he better quit. 'I'm sorry. I shouldn't have pried.'

'No, it's okay.'

Thick silence hung over them.

'Well, I better be going.'

'Thank you for visiting, Stan.'

116

They rose and walked to the door. She opened it. Stan bent down and lightly kissed her goodbye. When he turned around to leave, the doorway was blocked.

Stan smiled brightly. 'Hello, T.C.'

T.C.'s eyes blazed with anger. 'What the fuck—?' He spotted Laura and closed his mouth.

Stan patted T.C.'s bulging stomach. 'See you around, big guy.'

T.C. closed his eyes, wrestling with his temper to keep it in check. Stan made a hasty exit.

'Are you all right, T.C.?' Laura asked.

'Fine.'

'Come on in.'

'Laura, has he been around a lot?'

'Stan? He's been very supportive.'

'Uh-huh.'

'What's the matter, T.C.?'

'Just be careful with Stan Baskin.'

'I can take care of myself. Besides, he's been very kind.'

'Right. He's a real sweetheart.'

'Stan already told me you two don't get along.'

'It's nice to hear he's not a complete liar.'

'What happened between them, T.C.? What could separate brothers like that?'

'Not my story to tell.'

'Why not?'

'It's just not my place to talk about it, that's all.'

'Oh, I see,' Laura said with obvious annoyance. 'It's just your place to smear a man and then not offer a shred of evidence to back up your accusations.'

'I didn't realize I was testifying in front of a judge.'

'Listen, T.C., I don't need that shit. Stan Baskin happens to be family—'

'He happens to be scum.'

'I don't want to hear that.'

'Obviously.'

'And I don't believe it. When was the last time you spoke to the man?'

'At your house after the funeral.'

'You know what I mean. Before that.'

'Laura . . .'

'When?'

'I don't need to be subjected to your cross-examination.'

'When?'

'During my sophomore year of college. Ten years ago. Happy?'

'A man can change in ten years.'

'Not him, Laura. He's sick. He hated David.'

'You've never been more wrong. He loved him so much it hurts.'

'And you buy that crap?'

'He's his brother. Nothing he can do can change that.'

'So what?'

'So he's changed. He regrets the past. He feels guilty about whatever happened between David and him.'

'Christ, Laura, you sound like one of those pop psychologists who get murderers freed. How can you be so goddamn gullible?'

'Fuck off, T.C.'

'No, you fuck off.'

They both stopped, stared. He opened his mouth but before he could speak, she threw her arms around him. 'I'm sorry,' she began. 'I didn't mean . . .'

'It was my fault.'

She felt the tears start to force their way into her eyes. 'I know you're just trying to help. I could never have survived all this without you.'

'Forget it.' He gently pulled her away. 'Are you sure you want to go through the photo album now?'

She nodded. She had not had a chance to look at the photographs since they had taken them from the house. In truth, she was still not sure she possessed the strength to look at them by herself.

They carefully went through David's photo album. T.C. observed Laura as they turned each page. He was confused by his own feelings of guilt and doing what was right to help Laura. He was surprised at how fast her tears had stopped, how none were present now as she went through the pictures. There was no emotion on her face, just a pale blank look as though the earlier outburst had drained her. The lack of emotion frightened T.C. more than her tears.

She paused on one page for several minutes. T.C. looked over her shoulder at the picture of David's mother.

'What was she like, T.C.?'

'David's mother? I never knew her when she was healthy. She learned about her cancer during our freshman year. I know that she and David were very close. And I know he was devastated when she died.'

Laura stared at the photograph for another minute. Then she turned to the next page. It was empty.

T.C.'s hand reached down to the blank page. 'Was there a picture of . . .?'

She nodded. 'David's father.'

'Jesus. Talk about eerie.'

'I don't get it, T.C. Why rip up a picture of a man who's been dead for almost thirty years?'

'I don't know.'

'It doesn't make any sense.'

'Was there anything else in the picture?'

'I don't think so. It was just one of those faculty pictures they used in a yearbook.'

'Are you sure that's the only picture missing?'

They skimmed through the rest of the album, but there were no other blank pages.

'What could it be, T.C.?'

'Give me a second, Laura. I'm not much of a quick thinker. More of a plodder.' He took out a cigar. 'Do you mind?'

'Smoke away.'

He lit it. 'Okay, let's do this step by step. First, someone breaks into your house. Is he a burglar? No. If he was, he would have taken the money. Second, is he a fan who wants a few souvenirs of David? No. If he was, he would have taken David's NCAA ring or pictures of his playing days.'

'We know all this.'

'Just humor me for a minute.'

'Sorry.'

'Whoever broke in decided to remove a photograph of David's father.'

'And he looked in our diary,' Laura added.

'Right. Now what's the connection? What would make a person want to rip up a photograph of David's father and how is that related to looking at your schedule?'

'Beats me.'

T.C. paused, his hand rubbing his chin. 'What do

120

we know about David's father?'

'He committed suicide,' Laura replied.

'Right. I can semi-understand someone wanting a picture of him.'

'Huh?'

'Well, that part of David's life has been pretty much kept quiet. Maybe someone was doing an expose on David and couldn't dig up a picture of his father.'

'You're reaching.'

'I know. Plus, he didn't take the picture. He tore it up.'

'So where does that leave us, T.C.?'

T.C. took a deep puff and blew the smoke straight up over his head. Earlier, he thought he had understood why someone had broken in, why they had needed to see the schedule diary. That part had semi-made sense. But ripping up a picture of David's father? He shook his head.

'That leaves us,' he replied, 'very confused.'

*   *   *

The man watched the surgeon closely. He had seen him do this several times before, but he had never watched with anything more than idle curiosity. Now he studied the surgeon's movements closely, the way he slowly cut away the bandages, the way he unwrapped them, the way he removed the gauze. This time, the man was interested in seeing the end product.

'Just stay still,' the surgeon told the patient, 'and I'll be done in a minute.'

The man tried to glance over the surgeon's shoulder to see the face, but there were still too many bandages. With painstaking care, the surgeon peeled back the white tape. Layer by layer came off. He dipped chunks of cloth in alcohol and wiped the man's face with them. When he was finished, the surgeon stepped back so the man could see the patient.

'Jesus,' the man uttered.

The surgeon smiled. 'One of my better jobs.'

'You're not kidding, Hank. It's fantastic.'

For the first time since the operation, the man heard the patient speak. 'Can I have a mirror please?'

'And that voice. It's really incredible, Hank.'

'The mirror?'

The surgeon named Hank signaled to the nurse. 'Before I give this to you, young man, let me warn you: this is going to be a major shock. Do not panic. Many people feel disoriented when they first see the change. Many suffer an identity crisis.'

'Thank you,' the patient said tonelessly. 'Can I have the mirror now?'

It was the nurse who brought it over. The patient took it in his hands and gazed at his reflection. The man, the surgeon and the nurse all watched for his reaction. But there was none. The patient looked at his reflection as he would on any normal day. His expression remained unchanged.

'How do you like it?' the surgeon asked.

'You do very good work, Doctor. I assume your bill has been taken care of.'

'It has, thank you.'

'When can I get out of this bed?'

'Another day of rest is all I think you'll need.'

'And how long before I can start strenuous exercise?'

'Strenuous exercise? But why, if . . .?' He caught himself, remembering the danger in asking too many questions. 'If all goes okay, another week or so.'

CHAPTER SEVEN

Stan found a pay phone near Filene's Basement. He dug deep into his pockets and pulled out a roll of quarters. He dropped a few into the slot and dialed. After three rings, a receptionist answered the call.

'Charles Slackson, attorney-at-law. May I help you?'

'Let me speak to Charlie.'

'Whom shall I say is calling?'

'An old friend,' Stan snapped.

'I'm sorry. I'll need—'

'Just put him on, sweetheart, or I'll rip your tongue out of your air-filled head.'

There was a stunned silence. Stan listened to the click as she put him on hold. A few seconds later, a man picked up the line.

'Hello?'

'Charlie? It's me, Stan.'

'Jesus, Stan, did you have to scare my secretary half to death?'

'Sorry about that. I didn't want to give my name.'

'I don't blame you, old pal.'

'What do you mean?'

'The B Man is looking for you. And he is not in a very good mood about it.'

'So I figured.'

'Where the hell are you, Stan?'

123

'Don't worry about that. I need to ask you a legal question.'

'A legit one?'

'Yes.'

'I normally don't do legit cases. Scams are my specialty.'

'As I am well aware.'

'Don't tell me you've come up with a legitimate way for us to make some money, Stan. I prefer you as the sleazy con man that you are.'

'I'll try not to change.'

'Okay, what's the question?'

'You know of course that my brother kicked off in Australia.'

'Are you kidding? It was all over the news for weeks.'

'My question is about his estate. He didn't have a will so who gets his dough?'

'It depends. Is it true that your brother eloped with that Laura Ayars a few days before he drowned?'

'Yup.'

'Man, is she gorgeous or what? I used to have one of her calendars in my kitchen.'

'Super, Charlie. Now what about my brother's money?'

'Right. I got off track a little there. So they were officially married before he died?'

'Yes.'

'Then the news isn't too good for you, Stan.'

'What do you mean? I'm his only living blood relative.'

'Courts don't care much about blood. It's what we call the intestacy statute.'

'In layman's terms, Charlie.'

'In your case, it's simply this: no will and the widow gets everything.'

'Everything?'

'Everything.'

'Even if she's already loaded?'

'Even if she's the Aga Khan.'

'Shit!'

'Sorry, pal. How deep you in the hole to B Man this time?'

'Six feet under,' Stan muttered.

'You better think up a good scam in a hurry or learn how to become invisible. B Man doesn't like those who owe to hide from him.'

'I know, Charlie.'

'You held up well?'

'Well enough I suppose. All I need is a few more days. Listen, Charlie, there's a sure thing today at Aqueduct—'

'I've heard that before.'

'No, really. Just place this bet for me and—'

'No way, Stan. B Man has spread the word. No one is going to cover you.'

'But, Charlie—'

'Look, Stan, just keep me out of this. You're on your own. I gotta go now.'

Charlie hung up the phone. Stan thought for a moment. Then he smiled. He took out another quarter and made a second call.

*　　　*　　　*

Gloria Ayars felt light-headed as she walked down the stairs. She couldn't help it. For the first time since David's death, there was a reason to smile. True, she and her family were still in mourning.

She still wanted to cry constantly for their loss. But something nice had finally happened and there wasn't anything wrong with being happy about it.

Stan had just called her and asked her out for tomorrow night. It was not really a date, she kept reminding herself. It was just a friendly dinner. Nothing more. There was absolutely no reason to build it into something that it wasn't.

So why did she feel warm inside?

Gloria had not been with a man for so long. She had not even had a date, had not wanted to be near a man in a year. Not since . . . She closed her eyes. Why must she be reminded of that now? Why must she be reminded that she was not fit to be with someone like Stan? Why must she be reminded that she was only fit to be abused by filth and scum?

No! I'm not scum! That was in the past. That Gloria Ayars no longer exists. She's dead and buried, thank God . . .

'Just tell me what happened!'

Her father's authoritative shout jarred her back into reality. He was on the phone, angrily lecturing someone—probably one of the new interns at the hospital. Gloria began to move down the hall and away from his study so that she could not listen in.

'Did she kill David or didn't she?'

Gloria froze.

Her father's voice grew angry. 'Couldn't you stop her?'

He was silent now, allowing the whoever was on the other end to answer his question. When James spoke again, his voice was calmer, more in control.

'I know. I know. I'm sorry. I shouldn't have yelled like that.' Pause. 'I agree. It was probably suicide.'

Gloria felt her heart slam into her throat. She stopped breathing.

'No, that wouldn't do any good now,' he continued. 'Do you think she was telling the truth? Uh-huh. Right. I guess there is nothing we can do.' Pause. 'Don't talk that way.' His voice was angry again. 'Do you hear me? I said don't say that. It's not true. Not a word of it.' Pause. 'Never!'

Dr James Ayars slammed the phone down. Gloria continued to hold her breath, her back pushed up against the wall. There must be a million people named David, she reminded herself. Her father must have plenty of patients with that name.

*   *   *

The details of death.

Laura held her sister's hand tightly. Her eyes moved about the wood-paneled law office. The chairs were large and plush. Paintings of fox-hunting adorned the walls. The large desk in front of her was beautifully polished oak, the bookshelf behind it neatly arranged with law journals.

Clip was there. So was T.C. and Earl and Timmy and her father. Her mother, of course, had not been invited. Laura had however asked Stan to come. She was puzzled that he had not shown up.

Mr Averall Thompson, the Celtics' lawyer and long-time friend of Clip Arnstein, leaned forward. 'Let me make this as quick and simple as possible. Will that be okay, Mrs Baskin?'

Laura nodded to him.

'First, please accept my most sincere belated condolences on your loss.'

127

'Thank you.'

'And second, let me apologize for the delay in settling these matters. Whenever the deceased does not execute a will there is always some degree of confusion.'

'I understand, Mr Thompson. No apology is necessary.'

'Fine.' The senior law partner put on his reading glasses. 'In cases such as this, the widow is left all of the deceased's property. According to our study, you two already have most of your assets in joint accounts, so that should expedite matters. You both bought the house in Brookline. You have three joint accounts, two at banks and one at a financial institution. On top of that, David left a few mutual funds and stocks, his condominium in Boston, and that's about it.'

'And his account at Heritage of Boston Bank,' Laura added.

'Excuse me, Mrs Baskin?'

'David had an account at Heritage of Boston. There's about half a million dollars in it.'

The older man looked puzzled. 'Are you sure that wasn't liquidated?'

'Quite sure.'

Mr Thompson looked over the file in front of him. Laura glanced around the room. T.C. was looking straight down at his shoes. Most of the faces were mildly puzzled, more curious than concerned. The exception was her father. James Ayars's face drained of color, his eyes frightened and confused.

'I don't see anything about that in the file. Do you have the account number?'

'The statements are in David's condominium.'

Thompson leaned forward and buzzed his secretary. 'Beatrice?'

'Yes, Mr Thompson.'

'Call our contact at Heritage of Boston. See if they have an account there for a Mr David Baskin.'

'Right away, Mr Thompson.'

He leaned back. 'I'm very sorry about this, Mrs Baskin. I don't understand how we could have made a mistake like that. I am really very embarrassed.'

'I'm sure we'll straighten it all out.'

'I'm sure too.'

A moment later, the phone on the desk buzzed. 'Mr Thompson?'

'Yes, Beatrice.'

'I called the Heritage of Boston. There is no record of any account for a Mr David Baskin.'

Laura sat up. 'That's not possible.'

Averall Thompson smiled understandingly. 'Perhaps if you could come back with the bank account number . . .'

Maybe it was just her father's expression or the way T.C. kept staring at the ground, but Laura suddenly felt very uneasy. The money meant nothing to her. She already had more than she knew what to do with. But this was all very odd. Something was very wrong.

'Thank you, Mr Thompson.'

*　　　*　　　*

Laura managed to find the key with a shaking hand. T.C. had volunteered to accompany her but she had thought it would be best if she went alone. Now, standing in front of the door to David's apartment,

129

she wondered if she had done the right thing.

She placed the key in the lock and turned. The door opened into the darkened apartment. Laura hesitated. She was afraid to turn on the lights, afraid to face the painful memories readying to leap out at her.

She and David had spent many happy moments here, moments of pure joy that she knew she would never again experience. It wasn't fair. Blasphemous to say, but God had cheated her. Cheated her and hurt her in the worst way possible. He had made her happy, brought her up to the highest high. Then He tore her wings off and let her plummet back down to the hard surface below. One minute her David was alive and strong. The next minute he was gone. How could someone like David just be snatched away like that? How can everything suddenly be worth nothing?

It was all a cruel, sadistic trick.

She stepped in but still did not turn on the lights. She suddenly remembered the last time she had entered his apartment alone.

She and David had been going out for about three months and were already hopelessly in love:

She had stopped by to visit him on her way home from work, knocked on the door, and waited. No one came to the door.

Strange.

She had spoken to David only a few minutes earlier. Why would he have gone out? She tried the door and to her surprise it was unlocked. She smiled. He would never leave the door unlocked if he had gone out. David was too compulsive when it came to that kind of stuff. He must be in the shower.

She opened the door. The apartment was dark, just

like it would be two and a half years later when she opened it to search for his bank statements from the Heritage of Boston. Her eyes surveyed the darkened room. No one was there. She listened for the sound of the shower, but the apartment was silent.

That was when she heard the muffled scream.

The sound ripped into her stomach. She sprinted toward the bedroom where the anguished cry had originated.

'David?'

The next scream, though still muffled, was louder, more hideous than any sound Laura had ever heard.

She reached the bedroom. Her eyes quickly adjusted to the darkness. David was huddled in a corner of the bed, his head clasped hard between his hands, his body writhing in agony. He released another scream into the pillow.

She ran to him, her heart pounding like a sledgehammer in her chest. 'David, what is it?'

His face was contorted into a frightening picture of absolute agony. Laura had never seen pain like this, had never known it could exist. David's teeth were gritted, his color terrifyingly red as though his head were about to explode. He struggled, but he could not hold back. He dug his face into the pillow. The smothered shriek punctured Laura's heart. Panic filled her.

'I'm going to call the hospital.'

She tried to reach for the phone, but David's grip on her arm locked her into place.

'No!' David managed and then, once again, he turned his mouth into the pillow.

He released her as he once again screamed, his hands going back to the sides of his head. The effort of uttering that one word had cost him. He looked up, his tortured eyes finding hers. He worked up enough strength to say two more words:

'Hold me.'

She did. She held him, hugged him, soothed him, stroked him. She cried with him, and he hung on to her like a life-preserver. It took almost two hours before the pain began to loosen its strangle-hold on him. But Laura would not let go of David, would not risk allowing whatever had attacked him to come back and hurt him again.

'It's all right now, Laura.'

She still held on.

'I guess I should explain,' he said.

'Only if you want to,' she whispered, shaking.

'I do.'

She cradled his head. 'Do they come often?'

He shrugged. 'Once is often enough with these things. My doctor describes them as a combination of very bad cluster headaches and some sort of inoperable brain dysfunction.'

Dread washed through her. 'Brain dysfunction?'

'Like a cyst . . . or a tumor. But it's not that serious. I mean, it's not lethal. It can never do more than cause tremendous pain. My doctor said I was born with it, even though it never bothered me until my first year of college.'

'Can't medication control it?'

'Not really.'

'David, how bad do they get?'

He forced a smile on his worn face. 'I was never very good at feigning bravery. To be honest with you, that was probably the mildest attack I've ever had.'

Laura felt her heart sink at the thought.

'I guess that has something to do with you comforting me,' David continued. 'The attacks

132

usually start out like someone is using a trip-hammer on the sensitive nerves in my head. Then the pain grows until it feels like a thousand volts of electricity are being hurtled through my brain. Sometimes, I wish I could reach into my skull to stop it, but it's like trying to scratch an itch in a cast. And then sometimes the pain hits certain nerves that paralyze my body.'

'Isn't there anything we can do?'

'Just what you did. Hold me when it happens.'

'Do your teammates know?'

He shook his head. 'Only T.C. and my doctor know. I haven't even told Clip and Earl. I can usually sense when an attack is starting to come on so I make myself scarce. It helps to sit in a dark room. A lot of times I call T.C.' He swallowed and then looked up. 'T.C. can't help with the pain but sometimes it gets so bad I'm afraid I'll do something I may later regret. I don't mean to scare you. I just want you to understand the severity of these attacks.'

She was crying now, gripping him even tighter. 'I love you, David. I love you so much.'

'I love you too, Laura.' He closed his eyes. 'I need you so much.'

David's final attack came in October of 1988. During the last eight and a half months of his life, the torturous headaches never bothered him. David had been sure that Laura was somehow responsible, that she had somehow chased away whatever demon had been living inside of his brain. Even his doctor was amazed to discover that his cyst or tumor had died. Somehow, they had conquered David's demon.

Or had they?

Had the evil demon really been killed or had he just been waiting for the right time to strike? Had he merely faked his own demise until David was

133

vulnerable in the rough water? Had he then decided this was his opportunity to finish the game once and for all, to destroy David by paralyzing him in the treacherous ocean, to force him to go underwater until his lungs exploded?

T.C. had said no. Laura was not so sure.

She flicked on the light. Her eyes were wet. Even when David was alive, the thought of the agony he was forced to bear always made her tear.

She went into the bedroom half expecting to find him huddled on the bed, but of course, the room was empty. Then she headed into his study and over to the file cabinet she had bought him last year. The neatly labeled manila files gave the illusion at least that David was a somewhat organized individual. The illusion, however, was merely surface. He still lost bills, financial statements, important documents. David had always hated paperwork of any kind. He knew nothing of finance and wanted to know even less. 'You make both of our monetary decisions,' he had finally told her. 'You're the financial genius.'

The second drawer contained the financial statements. She pulled it open. She knew that his bank book and monthly reports from Heritage of Boston were filed behind the Gunther Mutual folder. She thumbed through the manila folders. Catalyst Energy, Davidson Fund, Equities with Recovery Corporation of America, Fredrickson and Associates, Gunther Mutual . . .

There was no Heritage of Boston.

She checked to make sure that it had not been placed out of order. Then she checked the other drawers. There was nothing on the Heritage of Boston.

She stood up. Her whole body was shaking. She needed to find answers and she needed to find them now. It was time to pay a visit to the Heritage of Boston.

*   *   *

T.C. and Laura parked the car and walked toward the entrance of the Heritage of Boston Bank. T.C. always felt odd walking with Laura. Here was one of the world's most beautiful women walking with a pudgy, nondescript shmoe in a wrinkled suit who was a good three inches shorter than she was. It must have made some spectacle.

'So you couldn't find the statements,' T.C. said. 'Big deal. Maybe he moved the account and got rid of them.'

'We're talking about David, remember? You know how bad he was when it came to financial matters.'

They waited for about ten minutes before a secretary ushered them into an office.

'I'm sorry for the delay,' the man behind the desk said. He stood and shook Laura's hand. 'I'm Richard Corsel, one of the bank's vice presidents. Please come in.'

He was young—no more than thirty—and something in his manner told Laura that he was not very happy to see them. 'Laura Baskin,' she said.

'I recognized you right away, Mrs Baskin. I'm very sorry to hear about your husband.'

'Thank you. This is Terry Conroy with the Boston Police Department.'

'Police? Is something wrong?'

'Nothing that I'm sure we can't work out,' Laura

replied. 'It involves an account my husband held here.'

'Yes?'

'I can't find the statements and I was hoping you could tell me what the current balance is.'

'One moment.' Richard Corsel tapped a few keys on his computer terminal. 'Your husband no longer has an account here, Mrs Baskin.'

'I'm sure he had one before we left for Australia a few weeks ago.'

'That's very possible, Mrs Baskin, but the account is closed.'

'Was the money withdrawn or transferred?'

Richard Corsel coughed into his fist. 'I'm not allowed to say.'

'By whose authority?'

'Your husband's.'

She sat forward. 'What?'

'When your husband cleared out his account, he left very specific stipulations. One of these was not to give out any information involving his funds.'

'But he's dead.'

'That does not alter his request.'

She glanced over at T.C. to make sure she was hearing right. 'When did he close the account?' she asked.

'I can't tell you that either. I'm sorry.'

'Mr Corsel, the money is missing. No one has any idea where it is being held.'

'I'm sorry. There's really nothing I can do.'

She peered into his eyes. They darted away from Laura's glare like scared birds. 'I want to know what happened to that account.'

'I can't tell you.'

T.C. stood. 'Let's go, Laura.'

'What are you talking about?' Laura raged. 'I'm not leaving until I find out what happened to that account.'

'Mr Corsel already said it's confidential.'

Richard Corsel nodded. 'Please, Mrs Baskin, I am only obeying your husband's wishes.'

'His wishes? He told you not to tell his wife what happened to his account?'

'I . . . I can't reveal that.'

'Mr Corsel, you are forcing my hand.'

His voice cracked. 'There is really nothing I can do.'

'Well there is something *I* can do,' Laura snapped. 'May I borrow your phone?'

'Of course.'

She dialed, waited, had the call transferred, and then she spoke. 'Sam? It's Laura. Thank you, it's nice to hear your voice too. I need you to do something for me. How much is Svengali holding in Heritage of Boston? I know it's a lot but can you give me a good estimation?'

Richard Corsel was turning white.

'Jesus, Laura,' T.C. interrupted, 'what the hell are you doing?'

'Wait outside, T.C. I don't want you to get involved in this.'

'But—'

'Please just do what I say.'

With a shrug T.C. stood and headed out. He slammed the door behind him, leaving Corsel alone to confront Laura.

'What's that, Sam? How many millions? Fine. Transfer it to First Boston. Tell the board of directors at Heritage of Boston that I was annoyed by the service of one of its vice presidents, a

Mr Richard Corsel. Tell them I also suspect he's involved in a scheme to rip me off. Right, that's C-O-R-S-E-L. Got that?'

'Wait!' Richard Corsel interrupted. 'Can't we talk about this?'

'Hold on a second, Sam. Excuse me?'

'Please, Mrs Baskin, just hang up and let's discuss this rationally.'

She turned back to the phone. 'Sam, if you don't hear from me in the next ten minutes, go ahead with the transaction.' She hung up. 'I'm listening.'

'Mrs Baskin, you are using blackmail.'

'I want to know what happened to that account, Mr Corsel, and believe me, I'll find out. This is no idle threat. If you still won't tell me after I transfer the Svengali funds, I'll have the press and my lawyers swarming all over the place. The media should love a story about a widow who wants to donate her late husband's earnings to charity and the bank that may have stolen the money.'

'Stolen?'

'The bank's reputation will be somewhat compromised, Mr Corsel, but eventually I will get the information.'

Richard Corsel looked like he had just lost a boxing match.

'By the way,' Laura added, 'Sam is very precise. I only have a few minutes left to stop him.'

Corsel lowered his head. 'I don't know where the account is exactly. You have to believe me.'

'Go on.'

'Your husband had me transfer the money to a bank in Switzerland.'

'When?'

He paused. 'Please, Mrs Baskin, I can't tell you.'

'Which bank in Switzerland?'

'Bank of Geneva. But I know it didn't stay there long so you can't make a claim there. And you may be able to threaten Heritage of Boston, but there's no way to budge a Swiss bank.'

'But why would David do something like that?'

He shrugged. 'I don't know.'

'Did he handle this transaction in person?'

'No, I spoke to him on the phone.'

'Are you sure it was David's voice?'

'Positive. I know your husband's voice very well—even with the static. Plus he used a code number only he knows.'

'784CF90821BC,' Laura stated.

'And obviously,' Richard Corsel replied, 'he trusted you with it.'

'David always told me everything, Mr Corsel,' she said. 'Now would you please hand me the phone? I have to call Sam.'

*   *   *

Laura recounted the conversation to T.C. as they headed back to the car.

'I can't believe you did that, Laura. I arrest people for doing that sort of thing.'

'Okay, guilty. So what do you think?'

'About Switzerland? I think Corsel is right. I've got a few friends at the FBI's office but I doubt we'll find out what happened to the account after it reached the Bank of Geneva.'

'But why would David do this?'

T.C. shrugged. 'Maybe he wanted to have some money stored away in case the bottom fell out.'

'And not tell me about it?'

'Maybe he was going to and didn't have a chance. You said he had the Heritage account recently. Maybe he made the transaction right before you eloped and decided a honeymoon was not the place to discuss finances.'

'Wait a second,' Laura began. She concentrated hard, trying to remember exactly. 'David came here to get some cash right before we left for Australia.'

'Then that's your answer, Laura. He made the transfer when he picked up the cash and just decided to tell you about it later.'

She shook her head. 'Something is still not right. David could barely balance his checkbook.'

'That's true, but—'

Laura stopped suddenly. 'Hold on.'

'What?'

'Corsel said that David made the transfer over the phone, not in person. He mentioned that there was static on the line.'

'So?'

'Don't you see?' Laura almost shouted. 'That means that David must have transferred his money while we were in Australia.'

*   *   *

Stan sat up and watched the television. Nothing on. Fat Oprah (or was she skinny this week?) was talking to some group of slobs who sexually assault their plants or something like that. Stan wasn't really listening. He was thinking. He needed to think up a score. A big one. And he needed to think of one in a hurry.

He was also thinking about the B Man.

The solution to his current money problems was

140

obvious: get the money from David's estate. But how? Everything was left to Laura. He could ask her for it but that would arouse her suspicion. She may be a bit naive, but she was far from stupid. Plus Stan was sure that fucking T.C. was filling her head with all kinds of nonsense about the past. No, Stan decided, he could not ask her directly. He would have to make her offer the money to him.

But how?

Knuckles rapped on the door.

Terror ran through Stan. He had used a fake name when he registered. No one knew he was here. He closed his eyes as the knock came again. Maybe it was just the maid. Maybe it was—

'Open up, Stan. I want to talk to you.'

—B Man.

Stan stood as though hypnotized. He was on the fourteenth floor so a window escape was out. But what the hell, he and B Man went back a long way. B Man had never hurt him before. He knew Stan was good for the money, and once Stan explained that he had a chance of getting his hands on serious money, B Man would give him more time. Stan turned the knob and opened the door.

'B Man!' Stan greeted him with a smile. 'How the hell are you, man? You look great.'

B Man stood in the doorway and smiled coolly. 'Thanks, Stan. It's nice to see you, too.'

Stan was always surprised by B Man's appearance. He hardly looked the part of a rough gangster. He had long, bleached-blond hair, a year-round tan, and teeth that were white enough for a tooth-polish commercial. His height and weight were average, maybe even a little on the small side. Even more unusual, the B Man had an

141

ivy league education and had lived for three years in Korea, where he trained six hours a day in Kung Fu or some shit like that.

That was his specialty: hand-to-hand combat. You could put three bruisers twice his size against him and B Man would slaughter them without breaking a sweat.

'Come in, B.'

'Thank you.' He stepped in and closed the door. His voice remained pleasant. 'What are you doing in Boston, Stan?'

'I told you I was going to go to my brother's funeral.'

'That was quite a while ago.'

'I know that, B Man, but I'm very close to scoring big.'

'I've heard that from you before.'

'No, really.'

B Man stood directly in front of Stan, their faces no more than six inches apart. 'You wouldn't be trying to avoid me, would you, Stan?'

'No way,' Stan argued. 'I would never do that.'

B Man just stared.

'Wh . . . What brings you to Boston, B?'

B Man strolled around the room. 'I have a little business here. One of my wrestlers is in town.'

'Roadhouse Rex?' Stan asked.

B Man nodded.

'Roadhouse is great,' Stan continued, trying to keep B Man's attention on the gruesome wrestler and off of himself. 'He can take a dive like nobody's business.'

'Roadhouse is the best,' B Man agreed with a hint of a smile. 'You should see him backstage. His trunk is filled with blood capsules, phony casts for

142

whatever ailment he plans on faking, you name it.' B Man turned and moved toward Stan. 'But we're getting off the subject, aren't we?'

'Off the subject?'

B Man just smiled. 'Stan, have you been trying to hide from me?'

Stan swallowed. 'You know me better than that, B Man. Like I said before, I told you I was coming to Boston.'

'True,' B Man agreed, 'but you forgot to mention that you were going to use an alias.'

'I just needed a little time. You see, my brother—'

'I know all about your brother.'

'Well, he was loaded. I'm going to get some of his money.'

B Man laughed. 'Who do you think you're talking to? I know what you did to him. I was there, remember? Your brother would never leave you a cent.'

'I know that, B Man. I'm going to get the money from his widow.'

'That model?'

'Yeah, B Man. She'll give me the money.'

'Fifty thousand dollars?'

'Right. No problem.'

B Man calmly walked toward the bed. 'But Stan, you're already very late.'

'Just tack on interest.'

'Oh I will. But you're past that now.'

'Come on, B Man. You know I'm good for it.'

B Man shook his head slowly. 'No, that's where you're wrong. I *think* you're good for it. But I don't know for sure. Perhaps a little incentive would help.'

'Incentive?'

There was no time for Stan to react. With frightening speed, B Man's hand shot out. The blow landed in the center of Stan's belly. The breath whooshed out of him. Stan fell to the ground, struggling to put oxygen back in his lungs.

B Man watched Stan writhe in pain. He calmly reached down and grabbed Stan's right hand. For a minute or two, he held the hand and waited for Stan to begin catching his breath.

'I'm sorry about all this, Stan.'

'Please . . .'

B Man clamped his hand over Stan's mouth. Then he pulled Stan's middle finger back until it nearly touched his wrist. The finger snapped like a twig. Stan felt the jagged edges of the bone rip into his skin. His head swam.

'One week, Stan,' the B Man said quietly. He held Stan's finger for another second and then gently placed the hand on the floor. The finger was already swelling, the bone nearly puncturing the skin.

'Do you hear me?'

Stan managed a nod. The pain was staggering.

'And you're not going to hide from me again, are you, Stan?'

He shook his head.

B Man smiled down at Stan. Then he raised his heel and slammed it with expert accuracy onto the broken finger. Again, B Man had to cover Stan's mouth to muffle the scream.

'I guess we understand each other now,' B Man said matter-of-factly. He turned toward the mirror, fixed his hair and then walked toward the door. 'Always a pleasure to see you, Stan. You have one week to come up with the money. And now it's sixty thousand dollars.'

*   *   *

Later that night, Laura sat in Serita's spare bedroom and looked out the window. What had happened? One moment the world was perfect and then she was suddenly thrust into Hell. What had she done? She hated the whole world right now. She hated everything about it. Sometimes, she even hated David for leaving her here alone when he knew that she could not survive without him.

Time limped by but it did not heal any wounds. Every time she felt like she was getting stronger, she would drive past a playground with kids playing basketball, or see lovers holding hands by the Charles River, or see a family taking a Sunday drive in their station wagon, and then the wounds would reopen and gush fresh blood.

And nothing made sense anymore. Their new house had been broken into but nothing was stolen. David's account had been mysteriously transferred to the Twilight Zone. Her father was acting peculiarly. And what was going on with T.C.? Since when had he been against using pressure tactics to get information?

Serita stepped in the room and turned on the light. 'What are you doing, Laura?' she asked.

'The usual,' Laura answered. 'I guess I just want to be alone.'

'You've been doing a lot of that the last couple of months. It's starting to get on my nerves.'

'I'm going to move out tomorrow, Serita. I think it's time I took care of myself.'

'Brave words, girl. So what are you going to do at your own place?'

Laura shrugged.

'If you're just going to mope around you might as well just stay here.' Serita tossed a newspaper onto Laura's lap. 'Read this.'

Laura glanced at the top of the page. 'The financial section? I didn't think business was your bit.'

'It's not,' Serita agreed. 'But I think you should read it.'

She did not have the strength. 'Why don't you just give me a quick rehash?'

'Okay, it's like this. Svengali slipped two points yesterday. That means it has dropped over ten points in the last two weeks. The reason it keeps sliding is because there is speculation that you don't have it anymore, that you're not going back.'

'I really don't care, Serita.'

'You listen to me. If you no longer give a shit about yourself, fine. But you have stockholders to protect, people who believed and invested in you. You can't just abandon them.'

Laura did not say anything. Her eyes never left the window.

'What the hell is the matter with you, Laura?'

Laura turned her gaze toward her friend. 'What's the matter with me?' she repeated. 'Don't you read the papers? My husband is dead, Serita. Can't you understand that? David is dead.'

'Of course I understand. But you're not dead, are you?' Serita crossed the room and sat on the chair next to her friend. 'Let me tell you something,' she continued. 'I remember everything there is to remember about you. I remember how you told

146

me all about those snotty little kids who picked on you because you were ugly, but you survived and showed them what you were all about. And I remember how those assholes from all the big companies laughed when you first started Svengali. They kept trying to knock you down, remember? But you stood up to them, Laura, and again you survived when everyone else counted you out. And me? I just sat back and cheered you on. You fought to make that company what it is today. You fought hard. It's your baby, Laura. Svengali is yours. Don't just give it up. David wouldn't want that. And he wouldn't want you to give up on yourself like this.'

David. Just hearing his name again pricked her eyes with tears.

'Honey, I know it's hard, but it's time to live again before everything you have—everything you worked so hard for—falls apart.' Serita stood and looked down at her friend. 'Besides, I happen to be your highest paid model. If Svengali goes under, I'm going to lose an important customer. You wouldn't want that.'

'Heaven forbid,' Laura replied with a hint of a smile. 'You know something?'

'What?'

'You're a good friend.'

'The best.'

Laura wrung her hands in her lap. 'Serita?'

'I'm right here.'

'I don't know what to do. I . . . I'm scared to go back.'

'I know, honey. I don't want to push you. Take one step at a time.'

Laura nodded but the doubts and fears remained burrowed in her mind. With a long and painful sigh, she sat up and reached for the phone. She dialed the number of Svengali's Director of Public Relations.

'Hello?'

'This is Laura,' she said, her voice quaking. 'Make an announcement that I will be back in the office tomorrow morning.'

*　　　*　　　*

'Line five, Dr Ayars.'

'Thank you.'

James Ayars picked up the receiver and pushed line five. 'Where the hell have you been?'

'Out.'

'I've been trying to reach you all day.'

'I'm not at your beck and call.'

'I didn't say you were.'

'What do you want?' the voice asked.

'I was at the settling of David's estate today,' James said.

'And?'

'Something rather odd came up about David's finances.'

'So?'

Dr James Ayars leaned forward. 'I'm no longer convinced that David committed suicide.'

CHAPTER EIGHT

'Estelle!'

'Yes, Laura?'

'Where the hell are the designs on winter shoes?

148

I asked for them ten minutes ago.'

'Right away.'

'And I want to see Marty Tribble now. This marketing scheme is for old ladies, for chrissake. I'm not trying to market the Bible Belt.'

'Will do.'

'And tell Hillary it's going to be a long night. These skirt patterns are all wrong, and we're going to be here until we get them right.'

'Got it.'

'And send Sandy up in about an hour. I have an idea for a new product line.'

'Sandy. One hour.'

'And tell accounting I want to see a tabulation of all transactions that took place during my absence. Something is wrong with my figures.'

'Right. Anything else, Laura?'

'I'd kill for a cup of coffee.'

'A cup of coffee it is.' Estelle turned to leave and then stopped. 'Laura?'

'Yes?'

'It's nice to have you back.'

'Thanks, Estelle.'

Estelle left. Laura looked at her desk and shook her head. What a mess. She scanned the piles, wondering what she should tackle next. Distribution was screwed up. The winter fashions were in disarray, and they had to be finished up in the next couple of days.

Laura sat back. Had coming back to work been a good idea? She was not sure. Yes, it was a welcome distraction. It kept her mind occupied. But everything felt a little out of place to her as though she were returning to her hometown after a long absence—familiar and yet foreign. If work was therapeutic, it would be a long, slow healing. Her hands still shook. Her heart still felt like it was being squeezed in a vise. But like Serita had told her, take one step at a time.

The phone buzzed.

'What is it, Estelle?'

'Visitor for you. A Mr Stan Baskin.'

'Send him in.'

Estelle opened her door and ushered Stan in. He greeted Laura with a warm smile. 'Good morning, kid. Nice to see you back at work.'

'This is a pleasant surprise, Stan. Sit down.'

'Are you sure I'm not interrupting?'

'Actually you are. But you are a most welcome interruption. I needed a break anyway.'

'You sure?'

'Positive.' Laura noticed that his right hand was all bandaged. 'What happened to your hand?'

'Oh, this? I slammed a car door on it. I've always been the klutz of the family.'

'It looks painful. Can I get you something?'

'No, it's fine. Really.'

Laura stood from behind her desk and moved toward the chair next to Stan. 'Why weren't you at the lawyer's office yesterday?'

Stan hesitated. 'I appreciated your invitation, but it wasn't my place.'

'You were his brother.'

'That might be true,' Stan allowed, 'but I wouldn't have felt right going. It was supposed to be for those David loved and cared for. I . . . I don't fit into that category.'

'That's not so,' Laura insisted. 'Whatever happened between you two does not erase the fact that you're his brother. Think of the childhood you

150

shared with him. Nothing can take that away. You belonged there, Stan. You're entitled to some of his estate.'

Stan slowly shook his head. 'I threw that all away, Laura. I don't want anything from David, except something he can never give me: his forgiveness.'

'If he were alive, I know he'd forgive you.'

'I'm not so sure.' He paused. 'Listen, Laura, I know you're busy so let me tell you what I came here for. I wanted to know if you'd have dinner with me tomorrow as a sort of Bon Voyage.'

'Bon Voyage?'

He nodded. 'I'm heading back to Michigan the next morning.'

'You're leaving?' she asked. Over the last month, she had gotten used to having Stan around. He was part of the family now, David's sole blood relative. She relied on him. 'Why? I thought you liked Boston.'

'I do. I love it. But the mall deal fell through. I can't raise the capital. And . . . I don't know . . . I feel like I don't belong here—like I'm intruding on David's family.'

'You're not intruding.'

'Be that as it may, will you join me tomorrow night?'

Laura leaned back. She clasped her hands together and leaned them against the bridge of her nose. 'Would you do me a favor, Stan?'

'Of course.'

'I don't know if you know this or not, but David did not have a legal will. The letter of the law leaves his entire estate to me. I want you to have some of it.'

'Laura, I can't.'

'I want you to build your mall with the basketball theme. How much do you think you need to get started?'

'Forget it.'

'Why?'

'I already told you. I don't deserve anything of David's.'

'Then do it for me. I need some new outlets for Svengali in his area. Your mall will be perfect.'

Stan shook his head, but Laura did not stop. 'You can name it after David, Stan. Think of it as a memorial to your love for him, a way of showing the world what he meant to you. Would a million dollars get the ball rolling?' Even as she said it, Laura felt a pang of discomfort. David's words came floating back to her.

We don't get along . . .

But she ignored the voice.

'Look, Laura, I don't feel right about this . . .'

'Then it's settled. I'll have my attorney write you out a check tomorrow afternoon. One million dollars of your brother's money will be yours. Agreed?'

He chuckled lightly. 'Laura, have you ever been called stubborn?'

'Frequently. Agreed?'

Stan shrugged. 'I don't know what to say.'

'Say yes,' Laura urged, while her mind churned in confusion. Was she doing the right thing? 'Say you'll cancel your flight back to Michigan. Say that you'll get cracking on this mall idea. Say that you still want to be part of this family.'

'Of course I still want to be part of this family.'

'Then say yes.'

Stan lowered his eyes and then slowly raised

them toward Laura. 'You won't regret this, Laura.'

Laura smiled uneasily. Won't regret? She thought that maybe she already did.

*   *   *

Clip Arnstein put out his cigar. He glanced across the table at his two star players. Earl was in his late twenties and just at the pinnacle of his career. He had led the league in scoring twice and rebounding once. He was also a consummate shot-blocker. But he had scored a lot of those points off great passes from David. He had been able to get open for many of those points because teams had often concentrated on trying to contain White Lightning.

Timmy Daniels was a few years younger. He was a shooting guard from Brigham Young University, a super all-around athlete who had a fiery intensity that matched David's. He liked to win, had to win, would do anything to win. His appearance may have reminded one of a little kid in the playground, but he was as tough as Clip had seen in his fifty years plus of basketball. And he could shoot. Now that David was gone, Timmy was probably the best outside shooter in the league.

Clip took out another cigar and bit off the end. 'I thought it was about time the three of us met in private.'

'What's up, Clip?' Timmy asked.

'I have the results of the team vote. You two are now the captains of the team.'

Timmy glanced over at Earl before speaking. 'I think I speak for both of us when I say that that's an honor we wish had never been bestowed on us.'

'I know,' Clip replied. 'But we all know the team

is not going to be the same without David. Hell, our lives aren't going to be the same. But we have to go on. The season starts in a couple of months and we have to get prepared. Rookie try-outs are next week.'

'What do you want us to do?' Timmy asked.

Clip tossed a file to both of his star players. 'Here's some info on our draft picks and free agents who are supposed to try out for the team.'

They both scanned the reports. When he was finished, Timmy closed the file. 'It's shit.'

Clip nodded his agreement. 'There wasn't a hell of a lot of talent in this year's draft, plus when you win a championship, you pick last. We've got a problem here, guys. We lost one of the league's best players. We don't even have a decent scorer from the forward spot now. We'll get crushed on the break without him. So my question is this: how are we going to find someone new on that list of players?'

'I don't know,' Tim responded. 'But you've been in tougher spots than this, Clip. You're famous for the last-minute deals you've made over the years. You're not called the Miracle Worker for nothing.'

Clip chuckled. 'Thanks for the vote of confidence. Earl, you haven't said anything. What do you think?'

'No one can replace David,' Earl said quietly.

'I know that,' the Miracle Worker replied. 'I'm not looking for a replacement. The team as a whole is going to have to shift perspective. Without David, you're not going to get those passes, Earl. We'll have to play a slower game, a more controlled game. You have to post up down low like you did at Notre Dame. And Timmy, your outside shot is

154

without question the best around. But we're going to need you to penetrate the middle and open it up. You're going to have to be more creative. But even with all that, we are still going to need more parts to make this machine run smoothly. I may have to make some trades.'

'Trades?' Timmy repeated. 'You can't break up this group.'

'It's a business, Tim. I traded three popular veterans to draft David and Earl, and I'll deal players if I have to.'

'Isn't there another alternative?'

Clip nodded. 'Sure.'

'What?'

The Miracle Worker stood. 'Hope for a miracle.'

*　　　*　　　*

Stan woke with a start. He wondered if he had had another bad dream. Impossible. No way. For the first time, everything was going his way.

He swung his legs over the bed and grabbed the clock. Three-thirty a.m. What a day he had had yesterday! As if duping Laura yesterday morning was not enough luck, the night had crowned him with yet another spectacular achievement. Maybe he should have held back. Maybe he should not have tempted the gods by stretching his luck, but oh man, he could not resist.

The woman lying next to him stirred and twisted her naked body toward him. Stan gasped at what he saw. His groin was reacting to just looking at her.

'How do you feel?' he asked her.

Gloria looked up at him with the eyes of a small animal. 'Very happy.'

'Me too,' he said. 'Do you know that you're the most beautiful woman I've ever seen?'

Her body quivered. 'Thank you.'

'I mean it. And it's been so long, Gloria. It's been so long that I can't remember ever feeling this close to someone.'

'Do you mean it, Stan?'

'Of course I do.'

'Please don't tease me.'

He lay back down and put his arm around her warm body. 'I would never do that, Gloria. I . . . I don't know if I should say this.'

'Please,' she urged.

'Well, this may sound corny, but I feel like last night was the start of something wonderful.'

'Really?'

'I hope I'm not being too forward,' he continued. 'Usually, I'm pretty shy and laid-back. I don't open to a person very easily. But it's just that I feel so right when I'm with you. Like I can say anything.'

She smiled hopefully. 'I feel the same way.'

'You do?'

Gloria nodded. 'I haven't been with a man in over a year.' She adjusted herself in the bed. Stan watched her. She had the nicest breasts he had ever seen. Large, round, firm. Mr Happy felt like a block of lead between his legs. 'I want to tell you something before we go on with this.'

'What is it?' Stan asked.

'It's about my past.'

'You already told me about that. It doesn't matter to me, Gloria.'

'Did I tell you about the last time I was with a man—or should I say men?'

Stan tried to hide the look of surprise on his face.

156

'You don't owe me any explanations.'

'Unfortunately, I do. Then you can leave if you want.'

About a year ago, Gloria was living on the West Coast with a dope dealer. For about the millionth time in her life, Gloria was sure she had found the right man. Tony may have been a dope dealer and a small-time pornographer, but he was not like the others. He was gentle. He genuinely cared for her. True, he had her hooked on drugs but she had been an addict even before they met. And Tony said she had it under control, that to go through withdrawal would be painful at this stage. So he kept giving her the needles with heroin and the cocaine for her nose because he cared, because he did not want to see her suffer.

But there were still fits of depression for Gloria. She had no self-esteem, no self-respect. But that wasn't so bad. Not as long as she could drug herself to a point where it did not matter. Sometimes, days would go by and she would not leave her bed. Sometimes, weeks would go by and she would not remember anything that had happened.

She had been living with Tony for about three months when he came home one day with a big-time dealer from Colombia. The three of them had dinner together but Gloria could not remember much about it. Tony had really given her some prime stuff and she was just flying. She did notice that the big-time dealer from Colombia was staring at her all the time. But that was nothing new. Men were always staring at her. And she was safe. Tony was there with her. And he loved her very much.

It was getting late and Gloria was feeling especially weary. 'Tony?'

157

'Yes, Gloria?'

'I'm going to go to sleep now. I'm really tired.'

'Okay. Say goodnight to our guest.'

She did. She held onto the railing as she steered her way up to the bedroom. She closed the door, took off her top and then slid off her pants.

'Guapa! Beautiful!'

She spun, trying to cover herself with her hands. The Colombian opened the door and stepped in. 'What are you doing up here?'

Tony stepped in from behind the Colombian. 'It's okay, baby.'

'What . . . What's going on?'

'Mr Enrique is a very important supplier, Gloria. He's asked for a little favor.'

'But Tony—'

'It's all right, baby. I'll be right here. It'll be fun.'

The wide-eyed Colombian quickly stripped down.

'Tony, I don't want to.'

Tony began to take off his clothes too. 'For me, Gloria. Please.'

Trembling, she turned toward the Colombian. He stood in front of her completely naked. He reached out a hand and grabbed her breast roughly. Pain shot through her. He lowered his mouth toward her nipple.

'Please don't.'

Gloria was forced back, tears pouring down her cheeks. Tony held her down as the Colombian did as he pleased.

Stan held her. 'It's over now, Gloria. It's over.'

'No it's not. I have to finish the story before I run out of nerve.'

The next morning, Gloria woke up feeling sore and dirty. She snorted a little cocaine and then made her way to the shower. She stayed under the powerful *spray until the hot water ran out. She still did not feel clean.*

Gloria did not cry that morning. For the first time, she saw clearly through the drugs. Nothing was different. Tony was not different. He was like Brad and Jeff and Stuart and Mike and J.J. and Kenny and all the others. He knew she was not worth loving, not worth caring for. She was just an object to abuse as he saw fit. And at long last, Gloria knew what she had to do. She finally realized how she could stop it. It was simple really.

She would kill herself.

She wondered how she should go about doing it. First she would call her sister Laura. She had not spoken to her for almost eight months but Gloria and Laura really loved one another. Her parents, well, they had given up on her a long time ago. But not Laura. It would be really nice to hear her voice one more time.

She picked up the phone and called. Laura was thrilled to hear from her. Laura thought it would be a great idea if they could get together soon. Gloria agreed. Maybe next week would be a good time.

'Is everything all right, Gloria?' Laura asked. 'Why don't you come home and stay with me for a while?'

Gloria declined the invitation, thanked her and hung up. Then she turned her attention to how she should kill herself. The answer came to her quickly. She would take a drug overdose. A friend of hers in San Francisco had done that about six months ago. Gloria resolved herself to her decision. Tomorrow night she would OD on heroin.

That night, Tony came home full of apologies and words of love. 'I was so stoned, baby. I didn't know what I was doing. I'm so sorry, Gloria. Please forgive me.'

'Do you really mean it, Tony?'

'Sure, honey. I never knew it would hurt you. I love you, baby. I would never do something to hurt you. You know that.'

And Gloria thought that maybe he was telling the truth. Maybe he did love her after all. Maybe he didn't understand how she felt about what had happened. If he did, he would never have made her do it.

Tony continued to talk to her, to soothe her. He had received a new shipment too. Prime stuff. And she needed a fix. Her whole body was craving for a little prick from Tony's needle. He shot her up with a very large amount of drugs.

Her mind became fuzzy, even more fuzzy than usual. She drifted back, her world spinning in a murky haze.

'How do you feel, honey?'

'I'm flying,' she replied with a smile. 'I'm flying.'

'Good, baby. That's real good.'

She felt his hand on her blouse. He was unbuttoning her top. He slipped it off and then he pulled down her shorts and panties. She began to giggle. 'You want to do it now?'

'Yeah, baby. I got something special planned.'

Special. That sounded nice. She closed her eyes as the drugs sped through her veins. It felt nice to be naked with Tony.

She felt him hold down her arms and legs. No reason to. She was not about to struggle, except that sometimes he liked that. The lights were suddenly very bright in her eyes. Tony must have pulled up the shade. But wait. How could he have pulled up the shades when he was holding her down?

Then she heard people speaking Spanish.

She opened her eyes but the harsh glare made her

close them again. She moved to shade them with her hand and that was when she realized that her hands and legs were tied to the bed.

'Tony?'

More whispered words. Some in Spanish. Some in English. And then laughter. She felt so tired she just wanted to go to sleep. She forced open her eyes and focused.

The Colombian smiled down at her. He was with six other men. They were all naked.

Now she struggled but the drugs and the knots were too strong. 'Tony?'

'I'm here, baby,' he laughed. 'Just enjoy.'

The men approached her, each stroking a different part of her body with their hands and tongues. She looked up and saw Tony holding a video camera. The rest was a blur of words and positions. Her body was turned over, twisted every which way, abused.

'Get her closer to the camera.' 'Put it in her mouth.' 'This is going to be the best film yet.' 'Bend her the other way.'

Gloria felt saliva and warm breath covering her face, her neck, her breasts, her thighs. Rough hands clawed at her.

Then a female voice shouted, 'STOP!'

Suddenly the men were being pulled off her. Gloria felt someone untying her arms. She managed to open her eyes and look up. But what she was seeing had to be a hallucination from the drug.

'Laura?' she called out.

'Just relax,' her sister said. 'You'll be all right.'

Gloria started to cry. Why hadn't she killed herself? Death would have been preferable to letting Laura see what her older sister had become.

David and T.C. had come with Laura. T.C.

whipped out his badge, causing the Colombians to scatter in every direction. David destroyed Tony's video recording.

'You're going to be all right, Gloria,' Laura said through her tears. She held her sister tightly. 'I'm going to help you now.'

Gloria raised her head. 'Now, if you want me to leave, I'll understand.'

What a fucking story! Stan thought. It gave him another goddamn hard-on! Stan moved toward her. 'Don't you understand, Gloria? None of that matters to me. I'm happy you want to be open with me, but that's all in the past now. You don't have to keep apologizing for it. It's the Gloria I know now that I care about. And I have something of a past myself. To be honest, I'm still not all I seem to be. But I'm trying, I really am. Will you help me, Gloria? Will you let me help you?'

They made love again and then Stan got dressed. He looked over at her body and felt Mr Happy start to stir yet again. Never had he been this horny for a chick's body. He had had plenty of women in his day but he had never seen a body like this. Soft skin, curvaceous and supple, flat stomach and, of course, the kind of breasts men fantasize about. There was only one thing that could arouse him more:

Laura.

But that conquest would come in time. Right now, he had to be careful with Gloria. Christ, what a story, he thought again. Talk about Miss Instability 1989. Stan didn't want to take the chance of letting Laura know about him laying her sister so he had convinced her not to tell anyone.

'Just for a little while,' he assured her. 'It's a

superstitious thing with me. I'm afraid if we tell the world something bad will happen.'

She had bought it. And besides, Gloria made an ideal safety valve in case something went wrong or if he needed another score. She had plenty of dough of her own.

They headed out of the hotel together. When they reached the street, Stan faced her. 'I'll see you tonight.'

Gloria nodded, her face beaming.

He bent down and kissed her passionately.

* * *

Across the street, a jogger wearing an Adidas sweatsuit watched the kiss from behind his zoom lens. He snapped a few more pictures and then he picked up the phone and dialed.

'What have you got?'

'He and Gloria Ayars just left,' he replied. 'They appeared rather chummy.'

'Keep following Baskin.'

'Okay, but I want to know what this is all about.'

'Don't worry about it. Just keep following him and call in if he does anything unusual.'

The jogger shrugged. 'Whatever you say, T.C.'

* * *

The phone buzzed.

'Yes, Estelle.'

'John Bort is here to see you.'

'Send him in.'

John Bort opened the door. 'You wanted to see me, boss?'

163

'Yes, John. Come in.'

'Something wrong with the security?'

'No, not at all,' Laura assured him.

'This place is wired better than Fort Knox, you know.'

'You're doing a super job, John. Please have a seat.'

'Thanks, boss.'

'You can call me Laura.'

'I prefer boss.'

She shrugged. 'Suit yourself.'

'What can I do for you?' he asked.

Laura tilted back her chair. 'You used to work for the FBI, right?'

'Thirty-three years with the agency,' he replied.

'So you've seen it all in your time.'

'Just about. What's this all about, boss?'

'My question deals with a bank transaction.'

'Huh?'

'Let me give you a hypothetical situation,' she continued. 'Suppose a large sum of money vanished—'

'Large amounts of money just don't vanish, boss.'

'True. Let's suppose a man transferred this large sum to Switzerland and they transferred it elsewhere. Now the man dies and there is no way to track down the money. What would you do?'

He thought for a moment. 'I'm not sure, boss. The man probably wanted to hide his money. Could be that he was afraid someone was after it—you know, a relative or something—and he wanted to make sure they couldn't get their hands on it. Or it could be that he had a mistress someplace and he wanted to take care of her without the family knowing about it.'

'What do you mean?'

'Well, let's say he knew he was going to die, right? His family would have a claim to the money. But he wants to leave a certain amount to somebody else without letting his family in on what he's doing.'

'Pretty far-fetched.'

'True enough, but I know a couple of guys who did it. Hell, if you think that's far-fetched, you oughta hear about the case in 1972 that was like this.'

'What happened?' Laura asked.

John Bort adjusted himself in the chair. 'This big informer dies in a fire right before giving his testimony. Arson. Knocked off by the mob, we figured. But something is weird: his money vanishes. Well, my partner and I check it out, check all over, but we can't locate the funds. Guess what happens?'

'What?'

'Two years later the same informer turns up dead . . . again! The son of a bitch hid all his money and then faked his own death! And we fell for it! He moved his money to Ireland and was living there under an assumed name for all that time. And we never knew. Unfortunately for him, the mob didn't fall for it. Somehow, they managed to find him.' John sat back with a smile and shook his head in disbelief. 'Ain't that the weirdest thing you ever heard?'

Laura did not respond. She was already dialing T.C.'s number.

*   *   *

165

The patient pushed the barbell over his head.

'That's enough for today,' the nurse said.

The patient lowered the bar and shook his head. 'Not by a long shot.'

'You're going to overdue it.'

The patient struggled and the bar went over his head. He was a bit out of shape but not nearly as bad as he feared. 'No chance.'

'You are being very stubborn.'

The patient performed two more repetitions. 'I've been cooped up in that goddamn bed for too long. I need to do a little exercise.'

'This is all highly irregular. We are supposed to imagine that this place is a hospital, not a health spa.' She moved over toward the curtain. 'Why don't you go for a walk outside? The only people who will see you are the locals.'

The patient looked surprised. 'I can start going outside?'

She sighed. 'If you promise not to overdo it.' She opened the closet and reached in. 'The doctor told me not to give this to you until you were ready.'

The patient put down the weights and watched her.

'Here,' the nurse said. 'The doctor said you would be anxious to get your hands on this.'

With a small grunt, she tossed the patient a basketball.

*　　　*　　　*

'I'm glad you called, Laura,' T.C. began as he entered her office. He was too jittery to sit on Laura's plush office furniture, so he paced around the room. 'I also wanted to talk to you.'

'About what?'

'You go first.'

She too was feeling somewhat jittery, but she stayed in her chair and performed her customary leg shake. She was not sure what she wanted to say. Nothing made sense anymore but maybe T.C. could help her figure out what was going on. Maybe T.C. could tell her why a man who knew nothing of finance worked out an elaborate scheme to have money disappear just days (or even hours) before his death. 'Do you know John Bort?'

'Your security chief? Sure. Good man. Hell of a storyteller.'

'Did you know he used to work for the FBI?'

'Sure.'

'Well, I asked him about the disappearing account.'

T.C. looked surprised. 'You told him about it?'

'No. I asked him about a hypothetical situation similar to ours.'

'What did he say?'

Laura told him about her short conversation with John Bort. When she finished, T.C. was more fidgety than ever.

'So what are you trying to say, Laura?'

'Nothing, I wanted your opinion.'

T.C. finally sat down. 'David's dead. You've got to come to terms with it.'

'I know that, but I want to know why he moved his money.'

'Like John said, maybe he had a reason for hiding it that we aren't aware of.'

Laura did not buy that. 'And where did he get this sudden know-how about transferring funds?'

'I don't know. He could have gone to some big

167

money expert or something.'

'And the timing? Isn't that a hell of a coincidence?'

T.C. took out a cigar, fighting to remain calm. 'So what do you think, Laura? I saw his body. David is dead. His ghost did not break into your house and rip up a photograph of his father. His ghost is not drinking Margaritas in Tahiti, living off secret bank accounts. There are a million more logical possibilities.'

The phone buzzed. 'Laura?'

'What is it, Estelle?'

'The accountant is here with the check for Mr Baskin.'

'I'll be with him in a minute.'

T.C.'s pale face gained color in a hurry. 'A check for Stan Baskin? What the hell is going on?'

'Nothing.'

'You're giving money to Stan Baskin?'

'Just drop it. You said you had something important to tell me.'

'Laura, you can't give him money.'

Laura wished he had never overheard Estelle's announcement. 'Like it or not, Stan Baskin is David's only living relative. He's entitled to some of his estate.'

'He's entitled to shit!'

'That's your opinion.'

T.C. stood quickly and once again began pacing. He was fuming. 'How much is he taking you for?'

'If you want to know the truth, I had to force him to accept it.'

'I'm sure you had to twist his arm. How much?'

'A million dollars. It's for a mall in David's name.'

T.C. wanted to laugh. 'He's using the mall scheme? And you fell for it?'

Now it was Laura who was getting angry. 'What are you talking about?'

'Just this: for someone so goddamn smart, you can be so fucking gullible.'

'Don't start this with me again, T.C. I am giving him the money.'

'No, you're not.' T.C. reached into his folder and tossed a photograph on Laura's desk.

Laura picked up the photograph. Her face twisted in confusion. She put down the picture and looked over to T.C.

'Now,' he said. 'I am going to tell you why David hated his brother.'

CHAPTER NINE

Laura could not believe what she was seeing. 'What is this supposed to mean?'

'It's a picture of Stan and your sister,' T.C. said.

'I can see that.'

'Gloria spent last night with him.'

'Jesus, you're a nosy bastard. Have you been following me too?'

'I'm not following Stan to be nosy. I'm following him because I know him.'

'And what great plot has your investigation revealed?'

'You're not going to like it.'

Laura shook her head in disbelief. 'You had the gall to criticize me for intimidating the guy at the bank and then you go around playing Peeping Tom with my sister? I can't believe it.'

'Are you ready to listen or do you want to keep calling me names?'

Laura looked at his eyes. A chill rushed through her. Suddenly, she was not so sure she wanted to hear what he had to say. 'Go ahead.'

T.C. was not sure where to begin. He lit another cigar and considered his words.

Stan Baskin had been scum for most of his life. He was a high-school delinquent who was fortunate enough to possess an enormous amount of superficial style and charm. It always got him through. He was intensely lazy, always looking for the easy way out, always looking for the easy money. Stan would do anything for money. Except work. He preferred setting up scams and cons and he was good. Damn good. Good enough to pilfer big bucks from his unsuspecting victims. But then his Achille's heel always took it away:

He gambled.

David tried to convince Stan to get help for his gambling problem. But Stan was like a drug addict or an alcoholic. He was sure he could stop any time he wanted. He just didn't want to stop. Especially when the Redskins were such a sure thing against the Vikings or Rambling Shoe in the fourth race could not lose. Maybe David should have tried harder. Maybe he should have forced him to get help, but it probably would not have done any good. Stan was naturally jealous of his brother. To Stan's way of seeing things, David had it all. His basketball talent was going to be his ticket to the easy money. Stan preferred to ignore the fact that David had worked hard and spent countless hours on his basketball and academics. But again, maybe that was understandable.

David and T.C. were freshmen when Stan got in over his head. Way over his head. It seemed that an especially large quantity of Stan's 'sure things' had not been so sure. He owed some very bad people a lot of money. He needed a major scam and he came up with a beauty.

It was March. Their mother was in the hospital with ovarian cancer. The basketball season was coming to an end. Everyone on campus was excited because the University of Michigan had reached the NCAA Final Four for the first time in God knows how long. There were constant fraternity parties and all anyone talked about was the big game against U.C.L.A. If Michigan could beat them, they would be in the finals.

Michigan was favored to win by three points.

Laura interrupted him. 'I don't know anything about gambling. What do you mean Michigan was favored by three points?'

'Let's say you bet on Michigan. In order to win your bet, Michigan must win by more than three points. If Michigan wins by less than three points or if U.C.L.A. wins, you lose your bet. Got it?'

Stan came up with a plan on the day of the game, a plan that involved David. Stan reasoned his baby brother would welcome the opportunity to help him out. And he wasn't asking much. All he wanted David to do was shave off a few points. What difference would it make to David if Michigan only won by two points instead of five? David didn't have to throw the game. All he had to do was keep it close.

David of course did not see it that way. 'I can't believe you're asking me this.'

'But I need your help.'

'No way, Stan. You got yourself into this. You get

171

yourself out. Then do yourself a favor. Get some help.'

'I will. I promise. Just do this one—'

'Bullshit. Get help and then we'll talk.'

The conversation became nasty and David threw Stan out.

'And that's what happened between them?' Laura asked.

T.C. shook his head. 'That's just the beginning.'

Stan had no money to gamble with. He had hoped to pay off his debt by convincing his rather unfriendly mob friends to bet on U.C.L.A. He had told them that David had promised to go along with his plan. Now Stan was in big trouble. He couldn't go back and tell the mob that he had lied and his brother had refused to do it. They would have done a slam dance on his ribs with a crowbar.

As one might have guessed, Michigan won big. Nine points to be exact. The mob was really steamed. They had lost major dough in Stan's scam and someone was going to pay for that. The word went out: find Stan Baskin.

But Stan knew how to survive no matter what the cost to others. He was already hiding in the outskirts of South Dakota. He knew that the mob would track him down eventually, but by then he would have the money. The mob however has never been known for its patience. They wanted blood. They wanted to recoup their losses. And they wanted to do it in a hurry. The mob wanted a fall guy and Stan Baskin was not around.

So they chose David.

The championship game between Michigan and Notre Dame was to take place two nights after the U.C.L.A. game. Everyone agreed that the teams were even and hence the game would be too close to predict. If you wanted to bet on it, you bet straight up. If your team won, you won the bet. It was that simple. The media meanwhile spent most of its time building up the confrontation between the two freshmen sensations, Michigan's David Baskin and Notre Dame's Earl Roberts.

It would be three years before that confrontation took place.

The mob's plan was simple. Get the money back by fixing the championship game. And how do you do that? Again, keep it simple. Bet on Notre Dame and then make sure Michigan's superstar cannot play.

The night before the game, David was sleeping in his hotel room—or at least trying to sleep. Who would blame him for tossing and turning the night before the biggest game of his life? This was the game he had dreamed of all his life and so sleep would come only in small spurts.

Around three a.m., the lock on David's door was jimmied open. Five men quickly entered.

David sat up. 'What the . . .?'

Before he could move, four of the men pinned him down on the bed. David struggled but he was dealing with professionals who had done this kind of thing plenty of times before. He didn't have a chance.

'Cover his mouth,' one whispered. 'I don't want anyone to hear him scream.'

David's eyes widened with fright as someone pushed a pillow into his face. He flailed his head back and forth in panic, but it was a worthless maneuver. He felt one of the men grab his right foot, one hand by the toes, the other on the heel.

'Hold him tight!'

The man twisted David's foot all the way around until he heard the ankle snap. Then he twisted it o

173

little farther for good measure. The bones in his foot grated against one another. David's scream was lost in the pillow.

The men quickly left. They had never even turned on the lights so David had no chance of identifying them. His ankle was badly broken. He was in a cast for two months. That week, David had two of his worst head attacks. They were so bad that T.C. feared for his friend's life.

Michigan lost to Notre Dame by fifteen points.

'There's more to this story, isn't there?'

T.C. nodded.

Stan could not hide forever. He needed to pay back his debt in a hurry. And he figured out a foolproof way of doing it.

The details are not important. No one ever found out for certain how Stan did what he did. But there are a million different ways to go about it. Stan might have gotten power of attorney. Mrs Baskin might have signed something while on some hospital medication. Who knows? What was important was the end result:

Stan stole the money from his mother.

Imagine a son who would wipe out his cancer-stricken mother's savings account to pay a gambling debt to the mob. Imagine a son who could leave his poor, sick mother penniless and without any way of paying off her medical bills while she lay dying in a hospital bed. It boggles the mind.

After that, David did his best to take care of her, but she was very ill and now she was also heartbroken over what her own son had done to her.

She died six months later. Stan never went to the funeral.

'Now do you understand, Laura?'

Laura just sat there. She felt drained by just

listening to the story. 'But this all happened years ago. I'm not going to defend it, but supposed you just looked at Gloria's past? What would you conclude? You'd say she's trouble, right?'

'Wrong. I may think she's weak or self-destructive, but she never meant to hurt anybody but herself. And more important, her past is just that. The past.'

T.C. opened up his folder. 'This is Stan's record. He's been arrested twice in the last three years for fraud. I called the arresting officer, a Lieutenant Robert Orian. He told me that Stan is well known for using his charm and good looks to seduce wealthy women. It's hardly an original bit. He bilks them for as much as he can and then gambles it away. He does however add a strange twist to the old game.'

'What?'

T.C. hesitated. 'He doesn't just walk away. He dumps them. He dumps them as cruelly as possible. Makes the woman feel like a worthless hunk of shit. One of his victims had a nervous breakdown. Another attempted suicide. Stan has been diagnosed as having a narcissistic personality disorder with a rather unhealthy hatred of the female sex. He knows how to hurt and degrade women, Laura, and he likes to do so.'

'Jesus.'

'I did a little more investigating,' T.C. continued. 'Stan owes again. He owes big bucks to some bookie with a propensity for breaking bones.'

Laura sat up. 'His hand?'

'Broken. Actually, it's just his finger. Very mean break. Stan needs the money fast. You're his new scam, Laura, but I'm not too worried about that.

You can handle yourself.'

T.C. lifted the picture of Stan kissing Gloria and handed it to Laura. 'But what about Gloria?'

*   *   *

The patient read Sunday's *Boston Globe*. He had always loved Sunday papers. During his college years, he and his roommates would emerge noon time Sunday from the dormitory after a particularly rough Saturday night, grab some brunch, and spread out with a few Sunday papers. By dinner time, the newspapers resembled a floor covering.

It was a tradition he continued to maintain.

He put down the *Parade Magazine* section and rummaged through the different sections until he found Sports. Usually he skipped the sports section, and that surprised a lot of people. But lately, he had changed his thinking.

Section C. Page 1. An article by Mike Logan. The patient had always liked Mike Logan. He was a good reporter who had a genuine love for his job and the Boston Celtics

CELTS GEARING UP FOR ROUGH ROAD
by Mike Logan

My team—our team—is in trouble, folks. Big trouble. You may remember last season's Eastern Conference play-offs. The Celtics barely squeaked by the Chicago Bulls and the Detroit Pistons. And I mean barely. No room to spare for mistakes.

Then the Boys from Beantown faced the Los Angeles Lakers for the NBA Championship. Let's face it. They should have lost. Had it not been for a last-minute miracle by David Baskin, the Celtics would not be the defending champions today.

Yes, other NBA teams are rising. And yes, the Celtics are sinking. Sinking fast.

It's not their fault. The David Baskin tragedy was not their doing. But excuses don't win championships. Great players, coaches and organization do. The coaching is no problem. The same with Clip Arnstein's organization.

Ah, but the players!

No one could argue about the talent of team center Earl Roberts or the outside shooting touch of Timmy Daniels or the ball-handling of Johnny Dennison. They're great. No doubt about it. But without White Lightning, this is just a good team. Not a great one. They need a great forward.

But how do they get one?

In the past Clip Arnstein, alias 'The Miracle Worker,' came up with something. And why not this time? After all, the Celtics still have the best organization in basketball. The Miracle Worker thrives in these situations. Usually he digs up a surprise draft pick. But this year, even Clip admits the draft picks are mediocre at best. Maybe he'll find a free agent. But no, the free agent camp has produced no superstars. Maybe he'll make another great trade. Uh-uh. The other teams don't want to help out the Celtics and most organizations are afraid of getting burned by Clip.

So what's left?

You got me. I'm a reporter. It's not my job, thank God. Clip Arnstein is the ageless genius and he doesn't even know. But when you've watched the Celtics as long as I have you start to believe in miracles. Somebody will come along. Somebody will be the Celtics Savior.

The patient looked up. He had a pretty good idea who that somebody might be.

*　　*　　*

'Stan Baskin is here to see you.'

Laura felt her leg begin to shake. 'Send him in.'

A few seconds later, Stan opened the door. He smiled brightly. 'Hi, Laura.'

She tried to keep an even tone. 'Come in, Stan.'

He closed the door behind him and kissed Laura on the cheek. 'You look as beautiful as always.'

'Thank you. Won't you sit down?'

He did so as the intercom buzzed.

'Laura?'

'Yes, Estelle?'

'Is it okay if I go to lunch now?'

'Go ahead.'

'I'll be back in an hour.'

Laura realized her leg was shaking more than usual. She made a conscious effort to stop it. 'I wanted to speak to you about your mall idea.'

'Yes?'

'Can you give me a few details on it?'

'Details?'

'Yes. I'd like to hear more about it.'

Stan sensed something different in her voice.

'Not much to tell. It will be gorgeous when it's finished. I'd say there will be about two hundred stores.'

'How many square feet?'

'Uh, I'm not sure.'

'Where is it going to be located?'

'In Boston.'

'Central Boston?'

'Sure.'

Laura leaned back. 'But there's no room to build something that large in central Boston. And you'll need a lot more than a million dollars to get started.'

'Right but—'

'Who's the contractor?'

'Contractor?'

'The builder.'

Stan's smile was flicking like an old light bulb. 'I forgot his name.'

'And your lawyer has secured permission from city hall?'

'Uh, just about . . .'

'Well, don't worry there. Teddy Hines at the mayor's office is in charge of building permits. I'll call him to make sure everything goes smoothly.'

His eyes darted around the room. 'Don't bother yourself with that, Laura.'

'No bother.' Laura started to feel more in control. 'Tell me about your last deal in Michigan.'

'To be honest it didn't go very well.'

'I see,' Laura replied evenly.

'I was operating a toy manufacturing company.'

'Really? What kind of toys?'

'Oh, standard stuff. I sold out.'

'Who bought it?'

'You wouldn't know them.'

'Try me.'

Stan realized that he was being cornered. He just wasn't sure what to do about it. 'Just a friend.'

'I see. How's your finger, Stan?'

'Better thanks.'

'Freak break, huh?'

Stan shrugged. 'Not that unusual.'

'Having a car door slam on just your middle finger, missing all the others completely? That's hardly a normal injury.'

For a moment they both just stopped and watched one another. Then Stan broke the silence. 'What's going on, Laura? Why all the questions?'

Laura took a deep breath. 'I had a talk with T.C.—'

'I told you he doesn't like me.'

'He told me what happened between you and David.'

Her words hit Stan like a splash of cold water. 'T.C. is exaggerating. You can't believe what he says.'

She lifted the file from her desk. 'And how about your arrest record? Did he make that up too?'

Stan swallowed. It was all unraveling. He was so damn close and now the bitch was stabbing him in the back. 'They were trumped-up charges. I haven't been a saint when it comes to women. I admit that. But I never stole from them and I never meant to hurt any of them. It's just that some women can't let go. You know how spiteful an ex-lover can be.'

Laura stood and walked from around her desk. 'Maybe that's so, Stan, but I don't want to take that chance. You've tried to take advantage of me and my family. And I've decided not to give you any of

David's money. I don't think he'd want me to.'

Stan's good hand clenched into a fist. He fought to maintain control, to keep his temper in check. 'Fine, Laura. Like I said before, I don't deserve it anyway.'

'One other thing.'

'Yes?'

'I'd like you to leave me and my family alone.'

Stan was fighting off panic now. 'You can't mean that. If I've done something in the past, that's one thing. As you yourself said, the past is the past. I am trying my best to make amends. Don't take away the only family I have.'

'I do mean it.' Her hand reached into her top drawer and pulled out a photograph of Stan kissing her sister. 'And I especially want you to leave Gloria alone.'

Stan glared down at the photograph. Anger finally nudged its way into his voice. 'How did you get that?'

'It's not important.'

'How did you get that?' he repeated.

Laura put the picture back in her drawer. 'Why not worry about other things, Stan? Like paying off the gentleman who broke your finger.'

Stan's face turned red. He tried to think of something to say that might salvage this situation. But it was pointless. Laura was just another in a long line of women who wanted to possess him. To own him. This was simply her way of taking control. Well, Stan My Man was not about to let her get away with it. It was time to turn the tide. To teach her a lesson. 'Okay, Laura, you win. I'm very sorry about everything. Please believe me.'

'Whatever.' She spun toward the window. 'Now

please leave.'

He stood and made his way to the door. 'Laura?'

Laura turned to face him. Her eyes widened when she saw his fist heading toward her face. She ducked. His knuckles skimmed the side of her temple. She fell to her knees. Dizziness and pain seared through her skull.

Stan stood over her. His fingers reached down and closed around her blouse. Laura pulled away and the thin material ripped.

'Oh, my God,' he began. His eyes grew large with lust as he gazed upon her. 'Oh sweet Jesus, your body is fantastic!'

Laura tried to roll away from him, but Stan followed. 'Relax, Laura,' he whispered. 'I'm not going to hurt you. I've been dying to do this to you since the first day we met. And you've been dying for it too. David wasn't a real man, Laura. Not by a long shot. But you're about to be fucked by a real man for the first time in your life.'

He looked down and unfastened his belt. It was a mistake on his part.

Laura saw the opening. She slammed her fist into his groin. Stan's eyes bulged. Laura scrambled to her feet, but she did not get far. His hand grabbed her ankle and tugged her back to the floor.

'You bitch!'

'Let go of me!' she screamed.

He did as she asked, his expression switching instantly from lustful to that of a confused child. 'But . . . but I thought you wanted me.'

She looked at him with horror in her eyes. He meant what he said. He really thought that she wanted him. 'I'd rather make love to a St Bernard.'

'You teasing little whore.'

She held the ripped parts of the blouse against her chest. 'Get out of here, Stan. Get out before I have you thrown in jail.'

He smiled crazily. 'You don't mean that, Laura. You still want me, don't you? Admit it. You're just jealous of Gloria.'

She started to crawl away slowly. 'You're slime. Get out of here. And leave my sister alone.'

He shook his head. 'Not until this is finished, Laura.'

Her eyes grew frightened. 'It's finished, Stan. Get out.'

Stan rose, his face pinched in confusion. He walked toward the door and opened it. 'Finished, Laura?' he repeated with a shake of his head. He turned to leave. 'Not by a long shot.'

*   *   *

Stan sprinted out of the building and onto the street. What the hell had happened? One minute he had a million dollars and the next it was gone.

Damn that fuckin' T.C.

But it was not just T.C.'s fault. It was that cold bitch sister-in-law who had truly betrayed him. And the reason was obvious. Laura did not care about his past. That was just an excuse. The real reason was jealousy. She was pissed off because he had fooled around with her sister and not with her. That was why she suddenly had a bug up her shapely ass. Oh yes, she wanted him. Craved him. And worse, her hubbie had just died so she could not blatantly come on to him. I mean, how would it look? Yes, Stan thought to himself, Laura was a bundle of frustrated cravings.

Cravings for him.

But right now, Stan was in big trouble. The B Man was after him and he had no way of paying him back. The million dollars was lost . . . for now anyway. He would have to hide, have to find a new scam, have to . . .

What the hell was he talking about?

He smiled. The game was not over. Not by a long shot. Stan My Man was still in control. He still held the winning ace:

Gloria Ayars, a.k.a. Miss Instability 1989.

He turned the corner and found a phone booth. He dropped a coin in the slot and dialed.

Gloria's voice answered. 'Hello?'

'Hello, beautiful.'

Her tone held its normal nervous quiver. 'Stan?'

'Yes, my love. How are you feeling on this fine day?'

'Fine. And you?' she ventured.

'Sinfully happy. I'm flying high.'

'Really?'

'Of course,' Stan replied. 'You're the best thing to happen to me in years. I can't wait to see you again.'

'I'll be off in a couple of hours,' enthused Gloria.

'Sorry. Can't wait that long. Let's meet right now.'

'Stan,' she said with a little laugh, 'I'm working.'

'Let's disappear for a few days. Just you and me.'

'That sounds wonderful.'

'Then let's do it. Let's go to someplace secluded and romantic.'

'I know just the place.'

'Where?'

'The Deerfield Inn. It's a small country inn about

an hour and a half from here.'

'Sounds perfect.'

'But, Stan, I can't just take off from here. I have work to do.'

His voice was filled with disappointment. 'I just thought it would be really special if we could share a few days alone together. I need to be alone with you so we can explore our feelings.'

'Can't you wait a few hours?'

He hesitated. 'I guess so. I shouldn't have pushed you like that. I'm sorry. I got a little excited because last night was so special for me. I understand if you don't feel the same way.'

'But I do feel the same way,' she assured him. Gloria thought for a moment, her hand wrapping the telephone chord around her fingers. 'Oh, why not? Let's do it.'

He almost laughed at her gullibility. 'Do you mean it?'

She smiled, feeling good about her decision. 'Sure. I'll just go tell Laura—'

'No,' he interrupted. 'Can't we just keep it our little secret? It makes it all the more spontaneous and secluded.'

'But she'll worry if I just disappear.'

'Leave her a note that you're going away for a few days. Just don't give her any details.'

There was a pause. 'I guess that'll be okay. But—'

'Great. I'll meet you downstairs in ten minutes. And Gloria?'

'Yes?'

'I feel really good about this.'

'So do I, Stan.'

Laura locked her office door. She moved toward her private bathroom, stripped out of her clothes and stepped into the shower. She was still dazed, still not sure she believed what had happened. The whole experience had a dream-like quality to it. Now she wondered if Stan had really attacked her or if her imagination was running rampant.

No. It had happened. Laura's imagination had never been that good.

She finished showering, stepped out and dried herself off. Tears began to swell in her eyes as the numbness subsided. Her shoulders heaved. She threw the torn clothes into a wastepaper basket and put on some fresh ones she kept in the closet. She sat on the bathroom stool, her arms wrapped around her in a self-hug. Her leg was shaking.

Help me, David. I need you so badly. Please come back and tell me what to do.

She continued to cry. She had handled Stan all wrong and now she was not sure what her next step should be.

Gloria.

Gloria was going to be devastated. What could Laura tell her?

'Gloria?'

'Yes, Laura?'

'The man you slept with last night was by far the largest piece of scum on the planet Earth. He makes your past boyfriends seem like Gandhi.'

There was no way she could do that. A few weeks ago it had seemed that Gloria would never trust a man again. Her past experiences had made her conclude that all men were out to destroy her.

Gloria must have very deep feelings for Stan Baskin if she had let him break down that wall of suspicion and fear.

What was Laura going to do?

The answer came to her. She would call Gloria's psychiatrist Dr Jennifer Harris. Dr Harris would know what to do. Though psychiatry had a strict rule protecting patient confidentiality, Gloria had insisted from the beginning that Laura be involved in her treatment. After seeing the two sisters together, Dr Harris had agreed.

Laura sat down at her desk and made the call. They exchanged pleasantries and then Laura told Jennifer Harris the entire story. She started with Stan's first visit at the funeral and ended with him storming out of her office.

When she was finished, Dr Harris was silent for a moment. 'Gloria has mentioned Stan Baskin to me. You're right. I think she is somewhat infatuated with him.'

'What should I do?' Laura asked.

'Gloria has not come close to risking a relationship with a man since her breakdown,' Dr Harris explained. 'If she finally did sleep with someone, it was by no means a quick decision. She's probably very scared right now, wondering if she made the right choice. But understand this, Laura: if she thought there was the slightest chance that Stan Baskin did not have strong feelings for her, she would have never risked it. In other words, there was no risk in her mind. Deep down, she was sure he cared about her.'

'But he's scum, Doctor.'

'Not exactly a medical term but I get your meaning. You have to tread very gently here,

Laura. You can't just burst into Gloria's office and tell her that the man she cares about is a louse.'

'But I can't just sit back and let her keep falling for him either. I have to tell her the truth.'

Again a pause. 'Yes and no.'

'I don't understand.'

'You might want to try subtle disapproval but I wouldn't go into too many specifics right away.'

'Why not?'

'Because if Gloria really has fallen for this man, then she won't listen to you. She'll get defensive and isolate herself from your words. You may actually end up pushing her toward Stan rather than away from him.'

'So what am I supposed to do?'

'You can help her, Laura, but in the end Gloria has to come through this by herself. We can't force her to see what she doesn't want to.'

Laura considered Dr Harris's words. 'Gloria can be stubborn,' she agreed.

'Yes, she can.'

'But I have to do something.'

'Agreed. But talk to her gently, Laura. Don't hit her with all of this at once. Don't force it on her. Help her see the truth on her own. And bring her in to my office as soon as you can.'

'Okay,' she replied. 'Thank you, Doctor.'

'Laura?'

'Yes?'

'How have you been lately?'

'Just fine.'

'No problems you want to discuss?'

'None. I'm doing just great.'

An uncomfortable silence traveled across the phone line. 'I have a free hour at noon,' Dr Harris finally said. 'How about coming down to my office for a little chat?'

'I don't think . . .' Laura stopped, swallowed. Her hands were shaking. 'That would be nice, Jennifer. Thank you.'

'I'll see you at noon. Goodbye, Laura.'

Laura replaced the receiver and headed down the hallway to Gloria's office. When she reached the door, a voice called out to her.

'Laura?'

It was Gloria's secretary. 'Yes?'

'Gloria's not here.'

'Where is she?'

The secretary shrugged and smiled. 'She just ran out of here with a beaming face. She left this note for you.'

Laura opened the envelope and read the note:

Laura,

I've gone away until Monday. Don't worry about me. I'll be fine. I'll call you when I get back. I love you.

Gloria

*   *   *

The man shaded his eyes from the harsh glare of the sun and watched the patient pace off twenty-three feet from the basket. The patient drew a line with chalk. Yeah, the man thought, that was about the spot where the three-point line was. Only the best shooters would dare launch a shot from that far away.

The patient began to shoot the ball, rebound, shoot the ball, rebound, shoot the ball. He moved effortlessly, his shooting motion almost a poetic flow. Shot after shot found its way through the metallic hoop with a swish. The ball hardly ever touched the rim.

'Looking good, Mark,' the man called out.

The patient stopped. His curly blond hair was getting long now. His eyes were ice blue. His nose was pointed, his cheekbones set high. His face was unusually handsome in a pretty-boy sort of way. He stood about six feet five and his build was rock solid. The patient had never tried weightlifting before but the effects were both enormous and immediate. His body was slimmer, his muscles more defined. He felt strong. 'Thanks.'

'Mind if I rebound a few?'

'I'd appreciate it.'

The patient named Mark shot. The man rebounded and tossed the ball out to him. 'Let me ask you something,' the man began.

'Go ahead.'

'How are you going to get a try-out?' he asked. 'You're a complete unknown.'

'I know.'

'So how are you going to do it?'

'I'm playing around with a few ideas,' the patient answered as he moved in for a hook shot.

'Like?'

Mark shrugged. 'Can you get me press credentials?'

'Sure. What do you need them for?'

'I'm working on it. I'll let you know.'

'Okay. One set of press credentials. Anything else?'

The patient continued to shoot, trying hard to look casual. 'How is everyone?'

'Everyone?'

'You know what I mean.'

'No, Mark, I really don't know.'

Mark did not take his eyes off the rim. 'You're right. Forget it.'

'It's forgotten.'

'The rules have to be followed.'

'Right,' the man agreed.

The patient continued shooting. The man continued rebounding. 'Mark?'

The patient stopped shooting.

'Everyone is doing badly.'

Mark's face caved in. 'Badly?'

The man nodded.

'I want to know—'

The man shook his head and began to walk back toward the house. 'I shouldn't have even said that.'

Mark clutched the ball to his chest like a child with a teddy bear. His large frame bent over. He collapsed heavily onto the asphalt surface. An awful mix of emotions whirled painfully through his head like a sharp propeller.

The man continued to walk away.

'T.C.?' Mark cried out.

The man stopped and turned around.

'Make sure nothing bad happens to them.'

The man called T.C. took out a cigar. 'I'll do my best,' he replied, even though he knew that he was powerless to do anything.

CHAPTER TEN

May 29, 1960
'Bastard.'

The gun exploded. A bullet sliced through Sinclair's skull. Blood splashed onto the walls, the sticky, red mist spraying the killer's face. Clumps of brain tissue flew out the other side of Sinclair's head. The dead body slid off the chair and onto the floor.

Standing over the bloodied corpse, the killer felt a strange exhilaration.

I killed him. I killed the bastard. He's dead. I didn't mean to do it, but I killed him. Plain and simple. I'm covered with blood, but oh, did he deserve it. Oh, was he asking for it.

The killer scanned the room. The music outside on the commons blasted so loudly that the students did not hear the bullet or, if they did, they must have thought it was a firecracker or a car backfiring. Still, time was short. The killer had to act fast.

Just relax. Don't panic. You're in control. Now just think. Something will come to you.

The killer looked at what had been a man's head. It was now an unrecognizable mass of blood, flesh and bone fragments.

I shot him in the head. That was good. That was smart. Now I can make it look like a suicide. Everyone knew the bastard had problems. A suicide would barely be questioned.

The killer locked the office door, wiped the gun clean of any fingerprints and placed the gun snugly in the dead man's hand.

There. It's done. Perfect. No one would ever suspect me. All I've got to do is sneak out the back before the police get here and—

The killer stopped abruptly, remembering something very bothersome.

What was the name of that T.V. show? Or was it a movie? Or a book? Not important. There was a situation similar to this one. A man was found dead with a bullet hole in his head and a gun in his hand. An apparent suicide. But the detective figured out it was really a murder. But how?

Fingers snapped. The killer smiled.

The detective had the victim's hand checked for traces of gunpowder or something like that. None was found. In fact, the hand showed absolutely no signs of trauma, so the victim could not possibly have fired the gun. Conclusion: he had been murdered.

Fear crept in along with an idea. The killer sprinted back toward the body, lifted the hand with the gun, and pressed Sinclair's finger on the trigger.

The gun fired. The bullet lodged into the wall near the bookshelf.

Relief settled onto the killer's face. The hand now had the gunpowder or whatever on it. The police would be here soon. They would investigate the matter completely and come up with one of two scenarios: 1) after shooting himself, Sinclair's hand spasmed in death, firing another bullet; 2) Sinclair had chickened out at first, pulled the gun away from his head as he fired, then worked up the courage to kill himself for real.

The killer headed out the back entrance and into the sunshine, confident that no one was watching.

That was wrong.

From behind the couch two scared eyes had seen

everything. But the killer did not look behind the couch. The killer just continued to make his escape, thinking:

I did it. I killed the bastard. And now he has left me no choice. There is only one way to right the wrong, only one way to put everything back in place.

The killer swallowed.

I have to kill again.

CHAPTER ELEVEN

Gloria had never been so happy. The weekend in Deerfield was turning out better than she could have imagined. There was no greater high than being in love. And this was love. Real love. This was not a contest where one combatant tried to abuse and hurt the other.

Real love.

True, they had only been together for a short time, but Gloria knew. She had never been so sure of anything in her life.

Gloria turned her gaze toward Stan. He smiled back at her. A warmth quickly spread throughout her body. She did not want to eat or sleep or do anything but be with Stan.

They strolled down the deserted street toward the Deerfield Inn. The small New England town was straight out of a postcard. It was September, still a little early for the leaves to change color, but the sparse population and the sun creeping through the thick branches more than made up for it. It was warm. Both of them wore shorts and a T-shirt. In their haste to get out of the city, Gloria had forgotten to bring a T-shirt, so she had to borrow one from Stan.

There were only twelve rooms in the Deerfield Inn's main building. The back annex held about a dozen more. But on this particular weekend, business was not too brisk, which suited Gloria just fine. Last night, they had dined, walked through the Deerfield Academy campus and sat quietly in front of the fireplace in the inn's back room. The silence worked on her like the most relaxing masseurs.

Stan put his arm around her shoulders. Gloria nestled in closer against his chest. She felt safe and snug and deliriously happy. The inn was coming into view around the corner.

Stan stopped and turned toward her. 'I love you, Gloria. I know we've only known each other a short time but—'

'I love you too.'

Her heart burst with joy as he bent down to kiss her. When he pulled back, she could see his face was troubled. 'What is it, Stan?'

His eyes swerved around for a moment. 'It's so beautiful out here. I wish we could stay here forever.'

'So do I.'

He nodded. 'It's time I told you everything about me, Gloria. The good and the bad.'

She hugged him. 'There is no bad.'

'Yes, there is.'

'You don't have to tell me.'

'Maybe that was true before I fell in love,' he said, 'but now I have no choice.'

She looked up at him with scared eyes. Stan stepped back and paused. 'I'm a gambler,' he began slowly. 'Baseball, football, horse-racing, you name it. It's a disease, Gloria, like what you went through with drugs. I have cravings that I can't control. Sure, I've tried to stop, but I just can't do it. I gamble and I gamble until I lose everything I have. And then I still can't stop. I borrow money and build up an even bigger debt which I can't pay back.'

He started to walk back toward the inn. Gloria followed silently, watching him stride purposefully. 'Sometimes, I do criminal things to pay the money back,' he continued. 'You see, the men who I owe money to are gangsters. They hurt people who are late with payments. I even owe them money now, and I still can't stop betting. Gloria, do you remember what it was like when you were cut off from drugs? Do you remember the cravings in your bloodstream until you thought the agony of withdrawal would drive you insane?'

Gloria nodded. She had felt those cravings. They had nearly killed her.

'Money to gamble with is my fix. I've tried to cure myself but I guess I don't have the strength you have.'

Gloria reached out for his hand. 'But that's because you've never had any support,' she assured him. 'I could never have done it without Laura. Not in a million years. But you can beat this thing, Stan. I know you can.'

Stan looked at her hopefully. 'Will you help me?'

She hugged him again. 'Of course I will. We'll beat it together.'

'I love you, Gloria.'

Her face lit up. 'I love you too.'

They walked together holding hands until Gloria spoke again.

'You said you owe money?' she began.

'Nothing for you to worry about.'

'But I have money, Stan. I can help.'

'No chance. I don't want you involved in this.'

'But—'

He gently put his finger up against her lip. 'End of discussion, my love.'

They reached the entrance to the Deerfield Inn. Stan kissed her again and they disappeared into the lobby.

*   *   *

Two men—one normal size, the other monstrously huge and hairy—watched the kiss from a parked car in front of the inn.

'Is that them?' the big man asked.

B Man nodded.

'Did you see her body?'

'Very attractive, Bart,' B Man agreed.

'She should be a movie star!' enthused Bart. 'Boy, I'd love to fuck her.'

B Man patted his giant friend on the back. 'Bart my boy,' he said, 'you might just get the chance.'

*   *   *

Gloria grabbed a quick shower. When she stepped out, Stan was there to dry her off.

'You are so incredibly beautiful,' he said. 'Am I getting repetitive?'

'Never. Say it again.'

He put down the towel and began to caress her body. 'You're beautiful.'

A knock at the door interrupted their foreplay.

'Talk about timing,' she said. She picked up the towel and tied it around her.

'Who is it?' Stan asked.

'Room service. A little champagne on the house.'

Stan smiled. 'Stay here, my little dove. And don't you dare put on one shred of clothing.'

Gloria giggled.

'I'm coming,' Stan said as he headed for the door. He turned the knob. Without warning, the door flew backward. The wood smacked Stan's forehead, knocking him to the floor.

B Man and his gorilla/henchman stepped in and quickly closed the door behind them. Gloria gasped.

The blond man smiled down at Stan. 'Isn't this nice?' B Man began. 'A nice quiet weekend in the country. Isn't this just wonderful, Bart?'

'Wonderful, B Man,' the gorilla agreed.

Stan struggled to his feet. 'What do you want?'

B Man ignored his question, circling instead toward the other side of the room where Gloria stood trembling. 'Who is this lovely lady?'

'Just leave her alone,' Stan said sternly. 'She's got nothing to do with this.'

'True enough,' B Man replied, turning back toward Stan. Gloria remained huddled by the wall, noticing that the ugly giant had not yet taken his eyes off of her. She had seen that leer before, and she suddenly felt very exposed in just a towel.

'Do you have the money?' B Man asked.

'I told you,' Stan replied. 'I'll have it for you in a week.'

'Not good enough.' B Man turned his attention back to Gloria who was still crouched against the corner, looking at Bart with frightened eyes. 'Did

Stan tell you how he hurt his finger, lovely lady?'

'I said leave her out of this.'

Again B Man ignored Stan. 'You see, lovely lady, Stan has not lived up to his obligations, his responsibilities. I found this most troubling. He left me no choice but to bend his middle finger back until it cracked in half. It was a most unpleasant noise.'

The blood drained from Gloria's face.

'Enough, B Man,' Stan shouted.

'But do not worry, lovely lady,' B Man continued. 'A broken finger is paradise compared to what I have in store for him now.' He signaled to his gorilla who was still staring at Gloria. The gorilla snapped out of his trance and began to walk toward Stan.

'Wait a second,' Stan said. 'Just let her get out of here. I don't want her involved in any of this.'

'I'm sorry, Stan,' B Man said with a slow shake of his head, 'but it's too late. Bart here has a crush on your lady friend.'

Bart leered at Gloria, spit forming in the corners of his lips.

Stan stepped forward, blocking Bart's path. 'Do what you want with me, B Man, but leave her alone.'

B Man looked at him, surprised. 'This is a switch, Stan. Since when do you care about somebody else?'

'None of your business. Just let her leave.'

B Man smiled. 'I'm curious, Stan. Suppose I promise to wipe away your debt if you let Bart have his way with your friend here? How would that sound?'

Stan stood firmly. 'Go to hell.'

'My, my, we really seem to be smitten. I admire that, Stan. I really do.' B Man smiled at Gloria, a smile that chilled her skin like cold gusts of wind. 'But alas, Bart is a faithful employee. And he asks so little of me, dear child. I would feel disloyal if I denied him this one small pleasure. You understand.'

B Man nodded toward Bart. The big man smiled at his helpless prey. Then Bart cocked his fist and slammed it into Stan's stomach. Stan collapsed on the ground.

Bart moved around the fallen man toward Gloria. He quickly cornered her, returning her look of mercy with one of pure lust. He licked his lips and reached out toward her towel.

'No!' she cried.

Bart's rough hands were no more than two inches away from her towel when he was tackled from behind. Stan had recovered. He attacked Bart with a fury. But Bart quickly flung Stan off of him. Stan's determination was no match for a man of Bart's size. Still, Stan kept fighting. He bravely grappled the much larger man, fighting to save Gloria from his savage assault.

Then B Man stepped in.

One man double his size would probably have been too much for Stan to handle. And now a second man had entered the ring. B Man quickly delivered a blow to the back of Stan's neck. Stan dropped to the floor.

'Run, Gloria!' Stan managed. 'Get out of here!'

Gloria tried to listen but her legs would not respond. She was frozen with fright as the two men began to kick Stan in the stomach.

Bart's face was red with rage. 'I'm going to kill

the son of a bitch!'

The two men continued their onslaught without pause. Their blows did not stop coming. Each kick and punch seemed to be well placed and not rushed. Grunts forced their way past Stan's lips. Gloria could also see blood trickling out of his mouth. His eyes rolled back and then closed.

'Stop!' she shouted. 'Leave him alone!'

B Man and Bart hesitated for a moment and looked up. Stan was not moving.

'Pl . . . Please,' she begged, 'I'll give you anything you want. Just leave him alone.'

B Man moved toward her. 'Sweetheart, he owes a hundred thousand dollars.'

'I'll write you a check. Just please don't hurt him anymore.'

B Man thought a moment. 'You want to help him?'

She nodded. Stan had risked his life for her. Sure, he had a problem. He had admitted it to her, had asked for her help. Once she paid off these criminals, she could help him heal in much the way Laura had helped her. 'Please. Don't hurt him anymore.'

B Man shrugged. 'Leave him alone, Bart. Wait for me downstairs.'

'But, B Man—'

'Go.'

Reluctantly, Bart left the room.

'My . . . my purse is in the bathroom,' Gloria stammered. 'I'll be right back.'

When she had gone into the other room, when she was completely out of sight, Stan raised his head toward B Man. Stan took the remains of the blood capsule out of his mouth and put it in his pocket.

'Thank Roadhouse for me,' Stan whispered.

Then the two men shared a smile and a wink.

*   *   *

Mark Seidman showed the press pass T.C. had secured for him to the security guard. He moved past him and sat on the wooden benches with the other reporters. Hellenic College in Brookline, Massachusetts was home of the Soaring Owls. Their basketball program had been dumped off the curriculum twelve years ago after yet another pitiful season. If they had drawn thirty people for a basketball game, including the players and coaches, it would have been considered a major sell-out. But Mark Seidman and the handful of spectators were not there to watch the Soaring (or Wingless, as the school newspaper had labeled them) Owls. No, the gymnasium at Hellenic College was better known for their current guests:

The Boston Celtics.

Here was where the final try-outs were held before the pre-season games began. The seventeen players on the court would be trimmed down to twelve soon, leaving five crushed dreams on this wooden floor in Brookline. The Celtics were having double sessions this week. That meant two practices a day. The morning practice was an intense workout, but in the afternoon the mood was a bit more relaxed. Members of the press with the proper credentials were encouraged to come in and watch the players for a while.

Today, Mark Seidman was one such reporter.

Celtics coach Roger Wainright ran the players

202

through a few simple drills and then gave the players time for free shooting. It was a quiet day for the Celtics. Mark counted only eight reporters in the stands. Not even Clip Arnstein was here. Mark watched the players shooting. Earl Roberts was working on his hookshot. Johnny Dennison dribbled laps around the court. And Timmy Daniels, the press's pick to be this year's best outside shooter, was practicing his long-range jumper with one of the towel boys rebounding for him.

Mark could see the smile on Coach Roger Wainright's face as he watched his young guard put shot after shot through the cylinder. Suddenly, an idea surged into Mark's head. He sat upright, mulling the idea over in his mind. It would work, he was sure of it. There was a big risk, but after all, what did he have to lose? He felt anxious, wanting to just get it over with. But Mark knew better than to try it today. No way. He would only get one chance. If he blew it . . . well, that was it. The end. Mark needed to get some money and wait until Clip Arnstein and the media were around. His scheme would fail without them.

Mark stood and stepped off the bleachers. He would have to wait until the team held its next press conference before putting his plan into action. The press conferences were usually the same—reporters asking about the team's chances of winning the championship, and Clip Arnstein answering with either a joke or a sports cliche. Occasionally, the press would ask about a trade rumor or a change in personnel, but for the most part, press conferences were routine and not very exciting events.

Mark Seidman was about to change all that.

Gloria came out of the bathroom with her checkbook in hand. She spotted Stan's body on the floor. He lay still, too still. She managed to write a check for $100,000 through her shaking fingers. She tore it out of the book and handed it to the bleached-blonde standing over Stan's body.

B Man smiled graciously as she cringed away from him. 'Thank you, lovely lady,' he said, pocketing the check. 'I assume you can cover this rather considerable sum?'

She nodded.

'I would not advise your calling the authorities or trying to stop payment after I depart. My reaction to such a move would be, well, let's say unpleasant. Do you understand?'

She nodded again, her eyes stained with fear.

'Good.' B Man looked down at Stan and shook his head. 'I'm not sure I understand what you see in this deadbeat. Frankly, I think you're being foolish.'

He smiled at her. She moved farther into the corner.

'Alas, life is full of choices,' B Man continued. 'You've made your bed, my dear, and repulsive as it might be, you have to sleep in it.' With a small bow (a custom he'd picked up in the Orient) B Man turned toward the door. 'I wish you both all the best. Goodbye for now, lovely lady.'

As soon as the door closed, Gloria raced across the room and knelt by Stan's still form.

'Stan?'

He groaned.

'Don't move. I'll call an ambulance.'

His hand reached out and grabbed hers. 'No.'

'But you're hurt.'

'Just a few knocks,' he said, forcing a smile onto his face. 'They're experts on inflicting pain and messing people up without leaving any real damage. I'll be fine.'

'What do you want me to do?'

'Just help me up.'

'Are you sure?'

'Positive,' Stan grimaced. 'I'll stand under a hot shower for a while and clean myself off.' He smiled at her encouragingly. 'It looks worse than it is, believe me.' With a struggle, Gloria helped him to his feet. He looked at her solemnly. 'I'm going to pay you back. Every last cent.'

'Don't worry about that now,' she replied.

'I mean it. Every cent. I'm so sorry about all this, Gloria. I would understand if you wanted to stop seeing me.'

'I don't want to stop seeing you,' she said.

'You don't?'

'No, of course not.'

'I'm not going to gamble anymore. I promise.'

'It won't be that easy, Stan. But I know you can stop if you really want to.'

'I do. I promise. I'll never gamble again.'

'Good,' Gloria answered. 'We're going to need a first-aid kit. Will you be okay while I run down to the front desk and get it?'

'Sure,' he managed. 'I'll be in the shower when you get back.'

She started toward the door. 'Gloria?' he called to her.

'Yes?'

'I love you,' he said.

'I love you, too, Stan.'

She closed the door. Stan listened to her footsteps echo down the hallway. He quickly moved toward the phone and dialed.

'Hi, it's Stan,' he said, 'Put five hundred dollars on Broadway Lew in the third race.'

*   *   *

Monday morning came to Brookline, Massachusetts. T.C. drove Mark through Brookline's town center on the way to the college's gymnasium. Mark had been silent for most of the trip, which was no surprise to T.C. After all, today was the big day. T.C. and Mark had spent nearly all the weekend going over the plan, trying to figure out a solution to every conceivable problem that could arise. T.C. thought that they had covered it all. The plan was actually very simple—and completely dependent on Mark.

Would he be able to pull it off?

Up ahead was the school's gym. T.C. glanced at his companion. Mark was stone-faced, his blue eyes staring straight ahead, his curly blond hair pushed back. He remained silent as he stepped out of the car.

'Thanks,' Mark said when he closed the door.

'Good luck,' T.C. answered.

T.C. watched Mark walk into the gym. The Boston cop realized that today was the biggest day in the life of Mark Seidman, that there was little room for mistakes. T.C. also knew that a few months ago, Mark's plan would have had no chance of failing. But a lot had happened in the last few months, things that had changed both of their perspectives and goals. A few months ago, Mark might have pulled this maneuver to bring happiness and joy into his life. But that was when things like happiness and joy meant something to him.

Now, this plan was his only chance for survival.

CHAPTER TWELVE

The intercom buzzed.

'Yes?' Laura replied.

'Gloria just arrived in her office,' Estelle announced.

'Thank you.'

Laura pushed back her chair. Gloria was back. With a deep sigh, Laura stood and made her way to the door. She walked past Estelle, who was typing a letter. Estelle did not look up. Her boss was in a mood this Monday morning—something to do with her sister—and when Laura was in a mood, it was best to be as inconspicuous as possible, lest one get in the way of her wrath.

'I'll be back. I'm not taking any calls.'

Laura disappeared around the corner, her back straight, her mind fighting off the mounting anger. She reminded herself of what Dr Harris had said about treading gently with Gloria. It was not going to be easy. Her sister had been missing all weekend, had just up and left without telling anyone where she was going. Of course, Laura told herself, it would be wrong for her to jump to any conclusions. She didn't even know for sure that her sister had spent the weekend with Stan.

Bullshit.

Laura fumed. To think she had been taken in by that demented psychopath . . . True, she had been vulnerable, but it frightened her that she could be so easily conned.

Laura entered the marketing department and knocked on a door that read Gloria Ayars.

A cheerful voice chirped, 'Come in.'

Laura peeked her head into the doorway. 'Hey, sis.'

Gloria crossed the room, her face bright. 'Laura! Come on in.'

'Thanks. How's it going?'

'Great,' Gloria replied. 'I'm sorry about running out on Friday.'

'No problem,' Laura said, plastering a fake smile onto her face. 'You've been working hard lately. You deserved a little time off.'

'Still, I feel bad about just leaving.'

'Forget it. Mind if I sit down?'

'Of course not.'

The two sisters sat down and faced one another, both smiling pleasantly like a couple of game-show hosts. Laura felt ridiculous. 'So did you have a good time on your mystery weekend?'

'The best!'

Laura tried to maintain the smile. 'Oh? Where did you go?'

'Up to the Deerfield Inn. Remember when we used to go there as kids?'

Laura remembered. 'Sounds like fun.'

'It was. Laura?'

'Yes?'

'I'm in love.'

Laura felt her heart sink, but she locked her smile onto autopilot. 'Really? Who's the lucky guy?'

'Stan!' Gloria enthused. 'Can you believe it? Isn't it great?'

Laura nodded mechanically. 'So when did all this start?'

'Last week. I know I haven't known him for long but he's so wonderful. He's so warm, caring, funny . . . well, you know him! He's just like David.'

Laura winced at the comparison. 'You should forget about David,' she said. 'You should judge Stan like you would any other man.'

'What do you mean?'

'Nothing really,' Laura ventured. 'I'm just saying that you should treat Stan Baskin the same as you would any other man you've only been seeing for a week. Don't behave differently just because he's David's brother.'

Gloria's puzzlement turned into a smile. 'Oh, I get it. You know about his past. You're worried about it.'

'Well maybe a little . . .'

'He told me all about it,' Gloria continued. 'I know all about his gambling problem. He's going to get help.'

Bullshit, Laura thought yet again. Dr Harris had told her not to push too hard so there was no way she could tell Gloria about all the wonderful things that warm, caring Stan had done to his family. She bit down on her tongue for a moment. 'Still, Gloria, you should keep both eyes open.'

'The past is the past, Laura. You said so yourself when he first came to Boston.'

'Yes, I know I did. I just want you to be careful, okay?'

'Careful?' Gloria repeated, her smile fleeing off her face. 'Stan and I are in love.'

'I'm not denying that,' Laura said, trying her best to sound diplomatic, 'but didn't you think the same thing in the past? What about that guy in California?'

Gloria's eyes narrowed. 'I'm not the same person I was back then.'

'I know,' Laura assured her, 'but maybe you shouldn't rush into anything.'

'Laura, what are you trying to say?'

'Nothing.'

'Come off it, Laura. It's his past that's bothering you, isn't it? I thought you said that the past was not important.'

'It's not. Really. But you shouldn't completely ignore it either.'

'Oh, now I see,' Gloria said slowly, her voice growing loud with anger. 'The past does matter! You're wondering why Stan would want someone with my past . . .'

'No, not at all!'

'A drugged-out slut! A no-good whore . . .'

'That's not true! That's not what I'm saying at all! The man who wins your heart will be the luckiest man in the world. I'm just not sure Stan Baskin is the right man.'

'And what makes you say that?' Gloria asked.

'I . . . nothing, Gloria. I just have a feeling, that's all.'

Gloria stood. 'Laura, you know how much I love you. I owe you my life.'

'You don't owe me anything. We're sisters. You've helped me. I've helped you.'

'Fine, but you want me to stop seeing Stan, right?'

Laura hesitated. 'I'm not exactly saying—'

'You don't fully approve,' Gloria tried.

'I'm not sure, that's all.'

'But you won't tell me why you feel this way.'

Silence.

'Look, Laura, I'm over thirty. Hard to believe, isn't it? Stan is just about forty. We're not children anymore. I love him, Laura. I love him very much.'

'I don't mean to try—'

'I really hoped you of all people would be happy for me,' Gloria interrupted. 'But if you're not, it doesn't change a thing. I'm in love and I'm going to keep on seeing him.'

'You don't know what you're saying,' Laura snapped. 'He's wrong for you.'

'Who the hell do you think you are?'

'He's crazy, Gloria! He hurts people! He's even—'

'I don't have to listen to this! You're not my keeper!'

Gloria stormed out of the office, slamming the door behind her.

Laura fell back in her chair. Good going, Laura. Way to be. Keep your cool. She sighed. Her whole body felt drained by the encounter. What was she supposed to do now?

She went over their conversation in her head. Something kept gnawing at Laura's subconscious, something her sister had said. Laura thought for a moment. When she realized what it was, her whole body went cold. Gloria's words of defense . . . they rang so familiar in Laura's ears. Perhaps it had something to do with the fact that Gloria was, after all, right. When you thought about it, what right did Laura have to interfere in Gloria's love life? Her sister was an adult. She had the right to do as she pleased. Laura replayed her conversation with Gloria in her mind one more time. The whole scenario reminded Laura of . . .

. . . of her and David.

Her throat clenched. The parallel dug painfully into her. Oh, God, hadn't her mother said the same thing to her about David? Hadn't she warned Laura to stay away from David, warned her without any discernible reason?

'Please, Laura, trust me. Stop seeing him.'

'But why?'

'I beg you. He's not right for you.'

Laura had not uttered a word to her mother since David's death. What had she been trying to say back then?

'We may get married.'

'Never, Laura. I will not let you marry that man under any conditions.'

But she had defied her mother. She had run off to Australia and married him anyway and now Laura understood something else: her words alone could never stop Gloria from seeing Stan, just as her mother had been powerless to stop her from seeing David.

Laura stared out the window. She wanted to sprint down the hallway, corner her sister, and force her to hear the awful truth. But she knew she could not. Had her mother been in a similar position? Was there something terrible she had wanted to tell Laura about David but for some reason couldn't? And now a crucial question poked at Laura's heart with a finger of bone, a question that finally had to be answered:

What had her mother been hiding about David?

Mark Seidman took his usual seat on the uncomfortable wooden benches. He spotted Timmy Daniels practicing his jumpshot. It was an impressive spectacle. Orange rainbow after orange rainbow ended with the ball dropping through the metal circle. Mark's eyes slid away from the basket and toward Clip Arnstein and the media who were standing off to the side admiring Timmy's flawless performance.

Mark continued to watch Clip Arnstein. The older man's arms were folded across his chest. He wore a floppy white hat, shorts and a green Celtics shirt. He looked more like an American tourist than a basketball legend.

'Nice shooting, kid,' Clip called out.

Timmy stopped and sprinted over to where Clip was holding the press conference. 'Thanks.'

The reporters crowded in. 'Are the Celtics going to repeat as champions, Clip?'

'I hope so.'

'Hope?'

'Doesn't pay to be too cocky,' Clip explained.

'Do you think you can pull it off without David Baskin?'

'Look, fellas, no team can lose a player like David and not feel it. A guy like White Lightning doesn't come around very often. Will we be contenders? Yeah, sure, of course we will. Will we be the champions? That, my friends, only time will tell. There are so many factors that come into making a champion. Healthy players and luck, to name just two.'

Mike Logan, the reporter from the *Boston Globe*

who had covered the Celtics for the last decade, stood up. 'Clip, last year you told us that David Baskin was the world's best outside shooter and Timmy Daniels was second.'

'And I was right, wasn't I, Mike? The three-point contest proved it.'

'No argument there,' Mike Logan agreed. 'My question is this: now that David is dead, is Timmy the world's best shooter?'

Before Clip could answer, a loud voice from the stands shouted, 'No!'

The reporters, the Celtics players, and Clip Arnstein turned toward the blonde heckler in the stands. 'Then who is?' Logan called back.

Mark stood. 'You're looking at him.'

*   *   *

Mary Ayars heard the doorbell chime. The sound echoed through the house, finding Mary in the kitchen with a glass of wine in her hand. Lately, Mary had been drinking a tad more than usual, a tad more than she should. She knew that she was dangerously close to having a drinking problem, that she should really cut back. But the pain of both her guilt and Laura's continuous rejection gnawed at the back of her brain until she craved just one more glass of white wine. Spanish white wine. Rioja was her favorite.

Mary glanced at the clock. Eleven a.m. Not even noon and she was already on her first glass.

The doorbell sounded again. Mary put down her drink, checked her face in the mirror, and headed toward the front door. She opened it and gasped.

'Laura!'

'Hello, Mother,' Laura replied politely. Her mother looked worn but still her beauty was dazzling. Laura noted that she still looked a good fifteen years younger than her true age of fifty.

Mary tried to gather herself. Her daughter had not uttered one word to her in months, not since she had eloped with . . . 'Your father isn't here.'

'I didn't come to see him. I came to see you.'

'Me?'

'I think we should talk.'

Mary stepped back and let her daughter enter. They moved into the den and sat down in chairs facing one another. Neither one spoke for several moments.

'I'm so sorry about David,' Mary began uneasily. She pressed her palms against her skirt. 'I've been so worried about you.'

'I'm doing okay.'

She reached out and took her daughter's hand. Tears started to gather in Mary's eyes. 'Please forgive me, Laura. I never meant to hurt you. You know I love you. You know I only want what's best for you.'

Laura kneeled forward and took her mother in her arms. 'It's okay, Mom,' she said softly. 'I know you were trying to help.'

'I love you so much, honey.'

'I love you, too,' Laura replied, feeling tremendous guilt for what she had put her mother through. 'I'm sorry I was so unforgiving.'

'No. You had every right to be.' Mary looked up hopefully. 'Oh, Laura, do you really forgive me? Is it really all behind us?'

Laura nodded. 'Mom?'

'Yes, honey.'

'I want to ask you something important.'

Mary dabbed her eyes with a tissue. 'What is it, baby?'

'Why didn't you like David?'

Mary felt her chest tighten. 'Oh, Laura, that's all in the past now.'

'I'd like to know.'

Mary's eyes darted around the room as though looking for a safe haven. 'It's not important now.'

'Mother . . .'

'You loved him, honey. I was wrong to interfere.'

'But you must have had a reason.'

'I guess I did at the time.'

'You guess?'

'You . . . you know how mothers are,' Mary said, her voice cracking. 'No man is good enough for my precious baby.'

'I dated men before David. You never interfered before.'

'But you were never serious about them,' Mary answered. 'Please, can't we talk about something else?'

Laura ignored her request. 'But that doesn't make any sense. You disliked David right away, the first time I mentioned his name to you. Why, Mother?'

A nervous shrug came off of Mary's beautiful shoulders. 'I never trusted athletes, I guess. But I was wrong, honey. He was a wonderful man. I'm sure he loved you very much.'

'What makes you say that now?'

'I . . . I don't know. I guess I just realized I was wrong.'

'When did this fact dawn on you, Mother?' Laura demanded. 'When he died?'

'No . . . I mean . . . Laura, please, I made a mistake. Can't we just put it behind us?'

'How can I, Mother?' Laura shouted. 'I lost the only man I ever loved. We were forced to secretly elope, and do you know why?'

'The press must have been hassling—'

'No, Mother! We were both used to handling the press. We eloped because my own mother swore the wedding would only take place over her dead body! That's why we took off for Australia and didn't tell you!'

Mary started to sob.

'And now David is dead.'

Mary's head snapped up. 'You can't blame me! I was just . . .'

'Just what, Mother? Don't you understand what happened? Because of some goddamn whim of yours, David and I felt shunned by my own mother. We ran away to Australia because of you!'

'Stop! Please!'

'And he drowned there, Mother. The man I loved perished there because you didn't like athletes, because—'

'I had my reasons!' Mary shouted back.

'What were they? What were your reasons?'

But the only answer Laura received was more sobbing, uncontrollable sobs that racked Mary's body. Her shoulders and chest heaved. Laura looked at the pitiful figure that was her mother and took hold of herself. What have I done, Laura asked herself? She had come here to forgive her mother, to release her from the undeserving torment she had suffered at Laura's hands over the last few months. Instead, Laura had attacked her with a vengeance that left them both trembling.

'I'm sorry, Mom. I didn't mean it. I just hurt all over and sometimes I just attack . . .'

She took her mother in her arms and together they both cried. Laura stroked her mother's hair. Some secrets defy death, Laura realized, and some truths are best kept buried deep in the past. Laura understood that. She knew the truth was not always a good thing. The truth could cause pain. Devastating pain. Pain that could destroy lives.

But that did not mean Laura would allow herself to be protected from the truth, to live a life where ignorance was bliss. Not when it came to David. After all, Laura's heart had already been torn from her chest. What further harm could the past do to her now? No, Laura decided, I will seek the truth.

And find it.

*   *   *

All eyes were on Mark Seidman. 'I can shoot better than any man alive.'

'Who the hell are you?' a reporter yelled out.

'Mark Seidman from the *Boston Eagle Weekly*.'

'The what?'

'Don't pay any attention to him, fellas,' Clip interrupted. 'He's just some pain-in-the-ass heckler. Ignore him. To answer your question, Mike, the finest shooter in the game today is Timmy Daniels.'

'Wanna bet?' shouted the blonde heckler.

Clip looked over to the security guards. 'Okay, that's it. Throw the bum out.' The uniformed guards strolled over to the bleachers.

Mark quickly stood. He reached into his pocket and pulled out a wad of green bills. 'Ten thousand dollars,' he shouted. 'One hundred portraits of Ben

Franklin on crisp, new bills says I can beat Timmy Daniels in a three-point shoot-out.'

The gymnasium fell silent. Mark watched Clip's face turned red with fury. 'I said throw the bum out!'

Reporters started snapping pictures. Mark waved the money. 'Ten thousand dollars for the charity of your choosing, Mr Arnstein. You put up zilch. Any charity you choose. No risk at all—unless you're a little afraid your shooting star's ego will be bruised by a stranger off the street.'

Timmy leaned toward Clip. 'Let me shut this punk up.'

'Yeah, Clip,' one of the reporters added. 'Let Tim take this kid's dough.'

Murmurs of agreement rippled through the gymnasium.

Clip's face was still red. 'You mind if I count the money, big mouth?'

'Not at all,' Mark replied. 'You can even hold it while we shoot.'

Mark walked down the bleachers and handed the money to Clip. He looked at the older man's angry eyes. If looks could kill. Whispers from the others: *'What do you figure?' 'Some wealthy punk with money to burn.' 'He's no reporter.' 'Rich bastard.' 'Yeah.' 'Timmy will teach him a lesson.' 'Weirdo.'*

Clip counted the money and then sighed. 'Okay, let's get this over with.'

A coin was tossed. Mark won and chose to shoot second. A ball boy quickly set up the balls in various positions over twenty feet away from the basket where only the finest shooters dare roam. Mike Logan watched with interest. He had covered last year's three-point contest before the All-Star

Game in Dallas. David Baskin had won, shattering his own record by hitting twenty-two shots in the one-minute time period. Twenty-two. It had been truly incredible. Timmy Daniels had placed second with twenty; Reggie Cooper of the Chicago Bulls was third with nineteen.

Timmy Daniels approached the first cart of basketballs on the left side of the basket, his eyes concentrating on nothing but the rim of the basket. He crouched and waited for the timer.

'One minute of shooting. Ready, go!'

Tim started shooting. He moved from the left side of the basket to the middle, his rainbow-like shots heading toward the cylinder.

Swish, swish, swish. Timmy shot as well as he had ever shot before.

'Thirty seconds!'

'He already has twelve!' someone shouted. 'He's heading for a record!'

Mark closed his eyes and hoped Tim would miss more often. But Timmy continued to shoot exceptionally well. His hands moved with precision, the same fast movement every time he shot.

'Time!'

The counter looked up. 'Holy shit! Twenty-three! A new record! He shattered White Lightning's record!'

Applause and cheers filled the small gymnasium. Timmy's teammates, including Earl Roberts, went over and congratulated their shooting champion. Clip patted him on the back. Reporters took notes. Even Timmy seemed somewhat taken aback by what he had done.

Clip reached into his pocket and took out a victory cigar. The small crowd went wild.

'Not so fast, Mr Arnstein.'

Clip looked past the front of his cigar at Mark. 'Son, you might as well just head on home now.'

Murmurs of agreement.

'Not yet,' Mark replied calmly. But he was worried. Timmy Daniels had indeed shot brilliantly. 'I still get my turn.'

'Why waste our time, son?'

'The name is Mark Seidman, Mr Arnstein, and this contest is not yet over.'

Clip lit his cigar. Everyone laughed. 'Well, let's get a move on, Mr Mark Seidman. There's a team practice being held up because of you.'

The ball boys quickly retrieved the balls and set them up for Mark's turn. He walked over to the left side of the basket and turned back toward Clip.

'Extra wager?' Mark asked.

'What? You crazy, son?'

'Extra wager or not?'

Clip smiled. 'Name it.'

'If I win, you give me a try-out with the team. If I lose, your charity gets another ten grand.'

Again the laughter echoed through the warm building. 'Done,' Clip shouted.

Mark nodded and waited; his muscles tensed. Everyone was watching him with mocking eyes. He could hear his heart pounding.

'Ready, go!'

Mark grabbed a ball off the rack and quickly launched his first shot. Too quickly. The ball banged off the rim. The crowd laughed. The next shot found its mark. So did the next, and the next . . .

'Not bad. He may even hit fifteen.'

'No way.'

. . . the next, the next . . .

221

'The kid can shoot.'

'He'll never even hit sixteen.'

... a miss, a make, a make, a make ...

'Funny way of shooting, huh?'

'Yeah. Quick release. Reminds me a little of Baskin.'

'Hey, Clip, what do you think?'

Clip Arnstein said nothing. He watched the awkward yet graceful shooting. Mark's hands were a blur.

'Thirty seconds.'

'Christ, the kid has ten!'

Everyone watched now as Mark moved toward another rack of basketballs. He was still behind Timmy Daniels and no one gave any serious consideration to the blonde's chances of beating him, but only seven professional players have broken the eighteen basket mark and the heckler had a real chance of hitting that milestone. Mark continued to shoot, ignoring his score, lost in the bliss of basketball. His shooting motion was fluid; the ball had perfect backspin as it dropped through the net.

'Time!'

Stunned silence. The counter looked up. 'Twenty-four,' he said softly. 'The kid just broke the record.'

Eyes swiveled as Clip Arnstein slowly strode toward the blonde stranger named Mark Seidman. No one spoke. Clip approached Mark and handed him back his money. Mark said nothing, his expression solemn.

'Impressive shooting, son.'

Mark did not respond.

'But there's a hell of a lot more to this game than

shooting.'

The blonde head nodded his agreement.

Clip eyed him. The kid had just beaten the NBA's best shooter and broken an NBA record. He should be celebrating. Instead, the kid stood there like he was attending a funeral. Clip shrugged, turning away from the bleak, haunted look in Mark's blue eyes. 'A bet is a bet,' he said after some time. 'Get on your practice gear.'

Mark jogged past the ugly, suspicious stares of his potential teammates, past the reporters. Mike Logan watched. The reporter could not believe what he had just seen. An amateur had just broken the three-point shooting record. And the weird style of his shot. Just like . . .

Logan took out his pad and wrote down a nickname just in case the kid made it.

White Lightning II.

CHAPTER THIRTEEN

May 30, 1960

Once again, it was time to kill. Victim Number Two.

Tears filled the killer's eyes. *I don't want to kill this one. I really don't want to. He was an innocent victim in all this.*

But maybe he wasn't. Maybe he was to blame. And maybe his death could finally lead to peace. Maybe his death would be a good thing in the long run. The innocent die all the time. Sacrifices must be made. Occasionally, the ends do justify the means. That was just the way of the world.

That argument was not very convincing.

The time had come. Without warning, the killer silently jammed the steel instrument of death into the helpless victim. Blood came pouring out in large doses, doses larger than the killer had expected. The dark red liquid seeped onto the floor, staining everything in its path.

It all ends so quickly, the killer thought, watching as Death claimed yet another life before its time.

The killer stood and turned toward the accomplice. The accomplice remained huddled in the shadows, watching with horrified eyes. 'Clean up the remains,' the killer said coolly. 'Make it fast.'

'Do I have to?'

'Yes. Now hurry.'

The accomplice had taken less than two steps when the door behind them flew open.

Both the killer and the accomplice gasped and spun around. A very young child peeked her head through the doorway. The little girl did not get a very good look at the room, but she saw blood. Lots of blood. Her scream pierced the silent room.

'Mommy! Mommy!'

'Get out of here, Gloria! Get out of here now!'

CHAPTER FOURTEEN

'Serita shimmers "minerally gorgeous" in this silver formal gown with a wide gold belt around her waist. The belt comes off for a more funsy look. Notice the dipping back . . .'

Serita spun to show the audience her stunning back. From behind the curtain, Laura watched her friend. A sign over the runway read:

Be your own SVENGALI!
Our new find: Mr Benito Spencer!

The well-known SV logo of Svengali adorned both ends of the sign. The ballroom at the New York Nikko Hotel was packed with some of the biggest names in fashion. Laura had arranged front-row seating for the most important critics, and tonight, the Palladium would throw a party for Mr Benito Spencer. Svengali's marketing department had been hard at work, making sure that the company's first show in nearly five months had plenty of positive publicity surrounding it.

Serita walked to the end of the runway, made a final turn, and headed back. No doubt about it, Laura thought, Serita was the best in the business. She thrived on the runway like an actress on the stage. With her back straight, her whole being giving off an aura of sophistication and elegance, Serita could make Hawaiian hula shirts look in vogue. And yet, Serita allowed the audience to peek under the unruffled facade and see that she was no mere mannequin, that she was real and having fun up there.

With one last look of total composure Serita made her grand exit. Once off stage, her cool expression changed completely.

'Out of my way,' Serita hissed as her casual runway stroll turned into a Carl Lewis-type sprint. On her way to the dressing room, her hands were busy working at unhooking the zippers. Four helpers raced after her. One managed to change Serita's earrings while she was still moving. Another touched on makeup. When Serita reached the dressing room (actually, part of the hotel's kitchen), the third helper slipped off the silver high-heeled shoes and replaced them with black shoes with a somewhat lower heel. Helper number four slid a white blouse over Serita's shoulders. Wild-eyed, Serita stood and dashed back toward the runway entrance with yet another helper trailing her with a pearl necklace. Serita stopped and rolled her eyes at Laura as the pearls were wrapped around her swanlike neck.

'I hate this,' she whispered toward Laura.

'Who are you kidding?' Laura asked. 'You love it.'

'True.'

Forty seconds after Serita had exited the runway wearing a silver formal gown with a gold belt, she stepped on again wearing a navy business suit complete with leather tie.

'Doesn't Serita look smart in the latest . . .'

'They love you!' exclaimed an assistant standing next to Benito Spencer. Spencer silenced his assistant with a sharp glare. He took a drag on his cigarette with enough intensity to inhale a tennis ball through a straw.

Laura turned and smiled reassuringly at her latest designer, Benito Spencer (his real name was Larry Schwartz). He was a thin-faced, long-haired twenty-three-year-old who had to know that today would decide his fashion future. The critics out in the audience, ordinary folks who just happened to have accumulated an enormous amount of power in the fashion world, would make or break Benito Spencer. Tomorrow morning, Benito would be the 'newest fashion genius' or a 'washed-up no-talent.' Despite all the publicity, that decision would be made by these critics, many of whom had never been able to achieve their own dream of finding a sponsor and having their own show like Benito. For Svengali, today was merely a small financial gamble. For Benito, it was much more.

The young designer stubbed out the cigarette and fidgeted with a dress, searching for some way to keep himself busy. Laura truly wished Benito the best. He was a sensitive man who she believed had tremendous talent. She was confident he would do well today.

Laura so used to look forward to the thrill of introducing a new talent to the fashion world. For weeks she would work on promoting new lines with the passion of a sculptor in front of a fresh piece of marble. She would stay late at the office and go over every detail of the presentation until everything was absolutely perfect. And when it was completed, when she could finally step back and look at the fruits of her long hours of labor, joy and a sense of fulfillment would fill her. But work no longer gave her such feelings. Now, life held no emotions like happiness, affection, passion. Now, life meant merely survival. It was an alternative to death—a welcome or unwelcome alternative, she could not say. Svengali was the life-preserver she clung to in her sea of despair. Work, like life, had become just a way of passing time, an occasional distraction from reality.

But work had never been like that before. She remembered the joy of preparing her previous fashion presentation when David was still alive. The show had taken place a few days before she and David had taken off for Australia—a lifetime ago. Every night during that long week, Laura had stayed in the Svengali office until nearly midnight. A few nights before the show at the Beverly Hills

Hotel, she sat alone in her office going over the show's seating. The seating was a crucial element in a good fashion show. If you snubbed a major critic and forgot to put him or her in one of the front rows, the presentation would flop no matter how good the designs were.

She had been working at her desk, her head lowered over the list of fashion magazines that would be attending. She knew the critic from *Vogue* was having a small tiff with the one from *Mademoiselle* so it would not pay to seat them next to one another. And the critic from . . .

Laura stopped. Though she knew the office was deserted, she felt eyes on her. She slowly raised her head toward the door.

'Hi,' David said softly.

She looked at him. There were tears nestled into the corners of his eyes. 'How long have you been standing there?' she asked.

'About five minutes.'

'Are you okay?'

He nodded. 'I'm fine. I just wanted to surprise you.'

'What's wrong, David?'

He smiled now. 'Nothing, my love. Nothing at all.'

'You're crying.'

'Just tearing, Laura.'

'Why?'

He shrugged, moved into the room, and embraced her. 'What can I tell you? I came in to surprise you. You've been working so hard lately and I thought a little break would be fun.'

'You thought right,' Laura added.

'Anyway, I came up to the door. You were sitting

there at work and . . . I don't know. I just love watching you. I love watching the way your head tilts when you're reading. I love the way you smile when you're thinking of a new idea. I love the way you brush back your hair with your finger. I even love the way your leg shakes. So I was watching you, mesmerized, and I was thinking about how beautiful you are and about how much I love you and all . . .'

Laura kissed him. 'You are the sweetest—'

'Don't you start, too,' David interrupted. 'Only so much corny stuff I can handle at one time.'

'I love you, David. I will love you forever.'

'This Svengali Special by Benito Spencer is perfect for the woman on the go. It can be worn with or without the jacket . . .'

Why had it all been cruelly snatched away from her?

The faces of the important critics in the front row blurred into one large mass of fleshy tones. More than two weeks had passed since Laura had confronted and made up with her mother, two weeks where Laura had done her best to bury herself in the preparation for this show. But still the conversation with her mother kept pricking at her mind with tiny needles. Her mother was hiding something, Laura was sure of it. Her mother was hiding something about David.

But what could it be? Could there have been something in David's past that he had kept from her? And if he had, how would Laura's mother know about it? And why wouldn't her mother say what it was? What could have happened to David that would explain all the peculiar happenings . . .?

Murder.

Laura's thoughts jerked wildly. She tried to push the thought away, but it remained anchored in her mind. T.C., Aunt Judy, her father—they were all acting so strangely . . .

Murder.

. . . as if they suspected something . . .

In the background the Svengali announcer: *'You're sure to be a hit in this red ensemble . . .'*

A half a million dollars was missing. $500,000. People would do crazy things for that kind of money. Cheat. Swindle. Deceive. Rob. Mug. Kidnap.

Murder.

Laura replayed her conversation with Richard Corsel at the bank.

'Your husband had me transfer the money to Switzerland.'

'When?'

'Please, I can't say.'

Why was Corsel so damn protective about telling her when? Unless . . . So many questions about David's death hounded her. He had drowned in the rough waters of the Pacific Ocean.

Drowned? David?

It didn't make any sense. She had listened to all their talk about the ocean's dangerous currents, but the excuse rang hollow in her ears. Rough currents or no rough currents, David was an excellent *and careful* swimmer. He would have checked the currents and tides before diving in. David may have been unpredictable but he never took foolish risks, especially when it concerned his health.

And a man like that drowned?

Murder.

The walls around her seemed to whisper that

word. $500,000 was missing, disappearing within a few days of David's death. Coincidence or . . .?

Murder.

And maybe T.C. and the others suspected the same thing. That would explain their strange behavior toward her. Were they trying to protect her from the truth? Is that the reason T.C. didn't approve of her strong-arm approach to handling Corsel at the bank? Had the devastation of David's death blinded her to the truth?

'The final ensemble is an innovative evening gown . . .'

Laura sat down. The Nikko Hotel and the fashion show evaporated from her mind, dissolving into the sounds of a distant background. Was she going crazy, or, for the first time, were events starting to make sense? Almost four months had painfully crawled by since David's death and Laura still could not accept it. People like David just don't up and die, her mind told her. It just doesn't happen. Not to David . . .

David, what happened to you? What did they do to you?

The fashion show finally came to an end. Serita moved toward Laura and sat down. 'I think it went well.'

Laura nodded.

Serita recognized the now-familiar blank expression on Laura's face, but now there was something more in her friend's glazed look. 'Uh-oh, what now?'

Laura turned to her. 'Something's not right, Serita.'

'What do you mean?'

Before she could answer, one of Benito

231

Spencer's helpers tapped Laura on the shoulder. 'Telephone call for you.'

'Take a message,' Laura said.

'It's a Mr Richard Corsel from some bank in Boston. He says it's urgent.'

*   *   *

Gloria gently dried off her face with a gray towel she grabbed from the rack. Interesting how Gloria's bathroom had been done all in gray. Her parents' was red. Laura's blue. The downstairs one yellow. Yet Gloria's was gray. She wondered if it had been an omen.

Well, not anymore.

She finished drying and draped the towel over the rack. She turned back toward the mirror, using her hands as a sort of comb in her thick blond hair. She studied her reflection for a moment and decided she had never looked or felt better. In fact, she felt so well that despite Dr Harris's protest, Gloria had cancelled the rest of her sessions. She no longer needed psychiatric help. Love was her cure from now on.

Gloria moved back into her bedroom, stepped over her two suitcases and headed down the stairs. When she reached the entrance to the den, she hesitated for a moment before going in.

Gloria turned the corner. Her parents were both reading on the couch. James Ayars's head tilted up when she came in. He glanced at her from behind his half-glasses. In his hands he held *The New England Journal of Medicine.* Beautiful Mary Ayars sat with her feet on a stool, her hair tied back away from her face. She was skimming through the most recent issue of the *New Yorker*.

'Hi,' Gloria began.

'Hello, dear,' her mother said, putting down her magazine. 'Is everything all right?'

'Everything's fine,' she responded. 'I just wanted to talk to you about something.'

Her father sat up. 'What is it?'

Gloria was not sure how to begin. 'You know how I've been spending the last few weeks with a friend?'

'Yes?' Mary said.

Gloria's words came quickly. 'Well, my friend is a man—and he's more than just a friend. We went up to the Deerfield Inn a couple of weekends ago and I've been with him every night since.'

Gloria watched her parents. As usual, her father's expression gave away nothing. Her mother's face, on the other hand, seemed to brighten.

'You've found a nice man?' Mary asked hopefully.

Gloria nodded. 'He's very special. We've decided to move in together.'

'I see,' Dr Ayars said.

'We're in love.'

'I see,' her father said again with a small nod.

'What's the young man's name, dear?' Mary asked, smiling.

Gloria pushed back her blonde mane. 'Stan Baskin.'

The smile vanished from her mother's face as if she had been slapped. 'What?'

'David's brother, Mom. Oh, that's right. You didn't meet him. He came to Boston for David's funeral . . . Dad, you met him, right?'

'Actually, I didn't,' James said matter-of-factly. 'There was so much confusion at the funeral and all, I didn't get the chance. But Laura told me what a comfort he has been to her.'

'He has,' Gloria agreed. She glanced toward her mother, whose lovely features were frozen in a look of terror.

James removed his reading glasses. 'So how did this all happen?'

'It just did,' Gloria shrugged. 'We're very much in love.'

Mary finally found her vocal chords. 'Honey, are you really sure about this? I mean, moving in with a man is a big step.'

'I know that, Mom, but I'm thirty-one years old. I'm not a child anymore. I love Stan.'

Panic colored Mary's eyes. 'But, Gloria, I don't think you should—'

'We wish you the best of luck,' her father interrupted, silencing his wife with a hard glare. 'If you're happy, we're happy.'

Oblivious to her mother's reservations, Gloria ran over and threw her arms around her father's neck and kissed him. Then she did the same to her mother. 'I love you both.'

'And we love you,' James said, smiling warmly. 'We'd love to meet this young man as soon as it's convenient for you. Bring him over for dinner one night.'

'No—!' Mary stopped, composed herself. 'I mean, only if you want to, Gloria. We don't want to pressure you into anything.'

'You're not pressuring me. I think that would be nice.'

'Good,' her father added.

'Dad, can you help me put my bags in the car?'

'Sure, honey. I'll be there in a second.'

Gloria left the room. James saved his page with a marker and gently placed the periodical on the coffee table. He sighed, slowly stood, and then turned toward his wife.

'I think it's time we talked.'

* * *

'I'm telling you there is something weird about that guy,' Earl Roberts said to Timmy Daniels.

'No kidding,' Timmy answered. 'I don't think I've heard him say five words since he beat me in that three-point contest two weeks ago.'

The two players took a sip of water from the fountain and headed back toward the court. Sweat drenched them both. For that matter, sweat drenched all fifteen of the players still in the Celtics camp. It was break time. All the players were scattered around the gym floor, catching their breath during the five-minute rest.

All save one.

Timmy collapsed onto the floor next to Earl. 'The guy doesn't say anything. Just plays and leaves.'

'That's fine with me,' Earl said.

'What makes you say that?'

'I don't like him. Something about him just ain't right.'

'Like?'

Earl shrugged. 'Let's face it. Mark Seidman is a great player. He can shoot and pass like nobody's business.'

'So?'

'So where the hell has he been? How can someone be that good and never have played college ball?'

Timmy positioned himself to watch Mark shoot. 'Got me. I think he told Clip that he went to school overseas. His family traveled around a lot or something.'

'Still,' Earl replied, 'nobody's ever heard of this guy. And he won't say a word to the press. They've been trying to get him to talk, but he just blows them off. What rookie does that? I mean, it's gonna be his first year in the NBA and he already acts like a prima donna with the media? I don't get it.'

Timmy nodded his agreement. 'It's every kid's dream to play in the NBA and he looks so goddamn sad all the time.'

The two teammates followed the ball as Mark swished jumpshot after jumpshot.

Earl wiped his sweaty face with a towel. 'There's something else that bothers me.'

'I know what you mean,' Timmy said.

'It's like he's trying to play like him on purpose. It's pissing me off.'

Timmy turned toward Earl. 'I don't think that's it,' he said. 'There's other players with that jumpshot.'

'Yeah,' Earl replied, as another of Mark's shots fell through the metallic hoop, 'but how many of them have that kind of accuracy?'

*　　　*　　　*

When Laura and Serita entered the Heritage of Boston Bank together, everyone stopped. Typewriters halted their clacking. Heads turned.

Eyes stared. Mouths dropped. Men gawked. Walking alone, Laura and Serita could make a man's eyes water; looking at them both at the same time could cause a cerebral accident.

'They're staring at us,' Serita whispered to her.

'You love it.'

'Always did.'

They moved past the bank clerks toward the executive office area. Heads, eyes, mouths, men followed them. When they were out of sight, Laura could hear the typewriters start up again.

An elderly secretary with gray-green hair looked up from her desk. She slipped on her glasses and narrowed her eyes suspiciously. A sign on her desk read Eleanor Tansmore. 'May I help you?'

'We'd like to see Mr Richard Corsel,' Laura said.

'I see,' Eleanor Tansmore replied. 'Do you have an appointment?'

'Not exactly,' Laura said, 'but he knows we're coming.'

'Well, Mr Corsel is very busy today. Perhaps you can call later and set up an appointment.'

'I have a better idea,' Serita interrupted. 'Why don't you buzz Mr Corsel and tell him we're here?'

'And whom shall I say is calling?'

Serita smiled devilishly. 'We're the two women Mr Corsel purchased from our, uh, agent. A Mr Tyrone Landreaux.'

'Excuse me?' the secretary said.

'One black, one white. Just like he ordered.'

'What?'

'Hurry, honey. Buzz him. My time is money. Big money, if you know what I mean.'

Eleanor Tansmore lifted the phone and smiled wryly. 'Did you bring your own whips and chains this time?' she asked Serita. 'You know how Mr Corsel hates to use his own.'

Serita looked at the woman in astonishment. 'Are you putting me on?'

'Yes.'

A smile of respect danced across Serita's lips. 'You're all right, Mrs T.'

'You're not so bad yourself,' Mrs Tansmore replied. 'Now sit down over there.'

'I'm sorry for my friend's behavior,' Laura interrupted, 'but if you could just tell Mr Corsel that Laura Baskin is here to see him, I think he'll make time to see us.'

'Laura Baskin? The model?'

'Former model,' Laura corrected.

'I read about your husband. I'm very sorry.'

'Thank you.'

Eleanor Tansmore looked toward Serita. 'And who is your witty companion?'

'Her bodyguard,' Serita replied.

The secretary smiled a phony secretary's smile. 'If you'll both sit down, I'll buzz Mr Corsel.'

Laura and Serita sat down. One of the office doors opened and a short executive with a thin mustache came out.

'That him?' Serita asked.

Laura shook her head no.

'Good.'

The executive stared at the two gorgeous women sitting in the waiting room. He sucked in his protruding stomach and smiled at them. Serita returned his greeting with a seductive wink. Then she slowly crossed her mile-long legs. The man nearly tripped over his own tongue. Serita laughed.

'Cut that out,' Laura warned.

'Sorry.'

'I swear, I can't take you anywhere.'

'I'm just trying to keep the mood light.'

'Knock it off.'

'Okay, but I've never seen you so uptight. It's not good for you, Laura. I'm just trying to keep you loose.'

'Serita?'

'What?'

'Am I crazy? I mean, all this conspiracy and murder stuff.'

Serita shrugged. 'Probably.'

'Thanks.'

'Look, Laura, you're not going to put this behind you until you figure out exactly what the hell happened. So go for it. Leave no stone unturned. If there's something weird going on, you'll find it. If not, you'll find that out too.'

Eleanor Tansmore came over. 'Mr Corsel will see you now.'

Laura rose. 'You coming?'

'Nah,' Serita answered with a smile, 'I'll wait here with my buddy Mrs T. Tear him apart on your own.'

'You're a good friend,' Laura said. She turned and headed down the hallway.

When Laura disappeared into Corsel's office, the smile vanished from Serita's face. She blinked away a tear. 'The best,' she whispered to herself.

*   *   *

Dr James Ayars faced his wife of thirty-three years. His mind flashed back to the first time they met. He had been an intern in Chicago, working a hundred hours a week when it was slow. At the time, he had been dating a bright student from the University of Chicago named Judy Simmons. Pretty little Judy Simmons. Nice girl. Auburn hair. Fine figure. Fun to be with. Young Dr Ayars had been very taken with Judy Simmons.

Until he met her younger sister Mary.

The first time Judy introduced him to Mary he felt a gurgling in the pit of his stomach. He had never seen such a beautiful creature in his life, never imagined such beauty existed. Mary Simmons smiled at him on that day, casting her powerful spell of sensuality upon him. The spell left him writhing and helpless in her presence. His eyes burned with unquenchable desire whenever he saw her. He knew that he would have to make her his wife. No matter what, he had to have her, possess her, cherish her . . .

The obsession had frightened him.

Of course it had not been that easy. There was Judy to consider, but sweet, kind Judy had understood. She stepped out of the way and wished them both the best of luck.

Now, some thirty-four years later, Mary was still ravishing. There were still times when James's stomach gurgled when he beheld her awesome beauty. Their marriage had had its share of problems (what marriage didn't?) but overall, James would say it had been excellent. They had raised two wonderful children. Life had been good . . .

. . . except . . .

'What's going on?' James asked his wife.

'Going on?' Mary repeated.

'You know what I mean. First you didn't approve

240

of David. Now you don't approve of his brother. Why?'

Mary swallowed. 'I . . . I'm not really sure. I just don't trust that family.'

'Why not?'

'I don't really know, James.'

'Mary, you've always been a good mother. I've always been very proud of the way you've handled our daughters. Do you remember when Gloria was having all her problems and I swore I would never let her back in this house again?'

Mary nodded.

'Well, I was wrong,' James said. 'And you knew it. But you knew fighting me on the subject would be worthless. So instead, you showered me with kind words. You made me understand that no matter what Gloria had done, she was still our daughter. Do you remember?'

Again, Mary nodded.

'Now I think it's my turn,' he continued. 'I think you should seriously look at the consequences of what you are doing. Look at what happened when you rejected David—'

'What?' Mary interrupted loudly. 'You're not blaming me, too?'

'Laura doesn't blame you,' he assured her gently, 'and neither do I. Laura is in pain right now. She lashes out and says things she doesn't mean.'

'It wasn't my fault,' she insisted. 'I was doing what I thought right.'

'What do you mean by that?' he asked. 'What did you have against David?'

'I was just doing what I thought was best.'

'Best for whom?' James asked.

She turned back to him, her eyes blazing

241

defiantly. 'For Laura.'

'And is the same true with Gloria and Stan? Are you doing what's best for Gloria?'

Mary closed her eyes tightly and leaned back. Thoughts flew aimlessly through her mind. She tried hard to concentrate but it was so difficult.

James was so wise sometimes, she thought. He was right, of course. This time, her words had not been said in the hopes of protecting her daughter. This time, she had put herself first. And that was wrong. Her daughters must always come first. Always.

Fear crawled around Mary's shoulders. Calm down, she told herself. After all, what harm could Stan Baskin cause her and her family now?

The answer made her shiver.

*   *   *

A nervous smile danced about Richard Corsel's face as he stood to greet Laura. His thin hair needed combing. His face needed a shave. He was hardly the neat and proper bank vice president Laura had encountered in the past.

'Mrs Baskin,' he said, his smile stretching for a moment before returning to its original state, 'it's a pleasure to see you again.'

'Thank you.'

'Please have a seat,' he continued. 'How are you feeling on this fine day?'

'Fine.'

'Good, good.' He looked around liked a caged animal searching for an opening. 'Can I get you something? Coffee?'

'No, thank you. Mr Corsel, you said on the

phone you have something urgent to tell me.'

His smile collapsed as if from exhaustion. 'I do—or at least I might.'

'I don't understand.'

He shook his head slowly. 'Neither do I, Mrs Baskin. Neither do I.'

'What do you mean?'

Corsel picked up a pen and then put it back down. 'I mean I looked through your husband's records again. Something might be wrong.'

'Wrong?'

'Might be wrong,' Richard Corsel corrected. He opened his desk drawer and took out a file. 'May I ask you a question, Mrs Baskin?'

Laura nodded.

Corsel leaned back in his chair. His gaze rested on the ceiling and stayed there. 'According to the newspapers, your husband went swimming on June 14 and drowned sometime that day between the hours of four and seven o'clock in the evening Australian time. Is that correct?'

'Yes.'

He nodded, his eyes still on the ceiling. 'There is a fifteen-hour time difference between here and Australia—we're fifteen hours behind them. That would mean Mr Baskin died sometime on June 14 between one a.m. and four a.m. Boston time.'

'Right.'

Corsel sat forward, but he still could not look at her. 'His call to me came on June 14 at eight thirty in the morning. That's nearly midnight in Australia, and at least five hours after he drowned.'

Cold fear seeped into Laura.

'Here,' Corsel continued, tossing the file at Laura. 'Read it. According to this, Mr Baskin called me several hours after his drowning.'

'Are you sure about the time? Could you have made a mistake?'

He shook his head. 'Not possible. Even though I recognized your husband's voice and he said the access code number, I insisted on verification due to the magnitude of the transaction.'

'What do you mean, verification?'

He swallowed. 'I asked him to give me the phone number of where he was so that I could call him back. A woman with an Aussie accent answered and transferred my call. The number is written there. There is also a copy of the phone bill which reconfirms the time.'

Laura skimmed through the file until she saw a phone number: 011–61–70–517–999. Then she saw the time of the call. Her heart fell deep into her stomach. How . . .? The call had been placed at 8:47 a.m. on June 14. Thirteen minutes before midnight in Australia. Several hours after David had drowned.

'The 011 is for a long-distance call,' Richard Corsel explained. 'Sixty-one is the country code for Australia. Seventy is the city code of Cairns.'

Cairns, Laura thought. That was where she had met with the Peterson Group, the meeting that had taken place while David drowned in nearby waters . . .

'I don't understand, Mr Corsel. How could David have placed a call to you five hours after he drowned?'

Corsel shrugged. 'I'm not a detective, Mrs Baskin. I only know the facts you see in front of you. As much as it pains me to say, I think you were right. Somehow, someone was able to get David's access code and imitate his voice well enough to fool me. I can't imagine what else it could be . . . unless, of course, the coroner was wrong about the time of death.'

Laura slumped back. If the coroner had been wrong, where had David been for all those hours? And why would David move around his money hours before taking a midnight swim?

'Can I keep this file, Mr Corsel?'

'I'd prefer if you just wrote down what you want to know for now. Of course, I'll keep trying to track down the missing money. Your husband . . . I mean, whoever made that call had this access code and insisted on absolute secrecy, so please, Mrs Baskin, I never showed this to you. This time I'm worried about something a lot more valuable than my job.'

Laura nodded. She understood what he meant.

*   *   *

When Laura and Serita arrived at Laura's place, Laura picked up the phone and dialed 011–61–70–517–999. She pictured her call traveling through thousands of miles of wires and satellite transmissions that led from Boston to a small city on the other side of the world in Australia. After a few seconds, a loud static came over the line. Then she heard the ringing of a telephone.

Laura gripped the phone impossibly tight and listened. The receiver on the other end was picked up after the third ring. A piercing feedback traveled halfway across the globe, followed by a young woman's voice:

'Pacific International Hotel. Can I help you?'

CHAPTER FIFTEEN

Laura hung up the phone without speaking.

'What is it, Laura?' Serita asked. 'Whose number is it?'

Laura remembered the hotel so well. The window from the Peterson office had given her a perfect view of the Martin Jetty's only high-rise structure. 'The Pacific International Hotel.'

Serita shrugged. 'So what does that mean?'

'The Pacific International Hotel is on the same street as the Peterson Group building,' Laura explained, her voice flat. 'The call to the bank was placed from a hotel less than a block from where I had my meeting.'

Serita leaned back in the chair. She kicked her shoes off her feet and across the room. 'This whole thing is getting kind of eerie, huh?'

Laura did not respond.

'I keep waiting for *Twilight Zone* music,' Serita said. 'So what's our next step? You gonna call T.C.?'

'Not yet,' Laura said.

'Why not?'

'Because I think he already suspects something.'

'What? How can that be?'

Laura shrugged. 'He's the professional, right? If I could figure it out, so could he.'

'So why not work together?' Serita suggested.

She shook her head. 'I don't think T.C. wants to find out what really happened . . . or else he already has and doesn't want me to know.'

'That doesn't make any sense, girl.'

'I know. It's just a feeling I can't shake.'

'Well, I think you better shake it and talk to him.'

'Maybe later,' Laura said. 'Right now, I think I'm going to take a shower and change.'

'Go ahead. I'll change when you're finished. Can I borrow that new white outfit of yours?'

'Sure. It'll probably look better on you anyway.'

'It's my ebony complexion.'

Laura smiled dully and headed into the bathroom. Serita waited for her friend to turn on the shower before picking up the phone and dialing.

'T.C.,' Serita said quietly, 'I need to talk to you.'

*　　　*　　　*

Stan Baskin looked out the window at the Charles River. In many ways, the new apartment was nothing special. It consisted of one bedroom, a living room, a bathroom, a kitchen, and a terrace. As far as Stan was concerned, you could get rid of the bedroom, the living room, the bathroom. Just leave him the terrace. The view soothed him like a gentle touch. Though he and Gloria had only moved in a couple of days ago, Stan had already spent what seemed like countless, blissful hours gazing at the Charles River. He watched the college couples stroll along her banks; he watched the crew boats from Harvard slice through her still waters. And at night, the Charles became a sparkling jewel of lights reflecting off of nearby buildings and onto her shiny, wet coat.

Usually, Gloria sat beside him and watched too. But she never disturbed him when he was lost in his own thoughts. Gloria had an uncanny knack for knowing when he wanted to talk and when he just wanted to be left alone. Right now, she was at Svengali's headquarters putting together a new marketing scheme for the teenage set. She would not be home for several hours yet.

Stan moved away from the window. He knew that he needed to find a job (or a good con) soon. The ten grand he had made from his part in the Deerfield Inn scam was running low. Shit, B Man had made a nice little profit on that one. He got the fifty grand Stan owed him, plus ten grand interest and another twenty grand net profit minus whatever minuscule amount he paid that Neanderthal Bart.

Stan picked up the newspaper from the couch. He had a tip about a horse in the seventh race named Breeze's Girl. The horse, his contact had assured him, could not lose. But somehow it did not feel right. Stan rarely, if ever, bet on a filly. Be they human or animal, females could not be depended upon to come through for you.

The clock read three o'clock. Gloria usually came home between six and seven. At least three more hours until she was back. Stan shook his head, wondering why he would be counting the hours until she returned. If he did not know himself better, he could swear that he sort of missed her. But of course that was impossible. Stan Baskin did not miss women. They missed him.

He moved back into the kitchen and poured himself a glass of orange juice. When he was a little kid, his mother squeezed him fresh orange juice every morning because she knew how much he loved it. His poor old lady. She had ended up dying of cancer. What an awful fuckin' disease, he thought. You're either lucky enough to be in remission or you get to stay in bed and wait for the cancer to claim your life, wait as the disease eats away at you from within. Or worse, the doctors make you go through that chemotherapy shit. No way would I go put up with that, Stan thought. If I'm ever in her shoes, I'd go out and buy myself the biggest gun I could find and press it against my temple and pull the trigger.

Bam.

Dead. Quick and painless. Just like what had happened to his dad—or so they all thought. Only Stan knew better.

Every morning Stan's mother squeezed him fresh orange juice. 'It's good for you,' she would say. But Stan needed no encouragement to drink the pulpy liquid with the little pits. He loved Grace Baskin's fresh-squeezed orange juice. But then his father died (was murdered) *and all that changed. Stan had been only ten years old at the time—David not yet two.*

The funeral had been jammed with thousands of people from the university: professors, deans, secretaries, students. All the neighbors were there too. Stan stood quietly next to his mother. She wore black and cried into a white handkerchief.

'We have to think of David now, Stan,' she said to him as they lowered the casket into the ground. 'We have to make up for the fact that he is going to grow up without a father. Do you understand?'

Stan nodded to his mother. But in truth, he did not understand. Why should David be the one to worry about? He had never even known their father. David had never played catch with their dad. He had never gone fishing or to museums or to ball parks or to movies or even to the dentist with him. Fact is, David wouldn't even remember Sinclair Baskin.

Grace Baskin did not see it that way. Never did. She decided to put all her energies into raising her precious David. She chose to be two parents for her youngest child, even if it left none for her oldest.

But Stan didn't care. Who needed her anyway? For that matter, who needed women? As he eventually learned, women are basically worthless and cruel. They could all be lumped into two basic groups; parasites who wanted to suck you dry, or ball-breaking bitches who used words like love and togetherness when all they wanted to do was possess and control and destroy.

Therein lies the beauty of Stan's livelihood (or scams, as those who did not understand liked to call it). He simply turned the tables on the female sex. He used women the same way they used men. And for that people wanted him to go to jail? How goddamn ridiculous! You talk about being equal and fair—why not arrest every gold-digging bitch who pretended she cared about a guy just to get his dough? Shit, there would be scarce few broads around then.

Yes, Stan had seen first hand the damage that a woman could do. He had learned from them. When he was just sixteen, he was seduced by a thirty-year-old divorcee named Concetta Caletti. Stan was convinced that Concetta was the smartest, most beautiful and sophisticated woman in the whole world. Young Stan Baskin was even foolish enough to think he was in love. He even went so far as to quit school and tell Concetta Caletti that he wanted to marry her. But Concetta laughed at his offer.

'You are only a boy,' the dark-skinned beauty said.

'I love you,' the sixteen-year-old Stan insisted.

'Love?' she said, her eyes scalding his heart. 'Who

250

taught you that word? You don't even know what love is.'

'Then show me,' he pleaded.

'There is no such thing,' she flared. *'Love is a word people toss around to fool themselves into believing that they are not alone in the world. It's a lie.'*

'But I love you, Concetta. I know I do.'

'Get out of here, Stan. You're just a kid. When you start making some real money, then we'll talk about love.' The sound of the doorbell jarred away the image of Concetta's angry face and left Stan standing alone in the present. He glanced at the clock. Still only three o'clock. Maybe Gloria had come home early from work.

Stan crossed the room and opened the door. His eyes widened when he saw who was standing in his doorway. 'Well, well, isn't this a nice surprise?'

Laura said nothing.

'Your sister isn't here, Laura. She's at the office.'

'I know that. I came to talk to you.'

'How nice.' Stan stepped back. 'Do come in.'

'I feel safer out in the hallway.'

'No trust?'

'None.'

'Well then, Laura, you can stand out there with the door closed in your pretty face. If you want to speak with me, you'll have to come in.'

Laura glared at him and then, hesitantly, she entered. Stan closed the door behind her. 'Would you like to sit down?' he asked.

'No.'

'Something to drink perhaps?'

'No, Stan,' she said impatiently.

'Fine. Then why don't we just get to the point? What can I do for you?'

251

'I want you to leave my sister alone.'

'I'm shocked,' Stan said sarcastically. 'Why on earth would you want to break up such a happy couple?'

'Stop playing games, Stan,' Laura snapped. 'Gloria is vulnerable. If you have a problem with me, fine, let's settle it. But leave my sister out of it.'

Stan smiled and moved closer to her. 'Do I detect a note of jealousy on your part, Laura?'

She stepped back. 'More like repulsion,' she replied.

'Quick, very quick. I like that. I really do. But your sister and I are in love now, Laura. Can someone place a value on that?'

'I'm sure you can,' Laura said wearily. 'How much?'

'Excuse me?'

'How much do you want?'

'I'm astonished, Laura, truly I am. Are you trying to bribe me?'

'Last time I ask: how much?'

'Oh no, Laura, it's not that easy. I want more than money this time.'

'Oh?'

'I can get all the money I need now. Your sister has plenty of dough. And now that Gloria and I are so close, I just know I can depend on my sweet sister-in-law to loan me a few bucks when I'm in need.'

'Why should I?'

Stan shrugged. 'Because I'm sure you want me to treat your sister kindly. You wouldn't want me to make her feel like a piece of shit. Or beat her. Or get her hooked on drugs again. I can do any of those things, Laura, and you know it. So I'll tell you

252

to pay up and you'll do it.'

Laura looked at him. 'I don't get it, Stan. What do you want?'

'I just told you.'

'But I already offered you money. You can just take it and run. That's always been your style in the past. Why are you taking the chance of hanging around?'

Stan felt rage course through him. His face reddened. 'Don't tempt me into doing something you may regret, Laura. Suppose I did just take off right now. Have you really thought that through? Have you really considered the consequences? What would it do to Gloria? What do you think it would do to her fragile emotional stability?'

Laura locked her eyes onto his. Frightening as it sounded, Stan was right. If he did run away, Gloria would suffer severe, maybe irreparable, emotional damage. But why would he care? Since when did Stan Baskin worry about someone else? No, there had to be another angle she wasn't seeing. Perhaps Stan figured that if he stayed around he could get money whenever he wanted. As long as he held Gloria hostage, so to speak, he could extort money. Weeks, months, whatever. But somehow that did not seem to fit. According to T.C., Stan usually liked to get the money up-front and screw what might be down the line.

'So what do you want, Stan?' Laura demanded. 'What is it going to take to get rid of you?'

Stan's eyes did not waver under her glare. 'You're so sure getting rid of me is the answer, aren't you, Laura? It must be wonderful to always know what to do, to always know what's right. Christ, suppose I told Gloria about our little conversation? How would you like that?'

'You wouldn't dare.'

'I wouldn't?'

'No, Stan, you wouldn't. You wouldn't risk losing your best money supply.'

Stan shook his head slowly. 'You're such a ball-buster, Laura. I sometimes wonder if David didn't take his last swim to get away from you for a little while.'

Laura's eyes blazed in a wrath of fury. 'You son of a bitch!'

'Temper, Laura, temper.'

'You listen to me, Stan, and you listen good. I'll go along with your sick little mind games because I happen to love my sister. I'll do what you say to protect her from your demented desires. But you leave David out of this, do you understand?'

He paused. 'Okay, fair enough. You see, Laura, I'm not unreasonable.'

She pushed her hair back off her face. 'I see, Stan. I see that you're a pig.'

Stan smiled. 'I understand how you feel, Laura, but remember: there's a fine line between love and hate. Between loathing and lust. Someday, you're going to have to stop denying yourself. Someday, you're going to have to face up to your true desires. And then I may not be around anymore. How will you feel then?'

'Blessed.'

He chuckled. 'Goodbye, Laura. For now. Maybe Gloria and I will have you over for dinner some night soon. Are you free this week?'

Laura tried to keep her voice even. 'No.'

Stan opened the door for her. 'What a pity. Where are you going to be?'

'None of your goddamn business,' she said while her true destination floated across her mind:

Australia.

*   *   *

Richard Corsel closed his files and locked them in the cabinet. He was getting closer to discovering the truth. A friend of his at the Bank of Geneva in Switzerland had learned that David Baskin's money had been split up into at least two accounts and transferred back to the United States. One was in Massachusetts. With a little luck Corsel could discover where the account was in less than a week.

'Goodnight, Mr Corsel,' his secretary said.

'Goodnight, Eleanor.'

Richard clutched his briefcase tightly and headed out toward the parking lot. It was already dark now. A gentle fall breeze blew through Boston, pushing Richard's hair in the opposite direction from where it had been combed. Never mind. The work day was over. He unbuttoned the top button of his shirt and sorted through his key ring in search of his car keys. Naomi had asked him to pick up her stuff at the cleaners. She had also reminded him to buy some white socks for the kids. Richard shook his head. He couldn't understand how his six-year-old twins could go through socks so fast. What the hell were they doing with them? Wearing them over their shoes?

With a tired sigh, he unlocked his car door and slid into the front seat. He tossed his briefcase into the passenger seat next to him. There would be traffic on the highways now. Maybe he should use the local roads. He put the key into the ignition . . .

. . . and a gloved hand grabbed the back of his neck.

'Hello, Richie,' a voice whispered in his ear.

Corsel's eyes bulged. 'Who the hell—?'

He was silenced by the sight of a large butcher's knife near his throat. 'Shhhh, Richie, not so loud. You wouldn't want to make me nervous, would you? My hand has a tendency to shake.'

As if for emphasis, the hand shook. The blade coarsely caressed the skin on Richard's neck.

'Who—?'

'Shhh, Richie, I'm doing the talking right now, okay? Don't turn around and don't try to get a glance of me in the rearview mirror. If you do, I'll kill you. Do you understand?'

The knife now rested quietly against Corsel's throat. He could feel the coldness of the metal. 'Y . . . Yes,' Richard managed. 'My wallet is in my jacket pocket.'

'I know that, Richie, but I'm really not interested in petty cash. I've got plenty of money of my own, you know what I mean?'

Richard swallowed, the knife moving along with his throat. 'Wh . . . What do you want?'

'You see, Richie, that's your problem. You ask a lot of questions, you know? You don't see me asking a lot of questions. I don't ask how Naomi's new job at the boutique is, do I? I don't ask how the twins Roger and Peter are doing at their new school, right? So why are you so interested in other people's business?'

The intruder's warm spittle pricked in Richard's right ear.

'Now the way I look at it, Richie, you can do one of two things. One, you can go about your usual business and keep snooping around into Baskin's money. That's up to you, Richie. I wouldn't want to pressure you. You do what you think is best for your family, but I should warn you: it would make me very unhappy if you continued to snoop, Richie. It's not nice. Do you know what I mean?'

Corsel felt his whole body quiver.

'Now let me give you choice number two. See how you like this one, Richie, and then make up your mind about what you want to do, okay? Choice two: you forget all about Baskin's little transaction with your bank. You can go back to business as usual and not speak to his wife about it anymore. In return, you and your family will live happily ever after. You will never see me again. Sound nice?'

Richard managed a nod.

'But don't decide now, Richie. Think over your two choices for a while before you make up your mind. I'll be able to figure out which option you chose and act accordingly. Any questions?'

Richard shook his head.

'That's it, Richie. You're learning already. I'm going to slip out the back door and disappear now. If you turn and see my face or if you decide to chat with the authorities, well, let's just say it would be an unwise move on your part. It may force me to get to know little Roger and Peter better. Do you understand, Richie?'

Corsel nodded again, tears streaming down his cheeks. He tried to stay calm. He pictured himself sitting at the breakfast table on a typical morning having a nice bowl of Cap'n Crunch with Naomi and Roger and Peter and . . .

. . . and the psycho in the backseat, his knife slashing across their throats. The screams, the sound of the blade ripping skin, blood spraying all over the place, his wife's blood, his children's blood.

Oh God, what do I do now? What do I . . .

Suddenly, the car door opened and the blade was off his throat. Richard was afraid to breathe. He listened to the car door slam closed. He shut his eyes and waited five minutes before opening them again.

When he reached home, Naomi lectured him for forgetting to pick up the laundry at the cleaners and for not buying the kids some white socks. Richard's response was to give all three of them a hug.

*   *   *

Earl's penthouse was something out of *Architectural Digest*. Literally. So much so that the magazine had devoted a cover story to what they called *The High-Rise in the Sky*. And it was gorgeous. Everything in the penthouse had been done in white. The walls, the chairs, the sofas, the tables, the carpet. The only smatterings of color were the large and varied assortment of paintings that adorned the walls. But somehow the white scheme worked and, more interesting to *Architectural Digest*, Earl had designed the penthouse totally by himself.

There were also plenty of windows, all of them offering a fantastic view of Boston. From the gleaming living room, Laura stared out at the lights of the Prudential Building. She moved her glance toward the harbor where occasional lights from boats broke up the blanket of darkness covering the sea. From way up atop this skyscraper you would never guess how dirty that harbor actually was. But God, she loved Boston. True, she had never really lived anywhere else. Her family had left Chicago and the Midwest when she was just an infant so she really could not make a comparison. But Boston was her city. And David's.

Earl came out of the kitchen, a Celtics apron tied around his waist. 'Dinner is served.'

'Good,' Serita answered, moving toward Laura and putting her arm around her friend's shoulder. 'I'm starved.'

'Well, then sit down and prepare yourself,' Earl said. 'The master chef has created a new masterpiece.'

Laura smiled and sat down. Earl was truly a renaissance man, she thought. Locked into his lanky, seven-foot frame was a man who played pro basketball, who decorated his own penthouse like a master designer, who cooked exotic dishes like a gourmet chef. He was even writing a book on his basketball experiences called *Slam Dunk.* 'Smells good. What is it?' Laura asked.

'A treat from the Orient. Thailand, to be more exact.' He lifted the silver cover. 'I call it Shrimp Chow Earl.'

'Mmmmm,' Serita hummed. 'Let me at it.'

The three friends began to devour the dish. It was, Laura thought, a delicious meal. Light yet spicy. Perfectly seasoned.

'This is really good,' she said.

Earl beamed. 'Thanks, Laura. It's been a while since you've let me cook for you.'

Laura nodded, not trusting her voice right away. She and David used to eat over Earl's at least once a week. 'I know.'

Earl smiled at her. 'But David never liked my cooking.'

'That's not true,' Laura argued. 'You're a fantastic cook.'

'True,' Earl replied, 'but David had the culinary instincts of a cashier at Burger King.'

Laura chuckled. 'Can't argue with that.'

'I think it was living with T.C. and his grubby cigars and greasy hamburgers that did his tastebuds in,' Earl continued. 'I used to always tell David that your body is your temple. Now take this dish for example. Fresh shrimp, mushrooms, broccoli and natural spices—none of that chemical shit. The crap some people put in their body—unbelievable.'

'What's for dessert?' Serita asked.

'Soybean pudding.'

'Yuck. I mean, I'm all in favor of health, honey, but let's not be extremists.'

Earl poured his two beautiful guests some Chinese beer and sat back to watch them chow down. He shook his head and smiled. 'It's like watching Dobermanns in front of raw meat. How do you two stay so skinny?'

'I work it off,' Serita answered.

'Nautilus machines?' he asked.

She winked. 'Wrong answer. Try again.'

'Let me think about it. Meanwhile, I better get some more food before Laura starts scratching the plate.'

'No really, Earl, this is enough,' Laura said.

'You sure? Chez Earl has an all-you-can-eat menu.'

'Positive. I'm stuffed.'

'Okay.'

Laura stared at the table that a lifetime ago had seen the four of them laugh themselves silly. Now the conversation rang hollow, the words stilted and uncomfortable in the bright room. 'How's the team look?' she asked.

Earl shrugged. 'Okay, I guess. We really miss David out there.'

'Any of the draft picks looking good?'

'None.'

'Free agents?'

'Just one.'

'Oh, I've read about him in the *Globe*,' Serita interjected. 'You must have seen it, Laura.'

'Sorry. I don't read the Sports too much anymore.'

'It was all over the place,' Serita continued. 'This guy just walked into the gym one day, put up ten grand to challenge Timmy to a shooting contest and won. This complete unknown even broke—' She cut herself off.

'Broke what?'

'Let's change the subject,' Earl tried.

'Broke what?' Laura repeated.

Earl glanced at Serita and then he released a long breath. 'He broke David's three-point shooting record.'

'What?' Laura asked. 'I remember when David set the mark. The press said it would never be broken.'

'I know,' Earl said softly.

'So who is he?'

'His name is Mark Seidman,' Earl said.

'And is he good?'

Earl nodded. 'Sure, he's a great player and all but . . .'

'But?'

'I don't know. The whole thing is weird.'

'Where did he play in college?' Laura asked.

261

'That's just it. He didn't. No one ever heard of this guy before.'

'No one? Are you trying to tell me the press hasn't dug up something on him yet?'

Earl shook his head. 'Not a thing. He claims he lived in Europe, that his family traveled around a lot or something.'

'And you don't believe it?'

He shrugged. 'I don't know. You mentioned the press before. Well, none of them have been able to substantiate his story. And Seidman refuses to talk to reporters—and you know how Clip feels about good relations with the press. But hell, Seidman doesn't talk to anyone. He just comes in, plays, and leaves. He's moody and quiet and then every once in a while, he'll say something off-hand—you know, impromptu—like he's one of us. He gets this really pitiful look in his eyes. Like he wants to belong. Then he goes back into his shell.'

'Could be nothing,' Laura said. 'Or it could be he's hiding something.'

'Could be,' Earl ventured. 'I guess I make him sound like some kind of fugitive from the law. Maybe he is. But I don't think so. It's just—I don't know—so weird. I don't like him, that's all.'

'How good is he?' Laura asked.

'Hard to say. It's pre-season. I've seen a lot of guys who were All-Stars in pre-season and then turned into bums.'

'But what do you think?'

Earl hesitated. He lifted his glass and took a tiny swig of beer. 'Aside from David, he could be the best player I've ever seen.'

Laura spotted the hurt look on his face. It was not easy for Earl to admit that someone could be in the same league with the friend he so admired. 'An unknown walk-on?' she said, shaking her head. 'It doesn't make sense.'

'He's incredible,' Earl went on. 'Velvet shooting touch, great passer . . . Hey, enough about Seidman. I have to talk to you about something important.'

'Ah, so this was not just a social invitation,' Laura said. 'And I thought you loved my company.'

Earl chuckled. 'It's only the hundredth time I've asked you to dinner in the past couple of months.'

'And I'm not too happy about that,' Serita joked. 'You trying to make me jealous?'

'I wish,' he replied. 'Laura, Clip asked me to speak to you.'

'About what?'

Earl lowered his head and played with his food. 'It's kind of difficult to talk about.'

'Go on, Earl.'

Tears filled the giant man's eyes. 'The Celtics and the city want to pay tribute to David. Opening game at the Garden is in a week. We play the Washington Bullets. At halftime, they're going to retire David's number and hang it with the others on the rafters.' Earl stopped and turned away. Laura put her hand on his arm.

'It's okay, Earl.'

Earl sniffled and faced her again. His eyes were red now. Laura glanced at Serita. She too was crying. 'The Mayor will declare it David Baskin Day. After the game, there's going to be a small gathering at the Blades and Boards for the players, families, press—the usual stuff. Clip wanted to make sure you and your whole family—David's brother too—will be there.'

Laura remained stone-faced. 'We'll be there. All

263

of us.'

'Good,' Earl managed, his eyes darting around the room. He stood, shaking. 'I'll be right back.' He nearly sprinted out of sight.

'Big chicken,' Serita managed between her own sobs. 'He's afraid to cry in front of you. He still does it almost every night, you know.'

'I know,' Laura said. But she did not cry along with her friends. Laura had learned that occasionally, when the pain became too great, her mental block came up automatically. Sure, she heard the sad words, saw the tears, but somewhere along the way to her heart, the pain veered away.

'I need to talk to you about something else, Serita. But you have to promise not to tell anyone—including Earl. Okay?'

'Okay,' she said, wiping her eyes with the corner of a napkin.

'I'm leaving for Australia tomorrow morning.'

'What?'

'I'll be flying out of Logan around noon.'

'Whoa, Laura, let's talk about this a second.'

'Nothing to talk about. You know what Corsel said. The threads are going to disappear if I don't get over there and figure out what happened. I have to go. You know that.'

'I'll go with you.'

'No. I want to go by myself.'

'But—'

'Let me put it another way. I don't want you to go.'

'Fuck you, too.'

They hugged then, tightly, fiercely. Earl came back into the room. He walked over to them and threw his arms around both of them. For a long

264

time, the three of them just held one another in comforting silence.

CHAPTER SIXTEEN

'Qantas flight 182 departing for Honolulu and Cairns is now boarding at gate 37. Those passengers with children or who need special care may board now.'

Laura glanced at her watch and saw that her flight was going to take off on time. No small miracle. LAX airport in Los Angeles was packed with travelers today. Laura watched the stone-faced passengers pace through the long corridors, striding purposefully and consistently in that way that only people in airports do. There were no Hare Krishnas in airports anymore. Linden LaRouche was the new air-terminal religion, the presidency being his holy grail. A man was selling bumper stickers—what one was supposed to do with a bumper sticker at the airport was beyond Laura—asking people to save the whale or harpoon Jane Fonda or some other nonsense. Another man sat behind a sign saying:

Roses are Red,
Violets are Blue,
I'm a Schizophrenic,
And So am I.

Laura shook her head. Los Angeles. The last time she had been in LAX airport, she was on her way to David's funeral; the time before that, she and David had stopped for one night as they headed toward their honeymoon. Funny how life works that way. She remembered how excited they had been, how they had rushed out of Los Angeles' immense airport and headed into the City of Angels to get their blood test at a nearby hospital.

'I hate needles,' David had told her.

'Chicken.'

'Needles and insects,' he said. 'When we're married, do you promise to kill all the household insects?'

'I'll put it in our vows.'

When the nurse handed Laura the results an hour later, David asked, 'Did we pass?'

Laura smiled as she read the report. Both of them had been deemed healthy by the State of California. They could get married with the state's blessing. 'Passed.'

'Not even a touch of V.D.?'

'Nope. Do you want to see it?'

'Blood test results? No way.'

'Whatever you say. We better get back to the airport. Our plane will be taking off soon.'

'Question.'

'What?'

'Do you know how long the flight is?' David asked.

'No.'

'I do,' he answered.

'Great. So why did you ask me?'

'More than thirteen hours,' he pronounced.

'So?'

'More than thirteen hours strapped into an airplane.'

'The point being?'

'Well, that's a long time, don't you think?'

'Yes,' she agreed.

'So we have a little time before we have to head to the airport, right?'

'Right.'

'Well, I think it would be good for both of us if we made a quick pit-stop in a nearby hotel for rest and rejuvenation—strictly for health reasons, of course.'

'Of course.'

'Well?'

'No,' Laura said firmly.

'No?'

'Stop pouting. I said no.'

'But thirteen hours is such a long time. I know you, Laura. I'm not sure you can hold out that long without . . .'

'Without what?'

'You know what I mean, Laura. I'm only thinking of you.'

'Your concern is touching.'

'So?'

She smiled and threw her arms around his neck. She kissed him passionately. 'Who needs a hotel room?' she murmured in his ear. 'I always wanted to try it in one of those little bathrooms . . .'

His eyes lit up. 'You don't mean . . .?'

'That's right,' she said. 'Right over the Pacific.'

'God, I love this woman.'

'Qantas flight 182 now asks all economy-class passengers to begin boarding.'

Laura stood and made her way to a pay phone, the happy memory melting down to a dull ache. She dialed the operator and charged the call to her credit-card number. The operator put the call through.

'Heritage of Boston,' a voice answered.

'Richard Corsel, please,' she said.

'Hold on, please.' She heard a ringing. Then

267

another voice came on. 'Mr Corsel's office.'

'This is Laura Baskin. I would like to speak with Mr Corsel please.'

There was a moment of hesitation. 'I'm sorry, Mrs Baskin. Mr Corsel is not in at the moment.'

'I called earlier. I was assured he would be in by now.'

'I'm sorry, Mrs Baskin. Would you like to leave a message?'

'Yes. Please tell him it's urgent that I speak with him. I'll call him tomorrow at ten in the morning.'

'Fine. I'll give him the message.'

Eleanor Tansmore put the receiver down and turned toward Richard Corsel. His face was white.

*   *   *

Laura slowly hung up the phone. Something strange was going on again. Richard Corsel was ducking her. But why? She looked toward the long line of passengers boarding the Boeing 747. There were still a few minutes left before take-off. She quickly placed another call.

'Hello?'

'Serita?'

'Laura, honey, where are you?'

'Los Angeles airport. I have to board in a minute. I need you to do me a favor.'

'Name it.'

'Corsel is avoiding me. Could you go over there and see what he's up to?'

'What makes you think he's avoiding you?'

'I'm getting the run-around when I call. They claim he's not in.'

'So? Maybe he's not.'

268

'Not likely. I had him checked out by my office. He hasn't missed a day in three years and he never works outside of the office.'

'Laura, you're sounding a bit paranoid. He contacted you, remember? Why would he be trying to avoid you?'

'I don't know,' Laura admitted, 'unless somebody . . . Serita, did you tell anybody about our visit to the bank?'

'Why would you ask that?'

'I don't know. Maybe someone found out we were there and scared him off.'

Serita remained silent.

'Did you tell someone, Serita?'

'Laura . . .'

'Tell me.'

'I only told T.C.,' Serita said. 'And I did that for your own good. You're scaring me with all this murder talk. I'm afraid you might be getting into something over your head.'

'Final call for Qantas flight 182 . . .'

'Is he the only person you told?'

'The only one. I swear. But call him, Laura. Please.'

'Does he know I'm going to Australia?'

'No.'

'Don't tell him. Whatever you do, don't tell him.'

'You don't think T.C. has something to do with all of this? He loved David.'

'Just don't tell him where I am,' Laura repeated. 'I have to go now. I'll call you soon.'

Before Serita could protest, Laura hung up and boarded the plane.

*   *   *

269

Mark Seidman stared at T.C. wild-eyed. 'You did what?'

'I had no choice,' T.C. replied.

'Had no choice? I thought you said no one else would get hurt.'

'I didn't hurt him. I just scared him.'

'You threatened his children, for chrissake.'

'Look, Mark, Corsel was your responsibility. You said he'd back us.'

'I misjudged him.'

'And in doing so, you risked everything. First he caved in and told Laura the money had been moved to Switzerland. Now he's told her that the transfer was made after Baskin's death.'

'But that's all he knows,' Mark countered. 'He can't tell her anything else.'

T.C. shook his head. 'That's where you're wrong. Corsel is a bright guy. He's moved up the company ladder rather swiftly. He promised Laura he'd check into it. He feels responsible.'

Mark Seidman began to pace, his fingers toying with his blond locks. 'There had to be another way. Christ, you threatened him at knifepoint.'

'I don't like it any better than you do,' T.C. snapped, 'but I had to stop him. Suppose he kept digging, Mark? Suppose he found out what happened to Baskin's money? The whole plan could be jeopardized.'

'But to threaten his kids . . .'

'Time was short. It was all I could think of. And even threatening his family wasn't enough.'

'What are you talking about?'

'Corsel already told Laura that Baskin called the bank hours *after* the drowning supposedly took

270

place. Now there is no way Laura will quit searching until she finds a satisfactory way to explain that.'

Mark turned away from T.C. and looked out a window. 'There's something else I don't understand, T.C.'

'What?'

'How come Laura hasn't come to you for help in all this?'

T.C. shrugged. 'I don't know. That's another part of our plan that has gone astray. I'm not sure she completely trusts me anymore.'

'But she can't suspect you have anything to do with the drown—'

'Maybe she does,' T.C. interrupted. 'Maybe she does.'

*   *   *

Richard Corsel sat in his office. He stared at the two pens jutting up from the marble holder on his desk. He had been doing that for most of the day. Try as he might, concentration would not come to him for even the briefest of moments.

Lack of sleep, he thought. The previous night had seemed endless. He wandered through his house, went downstairs and finished off the Shop-Rite All Natural Vanilla Ice Cream, reread the newspaper. He walked back up the stairs and quietly opened the twins' door. Roger and Peter were both asleep, their breathing steady and deep. Richard tiptoed over to Peter's bed. Peter still had his Red Sox cap on his head. Richard had bought the twins Red Sox caps when they went to Fenway Park last month to watch the Sox play the Detroit Tigers. What a day that had been. Peter almost

271

caught a fly ball; Roger had eaten so many hot dogs he came home with a stomach ache. Corsel smiled at his sleeping children. He gently took the hat off of Peter's sleeping head and laid it on the night table, next to the Garfield the Cat lamp.

He took a Sominex, counted sheep, even read boring bank newsletters. Nothing worked.

'Mr Corsel?' his intercom shrieked.

'Yes, Eleanor.'

'There's a call for you on line four.'

'I'm not taking any calls.'

'It's a Mr Phillipe Gaillaird from the Bank of Geneva. He said it's urgent.'

'Tell him I'm not here.'

'But—'

'Just tell him I'll call him back,' he said firmly.

There was a moment of silence. 'Yes, Mr Corsel.'

Richard leaned forward and lowered his face into his hands. He stood and crossed the room. He moved down the hallway and into the executive lavatory. The door swung onto an empty and silent bathroom. He walked over to the mirror and splashed cold water onto his face.

Richard realized that he would have to call Phillipe back. If not, Phillipe would keep calling the bank and that was no good. The psycho with the knife would not like that. No, Richard would have to reach Phillipe and tell him to forget the whole thing, to forget about tracing the Baskin account. The question was how. The psycho with the knife was clearly a pro with powerful connections. If he had learned all those things about Richard's family and his conversation with Laura Baskin, he might also have placed a bug on Richard's phone. The psycho might even have someone tailing him.

272

And if the psycho gets the wrong idea and thinks that Richard is still trying to trace David Baskin's account . . .

He let the thought hang in the air.

Richard had considered the possibility of calling the police or going to his superiors, but what could he say? His superiors would want to know why he had passed confidential information on to Laura in the first place; the police would be powerless in protecting his family from the well-connected psychopath who knew all about Naomi's new job and about Roger and Peter's school. But Richard also knew that as long as that guy was out there, the danger to his family would continue to exist. And what about Laura Baskin? Could he just turn his back on her without even giving her a hint about what kind of people she was up against? True, he had only met her twice, but he was convinced she would not give up easily on all this. Laura Baskin would push and push until . . .

He decided to let that thought hang in the air too.

What the hell should he do?

He went back to his office, grabbed his briefcase and went up to one of the bank clerks. He handed the young girl a twenty-dollar bill.

'I need change. All quarters.'

'All quarters?' the clerk repeated. 'Why?'

'I'm taking a long drive on a toll-infested road,' he said wearily. 'Just let me have them, please.'

With a shrug, the clerk counted out the quarters. 'There you go. Eighty quarters.'

He put them in his briefcase and headed outside. He grabbed a taxi, took a subway, changed trains and lines three times, and ended up near the

Bunker Hill Monument. He found a telephone booth. No way he could have been followed and no way the call could be traced—not when you used quarters from a telephone booth.

He placed the first group of quarters in the slot. Then he dialed Phillipe Gaillaird's private line at the Bank of Geneva in Switzerland.

'Gaillaird,' Phillipe answered.

'Phillipe? It's Richard.'

'How are you, my friend?' the accented voice asked. Gaillaird had been born in Paris but had lived in Geneva since he was seven. Two years ago, Phillipe Gaillaird had made a mistake transferring funds to the wrong bank in the United States. A big, multi-million-dollar mistake. The kind of mistake that could ruin a Swiss bank. Richard had traced the money down and gotten it back for him. Phillipe Gaillaird owed Richard Corsel for that favor and he was anxious to repay. Gaillaird did not fancy being in someone's debt. 'I tried to reach you earlier.'

'I got the message.'

'Where are you calling from, Richard? The connection is very poor.'

'Don't worry about it.'

'Usually your bank lines are so clear.'

'I'm not calling from the bank.'

'Oh, I see. Well, I have some information for you.'

Richard closed his eyes. 'Just forget it, Phillipe.'

'Pardon?'

'Forget I ever asked you about that account. I don't need to know anymore.'

'Are you sure, Richard?' Gaillaird asked. 'I have the name right here.'

'Positive.'

Phillipe paused. 'What's the matter?'

'Nothing. Just leave it alone.'

The Swiss banker's voice grew serious. 'You're calling from a pay phone?'

'Yes.'

'Listen, Richard, I've been working for Swiss banks all my life. I don't know what's going on over there, but I have my suspicions. Someone has got to you. That's okay. Don't confirm or deny it. It's none of my business and I don't want to know. But let me give you a piece of advice. You're at a phone booth. No one is going to know what is being said. You might as well find out who has the money from the Baskin account. If you never use the information, no one will be the wiser. If the tables turn, knowing the truth may save your hide.'

Richard's hand gripped the receiver tightly. His eyes darted madly. What Phillipe said made sense. 'Okay. Give me the name. But after this call, I don't think we should talk again.'

'I understand,' Phillipe said.

*   *   *

Laura handed the Australian official her quarantine form, located her luggage, and made her way through customs. She started to drag her suitcase toward the taxi stand when a large hand reached out and picked it up.

'Sheriff Rowe,' Laura exclaimed, 'this is a pleasant surprise.'

Graham smiled through his beard. He lifted the suitcase as if it were a candy bar. 'You called me, didn't ya?'

'Yes of course, but I didn't expect you to pick me up.'

The mammoth sheriff shrugged and began to lead her toward his squad car. Laura noticed that everyone around her was wearing shorts. The heat was oppressive, even by the normal standards of tropical Cairns. But then Laura saw the beauty of the place: the bright sun, the trees that looked as if they had been freshly painted green, the pure blue ocean, the golden-sanded beach. Memories rolled over her heavily.

'Slow day,' Graham explained. 'I had a choice of picking up a lovely young lady, or issuing fishing licenses to a bunch of hicks with no teeth. It wasn't an easy choice, mind you. The missus preferred I stay with the hicks.' He smiled again. 'She's seen your picture in the magazines.'

Laura returned the smile. 'Thank you for coming.'

He put her suitcase in the trunk and opened the passenger door. 'Where are you staying, Mrs Baskin?'

'Laura,' she corrected. 'I'm staying at the Pacific International, Sheriff.'

'Graham,' he corrected back. 'Now, Laura, why don't you tell me why you're here?'

*   *   *

During their time off, most models cannot wait to trade in their exotic work wardrobe for a comfortable ripped pair of jeans and tattered sweatshirt. Serita was not one of them. She liked designer clothes—the more outlandish, the better. Right now, she was buttoning up a skin-tight white

276

jumpsuit. When it came to clothes, white was her favorite. She liked the way it contrasted with her ebony skin tone, and judging by the reaction of most people who saw her, her preference was also theirs. On some women, Serita'a outfit might draw a few interested glances; on Serita, it drew mouth-dropping gapes.

And, of course, she loved that.

I should go into acting, Serita thought with a smile. I'm a big enough ham for it.

So she liked being noticed—what was wrong with that? The way the media played up her outgoing personality you'd have thought she started wars in the Middle East. Yes, she was brash, but so what? She never hurt anybody. She never bothered anybody. She was having fun and if they had a problem with that, if they were pissed off because she didn't want to be quiet and subdued and pristine and boring, then fuck them.

She grabbed her purse and headed toward the door. Laura. Her headstrong friend. What the hell was she doing running halfway around the world? Laura could be so goddamn stubborn sometimes. She was searching, investigating, but for what? The truth? What good could that do? Suppose there had been some foul play. Suppose David's death was not accidental. Would that really change things? Would that make Laura's bed warm or bring David back to life? Would that make the agony searing through Laura somehow let up?

No.

Serita knew that Laura would not stop searching until she was satisfied that she knew all the answers. And Laura was not easily satisfied. And, more to the point, this had become an almost welcome distraction for Laura, a way of diverting herself from the pain of reality. But the reality was still there. The reality would come back with a vengeance. When all this was over, David would still be dead . . .

. . . and if the drowning was not an accident, so might Laura.

Serita had visited the Heritage of Boston Bank earlier this morning. Corsel was nowhere to be found. Now she was heading for a four o'clock shoot by Quincy Market for a jeans company. She grabbed her coat off the hook, reached for the knob and opened the door.

'Hi, Serita.'

Serita jumped back, startled. 'T.C., you scared the hell out of me.'

'Sorry,' T.C. said. 'I guess I should have called first.'

'That's okay,' Serita replied. 'Something I can do for you?'

T.C. bit off the end of his cigar. He put the Dutch Masters in his mouth but did not light it right away. 'I was looking for Laura. Do you know where she is?'

Serita shrugged. 'She's not at Svengali?'

He shook his head slowly. 'I spoke to her secretary . . . what's her name again?'

'Estelle.'

'Right, Estelle. I spoke to Estelle. She told me Laura is out of the city for a few days. She said Laura is on some kind of sales trip.'

'And she didn't tell you where?'

'She claims she didn't know. Maybe Canada. She said it was a big fashion secret or something.' T.C. took out his lighter and flicked it on. He placed it

278

on the end of the cigar. The flame rose and fell in rhythm to his puffing for a few moments until the end of the cigar lit. 'I was hoping you could tell me where she went. I'm worried about her, Serita.'

'Worried? Why?'

T.C. took a deep breath. 'You know how you told me she's suspicious about David's death being a simple accident?'

'Yeah.'

'And how she even thought that I suspected the same thing?'

'Right.'

'Well,' T.C. said, 'she was right. I do suspect the same thing.'

Serita's eyes widened. 'You mean—'

'I mean that there is a very good chance that David's drowning was not accidental.'

Serita felt her body spasm. She moved back into the house and beckoned T.C. to follow. He closed the door and they both sat down. 'He was murdered?'

'*May* have been murdered,' T.C. corrected, 'or something else. We're talking theory here, remember?'

'What do you think happened?'

He scratched his neck and then looked forward. 'I don't know exactly. It could be that a few bad boys discovered they could get their hands on David's loot by knocking him off.'

'Do you have any idea who?'

'None. But whoever it was is well-connected and powerful. No amateur could pull this off. We're talking about some very nasty people here, people who wouldn't mind killing somebody who snoops around in their business. That's why I want to find

279

Laura.'

'You think she's in danger?'

'Think?' he repeated. 'Serita, this is Laura we're talking about. She's not a trained detective and let's face it, subtlety is not her strong suit. She's going to go busting around like a bull in a china shop. Very nasty people don't like that. Very nasty people have a way of making people like Laura disappear without a trace.'

Serita stood. 'I need a drink. You want something?'

'No.'

She grabbed the bottle of vodka she kept in the freezer and poured herself a shot.

'Serita,' T.C. began, his words coming slowly, 'did Laura say anything to you that might give us a clue to where she went?'

Tears worked their way into Serita's eyes, but she forced them back down. She was scared, but she had made a promise to Laura and, come hell or high water, Serita would stick to it. Besides, T.C. had raised a few interesting points. If David had been murdered, the killer was indeed well connected. He or she had learned David's confidential bank number and where David and Laura were honeymooning. He or she had the capability of pulling off a murder and executing a complicated money transfer through Switzerland. Not too many people fit that description. Not too many people could pull off such a crime. Serita only knew one person who could do it. Right now, that person was sitting in her living room wanting to know where Laura was.

'No,' she replied. 'Not a word.'

Laura told Graham Rowe the whole story. She started with the house being broken into, the open calendar on the desk, the missing photograph, the missing money, Richard Corsel, the money transfer to Switzerland—everything. By the time she finished, they were settled into the plush chairs in the sitting room of her suite at the Pacific International Hotel.

Graham began to pace back and forth, his head nodding as he listened to her words. He petted his beard with his hand. 'That's certainly a strange story, Laura.'

'I know.'

'Very strange,' he repeated, as though clarifying the notion in his own mind. 'You say that nobody knew David's bank number except the two of you?'

'Right.'

Graham peered at her. 'That would make you a pretty good suspect, wouldn't it?'

'No,' Laura said matter-of-factly. 'I'm the wife. I would have inherited everything anyway. There would have been no reason for me to go through the whole money-transfer scheme.'

He nodded at her. 'I didn't mean—'

'Please don't apologize,' she interrupted him. 'We have to explore every possible avenue. We might as well get rid of that one first.'

'True enough,' he replied. 'Now let me make another observation which you may find a tad more insightful than my first: you suspect your husband's mate T.C. may have something to do with this.'

Laura stood. 'What makes you say that?'

'Simple,' Graham said. 'If you still trusted him

281

completely, he'd be here with you. He was the first one you called when David disappeared. By your own definition, he's a good cop who was David's best mate. So why isn't he here investigating all of this?'

Laura glanced out the window. Down the block stood the Peterson building. Why had she gone to that damn meeting with the Petersons anyway? Why hadn't she just stayed with David? 'I don't know,' she said. 'I've always trusted T.C. and so did David. They were very close. I can't believe he would do anything to hurt David. He loved him. And yet . . .'

'Yet?'

'He's been acting so weird lately.'

'In what way?'

'There's been a lot of things. He keeps disappearing all the time. He tried to stop me from putting pressure on Corsel at the bank. He shoves away all the strange happenings as coincidence. And that's not like the T.C. I know. The T.C. I know would go through hell to trace down any clue, especially if it involved David.'

'So then he doesn't know you're here?' he asked.

She shook her head.

Graham sat back down. 'Well then, what do you say we get this investigation started?'

'What should we do first?'

'Do you have a photograph of David?'

She reached into her handbag and pulled out a photo of him she took last February. David's cheeks were red from the wind, his breath visible in the bitter winter morning. But his smile flashed brightly through the harsh weather. 'Here,' she said, handing it to him. 'What are you going to do

282

with it?'

'The call to the bank came from this hotel, right?' he said.

'So?'

'So,' Graham answered, 'we're in the hotel already. Let's see if any of the staff remember seeing David.'

*   *   *

They spent the next several hours interviewing the staff. Most were not even on duty on that fateful day in June; others did not recognize the man in the photograph.

'Now what?' Laura asked.

Graham thought a moment. 'Let's go to the bar on the second floor.'

'You think the bartender might have seen him?'

'Very doubtful,' the sheriff replied. 'I was thinking more along the lines of having a drink. Man is not a camel, you know.'

She followed him up the stairs. They sat on stools and waited for the barmaid to serve them. Laura looked at the woman behind the bar. She was young, not more than twenty-three or twenty-four. Very attractive in an Ivory Soap girl sort of way. Outdoorsy-looking. Well-toned body and long, auburn hair. The color of her hair reminded Laura of her aunt Judy.

'What can I get ya?' she asked Graham.

'A couple of Four Xs.'

'Coming right up.'

Laura nudged Graham. 'Four X?'

'It's a local beer. You like beer, don't you?'

She nodded. 'What do we do next, Graham?'

283

'Not sure yet. If no one recognizes him then it could be your banker Corsel was right. Someone disguised David's voice and called from here. The question is, who?'

The pretty bartender came back with two huge mugs filled with Four X beer, the foam spilling over the sides. 'Here you go.'

'Thanks, luv.' Graham took a sip. 'Mind if I ask you a question?'

'Not at all,' the bartender said. 'What can I do for you?'

Graham tossed the photograph toward her. 'Have you ever seen this man? He may have been in the hotel sometime in June.'

'June, you say? No, can't say I recognize him. Has he done something wrong? He's awful handsome for a criminal.'

Graham took back the picture. 'No, nothing wrong. We just need to know if he was in the hotel.'

'Handsome man,' she repeated. 'What's his name?'

'David Baskin.'

'The basketball player who drowned up the coast?'

Graham nodded. 'This is his widow, Laura.'

'I'm so sorry, ma'am. Really I am.'

'Thank you,' Laura said.

'But if you have any questions about him being here you oughta ask my Billy.'

'Who is Billy?' Graham asked.

'My beau. He's a big fan of American basketball. He watches it on the telly every week and once he starts watching, a crocodile gnawing at his leg can't get his attention.'

'And he saw Mr Baskin?'

'That's what he said,' the bartender continued. 'I didn't believe him at first. I mean, what would a basketball star be doing here? I said, "Billy, you're just making it up." So he says, "Oh, yeah," and hands me an autograph he got. Then I believed him.'

'Where is Billy now?'

The bartender checked the clock behind her. 'Should be arriving any minute now. He's a bellboy. You should be able to find him in the front lobby. Tall, skinny guy.'

Laura had already tossed money on the bar and was walking out of the bar when Graham thanked the girl and joined her.

*   *   *

'Billy?'

The tall, gangly youngster spun toward Graham's voice. He was as skinny as a poster child and Laura wondered where he found the strength to lug suitcases. He was an average-looking boy, red-faced from the sun and covered with the last remnants of what must have been bad acne. 'Yes?'

'Billy, my name is Sheriff Rowe. I'd like to ask you a few questions.'

The boy's eyes darted about the lobby. 'Have I done something wrong, Sheriff?'

'No, son. I just need to ask you a few questions about David Baskin.'

'David Baskin? What can I . . .? Wait a minute. You're Laura Ayars, aren't you?'

'Yes, I am.'

'You're even prettier in person than on the telly. I know all about you. I was your husband's biggest

285

fan—well, his biggest fan in Australia anyway.'

'Billy,' Graham said, 'did you see Mr Baskin in this hotel?'

'Sure did.'

'When?'

'On the day he died. He came right through these doors.'

'You're sure?'

Billy nodded. 'I got his autograph to prove it. He was a very nice fellow. I saw him come in and head straight for the elevator. I couldn't believe it. I mean, *the* David Baskin right here in this hotel. I play a little basketball myself but there was no one like White Lightning. Nobody. He was the greatest. So I sprinted over to the reception desk and grabbed a pen and piece of paper and asked him for his autograph. He said, "Sure, kid. What's your name?" I told him and then he signed it for me. He even scribbled the date.'

Laura's heart sank deep into her stomach. Whenever David had the time, he liked to put the date with his autograph because he read somewhere that it made it worth more to true collectors.

'Then what happened?' Graham asked.

'Like I said, he got in the elevator and went up. Didn't say a word to anybody else. He was nice and everything, but I could tell he was distracted.'

'What makes you say that?'

'I don't know. He just looked like he was in a trance or something.'

'Did you see him leave?'

'Not exactly.'

'What do you mean?'

Behind Billy, a group of tourists charged in

286

noisily after a full day boat trip to Green Island. 'While Mr Baskin was upstairs, I was working up the courage to talk to him when he came back down. I wanted to tell him that I thought he was the greatest basketball player in the world and that I loved watching him play. When he came down about an hour later, I was all psyched up to talk to him—until I saw his face.'

'What was wrong with his face?' Graham asked.

Billy shrugged. 'Can't say exactly. He was awful pale. That distracted face I was telling you about now looked pained—like somebody had danced on his guts with spiked heels. Or like he had just been told he has two months to live or something. I never seen such a change. He could barely walk when he got out of the elevator. I have to tell you, Sheriff, it was kind of scary.'

Laura felt her pulse quicken. What had happened to David when he went upstairs? Had the bastards drugged him or beaten him or threatened him or . . . or what? What could they have done to make her David react like this?

'Then what happened?'

'Well, I walked up to him and I said, "Are you okay, Mr Baskin?" but he didn't answer me. He just kept walking in a daze like a two-by-four had connected with the side of his head or something. I figured it was none of my business and I didn't want to get in trouble for bothering him so I just left him alone.'

'Did he leave the hotel?'

Billy scratched his head. 'That's the odd part. He wandered out and stumbled around the block a few times. He walked that way down the Esplanade. I watched him until he disappeared past that office

287

building.'

Laura swallowed. 'What office building?'

'The one on the next block.'

'The Peterson building?'

'Yeah, that's the one,' Billy confirmed. 'Anyway, a while later—I don't know, maybe a half-hour—he came staggering back into the hotel.'

'Did he go back up the elevator?' Graham asked.

Billy shook his head. 'He just wandered around some more. Then he asked me where the nearest phone was. I showed him.'

'A pay phone?'

'No. He said he needed to call the States. I brought him to one of the hotel operators to place the call.'

'Who was the operator?'

'Old Maggie. She died last month. She must have been two hundred years old.'

'What time was it by now?'

'Let's see. It must have been close to ten at night, I guess.'

'Then what?'

Billy took a deep breath. 'He finished his calls—'

'Calls?' Laura interrupted.

'Yeah, well, I wasn't listening in but I know he made at least two calls. I don't know if both connected or not. Anyway, he finished his calls and then he started doing his zombie bit in the lobby again. I was beginning to think this was all a little strange by now, but like I said, it was none of my business. He took off around ten thirty.'

Graham remembered that the call to the bank had been placed at midnight. 'Did he come back?'

'Can't say for sure, but maybe. When I got off at eleven thirty, I spotted him standing all by himself on the Marlin Jetty. He just stood there and stared out at the water. No one else was around. I know the newspapers said he drowned accidentally and I don't want to ruin a man's good name, but he wasn't looking at that water like a man who wanted to take a casual swim, if you get my meaning.'

Graham and Laura exchanged glances. They got his meaning.

*   *   *

Judy Simmons entered her apartment, dumped her luggage on the floor and collapsed into a nearby chair. A silly smile remained frozen on her face. All right, maybe goofy smile was a better description. No, Judy told herself, let's be honest about this. It's been so long since you've had this particular smile (or any smile for that matter) that you're forgetting what kind of smile this really is.

Judy thought about it a moment before remembering the correct terminology. It was hardly the vernacular an English professor should use to describe a facial expression but then again, it was succinct and appropriate for the occasion. Yes, the students of Colgate College would call it a 'Just F--ed' smile, the sort of look that comes over one's face after a particularly arousing session of sexual contact. To be more precise, a weekend's worth. Three times a day. Who would have thought that Professor Bealy would have such stamina?

She had started dating Colin Bealy, professor of geology, about a month ago. He was around fifty, divorced seven years with three grown children. He was short with a heavy beard, dark brown eyes and slight paunch. Though Colin Bealy was one

289

of the nation's most highly respected geology experts, Judy had been worried at first about their intellectual compatibility. How, she wondered, could a woman who taught the art of the written word of Shakespeare and Tolstoy date a man who was fascinated by a bunch of rocks? It didn't exactly have the romantic intrigue of a gothic novel— more like a manual on how to install a garage door opener.

But she was wrong about both Colin and geology. He was well read and closer to brilliant than very intelligent. As for geology, it was a far cry from a bunch of bearded men breaking rocks in search of an imprint from a sea shell. Geology was truly the study of the planet earth in all her natural glory, her history and her future.

Judy rewound her answering machine. The tape shrieked as it ran backward. She and Colin had been in New Hampshire for the past four days so there were quite a few messages on the machine. It had been a glorious little getaway. Finally, after all these years, had she finally found a wonderful guy to call her own?

That's not true. I almost had the best. Twice.

The tape stopped and turned itself on.

I almost had the best. Twice.

The first two calls were hang-ups. She hated those. Why couldn't the caller at least have the courtesy to say something? The next message was from one of her students asking for an extension on a paper due tomorrow.

Twice. I had the best twice.

With great effort, she pushed the tormenting thought away. That was when her sister's voice came on the machine.

'Judy, it's Mary. Please call me right away. It's very important I talk to you.'

Judy's silly/goofy/Just F- - -ed smile vanished. The panic in Mary's voice would have been picked up by a deaf mute. Judy pictured her sister making the call, the chord twisted around her hand, her beautiful eyes wide with alarm and fear. Something else must have gone wrong. Judy prayed it did not involve hurting Laura again. But how could it not? Laura was now enmeshed in the sins of the past as though she had partaken in them. She was entangled in a way she could never hope to escape. The combination of evil and the past made up an awesome foe, one that could cripple, mutilate, kill.

There were two more similar calls from Mary, each more pleading than the one before. Then Judy heard Laura's voice on the machine.

'Hi, Aunt Judy, it's me. I'm going away for a couple of days but I wanted to let you know that next Saturday the Celtics are going to retire David's number at the Boston Garden. I know how busy you are but I would very much appreciate it if you could be there. Bring Colin if you'd like. I'm anxious to meet him. I love you and I'll speak to you soon.'

'I love you too,' Judy said out loud. She wiped away a stray tear. Evil and the past. For David the pain was over. For Laura it had become a constant companion. Judy wondered how many great works of literature had taught her that life was not fair, not even remotely close to being an even-handed contest. Life was random, choosing to coddle some and destroy others without plan or justification. That was just how things worked. Accept it and move on.

Laura's message was the last one on the machine. Colin had a seminar on Saturday and would probably not be able to join her, but of course Judy would go to the ceremony. She had been very fond of David from the beginning and to Laura's initial surprise, Judy had even been a big fan of his.

'You're dating David Baskin?' Judy had said to her niece. 'I think he's the greatest player I've ever seen.'

'I never knew you liked basketball.'

'Love it. When I lived in Manhattan, I had season tickets to the Knicks games. I've followed your boyfriend's career since he was a Michigan Wolverine. You don't like basketball?'

'I do now.'

Judy laughed. 'Well, tell that handsome superstar that he better get me some tickets.'

'Will do. When you coming down this way?'

'In two weeks.'

'Will you stay with me?'

'Of course.'

'Great. I'll see you then, Aunt Judy.'

'Goodbye, Laura.'

Judy took a deep breath. Poor Laura. Poor David. She reached for the phone and dialed Mary's number.

'Hello?'

'Hello, Mary.'

'Where have you been?' Mary nearly shouted. 'I've been trying to reach you for days.'

'So I gathered. I went away for a few days.'

'Don't you call in for messages? Suppose somebody had to reach you in an emergency?'

Judy closed her eyes. 'I was distracted. I forgot. Now, what's the big problem?'

Mary did not answer right away. 'Stan Baskin.'

'David's brother?'

'Right.'

'What about him?'

'He's living with Gloria.'

Judy almost wanted to laugh. 'So?'

'So?' Mary shot back. 'Don't you realize what this means?'

Judy sighed deeply. 'Why don't you try being happy for Gloria, Mary? Hasn't she suffered enough? The situation is hardly the same as it was with David and Laura.'

Mary paused. 'I know,' she said quietly, 'and I want to do what's best for my daughter.'

'Is Stan Baskin a nice guy?'

'I don't know,' Mary admitted. 'I haven't even met him yet.'

Judy nodded. Now she understood why her sister was so upset. 'You're going to have to if they stay together.'

'I know. I'm just so scared. Suppose he recognizes—'

'It's been thirty years,' Judy cut in. 'And anyway, it's a risk we'll both have to take. For Gloria's sake.'

'Both?'

'Are you and Laura still speaking?'

'Yes.'

'Then she told you about the ceremony at Boston Garden on Saturday. I'm sure Stan Baskin will be there. So will I.'

'You're coming down for it?'

'Yes.'

'I'm so grateful, Judy. I need your support so badly.'

'I'm not coming down for you,' Judy said coldly.

'I'm coming down for Laura and to pay my respects to David.'

'Judy?'

'Yes?'

'It will never end, will it?' Mary began. 'Every time I think it's over, it comes back to haunt me. Was it that awful, Judy? Was what I did so terrible that it should harm my children like this? Was it that unforgivable?'

Judy thought for a moment. In truth, it was not so unforgivable. But sometimes this indiscriminate world did indeed have a pattern, a pattern like a set of dominoes. We knock down one small tile and without realizing it, we trigger a reaction that topples countless others. Had this particular chain reaction finally reached the last tile and stopped? Had David's death marked the end of this destructive chain? Judy hoped so.

But she doubted it very much.

CHAPTER SEVENTEEN

T.C. drove back to his office. Serita was good, damn good, but T.C. had been up against better. She was lying. No doubt about it. And she didn't feel good about doing it either. If she had been sure lying was the right thing to do, T.C. doubted her poker face would have revealed anything. Even now, T.C. was not nearly as confident as he pretended to be. But what else could he do? If he assumed she was telling the truth, it left him with nothing to go on. If he assumed she was lying, ah, well, that was a different story.

Okay, T.C. thought, let's assume Serita is lying. What does that mean? T.C. tried to organize the facts in his head. Fact 1: Laura had seen Corsel. Fact 2: She now knew about the timing of the money transfer. Fact 3: She had discovered that David's call had come from the Pacific International Hotel in Australia. Partial Conclusion: Knowing all of the above, Laura would never just give up and forget about it. Query: Where would she have gone next?

T.C. did not buy Estelle's story about Laura on some secret fashion trip. What kind of crap excuse was that? He could understand trying to hide a certain excursion from your competition, but from her family and friends? Hardly Laura's style. She trusted her friends. She would tell them, especially now when so many people were worried about her.

But she doesn't trust me.

Sad to say but T.C. had to accept the truth. Somewhere along the way, Laura's trust in him had disintegrated. She had not told him about her second visit to Corsel's office; she had not told him what she had learned about David's death. And if Laura had still trusted him, she would have. If she had still trusted him, Laura would have wanted his help.

T.C. shook his head. Those damn suspicions of hers just made everything all the more difficult. But all of this was an aside, an aside that was bringing him nowhere in a hurry. He had to find out where Laura was and what she was up to. He had questioned Laura's parents, her sister, her best friend. Nothing. Could Laura have really gone somewhere without telling anyone? And if so, why? Unless she wanted to protect them. Unless she was doing something that could prove dangerous to her family and friends. Unless . . .

He stopped his car and sprinted to a nearby phone booth. He put a quarter in and dialed the unlisted number. It was picked up after the second ring.

'Sherman's Paper Supplies.'

'Stu, it's T.C.'

Stuart Sherman repeated, 'Sherman's Paper Supplies.'

'Damn you FBI bigshots and your codes. Who the hell remembers? Can't you do a voice print or something?'

'We have a special on yellow paper today.'

T.C. thought. 'Oh right. Do you have any yellow paper with pink and aqua lines?'

There was a moment of silence. 'Hey, T.C. Long time no speak. What's happening?'

'Not much. Don't you ever get sick of playing spy with all those codes?'

'Nah,' Stu replied. 'It's the reason most of us join.'

T.C. laughed. 'And the reason I only work with you on special occasions.'

'What phone booth you at?'

T.C. squinted. 'The number is 617–555–4789.'

Stuart typed the number into his computer terminal. 'Okay, it's clean. What do you need?'

'Quick request. Can you tell me if Laura Baskin traveled on any flights from the United States to any city in Australia? She may have used the name Laura Ayars.'

'No problem,' Stu said. 'When do you need it by?'

'Right away. I'll hold.'

296

'Okay, but it'll take a few minutes. Say, how was the coroner we found for you in Australia?'

'He worked out well, but he was from Townsville, not Cairns.'

'Townsville?'

'It's about an hour flight from Cairns,' T.C. said. 'I had to fly him in.'

'Ah what the hell, T.C., this business wouldn't be any fun if there weren't a few bugs in the system. How about Hank? How did he do for you?'

'He's still the best surgeon around.'

'And the most discreet,' Stu added. He paused a second. 'Oh, and don't worry, T.C. I'm not going to ask you what this is all about. It's none of my business, right?'

'Right.'

'Besides I'm not a Celtics fan anyway.'

T.C. sighed. 'All right, Stu. I owe you one.'

'A big one,' Stu corrected. 'Hold on a sec. Let me check on this for you.'

T.C. listened to the hold music. He wondered what sort of subliminal message the FBI Special Branch put in its hold music. Something mind-warping no doubt. Stu was right. T.C. did owe him a major-league favor. If the company ever learned what T.C. had been up to, they would both be in serious trouble. But then again, T.C. had stuck his neck out for Stu plenty of times—especially the time when Stu had worked undercover for the Bandini family.

The Bandinis were a particularly vicious group of drug dealers who enjoyed torturing and executing those they did not like. And the Bandini family did not like Feds much. The last time they had discovered a Fed in their employment, the Bandinis tied him to stakes spreadeagle on the floor of an abandoned warehouse. Then they poured a bag of rats onto their helpless victim. The poor guy writhed in agony as he watched the vermin eat away at his stomach, his groin, his cheeks, watched until the rat's claws and small, sharp teeth shredded his eyes. When T.C. viewed the carcass a few days later, he had become physically ill for the first and only time in his career. The thought of that rotting cadaver still made him shudder.

Anyway, one of T.C.'s sources learned that the Bandinis had discovered Stuart Sherman was a Fed and were preparing an encore execution for his benefit. The FBI was able to pull Stu out just as he was heading to what would have been his final meeting with the Bandinis. After that Stu Sherman decided he preferred the computer and research end of the business. He no longer did field work.

Stu came back on the line. 'Got it, T.C.'

'I'm listening.'

'She's using the name Ayars,' Stu said. 'She left two days ago on a Qantas Airlines flight from Los Angeles to Cairns.'

T.C. rubbed his eyes. 'Stu, thanks a lot.'

'I'll just put it on your bill.'

*   *   *

Laura and Graham were back at the cocktail lounge. This time, they chose to sit in a quiet corner rather than at the bar. Laura studied the big man in front of her as he stroked his beard, his eyes fixed in concentration. What did she really know about Graham Rowe? How could she be so sure he wasn't involved in all this? After all, he had been

298

the police officer in charge of the investigation. If Laura could not even trust T.C., how could she rely on this stranger?

'Well, what have we got so far?' Graham asked, speaking as much to himself as Laura. 'Number one: David did not just go swimming like he wrote in his note.'

Laura remembered that note. *I will love you forever. Always remember that.* So serious for David. So foreboding. Had he somehow suspected that it would be the last note he would ever write? Had he somehow known that death was awaiting his imminent arrival?

Graham continued. 'Number two: the time of death estimated by the coroner was way off. We have an eyewitness who swore he saw David Baskin several hours after he supposedly drowned.' The sheriff flipped through his notebook, jotted something on a sheet of paper, and then continued. 'Number three: we know David took an elevator ride in this hotel. He was upstairs for approximately one hour. We can assume he visited someone during that time.'

Laura nodded. 'But who?'

'That's the question,' Graham agreed. 'But there are a few other things we should look into.'

'Like?'

'Like why was the coroner so far off with his estimation of David's death? And did he miss something else, like signs of foul play or . . .'

'Or?'

Graham's piercing eyes locked onto hers. 'Sorry, Laura, but we have to look into the possibility of suicide.'

Laura's tone remained even. 'Like I said before,

I want all possibilities explored—no matter where they lead.'

Graham nodded. 'Okay, let's get started.'

'What do we do first?'

The sheriff let a small laugh pass his lips. 'We?' he repeated. 'There's no chance I'm going to convince you to let me do this on my own, is there?'

'None.'

Graham shrugged. 'Well, I always wanted a beautiful partner,' he said. 'Okay, the first thing we should do is find Gina Cassler.'

'Who's she?'

'An old friend of mine,' Graham replied, 'and the owner and manager of this hotel.'

*   *   *

Gina Cassler was a stately-looking woman in her early sixties. Her neatly bunned hair was gray, her posture straight, her head held high in the air. She wore a gray business suit and her personal appearance was perfectly groomed and manicured. It made a shocking contrast with the cluttered desk she sat behind. Files and loose sheets of paper formed three-feet alps over what Laura assumed was a nice wood finish. Occasionally, papers floated onto the floor but Mrs Cassler didn't seem to mind.

'Jeez, Gina,' Graham said with a shake of his head, 'how can such a beautiful dame be such a slob?'

Gina waved her hand as if to dismiss him. 'Still a charmer, eh, Graham?'

'Trying.'

'And who is this lovely lady with you?'

Graham turned toward Laura. 'This is Laura

Baskin.'

'Ah, yes, the founder of Svengali,' Gina said, gently shaking Laura's hand. 'I bought one of your suits last time I was in San Francisco. I understand you're going to start marketing here in Australia.'

'Yes.'

'It'll be a big hit, I'm sure,' Gina said with a smile. 'Now what can I do for you, Graham?'

'We're investigating the death of Mrs Baskin's husband. Did you hear about it?'

'Of course,' Gina replied. 'It was all over the papers and telly. Such a terrible thing. We haven't had a drowning in this region in what? Three years, Graham?'

'Two and a half,' he corrected.

'Whatever. And I read he was a good swimmer.' She shook her head. 'I'm very sorry, really I am.'

'Thank you,' Laura said.

Graham cleared his throat. 'Gina, we need to see a list of your clientele for the time period surrounding Mr Baskin's death.'

Gina looked puzzled. 'A guest list you mean?'

'Right.'

'From June?'

'June 17th.'

'That's almost six months ago.'

'Five and a half,' Graham corrected.

'We don't have them.'

'What do you mean you don't have them?'

'We don't save daily rooming lists,' she explained. 'Sure, we have a customer list in the basement but it's not done by the dates they stayed here.'

'There's no way we can find out who stayed in the hotel on June 17th?'

'None. Unless . . . wait a sec.' Gina looked up, her face scrunched in concentration. A few moments later, her eyes widened and she snapped her fingers. 'Are you looking for a foreigner?'

'What does that have to do—'

'Just answer my question, Graham,' she interrupted impatiently. 'Are you looking for a foreigner?'

'Probably. Why?'

'The passport cards.'

'The what?'

'Each foreigner has to leave his passport at the front desk so we can fill out a passport card for them. Immigration collects them and keeps them at town hall.'

'Can you get the ones filled out on June 17th?'

'It would probably be faster if you made the request, Graham.'

The big sheriff shook his head. He did not want the government involved in this case yet. 'I'd appreciate it if you took care of it. Just say you need it for tax purposes or something.'

Gina shrugged. 'No worries. It'll probably take a couple of days. Red tape and all that, you know.'

'It's important,' Graham stressed. 'I also need to see your long-distance phone bills for that month.'

Gina released a long whistle. 'Look around you, Graham. Do I look like the type who saves old phone bills?'

Laura's eyes scanned the disheveled room and cluttered garbage cans. The answer was obvious.

'I need those phone bills.'

'My nephew works for the phone company in Cairns,' Gina said. 'He'll be in the office tomorrow. I'll give him a call.'

They thanked her and left.

'What next?' Laura asked. 'Do we go see the coroner?'

'Easier said than done.'

'What do you mean?'

The big sheriff opened the door for her. 'The coroner who handled your husband's case was not from around here.'

'He wasn't?'

Graham shook his head. 'He was flown in from a place called Townsville.'

*　　　*　　　*

Stan heard Gloria's key in the lock. He quickly rose and moved toward the door. When she opened it, Stan grabbed her and kissed her passionately.

'Welcome home.'

Gloria beamed. 'You certainly know how to greet somebody.'

He took her briefcase from her hand and put his arm around her shoulders. 'I missed you.'

'I missed you, too,' Gloria enthused. 'Mmmmm, what smells so good?'

Stan put the briefcase down and took her in his arms. 'I did a little grocery shopping and decided to cook us dinner.'

'You made dinner,' she asked, 'for me?'

He nodded. 'So how was work?'

'Good, but busy. Laura was away.'

'Where did she go?'

Gloria shrugged. 'I'm not sure. Estelle said she had some business to take care of somewhere and just decided to take off. What are you cooking in there? I'm starving.'

'Pasta Primavera.'

'Mmmm. I love pasta,' she enthused.

'It'll be ready in about fifteen minutes.'

Silently, Gloria took his hand in hers and led him onto the terrace. They sat on the love-seat together, their fingers still intertwined. Gloria closed her eyes for a moment and rested her head on his chest. 'I love this,' she said.

'What?'

'Everything about us. I've never been so happy.'

Stan gripped her hand. 'I feel the same.'

They sat back and just watched the Charles River. More than anything else about his relationship with Gloria, this part amazed Stan the most. They could just sit together without speaking, just enjoying the experience of being with one another. It didn't make any sense to him. Gloria was different from any woman he had ever known. She did not ramble on incessantly, trying to say something 'meaningful' or 'deep.' She did not pester him about not finding a job yet. She never even mentioned the one hundred thousand dollars he owed her. Gloria was content to just be with him. She demanded nothing of him and, as a result, he gave her more than he had ever given to a woman.

A few minutes later, Stan rose to get dinner ready. Gloria followed him into the kitchen. 'Laura left us a message,' she began.

I bet, Stan thought. 'Oh?'

'The Celtics are retiring David's number at the Boston Garden Saturday night. It's the Opening Game of the new season. She said she'd appreciate it if we were both there.'

'Both of us?'

Gloria nodded. 'You were his brother. I know you and Laura don't see eye-to-eye yet, but she'll come around.'

'Don't count on it.'

'I'd like to go, Stan. I think it's important that we're both there.'

Stan sprinkled a little Parmesan cheese over the pasta. 'Okay,' he said, 'tell your sister we would be honored to attend.'

'My parents will be there too. So will my aunt. It'll be a nice opportunity for you to meet them all.'

'I'd like that,' he said.

Gloria lit the candles and dimmed the lights. Stan watched her move about the room. Though he would never admit it to himself, he loved to watch her move, loved to watch everything she did. She was so goddamn kind and gentle that sometimes he wondered what she was truly up to. What was her angle on all this? What was she after? What did she want from him? Was her tenderness nothing but an unfamiliar ploy to lull him into an unprepared state, a state where she could get her hooks into him and take control?

Maybe.

But more important, what the hell was he doing? What was his angle? What did he want from Gloria? Laura had hit a raw nerve when she asked him about that. The truth was he was no longer sure what he was doing. He could score big bucks—major, major bucks—and hightail his ass out of here. He could score like he had never scored before and disappear into the sunset. But for some strange reason he stayed. He was out of money with the perfect opportunity to get his hands on plenty, but he chose not to.

Why?

What the hell was wrong with him? He should have dumped her already. He should have squeezed out every last dollar and been on his way, crushing Gloria's fragile spirit, leaving her crying or worse. But no, he had decided to stay around a while.

The phone interrupted their dinner. 'I'll get it,' Gloria said.

'No, it's probably for me,' Stan said. 'I'll just take it in the bedroom.'

Stan stood and moved into the bedroom, closing the door behind him. He knew who was on the other end of the connection. Dread filled him. He swallowed and lifted the receiver. 'Hello?'

'Stan My Man, how are you?'

Stan recognized the voice instantly. His face sunk. 'Hello, B Man.'

'Is that how you greet a good friend?' B Man asked. 'I'm insulted, Stan, really I am.'

'We're in the middle of dinner.'

'Oh how sweet,' he said. 'How perfectly domestic of you. I'm really impressed, Stan. What are you going to do after you eat, go out back and mow the lawn?'

Stan closed his eyes. 'What's up?'

'Not much,' B Man said. 'That's why I was calling you. Your contact tells me you haven't placed a bet in three days.'

'So?'

'So you're only two thousand down,' B Man continued. 'I usually don't cut you off until you reach the forty thousand mark.'

'I just haven't seen anything I've liked lately.'

'Save it, Stan,' the blonde bookie snarled. 'This is B Man you're talking to. You haven't missed a day

306

of betting in ten years.'

'So I've decided to take some time off. What's wrong with that?'

B Man laughed. 'You don't get it, do you, Stan? You just can't up and quit.'

'Who said anything about quitting?'

'Come on, Stan. Don't bullshit a bullshitter. Guys like you don't take time off. You're trying to quit.'

'And what if I am?'

'Why waste your time, Stan? You know you can't do it.'

'Why do you say that?'

B Man sighed. 'Stan, I've known plenty of guys like you. You're an addict. You can't quit. I understand what you're trying to do. You met this chick. You kind of like her, right?'

'You don't know what you're talking about,' Stan said. 'She's just another bimbo.'

'Sure, right. Whatever you say, Stan. Anyway, you're starting to like the simple life. You want to move out of the fast, dangerous lane for a while. But Stan, you're not the type. Eventually, you'll move back into the dangerous lane and pow! You'll smash your car. You're a screw-up, Stan. You can't change.'

'Leave me alone, B.'

'I will, Stan, because I know you'll be back. You'll look in tomorrow's paper and see a horse in the third that's a sure thing. Or you'll find a football game with a point spread that's just too juicy to pass up. Then the itch will come back and it will be so bad that you'll have to scratch. And once you scratch, you'll scratch again and again—

'Shut up!'

'—and I'll be right there to help you tear away

307

at your skin, Stan. Your old buddy B Man will be waiting with open arms and sharp claws.'

Stan's upper lip quivered. 'Just shut up!'

'I don't like being yelled at,' B Man warned, his voice low. 'I don't like it at all. Maybe I'll have to teach you a little lesson, Stan.'

'No, B—'

'Maybe I should pull your broken finger right out of the socket,' B Man continued. 'Or maybe I'll just grab your little blonde girlfriend, tie her down to a bed, and let Bart and a few of his buddies take turns on her. How does that sound?'

Stan's eyes flew open. 'I . . . I'm sorry, B Man. I didn't mean any disrespect.'

B Man's laugh chilled him. 'I know, Stan, I know. Give me a call when you feel the urge. In the meantime, enjoy your brief moments of joy. People like you don't get to experience this very often. When you're ready to go back to your home in the gutter, we'll be waiting to assist you.'

The phone went dead. Stan turned. Gloria was standing in the doorway. 'Is everything okay?' she asked.

He went to her and held her closely. 'Everything is fine,' he said.

She looked up at him. 'You've really given up gambling, haven't you?'

'Yes,' Stan said, and though it was the truth, he knew that B Man was right, that eventually it would be a lie.

CHAPTER EIGHTEEN

It had been the Garden of Eden. Then it became Hell. The transformation had been sudden. One moment, the Reef Resort Hotel was an idyllic honeymoon hideaway; the next, it was death. Staring at it now, the Reef Resort Hotel became hazy and unreal to Laura, as though she was seeing it in a dream. The building and grounds were all so familiar. She saw the bush, the gardens, the lobby—even the sunburned receptionist behind the desk. Laura remembered him well. He had handed her the last note David had ever written.

'Mrs Baskin!' the sunburned man cried out when he saw her. 'How nice to see you again!'

Laura smiled through her daze and shook the man's hand. 'Nice to see you.'

'Will you be staying long?'

Graham stepped between them. 'Only a few minutes.'

'How you doin', Sheriff?'

'Very well, Monty. You?'

'Can't complain,' he replied. 'Something I can do for you?'

Graham must have been a foot taller than Monty. He stared down at the smaller man. 'Do you remember the day David Baskin disappeared?'

'Yeah, sure,' the receptionist answered. 'What about it?'

'He handed you a note before he left, right?'

'Sure did,' Monty confirmed. 'Christ, that note was a regular riot. You remember it, Mrs Baskin? I read it to you over the phone when you called in. I was never so embarrassed in my life.'

'Then what happened?' Graham asked.

'What do you mean?'

'Did David return to the hotel?'

Monty nodded. 'Yeah, like I told Mrs Baskin. He came back for a little.'

'And then he left again?'

'Right.' Monty said.

'How long was he back?' Graham asked.

'Oh, I don't know. About an hour.'

'What time did Mr Baskin leave the hotel the second time?'

Monty thought a moment. 'Can't say for sure. Mr Baskin took off right after he got a phone call.'

Graham and Laura exchanged glances. 'What phone call?' Graham asked.

Monty shrugged. 'Don't rightly know really. I was doing the switchboard when a call came in for him. I just transferred the call to his room. Mr Baskin came down and rushed out of here a few minutes later.'

Graham wetted his lips. 'Can you tell me about the voice of the caller?'

'About the voice?'

'Sex, accent, anything.'

Monty thought a minute. 'Well, I don't remember the voice all that well. It was a long time ago. The only reason I remember it at all is because Mr Baskin was a celebrity and after I let the call go through, I kicked myself for not screening it for him. I mean, it could have been some reporter or obnoxious fan. But anyway, all the person said was "Mr Baskin's room, please." But I kinda remember the voice was hushed. Was it a man or a woman? Can't say for sure. But it was a Yankee accent all right. You can't hide that, no matter how hard you try.'

'Anything else?'

Monty shook his head. 'Oh, wait. One more thing. The call was local.'

'How could you tell?'

'The lines in this hotel are terrible when a call comes from overseas. But there was no static on the line. The call had to have been made from right around here.'

Graham thanked Monty and then he steered Laura toward a bamboo chair in the corner of the lobby. She sat silently, her bleak eyes staring out toward the pool and beach.

'Laura?'

Her head slowly swerved toward his voice. 'Yes?'

'You okay?'

She ignored the question. 'Somebody called him.'

'Seems that way,' Graham agreed. 'Let's try to put this little puzzle together and see what we come up with, okay?'

She nodded.

Graham began pacing in a tight circle. 'First step: you go to your meeting at the Peterson Building in Cairns. David gets dressed and goes outside for a little swim and basketball. Step two: you call the hotel. David is still out. He has left you an amusing little note. Step three: David comes back to the hotel. He goes up to his room. He receives a phone call from an American who was staying in the area—'

'That rules out T.C.,' Laura interrupted. 'There is no way he could have made that call locally and gotten back to Boston in time for my phone call.'

Graham pondered that for awhile. 'Seems logical to me. But that doesn't really tell us much. Just because he didn't place the call doesn't mean he wasn't involved in Mr Baskin's drowning. Now where was I?'

'David received a phone call.'

'Right. David receives a local phone call from an American. Then he quickly writes you a rather cryptic note and leaves the hotel. We can probably assume that he went out to meet the caller. That takes us to step four: David went to the Pacific International Hotel in Cairns.'

'Maybe a taxi driver remembers taking him,' Laura said.

'A long shot, but I'll check it out. Anyway, we have a witness who placed David at the hotel at about the right time so let's pick it up from there. Step five: David arrives at the hotel. He's a little distracted, probably from something the mystery caller said to him. He goes upstairs for about an hour, presumably to meet the caller. When David comes down, he's disoriented. Something happened upstairs that has upset him.'

'But what?' Laura asked, speaking more to herself than Graham.

'No idea,' the big man replied. 'David then takes a walk around the block. He may have even gone into the Peterson Building where you were having your meeting. Then he comes back to the hotel and places a couple of calls to the United States. Who did he call? I don't know. Maybe he didn't get through and decided to call later. He takes another walk around for a couple of hours. We have a witness who saw him standing by the beach at the Marlin Jetty at approximately eleven thirty at night.

From here, we have a blank space. The next time anyone saw him, he was dead. Your banker friend Corsel claims to have heard from him at midnight. Could be. Or could be David was already dead by then and the caller disguised his voice.'

Laura fidgeted in her seat. 'That no longer seems very likely, does it, Graham?'

Graham shook his head. 'Possible, yes. Likely, no. I think David came back to the hotel and placed a call to the bank. Why? I don't know. I think it had something to do with whomever he met in the Pacific International. Anyway, we'll know where David placed his calls for sure once Gina finds those phone bills. Also, we'll have to question the night porter and maybe the receptionist at the Peterson Building. They may also have seen David. This is just the beginning, Laura. A full investigation is not made in a single day.'

'So, what's next?'

Graham shrugged. 'How long are you planning on staying?'

'I have to leave tomorrow night. There's a ceremony being given in David's memory in Boston on Saturday.'

'Okay, no worries. What we have to do next is fill in those important gaps. We have to find out who David visited when he got to the Pacific International.'

'That's the real key, isn't it?' Laura asked. 'The identity of the mystery caller.'

'Sure seems that way to me,' Graham agreed.

'And what about this coroner?'

Graham checked his watch. 'Too late to call Dr Bivelli now. We'll reach him first thing in the morning.'

Laura swallowed and lowered her eyes. 'Graham, what do you think happened to my husband?'

Graham placed a large hand on her shoulder. 'I don't know, luv, but we'll find out.'

*   *   *

'Now?' Mark asked.

T.C. glanced at the clock behind Mark's head. 'Now.'

With a sigh, T.C. stood and walked over to the telephone. He dialed thirteen numbers and waited for the call to connect.

Mark began to pace. 'She's never going to buy that Baskin drowned anymore.'

'I know,' T.C. said. 'I'm working on it.'

After three rings the phone was picked up and an accented voice said, 'Bivelli residence.'

'Can I speak to Doctor Bivelli, please?'

'May I ask who's calling?'

'My name is Terry Conroy.'

'Hold on a moment, Mr Conroy.'

A few seconds later, Dr Bivelli picked up the phone. 'T.C.?'

'Yeah, Aaron, how's it going?'

'Not bad, mate. I didn't expect to hear from you so soon.'

'Yeah, well, things have come up.'

'What sort of things?'

'I need another favor.'

'You know I don't do favors,' Bivelli said. 'Stu told you that before you ever contacted me.'

'I know, Aaron. You're a true mercenary. But I've already paid you for this job.'

'You mean the Baskin drowning?'

314

'Bingo.'

'I thought everything went smooth as silk.'

'It did,' T.C. said. 'But now we've run into a minor obstacle. I just wanted to let you know that some people may come around asking questions.'

'After all this time?'

'Yep.'

'Well, that's just part of the job. No charge.'

'Just letting you know.'

'Appreciate it, T.C., but don't worry.'

'Good.'

'But,' Bivelli added, 'one of these days, I'd love to know the whole story.'

T.C. half smiled. Bivelli knew a little piece of what was going on. Stu another little piece. Hank still another. But none of them knew enough to put the whole story together. 'One of these days,' T.C. repeated.

*   *   *

Graham reached Dr Bivelli the following morning and set up an appointment for later that same day. Since all the flights between Cairns and Townsville were sold out, Laura chartered a small plane to take them into Townsville. At noon, they arrived at Townsville Memorial Hospital. The office of Aaron Bivelli, M.E., was, of course, on the basement level next to the morgue.

'Can I help you?' Dr Bivelli asked with solemn enthusiasm, as befitted his somewhat gruesome occupation. He was a short man in his late fifties, completely bald, a protruding paunch testing the buttons on his gray vest. His face was kind and reserved with a bright, trusting smile.

'My name is Graham Rowe. We spoke on the phone earlier.'

'Oh, yes,' Bivelli said. 'The sheriff of Palm's Cove.'

'And this is Laura Baskin.'

Dr Bivelli turned toward Laura, his face grim. 'I'm very sorry about your husband, Mrs Baskin.'

'Thank you.'

'Please,' Bivelli said with a wave of his hand, 'make yourself comfortable.' He walked around to his side of the desk. 'I reread your husband's file after I spoke with Sheriff Rowe this morning, Mrs Baskin. I truly hope I can be of some service.'

'Maybe you can help us clear up a couple of loose ends,' Graham said.

'I'll certainly try.'

'Let me begin by asking you this, Doctor. Could there have been foul play in the death of Mr David Baskin?'

Dr Bivelli sat back in his chair. 'That's a tough question, Sheriff. I mean, I guess it's a possibility but I doubt it heavily. First of all, Mr Baskin's lungs were filled with water when we found him. That means the cause of death was drowning. He was not killed first and then dumped into the ocean. How did he drown? Well, that's anyone's guess. He was bopped around a lot out there.'

'Bopped around a lot?' Laura asked.

'Yes, Mrs Baskin,' Dr Bivelli replied, turning his attention toward her. 'Your husband's body was brutally thrashed around by the rough waters. It was hurled against rocks and crunched against the surf. It was splattered against jagged coral and sliced up very badly. Fish probably gnawed on it.'

Laura's face blanched.

316

'I'm sorry, Mrs Baskin,' he added quickly. 'I'm a pathologist. I never had much use for proper bedside manner.'

Laura swallowed. 'That's okay. Please continue.'

'What I'm trying to say is that the body was in horrible shape when we found it. Could someone have knocked him on the head and dumped his body out to sea? Very doubtful but yes.'

'Why do you say very doubtful?' Laura asked.

'Because most of the time that's not how it works. Sometimes a man is murdered and his body is dumped in the water to make it look like an accidental drowning. Sometimes a man is killed and a large weight is tied to his body so that it won't be found for a while. But like I said before, David Baskin drowned and rarely is a man knocked out and then left in the water in the hopes he will end up dead. It's too risky. He may survive the ordeal by being rescued by a boat or by waking up or whatever.'

Graham nodded. 'You say Mr Baskin's body was in bad shape?'

'Yes.'

'Beyond recognition?'

Dr Bivelli eyed Laura. 'Pretty close.'

'How did you get a positive identification then?'

Dr Bivelli coughed into a fist. 'Two ways. First, that American policeman who was a friend of his'—he slipped on a pair of reading glasses and opened the file—'an Officer Terry Conroy, was able to recognize certain features. More important, his medical records were sent to me via a fax machine. The dental x-rays arrived the next day and confirmed what we already knew.' Bivelli looked down at the file again. 'According to Officer

Conroy, Mr Baskin should have been wearing a 1989 NBA championship ring, but we couldn't use that to i.d. him because his right hand . . . he wore the ring on his right hand, right, Mrs Baskin?'

She nodded. The ring. She had forgotten all about the last championship ring that had adorned David's hand. And that was the only piece of jewelry that he liked to wear—that and the wedding band they intended to buy when they returned from their honeymoon.

Bivelli cleared his throat again. 'Yes, well, his right hand was gone.'

'Gone?' Laura repeated.

Bivelli lowered his head. 'As I said, many parts of the deceased were badly damaged.'

'I see,' Graham replied. 'Let me ask you this, Doctor. How exact was the estimated time of death?'

'For a drowning like this, it's never more than guesswork,' Dr Bivelli continued. 'I could have been off by as much as twelve to fifteen hours.'

'You estimated the time of death to have been around seven p.m.,' Graham reminded him. 'Would it shock you to hear that we have an eyewitness who saw Mr Baskin at midnight?'

'Not at all, Sheriff,' Bivelli replied casually. 'Like I said earlier, dissecting a drowning victim with a battered body is not going to produce exact, scientific results. I wish it did. My time estimate was influenced in large part by statements made by Mrs Baskin. She said her husband went for a swim at around four or five in the afternoon. It would certainly be more logical to assume that he died within a few hours of that time than after midnight.'

Graham scratched at his beard. 'One last

318

question and then we'll be out of your way. Why were you called in on this case? Why wasn't the local coroner used?'

Bivelli shrugged. 'I can't say for sure, but I can make a guess.'

'Please do.'

'First off, Mr Baskin was a foreigner and a rather famous personality,' Bivelli began. 'When a death of that magnitude occurs, the Aussie government usually gets involved and I have done quite a bit of work for them in the past. They feel comfortable with me. Townsville is only about an hour flight from Cairns, so they probably thought I would be the better man for this particular situation.'

'Then Officer Terry Conroy of Boston didn't contact you?'

'No, he did not.'

Graham rose. Laura did the same. 'Thank you, Doctor Bivelli. You've been very helpful.'

'Anytime, Sheriff,' he replied with a firm handshake. 'And again, Mrs Baskin, please accept my most sincere condolences.'

They headed down the hall and into the elevator. When the door slid closed and the lift started to move upward, Laura turned to Graham. 'He's lying.'

Graham nodded. 'Like a rug.'

*   *   *

Judy stared at the photograph.

Tears welled in her eyes as she stared at the all-too-familiar images. How many years would this go on? How long would this black-and-white photograph be able to jab painfully into her heart?

319

God, how she had loved him. She had loved him like no other man before or since. Had he ever felt the same? Judy thought the answer was yes. She remembered a time when they were both deliriously happy, a time when they were so in love that nothing else mattered . . .

. . . until something took him away. Until something blinded him like a great flash of light.

I killed him. My jealousy pushed that gun against his head and pulled the trigger.

She had been so foolish, so impatient, so damn young. Why couldn't she just sit back and wait. Eventually, he would have realized his mistake and come back to her.

Why did I do it? Why couldn't I have just let it be?

But these were questions that had haunted her for thirty years, and still she had no answers. If only she could have it to do all over again. If only she hadn't acted so stupidly. She folded the photograph and put it back in her purse.

'Miss Simmons?'

She looked up. Her safety deposit box rested on the bank clerk's forearm. 'Would you like to follow me, please?' The bank clerk led Judy into a private room. 'When you're finished, just let me know.'

'Thank you.'

The bank clerk smiled and left. Judy turned toward her box. Her hand reached down and pulled back the top. The first thing she saw were some old treasury bonds her parents had left her. Her father had died suddenly years ago when he was only fifty-seven; her mother had passed away just last year. She missed them both terribly. So few people in this world love you unconditionally.

She thumbed past her birth certificate, the old

warranties, the useless financial statements. Then she spotted it. Her fingers reached down, gripped the leather cover and pulled. The small booklet came out. With shaking hands, Judy placed it on the table in front of her. She read the fading cover:

Diary 1960.

Since 1955, Judy had kept yearly diaries. All the events of her seemingly average life were kept safely tucked away on these blue-lined pages. And for the most part, average the words were— gibberish about the loss of her virginity, her first time experimenting with marijuana, her secret fantasies. In a phrase, her yearly journals contained nothing beyond the standard diary drivel.

But not 1960.

Judy kept all her diaries stacked neatly in a closet at home; all, that is, except for the one she now held in her hand. 1960—the one year she wished she could pull out of her life as she had pulled its diary away from the others. She had never mentioned anything about 1960 in her subsequent diaries. As far as her other writings were concerned, 1960 never existed. She had tried to keep the whole horrible incident locked in this one journal in some bizarre attempt to keep the rest of her life uncontaminated by that year.

It had not worked.

1960 had spread. It had poisoned them all. It occasionally disappeared from view for as much as a decade or two, but it was still there, always there, always waiting to rear its ugly head when they least expected it to.

Judy slowly flipped open the diary. She skimmed through the writings of January and February. Her teary eyes gazed upon the handwriting of the college-age Judy—so blithe and carefree with large, elaborate lettering that flowed smoothly from one end of the page to the other. Hard to believe the same person who was reading this diary had also written it:

March 18, 1960
I've never been so happy, never knew such happiness existed. Losing James has ended up being a blessing in disguise. Mary and James are happy and now I'm ecstatic! Could life be better? I doubt it. I am so filled with feelings of love . . .

*   *   *

Judy shook her head and turned the page. She barely recognized the author anymore—just a faint feeling of déjà vu for a friend now long dead. Who was this love-struck girl who had written such corny, cliched nonsense? If one of Judy's students had ever handed in trash like this, Judy would have written a giant 'See Me' on the top of the first page. But, alas, love was like that. By its definition, love called for corny cliches.

April 3, 1960
We're going to visit my family today. I don't expect them to be thrilled for me. I doubt they'll understand. But how can they deny the glow in my face? How can they be upset when they see how happy we are? They will have to accept us . . .

She smiled slightly. Reading the words, Judy once again felt the hope that had coursed through her young body so many years ago. How terrific life had been on that April morning. How beautiful the whole world had seemed. Even now, Judy could still feel that tingle of excitement in her stomach. Everything was going to work out. Everything was going to be perfect, just like it was supposed to be.

Her smile vanished. How naive she had been. How fragile and elusive the few moments of joy had proved to be. But on that wonderful April day, who could have blamed such a happy, trusting girl for being blind to the cruelty that awaited her?

May 29, 1960
Help me. God, what have I done? The whole situation has become too much for me to handle. It's completely out of control now. It's taking on a life all of its own, and I don't know where it will lead. I fear the worst, but what else could possibly happen . . .

What else, indeed. Judy turned away from the diary. She did not read anymore. May 30th was next. Her body felt cold. She could not bear to look at the words she had written on that day, could not bear to even think about that day.

May 30, 1960.
Her eyes closed in pain. Enough, already. Why was she tormenting herself like this? Why, when her relationship with Colin was bringing her true happiness for the first time in thirty years, had she come here in the first place? She should just let the past be; but, of course, that was not what the past wanted. It cried out, demanding that its secrets be set free. And one day, the past would have its way. One day, Judy would be dead and this safety deposit box would at last be opened. Its secrets would be let loose into the sunshine of truth where,

hopefully, they will wither and die. One day, this small booklet written by a hopeful, guileless young woman will let Laura know why her precious David had to leave her forever. And one day, Laura will learn what happened on May 29 and . . .

May 30, 1960.

Judy put the book back in the bottom of the box, closed it, and called for the clerk to take it back. She stood there and watched the clerk walk away with her most secret possession, not knowing that she would never see it again.

CHAPTER NINETEEN

Twenty-four hours had passed since Laura had kissed Graham's cheek, made him promise to call her as soon as he learned something, bade him goodbye, and boarded the Qantas Airways flight in Cairns. Now the Pan Am jet that had originated at LAX landed with a thud. Laura stared out the window, watching the blurry mass focus into Boston's Logan airport as the 747 coasted to a slower speed. She was exhausted, but Laura had not slept. Whenever she closed her eyes and tried, the same question kept nudging her awake.

What happened to David?

Laura still did not know. Her visit to Australia had given rise to more questions than it answered. Maybe some of these uncertainties would be resolved when they finally located the guest list or the phone bills from the Pacific International, but then what would she do? What was she searching for anyway? David was dead. What was the point in going through all of this?

She went through customs, found a taxi, and settled into the backseat. Her mind was still in Australia, still trying to figure out what David's last few hours had been like. Nothing made sense anymore. If someone had been after David's money, why had the bastards killed him? Why didn't they just hold him for ransom? Laura would have given them all the money they wanted and not said a word to anyone. But no, they chose to go through this elaborate scheme and kill David when the alternatives would have been much more profitable.

Why go to all that trouble? Unless . . .

Unless David wasn't killed for the money.

Laura sat up. Could that be? But why else would someone want to get rid of David? If his money was not the motive, what was? Laura's mind clawed around for the answer, but nothing came to her. Sure, there were people whom David had alienated. But enough to kill him? Not likely. How about someone who wanted him out of basketball? How about some big-time bookie who had bet against the Celtics once too often and thought David had double-crossed him? Highly unlikely. Besides, this was hardly the mob's style. If the mob had wanted David dead, they just would have sent some guy with a bent nose and a stiletto to do the job. There would have been no need for all this fancy cover-up.

The taxi reached the heart of the city, passing all the familiar landmarks Laura thought of as old friends. Had David really been murdered? When Laura mentally stepped back and viewed the evidence unbiased, she could see that most of it was circumstantial at best. So David visited someone in a hotel and made a few phone calls back home—big deal. It was a long stretch from those flimsy facts to concrete proof of a murder.

Laura glanced out the window. Reaching deeper into her mind, Laura wondered what she was really trying to find in all of this. Suppose David had been murdered. What would she do then? Would she hunt down the killers, demanding their blood like some character in a Charles Bronson film? Was she seeking vengeance, or was she just using this 'investigation' as an excuse to keep reality at bay for a little while?

Revenge had never been her game in the past. Laura's mind traveled back to Gloria's terrifying phone call from California last year. The two sisters spoke about nothing in particular, just catching up on what was going on in one another's lives. When Gloria finally said goodbye, Laura felt baseless panic. It was nothing her sister had said, nothing in the words they exchanged and yet the conversation kept gnawing at Laura. Something was wrong—not just the routine problems of life but seriously wrong. Deadly wrong. She decided to charter a plane and fly out to see her sister.

'Charter a plane?' David had said. 'Why the rush?'

'I can't explain it, David. You should have heard her voice. So lifeless. Like I was talking to someone who knew they were reaching the end.'

T.C. met them in the airport. They flew out to San Francisco and stormed in on a group of men gang-raping Gloria. After chasing the Colombians out of the house, David wanted to beat the shit out of Gloria's scuzzy boyfriend Tony and leave him for near-dead. T.C. concurred. But even though Tony had inflicted unimaginable horror onto her sister, Laura felt no need to strike back. She only wanted to save her sister. Revenge did not interest her.

So why the change now? Why was she all of sudden demanding her pound of flesh? She had no answer to that query. Maybe it was because David would have done the same if Laura had been the one killed. He had always fought those who harmed his loved ones with an intensity that sometimes frightened Laura. But maybe her motives were much simpler. Maybe she hoped this created conspiracy would distract her from the base issue: David's death. Be it murder or accident, David was dead. Nothing could change that simple fact. David was dead. Laura could say those three words easily enough, could think them, but they never truly sank in.

'Here we are, ma'am.'

Laura grabbed her suitcase from the trunk and paid the driver. A gust of cold wind ripped through her skin until it struck bone. By the time she reached the apartment door, the key was already in her hand. She put down her suitcase, opened the door, felt around for the light switch, found it, and flicked it up.

Nothing happened.

Laura moved the switch up and down a few times, but the light still did not come on. Strange. Maybe it was just a burned-out bulb. She shook her head. No way. This particular switch turned on the overhead light and two lamps. Slim chance all those bulbs blew out at the same time. It was more likely a blown fuse or a loose wire. With a sigh, she dragged her suitcase into the dark apartment.

There was no light at all except for the light from the hallway and—

—and the glow of light peeking out from under the bedroom door.

Laura's body went rigid. Sounds. Sounds were coming from behind the bedroom door.

Get out, Laura. Call the police.

But she did not do that. Instead, she felt her foot step forward. A strange thought propelled her toward the bedroom: whoever was behind the door had something to do with David's death. Behind that door could lurk what she had been seeking in Australia. If she ran away and called the police, the clue may have time to elude her and slip away forever. Now it was trapped in the bedroom. There was no way for it to escape without being seen.

She moved silently now, creeping slowly toward the door. The sounds became louder. Voices. Voices and a sound she couldn't quite place. The crack of light under the bedroom door flickered a few times but remained on. She slunk against the wall, sliding one foot forward at a time until she reached the door.

Laura held her breath. She could feel her heart beat wildly in her chest. She leaned her ear against the door. Voices. Unmistakable now. But what were they saying? And what the hell was she going to do now? Rush in like some kind of a superhero? Who did she think she was? Wonder Woman? What would she do—

The voices. Two of them. She looked down and saw the light sneaking under the door reflect against her foot. And then she heard that other noise again. Softly now. So like—

—cheering?

She closed her eyes and felt the relief wash through her. The glow of light. The sounds. It was the television. It was only the goddamn television. She shook her head and scolded her overactive imagination. David used to tease her about it all the time. 'You see conspiracy in everything, woman,' he would say whenever she came up with some harebrained scheme.

She took a deep breath and reached for the knob. She began to turn it when Laura had a momentary vision of the television being off when she left the apartment. During that split-second before the door opened, she had time to wonder why—when the whole apartment worked on one fuse—the television was now on and the lights were still out. But there was not enough time to think all of this through. The door opened and Laura's attention turned to the images on the television. Her face crumbled in anguish.

David.

It was a basketball game and there was David running up court. The voices were the CBS commentators for the NBA championship series.

'Baskin moves left, fakes, pivots, dishes off to Roberts. Roberts takes the big hook shot. No good. Rebound Lakers . . .'

But how . . .? She looked above the set and felt her legs almost give way. The VCR. She was watching the game on her videotape machine. Someone had been here, may still be in her apartment. She was about to turn around when she saw an envelope taped to the bottom of the screen. Laura's name had been scrawled across the front.

Above the envelope, David made a driving

left-handed lay-up. Time out, Los Angeles. The players all gathered around David to congratulate him. Laura watched David smile at Earl and she felt a sharp pain. David's smile. His wonderful, beautiful smile.

Her legs quivered as she crossed the room. She reached forward with her right hand and plucked the envelope off the television. She had still not tried the bedroom light switch but the television offered enough light to read. She ripped the envelope open and suddenly realized there may be fingerprints on it. Again, she shook her head no. Whoever had done this was a professional. He would not carelessly strew fingerprints around the apartment. Laura carefully lifted the note out of the envelope and read:

Laura,
I truly hope you enjoyed your little trip overseas. I missed you. This is just a friendly note to let you know that I can do whatever I want. You are not safe. Neither is your mother or your father or your sister. You can do nothing about it. But if you forget about me, I'll forget about you and your family. If not, I will kill them one by one. What do you say?

A friend

P.S. Look under your pillow.

Thick bile settled into Laura's throat. She moved toward the bed and tried the lamp. This time, the light went on. The sudden brightness made Laura shade her eyes. She reread the note and lifted her pillow. She squinted at the object under it.

Her scream pierced the still night.

330

The lamp's light reflected the gold into her eyes. But it didn't matter. Laura could still make out the inscription on David's ring:

1989 NBA CHAMPIONS—BOSTON CELTICS

*   *   *

The blood. So much blood . . .
    'Mommy! Mommy!'
    'Get out of here, Gloria! Get out of here now!'
    So much blood. Everywhere blood . . .
Gloria screamed.

'What? Wha . . . Gloria?'

She shot up in the bed. Her eyes flew open. Her body went stiff.

Stan shook himself awake. 'Gloria?'

Her breathing came in spurts.

'It's all over now,' Stan whispered softly. He moved over and put his arm around her. She hesitated and then snuggled up to him. He felt her tremble against his chest. 'It's okay now, sweetheart. It's all over.'

She looked up at him with the eyes of a cornered animal.

'Are you okay?' he asked.

'Y . . . Yes.'

'Bad dream?'

She nodded, her breathing beginning to even now.

'Do you want to tell me about it?'

Gloria nodded again but did not speak for nearly a minute.

'You don't have to tell me if you don't want to,' he said.

'No,' she answered, her voice shaky. 'I do. I'm

331

just not sure how to begin. You see'—she hesitated, searching for the right words, any words really—'it's not the first time I've had this dream.'

'Oh?'

'When I was young, I had it a lot. I used to wake up screaming and crying and I wouldn't be able to stop. I remember how my mom and dad would come in and try to calm me down. They would try to hold me and tell me it was just a dream, but nothing they could do would comfort me. Then Laura would come running in—she was just a fat little kid back then, if you can believe it—and somehow she'd be able to soothe me. I wouldn't go back to sleep until Laura promised to stay with me. She would crawl in the bed and hold my hand. Only then would I be able to sleep.'

Stan smiled gently. 'Do you think I can take Laura's place for tonight?'

She returned the smile. 'I think so.'

Stan looked at her. God, she was good-looking. Cute and built with a body that didn't rest for a minute. He stared at the thin material of her negligee and at her delicious cleavage. Gloria turned him on like no other chick in the world—except for her younger sister. And that, friends and fans of ol' Stan My Man, was the reason he stayed. Yes, folks, he had figured it out last night. B Man didn't know what the fuck he was talking about. Stan wasn't falling for this chick. It was just that, well, she was hot in the sack, and more important, little Miss Instability was a rung on the ladder to his ultimate achievement:

Screwing the delectable Laura Ayars-Baskin.

But even as he thought the words, Stan knew that they were not true. Like it or not, Gloria meant

332

something to him.

'Tell me about your dream,' he said.

Gloria lowered her head and gripped him tighter. 'I don't remember it very well.'

'What do you remember?'

She shrugged nervously. 'Blood.'

'Blood?'

She nodded. 'I'm a little girl in the dream—no more than five or six. We hadn't moved to Boston yet. We were still living in this little house in the suburbs of Chicago. It's late at night and I'm walking down the hall when I hear a noise from my parents' bedroom. I slowly move toward the door, turn the knob, and . . .'

'And?'

Gloria shook her head. 'I always scream and wake up before I can really see what's going on. I only remember blood. I remember it flowing and oozing everywhere. And someone's watching it all with an awful, hideous smile and, and—'

'Shhh, it's okay now.'

She took in deep breaths and struggled to put on a nervous smile. 'Sounds crazy, huh?'

'Not at all,' Stan assured her. 'We all have our childhood nightmares.'

She sat up and faced him. 'Do you?'

'Sure. Well, not exactly a nightmare.'

'What, then?'

He lay back, his eyes staring up. 'Something very strange happened to me when I was about ten years old.'

'What?'

Stan continued to gaze at the ceiling. He wondered why he was about to tell Gloria a secret he had kept locked within himself for nearly thirty years—especially when he had just convinced himself that Gloria didn't mean a mule's load of shit to him. And he had sworn to himself that he would never tell another soul this story. Never. But David was dead now. So was his mother. How could the truth hurt him anymore? He lowered his eyes toward her and just stared for a long moment. 'I saw my father being murdered.'

Gloria gasped. 'But . . . but I thought David said he—'

'Committed suicide? I know. That's what everyone thought. But he didn't. Somebody shot my father in the head and then put the gun in his hand to make it look like a suicide.'

Gloria's face turned white. 'But . . . I don't understand. How did you get away?'

'Simple,' Stan continued. 'No one saw me. I was hiding behind the couch. You see, I used to play in my dad's office all the time, even though it drove him crazy. He used to get so pissed off when I sneaked in there and messed up all his important papers with my little games. So when I heard him coming back early, I quickly hid behind the couch. But I saw the whole thing. I saw the gun pressed against my dad's temple. I saw the blood shoot out from his head. I'll never forget that sight, Gloria. Never.'

'But why didn't you tell anybody?' she asked.

Stan shrugged. 'Good question. I don't know really. At first, I was in shock. And then I was so scared.'

'Scared?'

'Of the killer. I was afraid the killer was going to come after me, too. And one other thing.'

'Yes?'

'I think the police knew my father hadn't committed suicide.'

'But why—?'

'Because of pressures from the college board. You see, my father taught at Brinlen College—'

'Brinlen? That's near where we lived in Chicago.'

'It's in the Chicago suburbs,' Stan agreed. 'Anyway, Brinlen was one of those elite schools for the preppie upper class. A suicide would be a bad enough scandal for the school, but a murder? That would have been devastating to the college's haughty image.'

Gloria sat back. 'I don't know what to say.'

'Don't say anything,' he replied. 'And please don't tell another soul.'

'Never,' she promised. 'Stan, can I ask one more question?'

'Sure,' he said softly.

She moved her fingers across his hair in long, soothing strokes. 'Did you recognize the killer? I mean, was it somebody you knew?'

'No,' he replied, 'but I still remember the face.' Stan closed his eyes. Oh yes, he remembered the face, that twisted expression of pain that still haunted his dreams. He was sure he would never see that face again.

He was wrong.

*   *   *

'Let me get this straight,' the taller of the two police officers who had responded to Laura's call began. He was ultra-thin, almost emaciated, with a bobbing Adam's apple. He strongly resembled Ichabod Crane. 'You were out of town for a couple of days,

335

correct?'

'Yes,' Laura replied.

'You flew back home and took a taxi to your apartment. You headed up the elevator, got out, walked to your door—was the door locked?'

'Yes.'

'Okay, door locked,' he repeated, writing in a small pad. 'Where were you coming from, Mrs Baskin?'

'What difference does that make?'

'Well, its—'

A voice interrupted him. 'I'll handle this, Sleepy.'

The tall officer nicknamed Sleepy (short for Sleepy Hollow) spun toward the voice. 'Hey, T.C.! How's it going?'

'Not bad, Sleepy,' T.C. answered. 'What's going on here?'

'Break-in,' Sleepy said.

'You mind if I take over?'

Sleepy shrugged. 'All yours. Joe's in the other room. We checked around. No fingerprints. It's kinda weird, T.C. Some guy breaks in, turns on the VCR—'

'Thanks, Sleepy. I'll take it from here.' T.C. glanced quickly at Laura. She was staring back with fury in her eyes.

'Suit yourself,' Sleepy said. 'Joe,' he shouted, 'let's go.'

'Huh?' Joe called back.

'T.C.'s here. He feels like taking over.'

Joe came out from the bedroom and greeted T.C. He and Sleepy quickly left, closing the door behind them and leaving Laura and T.C. alone in the apartment. Neither spoke. T.C. stood and stared at the closed door; Laura kept her eyes on

336

him. After some time had passed, T.C. swung his line of vision toward her.

'You don't trust me anymore, do you, Laura?'

Laura tried to hide her panic. 'Should I?'

'I wish you had, Laura,' he said. 'I wish you did.' He took a cigar out of his shirt pocket. 'Do you mind?'

She shook her head.

He lit the stogie and puffed. 'What happened here?'

'My house was broken into.'

'And?'

'And that's all.'

T.C. shook his head. 'Laura, I'm going to find out anyway. Wouldn't it be easier if you just told me?'

She continued to study his face. *Did you kill my husband, T.C? Were you somehow involved in his death? How could you, you who he trusted and loved so?* 'I was away for a few days. When I came home, the VCR was playing the last game David played in.'

'The tape was still on?'

'Yes.'

'Then whoever broke in timed the whole thing. He knew when you were coming home.'

'Sounds logical,' Laura agreed.

'Who knew your schedule?'

'Nobody.'

'Are you sure?'

'Just Serita.'

'Well, we can rule out her. Where were you anyhow?'

'On business.'

T.C. looked at her for a long moment. 'You

337

really don't trust me, do you, Laura?'

'I don't know what to think.'

'Do you honestly believe I would do something to hurt David?'

Laura hesitated, her mind tugging her thoughts from one extreme to the other. *No, I don't think that. In a million years, David would never believe you would do anything to harm him. He would prefer death to your betrayal. But could you have done it, T.C? Is it even a possibility? If I look at the facts coldly, you have to be my major suspect. But when I look at your face, when I remember the times you and David shared* . . . 'No, I don't think you could hurt him.'

T.C. released a long breath. The relief on his face was visible. 'So where were you?'

'I was in Australia.'

'I know.'

'You know? How could you have—'

'I have my sources,' he explained.

'T.C.,' she said slowly, 'do you think David was murdered?'

His simple answer tore a hole through her heart. 'Yes.'

She felt his words dry up her throat. 'Did you kill my husband?'

'No.'

'Who did?'

T.C. shrugged. He crossed the room and glanced out the window. 'I don't know. Yet.'

'Yet? You mean you're close to finding out?'

'I *was* a lot closer before you started stumbling around Australia.'

'How did you know about that?' Laura asked again.

'Come on, Laura,' he began. 'Open your eyes and take a look around. You're playing in the big leagues now. Do you think I'm the only one who knew about your trip? Do you think that whoever broke into your place was an amateur?'

'So how did you find out?' she insisted.

'Believe me,' he said, 'it was no problem for me and more important, it was no problem for them. You're out of your league here, Laura. Stop playing games and tell me what you learned over there.'

Laura stared at him for a brief moment and then everything spilled out all at once. She did not hold anything back. If T.C. had killed David, then she did not care what else happened. *Et tu, Brute.* But he had not killed David. She was sure of it. He had loved David. No one was that good of an actor. Laura may have been burned by Stan, but she had known T.C. for years, had seen him interact with David under all kinds of circumstances. No, there was no way he could hurt David. His strange behavior was clearly a case of him trying to protect her from something—not because he was trying to cover up a murder plot.

And God, it felt good to trust him again. It felt good to let it all out, to share her secrets and fears, to once again be able to lean ever so slightly on him.

When she finished speaking, Laura handed T.C. the ring she found under the pillow.

'Did you show this to Sleepy or Joe?' T.C. asked.

She shook her head. 'I was going to, but I wasn't sure I should. What does it mean, T.C.? What's going on here?'

T.C. stubbed out his cigar, picked at the ashes with the end of a used match and sat down. He examined the ring like a jeweler pricing a diamond. 'There are things,' he began, 'I didn't want to tell you—things you're better off not knowing.'

'Like what?'

'Please, Laura, just let it rest.'

'Why didn't you tell me David was murdered?'

'I was just looking out for your welfare.'

'How? By coddling me? By lying to me?'

'By protecting you,' he corrected. 'Laura, look what these people have pulled off. Christ, they even timed your return to the apartment. And what good would telling you have done? You've already put your life in jeopardy and now you've chased away the killer. I wanted them to think they were in the clear. It makes them careless.'

'What are you saying?'

'Stay out.'

Laura's voice was nearly a whisper. 'I can't.'

'For your sake.'

'I don't care—'

'About yourself?' T.C. interrupted. 'Well, David would. David wouldn't want anything to happen to you. He loved you, Laura. He made me promise to watch out for you.'

Laura closed her eyes, trying to silence him by turning away.

'And what about your family?' he continued. 'Are you willing to put them in danger too?'

Laura remembered the note taped to the television. 'Do you really think the killer would . . .'

'Go after them? These guys play for keeps, Laura. They kill people as easily as they say hello.'

'But why? Why did they kill David?'

T.C. thought for a moment and then shrugged his shoulders. 'I don't know, Laura. But I intend to find out.'

*   *   *

Graham Rowe clicked on the fan. Damn, it was hot. Living in Palm Cove, you get used to hot but today was one for the record books. The humidity was thick enough to coat your skin.

He sat back in the chair and glanced around the office. There was paperwork to do and Graham hated paperwork. He glanced at his guns, the empty cell, anything as long as it would help him avoid doing that damn paperwork for another minute and a half.

He felt sticky, his shirt pasted to his skin. He pulled the front of it away from his body for a second and then let it drop back. Yuck. He was in desperate need of a shower. Maybe he should run home and quickly shower and change. That would make him feel better. Then he could come right back and be ready to really get down and do the entire week's paperwork with no worries. Yes, that's what he should do. No worries.

He started to rise, stopped, sat back down, smiled. *You are one major procrastinator, Sheriff Rowe. You should be ashamed of yourself—trying to sneak out of here like that to shower and change clothes. You know very well that in this friggin' heat your fresh clothes will be as sopped as these before you finish the walk back to the car.*

With a sigh, he reached for the stack of fishing licenses. He began to thumb through them when the phone rang.

'Sheriff's Office.'

'Graham? Is that you?'

341

Graham recognized Gina Cassler's voice immediately. 'How's it going, Gina?'

'Answering your own phone, Graham?'

'This isn't a hotel, luv. I don't have a receptionist. What's up?'

'We should have the passport cards in another day or so,' Gina began, 'but my nephew came through already. I have the phone bills right here.'

The sheriff felt a jolt of excitement race through him. 'Any calls to America late that night?'

'Yes,' she answered. 'And they were made from the lobby phone at right about the time you expected.'

'Sweet Jesus,' Graham said softly. He cradled the phone on his shoulder and reached for his car keys. 'I'm on my way over there now.'

CHAPTER TWENTY

Hordes of Celtics fans beset the entrance ramps of the Boston Garden for the long-awaited opening game. They scrambled through the stairwells, the concession stands, the long aisles. Wealthy season-ticket holders with their courtside seats greeted the long-time ushers like old friends at a reunion. The masses in the upper deck stared in familiar awe at the championship banners and retired numbers that hung from the rafters. At halftime of tonight's game, two new banners would be added to this historic collection: the 1989 Championship and David Baskin's uniform.

Six months had passed since David had led the Celtics to that NBA championship flag. Six months had passed since White Lightning had been awarded the league's Most Valuable Player Award. And six months had passed since David Baskin had drowned off the coast of Australia.

The mood was ambivalent. The fans were in a quiet and yet frenzied state. A slight hush glided across the parquet floor, for things were not the same on this cool November evening:

White Lightning would strike no more.

Laura and Serita stood by the court-level entrance. From this spot the players would soon sprint out to the deafening ovation (Celtics) and boos (visitors) of the fans. Tears prickled Laura's eyes as she peeked out at the familiar arena. She had not been here since the championship series last season, but nothing had changed. The paint was still chipped, the climate still unbearably stifling.

Two security guards stood next to her. Serita took her hand. 'Ready?' she asked.

Laura nodded. The two guards whisked them out of their protective hideaway and into the bright glare of the Garden's spotlights. Laura and Serita tried not to move too quickly, tried not to look too conspicuous. No one seemed to have noticed them, or if they had they did not say anything. Laura proceeded forward without turning her head to the left or right. She could sense rather than hear the crowd quieting, but she dismissed that as a by-product of her overactive imagination. Still, something was strange. No one was staring at them. No one was catcalling. No one was pointing.

When they reached their seats, Laura saw that Stan and Gloria were already there. Stan stood and smiled brightly. 'Ah, Laura, how nice to see you again.' He took her hand and kissed it lightly.

Laura closed her eyes to avoid Stan's customary smirk. Not now, she told herself. Not tonight. For one night, pretend he is David's brother and not some maggot. 'Thank you, Stan. This is my friend Serita.'

Stan turned his attention toward Serita. 'Another lovely creature,' he said, taking her hand and kissing it. 'Sitting with three such ravishing beauties—I will surely be the envy of every man in the arena.'

Serita choked back a laugh. She and Laura exchanged kisses with Gloria and then took their seats. Serita leaned over and whispered, 'Is he for real?'

Laura shrugged.

Stan hopped out of his seat and into the aisle. 'I'm going to grab some popcorn. Would you ladies care for anything?'

'No thank you,' Laura said flatly.

'Nothing for me,' Gloria added.

Serita said, 'Can you get me a soda?'

'Sure,' Stan replied. 'What kind?'

'Diet Coke.'

'Diet?' Stan repeated, his smile on automatic. 'Why would someone with your figure need diet?'

Serita rolled her eyes toward the ceiling and held back a chuckle. She waited until Stan had headed out of earshot before leaning toward Laura. 'Another good line,' she said in a whisper dripping with sarcasm.

Laura shushed her and turned toward her sister. 'How are you, Gloria?'

'I'm doing great,' Gloria said. 'How was your trip?'

'Productive, I guess. Where are Mom and Dad?'

'They were going to pick up Aunt Judy at the Sheraton,' Gloria answered. 'They should be here any minute.'

'Good.'

'Laura,' Gloria continued, 'I want to ask you a favor.'

Laura's eyes met her sister's, knowing what Gloria was going to say and wondering what she should say in return. 'Name it.'

'It's about Stan.'

'What about him?'

'I know you two have your trouble,' she began. 'I don't know what it's all about, but I love him, Laura, really love him. Can't you give him another chance? For me? Please?'

Laura took a deep breath, a maneuver she used frequently to stall for a little extra time. It worked. When she finally opened her mouth, her reply was interrupted by the arrival of her parents and her aunt. Laura, Gloria and Serita greeted James, Mary and Judy. Everyone busily exchanged embraces and kisses. Laura hugged each one of them tightly, holding on for a few extra moments as though she were gaining strength from each embrace. It felt nice.

James returned her hug with surprising vigor. 'How's my little girl?'

'I'm fine, Daddy,' Laura said.

'Bullshit,' he whispered.

Laura managed a small laugh. 'I miss him so much,' she whispered back.

'I know, honey,' he said. 'I know.'

They managed to release one another. Laura looked at her father. David's death had aged him too. James Ayars's face was a bit more worn; a few new worry lines had been etched into it. As always, he was dressed immaculately. His suit was covered with a Burberry trenchcoat, matching scarf, matching hat, matching gloves.

Mary was taking off her heavy overcoat. Laura noticed that her mother still trembled fiercely. The combination of sleepless nights and a few too many wines with dinner had continued to change Mary's rosy complexion into a pasty one.

'Where's your new young man?' James asked Gloria.

Gloria beamed. 'He'll be here in a minute. He just went to get some popcorn.'

Dr Ayars smiled encouragingly at his oldest daughter. 'We're all looking forward to meeting him.'

'I just know you're going to like him,' Gloria added.

'I'm sure we will,' he replied gently.

Laura eyed her mother with concern. Despite the Garden heat, Mary's body trembled like she had been left out in the frigid cold. 'Are you okay?' she asked her mother.

Mary tried to force on a smile but it never made it to her eyes. 'Just a little cold. Nothing to worry about.'

For a moment, no one spoke. They all just glanced around the Garden, glanced at the parquet floor, glanced at one another.

'There he is!' Gloria cried.

Laura looked behind them. Stan moved briskly down the stairs. He smiled at Gloria as if he only had eyes for her. What a slug, Laura thought, but she had to admit to herself that his lovesick puppy act was good. Very good.

Heads swirled in the general direction of Stan as he continued his trip down the aisle. He was practically skipping, joy in his every step. He bounced down to their row and greeted Gloria with a quick kiss on the cheek. Gloria blushed and grabbed his hand.

'Mom, Dad, Aunt Judy,' she began, 'I'd like you to meet Stan Baskin.'

Stan turned toward them, stuck out his hand and froze. His smile disappeared. The color in his face ebbed away. His mouth dropped open.

Mary and Judy stared back at him with looks that mirrored his own. Only James ignored Stan's expression. Dr Ayars stood and took the outstretched hand. 'Nice to meet you, Stan,' he said.

Like a boxer who uses the standing eight count to get his bearings back, Stan began to recover. His smile returned, though not to its original potency. He shook James's hand. 'Pleasure to meet you, sir.' He then greeted Judy and Mary cordially, not meeting their eyes and they not meeting his. Finally, he sat down.

'What the hell was that all about?' Serita whispered to Laura.

'Beats me,' Laura replied. 'Weird, huh?'

'At the very least.'

Laura watched her mother visibly sag and now even Aunt Judy looked worn. What the hell was going on? An uncomfortable silence hung over them. The seat on Laura's left was left open for T.C., who had told her he was going to be a little late. Laura wished he were here. She'd like to know what he would have made of Stan's introduction to her family.

An uncomfortable silence circled around them until Laura turned toward Judy. 'Tell us about Colin,' she said.

Judy seemed relieved at the break in tension. 'He's a geology professor at Colgate. Head of the department.'

'And?' Serita encouraged.

Judy smiled. 'And he's terrific.'

'That's wonderful,' Gloria enthused.

'Yeah, well, enough about me,' Judy said. 'I hear the Celtics got a great prospect in this Seidman kid.'

Mary Ayars tried her best to pretend everything was normal, that everything was just fine. 'You're not still a basketball nut, are you, Judy?'

'Are you kidding?' Judy answered, also trying like hell to keep the mood upbeat. Between David's memorial and Stan's reaction to seeing them . . . 'I got tickets to the Final Four already and I put in MSG so I'll be able to see all the Knicks games this year.'

Mary looked puzzled. 'What is a Knick? And what on earth is an MSG?' she asked.

Judy chuckled. 'Forget it.'

Their conversation came to a halt when the loud-speaker blared, 'Ladies and gentlemen, the 1989–90 Boston Celtics!'

A sudden roar blared out from all points, consuming the arena in waves of sound. Twelve men with green warm-ups jogged onto the court and the roar became impossibly louder. For a split second Laura looked for David on the familiar parquet floor. When she realized that he was not there, that he would never again be there, the familiar pain ripped into her heart.

348

The players circled the floor a few times and then some began to stretch out while others grabbed basketballs from the rack and took some shots. Laura spotted Earl standing under the basket. He half waved in their direction. Serita returned the wave by blowing him a kiss and winking suggestively. Laura scanned the other familiar faces. David's teammates all caught her eye and smiled warmly, sadly. Timmy Daniels, Johnny Dennison, Mac Kevlin, Robert Frederickson . . . all except one.

Number thirty.

Number thirty was the only face Laura did not recognize. He was about six-five with curly, blonde hair. His body was well-toned and defined—a nearly perfect physique. She watched as he took lay-ups in a relaxed manner, flipping the ball casually onto the backboard without really looking, knowing it would hit on the precise angle and go in. Laura realized that this had to be the rookie Earl and Serita had talked about last week. What was his name again? Aunt Judy had just mentioned it. Seidman. Mark Seidman. The man from nowhere.

Mark Seidman.

As though hypnotized, Laura watched the new Celtic weave through the lay-up drill: waiting on line, shooting, waiting on line, rebounding. Mark Seidman moved smoothly and without hesitation. He seemed loose, incredibly loose for a first-game rookie whom the press had built up as the Celtics' new savior.

T.C. arrived as the referee tossed the ball in the air to begin the game. He said hello to everybody (except Stan) and gently slid past them (except Stan—T.C. purposely stepped on his foot). 'Sorry about that, Stan ol' boy,' he said with deep regret. 'It was an accident.'

T.C. Ignored Stan's angry glare and collapsed heavily into the empty seat next to Laura. 'How's it going, champ?'

'Not bad,' Laura said.

'Sorry about being late.'

'You only missed the opening tap.'

They turned their attention toward the game. Johnny Dennison passed the ball to Timmy Daniels. Timmy looked around before tossing it inside to Big Mac Kevlin. Mac was double-teamed. He passed it out to Mark Seidman. Seidman was trapped in the corner.

'He's going to have to shoot,' T.C. remarked. 'The shot clock is ticking down.'

As if on cue, Mark Seidman leaped in the air, twisted, and took a fade-away jumpshot. The ball touched the backboard and fell in, Laura felt the breath shoot out of her. Her stomach coiled in pain. That jumpshot. That damn fade-away jumpshot— no wonder they call him White Lightning II.

'Jesus, T.C., did you see that?'

T.C. nodded. 'Hell of a good shot.'

'Unbelievable,' Judy uttered from their left, her voice cracking.

Mary did not pay attention to the game. Her eyes darted about, sneaking glances in Stan's general direction. Stan's concentration also wandered away from the parquet floor and toward those with whom he was seated. He gripped Gloria's hand tightly, his face frighteningly pale.

'You know anything about him?' Laura asked.

'Seidman?' T.C. replied with a shake of his head. 'Just what I read in the papers. Earl mentioned him to me a couple of times. He said he's quiet, keeps to himself.'

The game continued with Mark Seidman playing like a man possessed. He scored eight points in the first quarter and added three assists and four rebounds. The Celtics led by seven. By the end of the first half, the Mark Seidman-led Celtics had upped their lead to twelve.

Halftime activities pushed by in a murky haze. Laura walked onto the basketball court, silence and stillness devouring the entire arena around her. She went through the motions, accepted the solemn words, watched with a quivering lower lip as Earl and Timmy hoisted David's uniform up into the rafters.

But Judy Simmons did not watch the proceedings too closely. Instead, she kept her eye on Mark Seidman, trying to see his reaction to David Baskin's memorial. His expression did not change, but Judy noticed that his eyes never went anywhere near Laura.

Thoughts—wild, crazy thoughts—dashed and bounced across Judy's mind. She tried to reach out and grab a few of those irrational thoughts, tried to organize them and create a cohesive theory. But they managed to elude her.

Separately, Judy knew the facts meant nothing. There were plenty of guys who had successfully duplicated David's fadeaway jumpshot. There was that guy from U.C.L.A. and the point guard from Seattle. And what about that power forward on the Phoenix Suns? Basketball players everywhere were trying to perfect the White Lightning jumpshot, that quick release that made it impossible to block. No, that alone would make absolutely nobody suspicious.

But that was the problem. It was too perfect. Nobody would be suspicious. Unless of course you knew the background of the situation. Unless you understood completely the strength of the past and how it could twist reality into unrecognizable shapes.

Laura moved back toward her seat, her head high, her eyes dry. There would be no tears now, Judy thought. The tears would come later, when she was alone and away from everyone. Judy kissed Laura's cheek, trying like hell to dismiss the crazy ideas that kept circulating in her head. After all, she was probably wrong. She was letting her overly suspicious nature get the best of her. Better to think it through carefully before jumping to any conclusions. Better to look at the whole situation coldly before crossing into uncharted minefields.

But if her suspicions were correct, she would have to trample through that minefield no matter what the costs. If her suspicions were correct, the ghosts of the past were going to rise up yet again and demand to be faced. They would cry out one last time for vengeance and finally, at long last, that lust would be quenched. And this time, there would be no place to run and hide, no one to sacrifice to the ghosts. This time, the guilty would be destroyed.

*   *   *

Mark lowered his head into his hands. He sat on a bench in front of his locker, trying to dismiss the noise of the media frenzy that surrounded him on all sides. Most of the reporters had already left him alone, knowing his reputation for not talking to

352

the press and moving on to the more fruitful and talkative pastures of Earl Roberts, Timmy Daniels and Mac Kevlin.

But it had been Mark Seidman's game. In his debut, Mark had netted 27 points, twelve rebounds and eight assists as the Celtics coasted to a 117–102 victory over Washington. Normally, the press would pounce upon such a subject no matter what that subject requested, but for the most part they kept away from him, respecting his desire for solitude. They milled about the other players in the locker room, stealing quick peeks at Mark as if he were a grenade with the pin half out. Who could have imagined that the budding hopeful would more than fill expectations in his Boston Garden debut? Doing well in pre-season was one thing. To face the opening game crowd at Boston Garden as a rookie and dismantle the competition . . . that was something else. But Mark looked more like a weathered veteran than a rookie. His intensity on the court was amazing and downright eerie. He never slapped his teammates five, never celebrated a good shot, never smiled, never showed emotion of any kind. It made no sense. Here was a rookie playing in front of a sell-out crowd in the home of basketball legends and he stalked the parquet floor in a cold, unfeeling, technocratic manner. And yet, there was still a beauty to his game, the unmistakable grace of a master at his craft.

Clip Arnstein came into the locker room, a famous victory cigar clenched between his teeth. The press sprinted toward him. 'What did you think of the game, Clip?' a reporter asked.

Clip smiled. 'I'm smoking a cigar, aren't I?'

'And how about the play of Mark Seidman?'

His answer was an even bigger smile. 'And you can quote me on that, fellas. Now do me a favor, will you? Get out of here for a while. The guys have to get dressed and head down to the reception.'

Normally, the press would protest. But not tonight. They knew that the Celtics were heading to a reception for David Baskin's family. David had been a favorite of the press: colorful, off-the-wall, fun, polite, and always willing to say something outrageous. White Lightning had the ability to be engaging with the media while not appearing egomaniacal.

The reporters filed out without another word. The players dressed quickly now, silently. But Mark just continued to sit with his head between his hands. Clip headed over to the corner locker where Mark sat alone, away from his teammates. He put his hand on Mark's shoulder as several players left the room and headed upstairs.

'Are you okay?' Clip asked.

Mark nodded.

'Look, I know you don't like making appearances or talking to the press. Fine, that's up to you. But David meant a lot to these guys. I know you're not a social guy, and I guess you don't want to make friends with your teammates. That's also up to you. As long as you're doing your job, I won't say anything. You understand?'

Mark looked up. 'Yes.'

'So while I don't like your closed-mouth act, I let it go,' Clip continued. 'But I don't want you to do something that will alienate your teammates.'

The last of the Celtics filed out, leaving Clip and Mark alone in the towel-cluttered locker room. 'As long as I do the job on the court,' Mark began, 'what's the difference?'

'I'm not saying that you have to be buddy-buddy with the other guys. But it doesn't pay to piss them off . . .'

'But—'

'Or me,' Clip pronounced, his voice getting louder and shakier. His face turned deep scarlet. 'I've got to draw the line somewhere, Mark, and I don't give a shit how great of a player you are. David Baskin meant a lot to these guys—and to me. If you're disrespectful to his memory, I don't care if you're the Messiah. I'll sit you so far down the bench you'll be lucky to see the game. Is that understood?'

Mark wanted so much to stand up and hug the angry, frail-looking man who stood before him. 'I guess so.'

Clip calmed down, the scarlet ebbing away from his complexion. His voice softened. 'You're already being compared with David,' he said. 'You shoot like him, you move like him, and you've taken his position.' He stood and moved toward the door. 'Get dressed now. We'll go together.'

Mark nodded. Any further resistance would only draw attention to himself. He began to shiver uncontrollably, frightened of entering the Blades and Boards Club. His teammates would be there. T.C. would be there. But most of all, the row of people who had been sitting with T.C. would be there. He had managed to avoid even looking in that direction, not even catching the eye of T.C. for fear he would see someone else. And though he had not seen her, he knew that she had been there, could feel her from the moment she had entered the building. Now his body felt cold as he realized that, like it or not, Mark Seidman would have to face her for the first time. The pit of his stomach contracted.

At long last, Mark Seidman would meet Laura Baskin.

CHAPTER TWENTY-ONE

Laura stood with Earl and Serita. She had already greeted David's old teammates with embraces and kind words. All of them were there, except for Clip and that mystery guy. Laura could still not believe what she had seen on the court. It was more than Mark Seidman's play, fantastic as it had been. Now she understood what Earl had been talking about at his penthouse. There was something disquieting about Seidman. The way he played—so like David technically but without one slice of emotion. Emotion had always propelled David to play his best. He fed off his affection for his teammates and off his love for the game. His face showed it in every jumpshot, every pass, every rebound. But Mark Seidman seemed motivated by something else, something abstract and impersonal. He looked like a reluctant warrior trying to survive the fiercest of battles so he could just go home.

But then again, he was so like David. Mark Seidman had taken David's place in the line-up, played the same position, displayed the same unshakable concentration, but weirdest of all, he had that quick-release jumpshot. Like David, Mark Seidman made the ball appear to float gently toward the basket, as though an invisible hand were guiding it in the air. Laura could not take her eyes off him. Every move Mark Seidman made on the court jabbed at her insides. So like David. So like her wonderful, beautiful David. Even now Laura felt herself trembling.

She stopped herself as Clip entered the room, shaking off her ridiculous thoughts about the Celtics rookie. Clip turned toward her. His smile reached his sad eyes. It was a soothing smile, the smile of an old friend who had come to help. She began to make her way to where he stood.

Then Mark Seidman walked in.

Laura froze. She did not glance at him just yet. She could not explain why she felt it necessary to avoid seeing him. But she did. Clip took Mark Seidman's arm and began to whisk him about the room, introducing him to Laura's parents, Serita and T.C. Finally, Clip brought Mark Seidman over to where she stood.

'Laura, this is Mark Seidman,' he said. 'Mark, this is Laura Baskin.'

She slowly lifted her head toward him. Without warning, her gaze locked onto his. A powerful blow struck her midsection. Her eyes dodged for cover from the onslaught while his did the same. She had looked at him for less than a split second, but there was no mistaking the unspeakable pain in his contorted eyes.

'Congratulations on a good game,' she managed.

'Thank you,' came his soft voice. 'I'm sorry about your husband.' They shook hands. Mark's face flushed with her touch. He quickly released his grip. 'Please excuse me.'

Clip tried to keep hold of Mark's arm by subtly locking him in place, but Mark slipped through and hurried to the other side of the room. Embarrassed, Clip raised his hands toward Laura and shrugged. 'What can I tell you?' he said. 'Mark is painfully shy.'

'Earl told me,' Laura replied.

'He's a strange sort. Good player though.'

Laura nodded. Clip excused himself and made his way toward the Celtics coaching staff.

That was when Laura spotted Stan wobbling toward her.

After downing a good number of beers during the game, Stan had been hanging out near the fully stocked bar throughout the reception. Now Stan was most definitely drunk. Completely inebriated. He could barely stand. Laura scanned the room. Gloria was nowhere to be seen.

When Stan finally reached where she was standing, he threw his arm around her shoulders, leaned over, and quickly kissed her. 'You've got some hot bod, Laura.'

'Bastard!' she hissed.

'Now, now, don't make a scene,' Stan slurred, his arm still around her for support. 'It was only a peck on the cheek.'

'What do you want, Stan?'

Stan teetered but steadied himself quickly. He kept his arm around Laura's neck and pulled her closer to him. 'God, you're rude, sis. Has anyone ever told you that before?'

'You're drunk.'

'No shit, Sherlock. I'm drunk. So what? Does that mean I can't come over and say hello and see how you're holding up? Can't you at least be civil on a tragic occasion like this?'

Laura chortled. 'You'd spit on David's grave for

a dollar.'

He pulled her closer and whispered, 'Or even half that much.'

Laura considered slamming her fist into his groin, as she had done that day he attacked her in her office, but the thought of making a scene and then trying to explain her behavior kept her temper in check. Instead, she smiled as though nothing was wrong and said, 'Get away from me, pig.'

'But, Laura, I have good news for you. The charade is about to end.'

'Where's Gloria?'

'Powdering her nose. But listen to me. It's over. Tonight.'

'What are you babbling about?'

His body swayed back and forth. 'I don't need you or your sister's goddamn money anymore.'

'Stan, I don't know what you're talking about nor do I care. Just get the hell away from me.'

'All in good time,' he said. 'But don't you understand? It's over. I'm leaving.'

'Great. Nice knowing you. Bye.'

Stan smiled, his red eyes trying to focus in on hers. 'Aren't you forgetting one small detail?'

'Such as?'

'Gloria.'

'What about her?'

He shrugged, nearly toppling from the effort. 'She loves me, you know. I can let her down nice and easy. Tell her how I'm not good enough for her and all that bullshit. Or I can crush her, tell her that I was just using her, that's she's nothing but a useless whore.'

Laura let the rage build inside her but her face remained calm. 'If you do that,' she said evenly, 'I'll kill you. I swear it.'

'Threats, Laura? You should know better than that.'

'What do you want, Stan? I thought you said you didn't need money anymore. And why the hell were you acting so weird at the game?'

'Patience, my lovely flower. You are indeed correct. I do not need your money.'

'Then why don't you just leave my sister in peace?'

'Nothing would please me more. But life is not that easy. First, you must do something for me.' Stan grabbed her by the shoulders, turning her body so that they faced one another.

'What?' she asked.

He smiled. 'I want you to sleep with me. Just once. Do me that one little favor and I won't harm your sister.'

As Laura felt herself begin to gag, she realized that to an onlooker she and Stan appeared to be just a happy, good-looking couple. They were both smiling, facing one another, Stan standing close with his hands on her shoulders. Appearance vs. reality. People were probably smiling sweetly at them, commenting on what a nice couple they made . . .

. . . but right now, Laura was looking at Mark Seidman and he did not appear to be smiling. For the first time that evening, Mark Seidman's cool exterior had cracked. Laura was puzzled. Mark Seidman stood behind Stan, glaring at them, his face twisted into a look of intense hatred.

Why?

'Well,' Stan said, his breath reeking from liquor, 'I'm waiting.'

Laura's eyes swung back to his. 'You're drunk.'

'That fact has already been established,' he replied. 'I'm still waiting for an answer.'

'How about this? Go to hell.'

Stan shook his head. 'You're not being smart, Laura. Really you're not. You should think this through first.'

'Think *this* through, Stan: you are the most repulsive creature I have ever met. I hate you.'

'Do you know why you hate me?'

'Do you want the list in any particular order?'

He laughed. His feet shuffled underneath him, allowing him to maintain his balance. 'Laura, why don't you stop deceiving yourself? Admit to yourself at least why you hate me.'

'Okay, Stan, I'll bite. Why do I hate you?'

'It's because you find me attractive,' he said, spittle flying with his words. 'Very attractive. You want me, Laura. You want me very badly. And that makes you feel guilty. It makes you feel like you're being disloyal to David. So how do you compensate for that? You create this ugly illusion, an illusion you're able to hate.'

'You're sick, Stan,' Laura shot back. 'When I first saw you with Gloria tonight, I was actually stupid enough to think that maybe you did give a half a damn about her. But I won't ever forget the truth, Stan. I won't ever forget you're a piece of shit.'

His smile did not waver. 'Yes, but a piece of shit who is going to have his way with you.'

'Not a chance.'

'Ah, Laura, you're using emotion again. Didn't I warn you about that? Pretend this is a business decision. If you sleep with me tonight, I'm gone forever. I will be nothing but a pleasant memory for

Gloria. If you don't, I'll destroy her. Think about it, Laura. What is Gloria's life worth to you? Does she matter so little that you wouldn't sacrifice your widow-virginity for her?'

Laura said nothing.

Stan's smirk of satisfaction raked across her heart painfully. 'I see you're starting to think about this practically. That's smart, Laura. Just one quick boff and I'm history. You can even close your eyes if you want. And of course, if your lovely bod decides it can't just have Stan for one night, that it craves more of what I have, I'll stay with you for a while. We'll make it our little secret.'

Laura swallowed away her nausea, not believing what she was about to say. 'What guarantee do I have you will actually leave?'

Stan smiled. He had her. 'You don't trust me?'

'Not at all.'

'Well, you're going to have to, my love,' he explained. 'Life is a gamble. You'll have to make your choice and live with it. But either way, I'm leaving tomorrow. So if you find Gloria in the bathroom with her arteries bursting blood, you know you made the wrong decision.'

Across the room, Laura spotted Gloria. Her sister began to walk toward them.

'I'll meet you at your place at midnight,' Stan whispered.

Laura watched him stagger toward her sister. Gloria looked so beautiful, so happy, so delicate, eyeing Stan worriedly as he stumbled his way toward her. She is concerned for his welfare, Laura thought, concerned about that no-good son of a bitch. And Laura could do nothing about it. She was powerless against him and right now that meant just one thing.

Laura turned away. David was already dead. She had arrived too late to save him from the clutches of the Pacific or a still unknown murderer. But Gloria was still with her, still alive.

And Laura still had the opportunity to save her.

*   *   *

Anger glazed Mark's eyes as he glared at Laura and Stan. He still could not believe it. Stan. Stan was here in Boston. Why the hell hadn't T.C. told him? But the answer was obvious. Now that David Baskin was dead, Mark Seidman was to be told nothing.

A familiar voice snapped him out of his semi-trance. 'Excuse me.'

Mark swiveled his head toward a tall woman with auburn hair. Judy Simmons. He had figured Judy was going to show up for this event, and that made him very afraid. Laura's aunt was no fool and, more to the point, Mark was sure that she was the only person who had any real chance of discovering what had really happened to David Baskin.

'Yes, Miss . . .' he feigned forgetting her name.

'Simmons,' Judy finished for him. 'Judy Simmons. I'm Laura Baskin's aunt.'

'Yes, of course.'

She scrutinized him closely, spending a long time on his face. 'I just wanted to say, Mr Seidman, that you played a wonderful game tonight.'

'Thank you.'

'Where did you learn to play like that?'

Mark shrugged. 'Nowhere special. Around.'

'Well you play like no rookie I've ever seen.' She stopped, her eyes narrowing. 'You look very familiar to me, Mr Seidman. Have we met before?'

'I don't believe so.'

'Funny, I know I've seen you somewhere,' she continued. 'Were you ever on the campus of Colgate College?'

'No.'

'Maybe I knew your mother. Yes, that's it. Seidman, Seidman. Even the name rings a bell.'

'My mother died a good number of years ago.'

Once again, Judy studied his face. She had seen his reaction at Laura's conversing with Stan Baskin, but this time, his expression remained composed. 'I'm sorry.'

'Will you excuse me, ma'am?'

Judy simply stared at him, saying nothing. Her eyes did not wander off his face as he smiled weakly, nodded, and moved toward the exit.

It can't be, she told herself. *Just calm yourself down. Mark Seidman is just another amazing sports story. That's all. Stop making something out of nothing.*

But she knew it was not true.

＊   ＊   ＊

Stan stumbled down the empty hallway at the Boston Garden and into the abandoned men's room on the top floor. He had been drunk plenty of times before, plenty, but man, did he feel out of control and sick tonight. His head spun like a 78 on an old victrola. His mouth felt like someone had poured sand down his throat. And his stomach, his goddamn stomach felt like a training ground for grenade launchers.

He looked at himself in the mirror, fear clutching

his neck and throat. There was more than just booze working on his head, his mouth, his stomach. He had never been so terrified in all of his life, and yet an opportunity had sprung forward that exhilarated him. Money. All he wanted. All he needed. It was right in front of him now. He would ask for one hundred grand right off the bat and then cash in on new installments whenever he deemed it necessary. He could have everything he ever wanted if . . .

. . . if he would only shake hands with the devil.

Stan staggered away from the mirror. Sometimes he was such an idiot, especially when it came to Laura. When was he going to learn to keep his big mouth under control? Christ, he was drunk. Maybe he should apologize for what he said, but no, that would do no good. Laura would just spit on him. Why did he always do things like that? Why did he always slide backwards into his darkened, vile pit whenever he was one step away from getting out of it for good? He had drunk too much, seen Laura, and wham, his lust for vengeance on David rose up in him. Why? The poor guy was dead now. Why in the face of Laura's awesome beauty did his old hatred always emerge anew?

He unzipped his fly in front of the urinal. The truth was he did not want to leave quite yet. He could have the money and keep Gloria—though it could get a little messy. After all, the source of his money supply was a member of her family.

Yes, blackmail was on his mind, plain and simple. But this was no ordinary blackmail scheme. He was not planning on blackmailing an ordinary wrongdoer.

He was going to blackmail his father's murderer.

Stan grabbed onto the sides of the urinal and steadied himself. Sweat made his clothes cling to his skin uncomfortably. After all these years he had finally seen his father's killer again. Most sons would cry for blood against such a demon. They would demand biblical justice, an eye for an eye, death. But not Stan. Too many years had passed to play vengeful gunslinger and frankly, Stan was gutless in the ways of violence, always had been. He could report it to the police, but who would believe him? Who would trust the word of a man who waited thirty years to let anyone know that he had witnessed his father's murder? And with his police record? No way. Forget it.

No, Stan decided, he would have to wreak his own type of vengeance against the killer of his happy childhood. He would let the murderer live in constant fear of being discovered—and make a nice profit for himself in the process.

A rush of nausea swept through him. Sure as God made green apples he was going to vomit. No doubt about it. He hated throwing up but then again, who likes it? It had to be done. Best to get it over with. Besides, maybe he'd feel better after sacrificing a few of those Molotov cocktails to the porcelain gods.

He wove toward the stall, his right shoulder ramming against the metallic side. If he were sober, Stan undoubtedly would have noticed the throbbing pain in his shoulder blade. Fortunately, the alcohol snuffed it out. Stan dropped to his knees, clutched the cold toilet on either side and waited.

That was when he felt someone grab him by the hair.

'What the—?'

The rest of his words were lost in the icy water. Whoever had grabbed him was strong. Stan's face lunged forward into the toilet bowl, crashing into the bottom. He could no longer breathe. Panicked, he shook his head back and forth violently, but he could not get free from the vise-like grip, could not find an air-pocket so that he could gather even one more breath into his heaving chest.

'You son of a bitch!'

Stan could barely make out the words being shouted at him, the toilet water splashing against his ears. *I'm going to die*, he thought. *I'm going to drown in a fuckin' toilet.*

His lungs were ready to burst. Water seeped down his throat. He felt himself choke. His eyes bulged. Thoughts flew out of his mind, replaced by primitive instinct. One primitive instinct. The instinct of survival. He became like any other mammal trapped underwater and unable to breathe. He jerked and bucked and kicked out, but the hand on his head held him down. The assailant shoved Stan's face further into the water, crushing his nose against the hard bottom of the bowl. Stan saw his own blood flow past him.

His throat burned. His eyes rolled into the back of his head. Death. Drowning. Like David. Is this what it was like, little brother? Is this . . .?

The powerful grip pulled Stan's head out of the water and dropped it like an inanimate object. His skull bounced off the porcelain seat and crashed onto the tile floor, but Stan did not notice or care. He gasped and wretched uncontrollably, his hand wrapped around his throat in some bizarre attempt to lessen the pain. He rolled on the floor, desperately trying to put some oxygen back into his sore lungs.

Then he felt the hand clutch his hair again.

'Oh God, please,' he managed.

The hand roughly jerked his head back toward the rim of the bowl. It began to push his face downward, stopping less than an inch above the water. Stan's chest still heaved spasmodically.

'No, please . . .'

Stan felt the assailant lower himself toward him, the hold never loosening. Warm breath pricked Stan's ear and neck. 'If you ever go near her again,' the male voice said slowly, 'I'll kill you.'

The punch came from nowhere. Stan's head snapped back from the blow. His body went limp. He slid to the floor as unconsciousness mercifully kicked in.

*　　　*　　　*

Mark looked down past his shaking hands to Stan's still form below him. He clenched his fists, trying to fight off his turbid fury against the no-good son of a bitch. He had never lost control like that, never knew he was capable of such violence against any man. But then again, Stan Baskin was not just any man.

With one foot, Mark flipped Stan onto his back. Stan's face was covered with blood. Nothing to worry about really. He had not hit him with anything near full force, but in Stan's inebriated state a love tap would have been enough to knock him out. He still could not believe his eyes. Stan was back. Stan had always been scum and judging by the bits and pieces of conversation between Laura and Stan he had overheard, nothing had changed. Stan was still a sick, demented man.

Why had Stan come to Boston? The answer was fairly obvious: money. Stan figured that the wealthy widow of his late brother would be an easy mark for his cunning ways. And, Mark realized with mounting rage, the fact that Laura happened to be lonely, vulnerable and gorgeous just made her all the more irresistible to lure into his lair.

Son of a bitch.

There was a knock on the door. 'Mark? You in there?'

Mark quickly moved out of the stall. 'Are you alone, T.C.?'

'Yes.'

He reached the door and pulled back the deadbolt. T.C. entered. Mark slammed the door behind him and replaced the lock.

'What the hell is going on?' T.C. asked. Then he spotted the open stall door. Glancing into the cubicle, he found Stan's crumbled body on the floor.

T.C. whistled. 'What did you do to him?'

'Played a little game of dunk. Why the hell didn't you tell me he was here?'

T.C. turned away from the tile floor and shrugged. 'It was none of your business.'

'None of my business? Don't you think you're taking this—'

That was when it hit him. Mark clutched his head between his hands, his fingers clawing at his temples. Pain came at him in great, unbearable waves. He sunk to his knees.

T.C. acted without hesitation. He sprinted toward Mark. 'It's okay, Mark. I'm right here.'

Mark looked up at him with eyes distorted

369

by pure agony. T.C. placed his arm around his shoulder and helped his friend to his feet. While pain consumed Mark's every nerve, naked fear seeped into T.C.

It's back, T.C. thought. *The demon is back.*

*   *   *

Laura excused herself and moved toward the Blades and Boards Club exit. She just needed a moment away from the crush of family and friends, a few seconds to be by herself and think about David. Evenings like these had a way of going by in a murky haze, but Laura knew that she could only block so long before her protective wall crumbled and reality flowed back in.

She strolled aimlessly down the vacant hall, her mind filled with images of David. She had learned over the past six months that people handle death differently. Some wear their grief on their sleeve. Others try to avoid pain by pretending that nothing ever happened, that the beloved never existed. Laura guessed she fell into a third category. Friends had told her to try to put the tragedy behind her—best to move on, they had said. She understood their reasoning and probably would have offered similar advice if she had been the bereaved friend rather than the widow. But Laura did not want to forget David. She found an odd sort of comfort in thinking about him, in remembering every moment she spent with him. And yes, she cried when she went through photo albums, when she thought of how much he had to live for, when she thought of the happy family that would never be. But crying was okay. There was nothing wrong with crying.

370

Better to cry than to pretend David did not exist. Better to cry than to feel nothing.

T.C.'s voice jolted Laura away from her thoughts and back into the darkened hallway in Boston Garden. His voice was low. She moved closer and tried to listen.

'It's okay,' he said. 'I got you.'

She cocked her head to the side. What was T.C. doing out here? Laura peered around the corner and spotted him right away. Her eyes grew puzzled. T.C. half dragged, half carried Mark Seidman down the hallway. Mark's legs were not functioning. His hands gripped his head as if it were about to split open. A scream was cut off when T.C. clamped his hand over Mark's mouth.

'Hang in there, old buddy. Just lean on me. I'll have you home soon.'

Mark's reply began with another muffled cry. 'I didn't want to see her, T.C. I didn't want to go near her.'

'I know, Mark. I know.'

Laura stood in frozen horror as the two men disappeared around the corner, remembering that T.C. had told her just a few hours ago that he had never met Mark Seidman.

CHAPTER TWENTY-TWO

Judy paced the living room of her one-level home. She had lived in campus housing for over a decade now and she liked it well enough. It was small but there was still a bedroom, a living room, a kitchen, and an office—plenty of space for her. More rooms would have just meant more places to store mess.

Her mind kept racing through the events of the previous night at the Boston Garden. She would think it over, mentally rewind, review what she had seen and heard, try to draw conclusions. Mark Seidman's first jumpshot had set her mind in a whirling, terrifying spin and now it would not stop. Could it be? Could Mark Seidman have pulled it off? It seemed incredible to her but when she thought the whole scenario through, only one conclusion made sense.

Judy reached into her wallet and grabbed out the familiar old photograph. The picture trembled in her hand. She stared at the image of a young, glowing Judy in an embrace with a somewhat older man. The black-and-white photograph had been taken after a faculty softball game on a bright, beautiful Chicago afternoon in 1960. The older man still held the bat in his free hand. His baseball cap was tilted to the side, a smile plastered across his handsome face.

The older man was David's father.

Judy continued to stare, remembering the very moment the photograph had been snapped. She and Sinclair had known each other for about two months on that sunny day and both of them were in love. Neither one of them planned it to happen that way. Neither one of them wanted to hurt anybody. But there had been an instant chemistry there, the kind of reaction that could make a level-headed, proper young woman like Judy fall for a married man.

Yes, Judy heard about Sinclair's reputation as a major womanizer. Yes, she knew that this was not his first experience with adultery, but all the others had been nothing more than empty-headed campus beauties whom he could have fun with and dispense with quickly. Judy was different. While attractive enough, she was certainly no head-turner and, more to the point, their affair was now four months old. Sinclair Baskin loved her, she knew, and he was going to get divorced. Yes, it would be messy. No, her parents would not understand or be supportive at first. But love conquers all, right? What could be stronger than love?

As it turned out, love proved no match for jealousy, beauty, deceit and rage.

The affair had been tough on Sinclair too. He had a ten-year-old boy and an infant son, both of whom he loved dearly. Judy smiled sadly. Little, mischievous Stan was now forty years old. The little baby boy named David had grown up to be a wonderful young man and a sport's hero. How proud Sinclair would have been of David. How crushed he would have been when David drowned . . .

But of course, that would never have happened. If Sinclair were here, David would be too.

Judy continued to gaze at the familiar photograph. Her thoughts glided easily from the past to the present. Such a thin line separated

Boston in 1990 from Chicago in 1960. Her beautiful niece had also loved a Baskin man. David Baskin. Sinclair's baby boy. Laura had put her whole life into loving him. Her dreams, her hopes, her love, her life—all gone now. Gone.

But there were major differences between Judy's tragedy and Laura's. For one, David had loved Laura with everything he had, no questions asked. In the end, Judy could not say the same thing about Sinclair. But more important, Laura was completely blameless in the death of the man she loved.

Judy was not.

Damn you, Sinclair Baskin. Why did you make that one dreaded mistake? And why was I so stupid? Why did I react so impulsively and strike without thinking? Everything was perfect, you idiot. Perfect.

Gone. Dead. Over. For Judy, there was nothing left. But what about Laura?

Her hand reached for the telephone. There still might be hope for Laura. She grabbed the receiver, picked it up, dialed.

Her decision was made.

*   *   *

When practice ended, Mark Seidman silently showered and dressed. The locker room was quiet, the players still somber from last night's ceremony. No tape deck blasted the latest long-play single from Chaka Khan or Samantha Fox. There was little conversation going on, which made it easier for Mark to avoid conversing with his teammates. In the past, Mark had always enjoyed the camaraderie of his teammates. He recognized that there was a direct correlation between winning basketball

374

games and having fun. When basketball became merely a job, the level of play always dropped off.

All that being said, Mark could not get himself to warm up to his teammates, nor did they accept him with open arms. It bothered him, and yet he knew that getting friendly with any of them could be catastrophic. Earl was not stupid. Neither was Timmy, Mac or Johnny. While he doubted that they could ever put the whole thing together, the risk was still too great.

He grabbed his gym bag and headed toward the exit. As he passed by Earl's locker, he heard, 'See you tomorrow, Mark.'

Earl had barely spoken a word to him all season. 'Yeah,' Mark said unsurely, 'see you tomorrow, Earl.'

'Nice game last night.'

Mark swallowed. 'You too.'

They both stood uncomfortably. With an uneasy smile Mark turned away. He pushed the door open and vanished into the lobby.

One of the towel boys ran after him. 'Mark?'

He turned. 'Yes?'

'There's a telephone call for you.'

'Tell whoever it is I'm not here.'

'She said it's urgent.'

'She?'

The boy nodded. 'She said you would know her. Judy Simmons.'

Mark felt something rip through his stomach.

'You all right, Mark?'

He nodded, his body numb. 'I'm fine,' he said. 'I'll take the call in room five.'

Mark tried to remain calm, composed, unruffled. He reached room five, closed the door for privacy, and picked up the phone.

'Hello?'

'Mr Seidman?'

'Yes?'

'This is Judy Simmons. We met last night.'

His mouth felt incredibly dry. 'Yes, of course. Is there something I can do for you, Miss Simmons?'

'How do you know I'm not married?'

'Excuse me?'

'You just called me "Miss". How do you know I'm not married?'

Mark closed his eyes. Every word had to be watched before it passed his lips. 'I . . . I noticed last night that you weren't wearing a wedding band.'

She paused as if she were mulling over his explanation. 'I see.'

'You said it was urgent.'

'It is,' she said. 'Do you mind if I call you Mark?'

'Please do.'

'Good,' Judy replied. She hesitated for a brief moment before speaking again. 'Do you mind if I call you David?'

Her words hit him like a powerful blow. *Just keep cool, Mark. Just keep cool.* 'Is this some kind of joke?'

'No.'

'Look, I don't know what this is all about, but I do not appreciate your calling me under the pretense of an emergency—'

'Don't play games with me, David,' she interrupted. 'That is your real name, isn't it? David Baskin.'

'No, it is not,' he shot back confidently. But he was scared, oh so scared. 'I don't know what you're talking about and frankly, I don't care. I'm sick of

376

hearing the man's name already. I know that your family has suffered a tragedy, Miss Simmons, and I know that my jumpshot is similar to his. But I am Mark Seidman, not David Baskin. Do you hear me? I am not your niece's dead husband.'

'Wait a sec—'

'No, you wait a second. Tragedies happen, Miss Simmons. They are indiscriminate and cruel. I know that the death of a man as young and healthy as David Baskin is hard for everyone to accept. The press and fans can't even accept it. They call me White Lightning II as if I were David reincarnated. I'm sick of it, do you hear me? Do yourself a favor. Accept the truth and help your family do the same. David Baskin is dead. I happened to replace him on the basketball court. That's all.'

There was a long silence before Judy spoke again. 'You don't understand anything, do you?'

'What do you mean?'

'I mean that you think you know what you're doing, but you don't. There are things about this whole situation that have been kept from you.'

'I don't know what you're talking—'

'Fine, Mr Seidman or whatever your name is. If you want to continue your strategy of feigning ignorance, I am truly left with no defense. But if you want to learn what really happened thirty years ago, if you ever want to save Laura from unspeakable cruelty, come up to Colgate tomorrow evening at seven. I'll explain everything to you then. After you listen to what I have to say, I will live with whatever decision you make. I will never speak of this again. But if you do not come, I am left with no choice but to find another way of handling this. You may not like what I come up with.'

Mark swallowed hard. A tear came to his eye.

'Tomorrow night, Mr Seidman. Seven p.m.'

She hung up. Mark quietly replaced the receiver and moved toward the car waiting for him outside. He opened the passenger door and got in. 'I just got a call from Judy Simmons.'

T.C.'s reaction was swift and predictable. 'What did she say?'

'She thinks I'm David Baskin. She says Baskin was not told the whole truth.'

'Not told the truth? What the hell does that mean?'

'I'm not sure. She said it had to do with what happened thirty years ago.'

T.C. bit off the end of a cigar. 'Interesting, no?'

Mark shrugged. 'Depends on what she means.'

'Could she be right?' T.C. asked. 'Could Baskin have been deceived?'

'You're the detective. You tell me. I mean, I guess it's possible. But how? And more important, why? What would have been gained?'

'I don't know,' T.C. agreed, 'but she really has no idea what Baskin knew, does she?'

'Meaning?'

'Meaning she might think Baskin didn't know the whole story when in fact he did.'

The car pulled out of the parking lot. Mark stared out the side window. 'She also said that if I ever wanted to save Laura from what she called unspeakable cruelty, I should go to Colgate tomorrow night.'

'What else did she say?'

'That if I did not go, she would find another way of handling it.'

'She said that?'

378

Mark nodded.

T.C. gripped the wheel firmly, his face tightening. 'Well, we certainly can't let her do that, now can we?'

*   *   *

Riiiiing. Riiiiing. Wake up, Stan! Time to call your daddy's murderer!

'Ooooooh, my fuckin' head.'

Stan rolled over onto his back. What a goddamn hangover. Just like the good old days. His hand reached out, smacked the alarm clock and pulled it toward him.

One p.m.

He put the clock back onto the night-table. Breathing through his nose hurt like a son of a bitch. It was probably broken. He'd have to get it taken care of at the hospital. Later. He had things to do now.

He stood and walked over to the mirror. His face looked like shit. Both his eyes were black from the broken nose, and his complexion was white from vomiting up a storm last night. Bits and pieces of the incident in the bathroom came to him, but it was all so fuzzy. A man jumps him, dunks his head in a toilet bowl till he nearly drowns him, then knocks him out. Strange but true. And what had the guy said to him? Something about keeping away from 'her.' He assumed 'her' meant Laura.

Stan wondered if Laura could have hired the guy. Doubtful. The most obvious suspect was T.C., but that was not T.C.'s voice he heard whispering in his ear.

His mind replayed his conversation with Laura,

wondering for the zillionth time how he could have been so stupid. Why create an adversary in a woman as powerful as Laura? Why not just forget about her and go on? He was happy with Gloria. He was going to have all the money he wanted. So why screw it all up? Why did he always need to mess up his life?

But, alas, that was his way. Stan always managed to keep one foot firmly placed in dung. He would try like hell to pull it out. He would pull and tug, straining with everything he had. His foot would slowly come loose from the filth, lift in the air, and then Stan would notice that his other foot was now firmly entrenched in another pile of dung.

Stan headed into the den and collapsed on the couch. That was enough life analysis for one morning, thank you. He sat down by the phone and rubbed his hands together nervously. A thin film of sweat coated his body.

It was time to place that little call.

For a brief moment, he felt repulsion at what he was about to do. How he could just let the murder of his father slide. How he could allow himself to be bought off by his father's killer. His father had been one of the very few people in this world who truly loved him. Maybe the only one.

Stan reached for the bottle of vodka and poured himself a healthy shot. Better not to think about it like that. Better to consider the phone call a normal business transaction, a very profitable one. Yes, that was the best way to look at it.

He went back into the bathroom, shaved, showered, sprinkled on a few dabs of Old Spice and threw on a sweatsuit. After he finished a glass of fresh-squeezed orange juice (with a touch of vodka for taste), he picked up the phone and called his father's murderer.

*   *   *

Judy hung up the phone on Mark Seidman and renewed her pacing. What next? The answer was pretty clear: call the one person in the world who would not think she was crazy, the one person who would understand her suspicions. And it just so happened that that one person loved Laura more than life itself.

James.

She and James had spoken a few times once they had realized that David's death had been no accident, that he had in all likelihood committed suicide. They had even considered the possibility that Mary was somehow responsible for the drowning. Now Judy realized that they had only skimmed the surface in their skepticism over David's 'accidental' death. The rumblings underneath were just beginning to show. It scared Judy and it brought her hope. She knew that James would feel the same but the truth was that they both loved Laura and wanted what was best for her. James might even figure out a way of salvaging the situation without bringing back the past.

Maybe. But not likely.

'Let me speak to Dr Ayars, please. This is his sister-in-law.'

'Please hold.'

A moment later, James's voice came through. 'Judy?'

So authoritative, so controlled—it had been part of the reason she had fallen for him all those years ago. Her heart had been brutally crushed when she lost him to Mary, though she never let it show. She stepped aside gracefully as poor, sweet Judy had always done, stepped out of her leading role as fiancée and into the bit part of Mary's maid of honor. She met Sinclair Baskin a few months after losing James. He mended her heart to the stage where she was able to forget all about Mary's husband.

A few months later, her heart was crushed again, never to recover.

'I need to speak to you,' she said. 'Are you alone?'

'Yes. What is it?'

She took a deep breath, not really sure how to begin. 'Did you notice anything strange at the game last night?'

'What do you mean?'

'I mean anything unusual.'

'I've got a dozen patients in the waiting room, Judy. Can we please stop playing cat-and-mouse?'

Again she wondered what to say. 'Did you notice Mark Seidman?'

'The rookie? Of course. Brilliant player.'

'And his jumpshot?'

'What about it?'

'Didn't it look familiar?'

'It was like David's. So what? What are you getting at—?' He stopped speaking. His mouth dropped open. When he was finally able to talk again, his words came softly. 'You don't mean . . .'

'I do.'

'But how? It makes no sense.'

'It makes perfect sense. Think about it a second. Didn't you call me after that meeting with David's attorney and say that you were no longer sure David committed suicide?'

'Yes,' James agreed, 'but that was because his money was missing. I thought there was a remote possibility that someone had murdered him to get it.'

'Think it through again, James. Wouldn't a murder be a terribly strange coincidence?'

'Maybe,' James allowed, 'but what you're suggesting is preposterous.'

'Is it? Or is it the only answer that completely fits?'

'How could David have possibly pulled it off?'

'Not easily, I assure you. He would have needed help. Probably from T.C.—'

'—who was the first one to get over to Australia when Laura discovered that David was missing,' James added.

'Exactly.'

'But we have to admit it's a pretty wild theory, Judy. And that's all it is right now: theory. There's not one shred of proof. We can't just go off half-cocked on a supposition. Think of the repercussions involved.'

'I know all about the repercussions.'

'Then what do you think we should do?'

Judy sighed. As usual James was right. In the end, this was only another in a series of crazy hypotheses by a frustrated English teacher. 'We'll move slowly, but it has to be investigated.'

'The sooner, the better,' James said. 'This can't wait. I'll go to the bank and try to track down the missing money.'

'Good.'

Pause. 'Have you spoken to Mary?' he asked.

'Are you joking? Who knows how she'd react?'

'I agree. Goodbye, Judy.'

'Good luck, James. Let me know what you find out.'

*   *   *

Graham Rowe scanned the telephone bill. He could have gotten the bill from the phone company, but if he had made that request, the government might just want to find out what he was investigating. And if something big was going on, if Dr Bivelli and the Aussie Feds were working with this T.C. fella, poking his nose where it didn't belong could prove hazardous to his health.

This is not my cup of tea, Graham thought. He was a simple, small-town sheriff. He liked fishing, hunting, and downing a few Fosters at Luke's Pub in town. Not too many, mind you, but a nice cold one now and again helps set a man straight.

Conspiracy, complications, murders—he avoided them like a leper colony. And what was he risking his neck for anyway? From the looks of things, the actual drowning occurred in Cairns. They had a whole police department over there. He could just hand the whole thing over to them, sit back in his chair, and catch a little cat-nap.

You'd like that, Graham ol' boy, wouldn't you? he thought. But in truth, David Baskin had been vacationing in his jurisdiction. His wife had come to him for help. She could be in real trouble and Graham Rowe was not the sort of man who turned away from a woman in danger.

He grabbed a pen and circled all the calls on the bill that had gone to the United States. There were a total of seven made on June 17th. The big sheriff had all seven numbers checked out quickly. Three were tourists calling their family in California. One was to Texas. One was even to something called SportsPhone in Cleveland. As he expected, dead ends.

The same however could not be said for the last two calls, both placed to the Boston area from the phone extension in the lobby—the same extension that Baskin had used. Once again, Graham stared at his findings and wished they would change.

Damn. Why did it have to be this way?

He shook his head. No use in putting it off. He might as well call Laura and get it over with. She was about to be one unhappy little lady.

The call connected rapidly. In a matter of seconds, he heard Laura pick up the phone. 'Hello, luv,' he said.

'Graham?' Laura asked, 'is that you?'

He tried to sound jovial. Why he did so he had no idea. 'You know somebody else with an Aussie accent?'

'Have you learned anything? Have they found the passport cards?'

'Yes and no.'

'Give me the no first.'

'No, the passport cards have not been located yet. We should have them sometime tomorrow.'

'And the yes?'

He let go a long sigh. 'We have the phone bill.'

'Were calls placed to Boston?'

He closed his eyes. 'Yes. Two of them. Both from the lobby of the hotel.'

Laura's pulse quickened. 'Who did he call, Graham?'

'One of the calls we already knew about. As we expected, he did call the Heritage of Boston Bank.'

'And the other call?'

He could hear the eager and troubled tone in her voice. 'Laura, he called T.C. They spoke for nearly an hour.'

Graham's words rammed into her midsection. All her worst fears had come full circle. Another lie from T.C. Last night, he claimed that he had never met Mark Seidman. When she saw them sneak out together, she felt a knowing dread crawl over her. He had lied. Somehow, Mark Seidman was connected with all of this. Somehow, the Celtics rookie had a part in this little plot.

'Laura? You still there?'

'Yes, Graham. Is there anything else?'

'Not yet.'

'Thank you for calling.'

'No worries. But Laura, let's take this slowly, shall we? If T.C. does have something to do with this, it might not pay to let on quite yet. In fact, it might be rather dangerous.'

Laura remembered what T.C. had said to her just a few days ago. *You've already put your life in jeopardy and now you've chased away the killer. I wanted them to think they were in the clear. It makes them careless.*

Careless, huh? Maybe it was time to put the shoe on the other foot. Maybe she should let T.C. think he was safe in his web of lies, let him think she had given up on going after the truth behind David's drowning. And then maybe, just maybe, he would be the one to get careless.

'I'll be careful,' she said.

Richard Corsel sat with his fingers on the computer keyboard. He was not typing, not just at this second. For the third time that day, the super-advanced Heritage of Boston Bank computer system had gone down. Richard stared at the blank screen.

'Mr Corsel?'

Richard sighed and swiveled his chair toward the intercom. 'Yes, Mrs Tansmore?'

'There is a gentleman here to see you. A Dr James Ayars.'

'Does he have an appointment?'

'No.'

'Do you know what he wants?'

'He says he wants to talk to you about his son-in-law's account here.'

'Who is his son-in-law?'

'David Baskin.'

Richard tried to swallow but his mouth was too dry. His mind flashed back to the knife at his throat, to the threats against his twin boys and his wife. Despite those threats, Richard had found out where the money had been transferred to after Switzerland. Somebody now had David Baskin's half a million dollars and Richard knew who that somebody was.

But what could he do about it? The psycho with the knife had threatened his children, for chrissake. Laura Baskin was a wealthy woman. She would get along fine without ever learning what happened to the missing money. He had to keep silent. He had to protect his family. And besides, what good would telling her do? The psycho was powerfully connected. He knew all about Richard's personal

387

life as well as his conversations with Laura. It would not pay for him to piss off these kind of people. The same was true for Laura Baskin.

Of course, there was one giant hole in Richard's theory. Suppose the psycho and his companions were not through with Laura Baskin? If they had murdered David for his money, who was to say that Laura was not going to be the follow-up? And what if they decided that Richard Corsel knew too much? What if they decided to make sure he kept silent by turning Naomi into a widow?

His mind writhed in confusion. 'Send him in.'

A moment later, James Ayars came through the door. He looked, Richard thought, remarkably like a doctor. Well-groomed, neatly dressed, gray-haired, good-looking, serious—a TV doctor for the nineties. Richard stood and shook his hand.

'Please sit down, Dr Ayars.'

'Thank you.'

'Is there something I can do for you?'

James got right to the point. 'I would like to know about Mr Baskin's missing account.'

'I'm afraid I don't understand.'

'David Baskin was my son-in-law. Before he died, a great deal of money was transferred out of his account. It disappeared, so to speak. I would like to know where it went to.'

Richard almost breathed a sigh of relief. Obviously, Laura had been smart enough not to endanger her father by telling him what she had learned. 'I'm sorry, Dr Ayars. That's confidential information.'

'Confidential?'

Richard nodded. 'Suppose, Doctor, that you transferred money out of this bank. Would you

388

want any relative to be able to come in and find out about it?'

'Fair enough,' Dr Ayars agreed, 'but Mr Baskin is deceased.'

'That does not change his rights.'

'But certainly the next of kin has a right to know what happened to his money.'

'In most cases, yes. But you are not next of kin, Dr Ayars. Your daughter is.'

'I understand that, but my daughter has gone through a terrible ordeal these past few months. Couldn't I act as her proxy?'

'You could,' Richard replied, 'if you had her power of attorney.'

Dr Ayars leaned forward, his face clouded. 'Have you learned anything new about this matter?'

'I'm sorry. That's also confidential.'

James settled back into the chair. 'I respect what you're saying, Mr Corsel,' he said in a quiet voice, 'but I suspect there may be more to this money transfer than meets the eye. There could be something else at stake here, something very dangerous, something that could hurt my daughter. I need to know what happened to that money.'

The two men stared at each other for a moment. 'I wish I could help you,' Richard said, 'but this situation involves bending more than a few bank rules. You're asking Heritage of Boston to break the law.'

'Then how do I find out what happened?'

'I suggest you speak to your daughter about this.'

James realized it was useless to push any further. 'Thank you, Mr Corsel,' he said as he turned to leave. Once out in the lobby, James wondered what his next step should be. Either way he looked at it, if Judy's crazy suspicions were right or wrong, his daughter was going to continue to suffer. James would do anything to help Laura, to shield her from any more pain, but what could he do to help?

Whatever it took.

James found his car and pulled out of the lot. His daughter had gone through enough torment. He would not let her go through any more—no matter what the cost.

*   *   *

An argument had raged in Judy's mind all day. Should she call Laura or not? If Judy was wrong about Mark Seidman, calling Laura could be catastrophic. It could re-open old wounds and help the present ones gush anew. It could cause irrevocable harm. And to face facts, Judy did not know the whole story of Mark Seidman. More specifically, everything her mind had dreamed up boiled down to little more than creative conjecture. Being logical, Judy knew that she should not contact Laura yet.

So how come she was dialing her niece's phone number?

In a strange way, it was time for Judy to stop worrying about what might be best for Laura. Trying to protect her could take away Laura's one last chance for true survival. The risk had to be taken. Judy had no choice. If she were wrong, Judy would be harming Laura by telling her. But if she were right and chose not to tell Laura, then she would be guilty of perpetrating the worst possible crime against her niece.

Judy's hand gripped the receiver impossibly tight

390

as the first ring echoed into her ear.

'Hello?'

Judy's vocal chords froze.

Laura repeated her greeting. 'Hello? Hello?'

'Laura?'

'Aunt Judy?'

'Yes.'

'Why didn't you answer me?'

'Bad connection. Sorry.'

'Forget it. How are you?'

'I'm fine, thank you. And you?'

'Doing okay. Thanks for coming last night. It meant a lot to me.'

'No thanks necessary. You know how I loved David.'

Silence hung uncomfortably in the air. 'This isn't a social call, Aunt Judy, is it?'

What to say? How to say it? 'Not exactly, Laura.'

'Does it involve last night?'

'Yes.'

There was another lull. 'I'm listening.'

Just dive in, Judy. There is no easy way. 'It's about David's death.'

Judy's words sliced through the phone line like a scythe. Laura's face fell, her voice barely a whisper. 'What?'

'It's about David's death. It's probably nothing—'

'What about David's death?'

'Laura, I know this is a shock for you. Just bear with me, okay?'

She could hear Laura's breathing start to settle. 'Go on.'

'There are things,' Judy began, 'that you know nothing about. Things that happened many years ago.'

'Many years ago? But David drowned in June.'

'I know that,' Judy continued, trying like hell to keep an even tone, trying not to get too emotional and start screaming, screaming until she could not stop. 'But sometimes the past can overlap with the present, Laura. That was what happened with David.'

'I don't understand.'

'I know you don't, sweetheart.'

'Are you trying to say that David did something in the past that caused his death?'

'No, not David. He was an innocent victim.'

'Then why—?'

'Listen to me, Laura. I need to talk to you, to show you what I mean.'

'Show me?'

'David might be here . . .' She stopped herself. An idea had surged into her head, and her mouth had moved with too much speed. This was a dangerous game she was playing, putting the two of them together, but maybe it was the only way to find out if her theory was true. 'I have some photographs and stuff, but we can't go over this all on the telephone. Can you come here tomorrow evening? Seven o'clock?'

'I'll fly up right now. I'll be there in a couple of hours—'

'No,' Judy cut in. 'I want you to be here tomorrow night at seven p.m. Don't come any earlier.'

'Why seven p.m.?'

'Please, Laura, just trust me on this, okay?'

'But I want to know—'

'Tomorrow. Seven p.m. I love you, Laura.'

'I love you too, Aunt Judy.'

Laura heard the phone click. She replaced the receiver and turned to her guest. Sitting in front of Laura was her mother. The color in Mary's face had drained away in the last minute or two, leaving a skeletal death mask in its place.

CHAPTER TWENTY-THREE

Fire. Satan's soothing bath water. Emblem of Hell. Instrument of mass destruction. Fire devoured everything in its path without concern for value or worth. Fire scorched the skin, fused the flesh to bones, choked the life out of lungs, eventually leading to . . .

The killer drove past the Connecticut state line and into New York on the way to Colgate College.

. . . Death.

I often wonder about Death. What is it, really? No one has any idea, do they? People have speculated since the beginning of time, but each original concept of the hereafter has been as absurd as the one before. How did Hamlet put it before his own demise? Didn't he describe death as 'an undiscovered country from whose bourn no traveler returns?' Is that what we fear, the unknown quantity of the Great Beyond? Was it a glorious Heaven, a destructive Hell, a great black nothingness, or all of the above?

Tears stood in the killer's eyes, tears of regret and sadness.

I have sent people to the mysterious other world. I have handed two souls to the Grim Reaper, never to return . . .

Three, if I include David.

The killer's body trembled, rage pulsing through

393

its veins and arteries. One simple word was shouted. 'No!'

No! I will not take the blame for that. I did not kill him. People react to their situation. David Baskin did what he thought best. And that was a shame. Despite his father, I couldn't help but admire David Baskin. And I am not a murderer. Not in my heart. I never meant to hurt anybody, not really. Yes, I killed Sinclair Baskin. I put a gun against his forehead and I pulled the trigger, but it was an act spawned from a thoughtless fury against a man who deserved to die. Like David Baskin, I reacted to a set of circumstances. And as far as my second murder is concerned—

The steering-wheel spun in the killer's hands, nearly driving the car off the road.

The second murder. What about the cruel butchery of my second, nameless victim? Can I dismiss that as easily as the death of Sinclair Baskin? No. Guilt will burn eternally inside me for slaying that unstained soul. Why did I have to do it? He was, after all, an innocent victim. My only solace comes from a Machiavellian concept: the ends justify the means. History would say that the decision was a clever one and in the end, I have to agree. Just look at Laura if you don't believe me.

The killer glanced at the map, spotting the exit leading to Hamilton, New York. Hamilton was the home of Colgate College.

Thirty years ago. All of that had happened over three decades ago. Kennedy had still been alive. Incredible. So long ago and still not an hour goes by when I am not reminded of my days in Chicago. They haunt my every step, my every dream, though I do step and sleep with a clear conscience. But I had thought, hoped, prayed that all of the secrets of the past had been laid to rest years ago. I assumed that the past was just that—the past. I never expected it to hurt me again.

Or did I?

In the back of my mind, didn't I know that the past would survive and resurface one day? I guess I did. But all of a sudden, horrible secrets are coming at me, tidal-waving at me, laughing and taunting and threatening to destroy everything I cherish. Stan Baskin, a man frighteningly like his father, wants to blackmail me. I will deal with him tomorrow night. Deal with him brutally.

And Judy. After all these years, Judy wants to talk about the past. Why? Why couldn't she just let it be? Why does she insist on keeping the past alive, on helping it thrive with its full wrath intact?

The car exited the highway. The container of kerosene rolled back and forth in the trunk, making a clanking noise when it hit the metallic sides. A book of matches sat on the dashboard. Hamilton was not very far off now.

First Judy.

Then Stan.

Then . . .?

*   *   *

Judy made herself a cup of tea and sat in the kitchen. Her eyes glanced at the clock for the third time in the last four minutes:

6:20 p.m.

If everything went according to schedule, Mark Seidman and Laura would both be arriving in about forty minutes. She realized that she had created a volatile situation by telling them both to be here at the same time. The last few hours had been spent questioning that decision. Judy carefully weighed the risks against the rewards and realized that there was no contest. She had to do it. Enough time had been wasted, enough lives thrashed apart and left to decay in the hot sun.

She took out the Lipton tea bag, read the little health tip on the tag, and tossed it into the garbage can. A half-teaspoon of sugar and a drop of milk were added. She had hoped to brew up some nice herbal tea. One of the students in her seminar on nineteenth-century American poetry had spent a semester in the Orient and had brought her back a whole slew of wonderful teas from mainland China. But, alas, Judy had used them all up already. So it was back to Lipton for today. Tomorrow she would go out to that avant-garde gourmet shop in town and pick up some new herbs.

Tomorrow.

Like the corny lyrics to that song in *Annie*, she realized that tomorrow was only a day away. And yet, it was a lifetime. The Judy that drank tea tomorrow would live in a different world from the one who sat at her table right now. Nothing would be the same. Her life and the lives of those she held dear would be eternally altered—for better or for worse she could not say.

She sipped the tea, enjoying the feel of the hot liquid sliding down her throat. The hands on the kitchen clock kept trudging forward. Judy was not sure if they were moving too slowly or too quickly. She only knew that the future was coming. Her emotions darted from one extreme to the other. One minute, the wait made her nearly burst with anticipation; the next, she dreaded the thought of hearing the inevitable knock on her door.

She picked the key ring off the table and held it in front of her. Four keys hung off it: two for the car, one for the house and one for the safety deposit box that held her diary from 1960. Laura was about to learn all about the contents of that diary. She was about to discover the secrets that had been kept from her for so many years. And once she did, Judy prayed it would all be over.

But would it?

Judy took another sip of tea. It tasted bitter.

*   *   *

Laura's leg shook, but as usual she did not realize it.

Damn. How much longer before this plane lands? Anxiousness overwhelmed her. She found herself biting her nails, craving a cigarette, reading the boring airline magazine, memorizing the emergency exit locations on the plastic card, learning how to throw up into a paper bag in three different languages.

All of this for a lousy one-hour flight to Hamilton.

The leg continued to rock. The blue-haired woman seated next to her shot Laura an annoyed glance.

Laura stopped her leg. 'Sorry,' she said.

The blue-haired woman said nothing.

Laura turned back toward the airline magazine. She flipped mindlessly through the pages. There had been no reply to the numerous calls she had placed to Judy last night, save Judy's voice on an answering machine. What had she meant last night? David had been dead for over six months. Now, after all this time, Judy wanted to tell her something about his death. But what? What could her aunt possibly know about David's death?

And the tone of her voice—so frightened, no more than that. Petrified. And what was all the cloak-and-dagger stuff? What was so important that Aunt Judy could not say it over the telephone? What kind of photographs did she want to show her? What was all this talk of the past? Why did Aunt Judy want Laura to wait until 7:00 p.m. today to see her? And how could all of this possibly be connected to David's death in June?

Too many questions. Too few answers.

The blue-haired woman coughed in undisguised irritation.

Laura looked down at her leg. Old Faithful was boogeying again. Her hand reached out and took hold of her knee. The leg slowed before coming to a complete stop.

'Sorry,' Laura offered again.

Ms Bad Dye glared at her.

Laura returned the glare. Well, fuck you too, lady.

She turned back toward her magazine and continued not to read it. The same thoughts kept racing through her brain. Her suspicions about David's death now traveled down a new and frightening avenue. Intuition now steered her. No longer did things merely appear wrong—they *felt* wrong. There was a danger here, a danger more horrifying than Laura had previously imagined. She had arrived at a locked closet that held something terrible, something evil, something that threatened to destroy them all. She wanted to run away, to forget that she had ever found this locked door, but her feet were frozen to the floor. Without conscious thought, her hand reached for the deadbolt. She would soon unlock the closet door, turn the knob, peer inside. There was no turning back now. It was too late to stop.

What was behind the locked door? Laura did not know. In a few minutes the plane would land in Ithaca. A taxi would take her to Aunt Judy. Once there, the closet door would be opened.

*　　　*　　　*

The killer read the sign:
COLGATE COLLEGE

The car turned right and entered the campus. The campus was storybook small college. Buildings that would be covered with ivy if it were not for the snow dotted the barren campus. The place reeked of liberal arts. Students here engaged in intellectual discussions on Hobbes and Locke, on Hegel and Marx, on Tennyson and Browning, on Potok and Bellow. During the day, they went to classes, met friends in the cafeteria, picked up mail at the P.O. At night, they studied in the library, flirted during strategic study breaks, had a few beers at a frat house, engaged in whatever with members of the opposite sex.

To these undergrads, nothing existed outside of the campus. Somehow, the whole world with all its problems and complexities had shrunk down into the boundaries of this idyllic, upstate campus. And life would never be this good again for most of them. They would never again have a chance to care so passionately about things that did not affect

399

them. They would never again be able to enjoy a dress rehearsal for the real world.

The car slowed. There were very few students around right now. That was good. That was what the killer wanted.

I'm here, I can't believe I'm here. I can't believe what I am about to do.

The temperature had to be below zero with the wind-chill factor. Icicles hung off the gutters on the library. The snow had to be nearly a foot deep. The killer braked at a speed bump and looked out the passenger window for a brief moment. Without warning, the tears returned.

Why do I have to do this? Why? Isn't there another answer?

But the killer knew that the answer was no. The past was using Judy as its outlet into the present, and so she had to be stopped. She had to be silenced before she could tell Laura what had happened thirty years ago.

Light flurries gently kissed the front windshield. Another left and the car entered the faculty housing area. Up ahead, the killer could now see the small brick building inside of which Judy Simmons was sitting at the kitchen table, drinking Lipton tea.

*   *   *

Laura hurried off the plane and across the small terminal. Had the flight been bumpy or smooth? Good or bad? Had they served food or drinks or nothing? Laura did not know the answer to any of those questions. She did not know what type of airplane she had been on, what airline she had used, what seat she had been in. The only memory that made its way past her murky haze was of a blue-haired woman dressed in Early Mayberry who resembled a waitress at a roadside diner. The woman had spent the flight alternating between practicing her look of disgust and snoring as she cat-napped. A pleasant companion.

But Ms Psychedelic Hairdo had been a welcome distraction from the agony of the unknown. Minutes on the plane aged Laura like years. Her hair was a mess, her thin layer of makeup smeared on her face like so much finger-paint. Laura did not realize any of this. She did not care. Laura had but one mission: get to Aunt Judy's house. That was all she was concerned with right now.

Laura glanced at her watch. It was nearly six-twenty and she wanted to be at Judy's promptly at seven o'clock. She picked up her pace and realized that she was nearly sprinting. A sign said the taxi stand was on her right. She veered and the electric glass doors opened. Cold wind whipped her face and neck. Up ahead, she spotted a sole taxi waiting at the stand. She broke out into a full run now, heading in a straight line toward the yellow cab. Her legs pumped hard, lifting her feet up and over the snow banks.

When she reached the car, her hand grabbed the door handle and pulled. Nothing happened. The door was locked. She lowered her head and squinted into the locked taxi. She was greeted with a now-familiar glare. Inside the taxi, taking off a heavy overcoat and jabbering with the driver while staring at Laura, was the blue-haired woman from the plane.

Laura stepped back as the taxi drove off.

*   *   *

The killer parked the car in a wooded area behind Judy's house. No one would be able to see it there. Entering and exiting without being seen was very important. No witnesses. No one must see a thing.

The killer stepped out of the car and opened the trunk. A quick look around proved no one was in the area. Good. Very good. A hand reached into the trunk and pulled out a kerosene container. The hand shook wildly, spilling some of the flammable liquid onto the snow.

Stop that shaking. This is no time to go soft. Brace yourself. Steady yourself. Don't be weak. Not now. This is too important. It has to be done.

Through the woods, the killer could make out the brick building where Judy lived. The house was a hundred yards away, then fifty, then twenty. One foot stepped, the other messed up the tracks. No use in letting the police see the shoe size in a snowprint.

A few seconds later, the killer was in the backyard. The container of kerosene was placed behind a garbage can. But just for the moment. Soon the kerosene would help light Judy's house in a bonfire of death.

The killer moved toward the back door and prepared to knock. A quick glance in a window revealed Judy having a cup of tea in the kitchen.

It was to be the last cup of tea Judy would ever have.

*   *   *

Judy looked up sharply from the kitchen table. She

402

could hear footsteps trudging through the deep snow outside of her window. Someone was outside in the backyard. Someone was walking around back there. Someone was heading toward her back door.

A chill glided through her. She sat up straight, wondering why anybody would come through the back when the front path was cleanly shoveled. No one ever used her back door. The only things back there were woods and shrubs and now snow.

Unease fell over her. She glanced at the clock: 6:45 p.m. It could be Laura or, more probably, Mark. Mark would not want to be seen coming here. He would not want anyone to make the connection between Judy and himself.

The knock on the door startled her. It had to be Mark Seidman, she thought now, her pulse racing fast. She grabbed her empty cup and stood. She put the cup in the sink as she made her way to the back door.

Judy's hand reached up and pulled away the chain-lock. She grabbed the knob and turned it. Slowly, the door swung open. When Judy looked out, a face in front of her smiled brightly.

'Hello, Judy.'

*   *   *

'Say, you're that model, aren't you? Laura Ayars, right?'

It had taken Laura another ten minutes to dig up a taxi. 'Yes. How much longer until we get there?'

The driver let go a laugh. 'Laura Ayars in my cab. My wife will never believe it. I bought your swimsuit calendar one year.'

'Great. Can we go any faster?'

He shook his head. 'I'd like to. I mean, that way I can get more fares. More fares means more money, you know? And I like driving fast. I mean, I'm no New York City cabbie. They're crazy. Have you ever been in a New York taxi?'

'Yes.'

'Well, then you know what I mean. They're crazy. But back to your question. I'd like to go faster. I really would, but I already got two speeding tickets this month. Can you believe that, Laura? Can I call you Laura?'

'Please do.'

'Two speeding tickets, Laura. Cops around here have nothing better to do than protect sheep from college pranks and give a guy trying to make an honest buck a hard time. But hell, they don't bother me much. The problem, Laura, is the snow and ice. I took a turn too quickly around here last year and ended up in a ditch. No kidding. I must have driven on that stretch of road a million times, knew it better than the back of my hand. But this time, it was a coat of ice. Whoosh, the car went right over . . .'

Laura tuned him out. She watched out the window as the car traveled along a seemingly empty road. Only occasionally did another car go past them in the opposite direction. There were no vehicles in front or behind them—just snow piled high on the side of the road.

The land was still, peaceful, quiet. Laura soaked in the tranquillity. She had always liked visiting this area. Her mind and body let the surroundings work on her tense muscles. Yes, it was a beautiful place to visit for a few days. Stay longer than that and you start going stir crazy. Solitude was nice every once in a while, but as a way of life? Uh, uh. Not for her.

'Faculty housing, right?'

'Right.' Laura said.

The taxi pulled onto the campus grounds and headed toward the left. Laura looked around the still campus, her thoughts on David. She couldn't help but feel that all of this was coming to an end, that she would soon know what had really happened to David in Australia. And then what? She would be alone. David would still be gone and Laura would be left with no potent distraction. But it was better not to think too far ahead, better not to consider the future.

The taxi slowed to a stop. 'We're here,' the driver said cheerily.

Laura looked out at Judy's small home. There was no movement anywhere in sight. She quickly paid the driver and slipped her arms into the sleeves of her coat. She left the comfort of the taxi's heater and headed into the cold of northern New York. The taxi drove off as she headed up the path.

Her hands dove into her pockets, her arms huddling against her sides in order to keep warm. As she moved closer to the house, she still saw no movement. One hand came out of the pocket just long enough for Laura to catch a glimpse of her watch.

Seven o'clock on the button.

When she reached the door, Laura rang the doorbell. She could hear the chime echo through the small dwelling before fading away into silence. There were no further sounds. She tried it again, waiting anxiously to hear footsteps heading her way.

No dice.

She tried the bell one more time, waited, but still no one came toward the door. She heard nothing—

No. That was not exactly true. She heard a shuffling noise.

'Aunt Judy?' she shouted.

No answer. No sounds at all. The shuffling noise, if there had indeed been a shuffling noise, was now gone. Laura reached forward and tried the door. The knob turned easily in her hand. The door was unlocked.

Two things occurred simultaneously as Laura pushed open the door and walked into Judy's house: the killer sneaked out the back, and Laura detected the not-so-unpleasant odor of kerosene.

CHAPTER TWENTY-FOUR

'Well, well, what have we got here?'

'Shit! It's the sheriff!'

Graham Rowe approached the two youths. It had not taken him long to find them. Old Mrs Kelcher had pinpointed the spot on Route 7 where the eggs had first catapulted toward her car. Right away he knew the perpetrators of said offense had to be hiding on top of Wreck's Pointe. Pain in the ass getting the car up here. No one ever drove the old, unpaved road to Wreck's Pointe, but if the good folks of Palm Cove thought that Sheriff Graham Rowe was about to scale the side of a mountain to catch a couple of punks chucking eggs, they had another think coming. 'Throwing eggs at passing cars, boys?'

The taller of the two boys stood. An egg was

406

still in his hand. 'We didn't mean no harm, Sheriff Rowe.'

'Well, you caused it, Tommy. Aren't you boys a little old to still be into this kiddie crap?'

Both boys, brothers actually, lowered their heads.

'What's your dad going to say about this? Tommy? Josh?'

Neither spoke.

Graham took a step toward them. He readied himself for his standard lecture designed for the chronic mischief-maker—his stern man-to-punk chat, so to speak—when the radio in his squad car squawked his name. Graham sighed heavily. 'Get out of here, the both of you. If I catch either of you causing trouble again, I'm going to stick you in a cage with a hungry crocodile. You understand?'

'Yes, sir, Sheriff.'

'Yes, Sheriff.'

'Good. Now get lost.'

The brothers ran down the hill and out of sight.

Graham heard the radio shriek his name again. Damn radio was a piece of crap. Had more static than a cheap sweater rubbed on an even cheaper carpet. Graham half sprinted toward the car and picked up the microphone. 'Sheriff Rowe here. What's up?'

His deputy's voice was barely intelligible through the blown speaker. 'Mrs Cassler from the Pacific International Hotel called for you.'

'And?'

'And she wants you over there right away.'

'What's up?'

'She has the passport cards you were looking for.'

Graham had already started his car. Now he turned on his siren and slammed his foot on the gas pedal. 'Tell her I'm on my way.'

*   *   *

The killer stood over Judy's still body. The first murder weapon had been a gun. The second, a sharp blade. Now the third, the third weapon was . . .

. . . *Fire.*

Judy's breathing came steadily. Her eyes were closed. She almost looked as though she were sleeping, her chest rising and falling as though in heavy slumber. But Judy's body was still, oh so still. A small pool of blood had formed on the floor near the back of her skull where a bronze bust of Keats had made impact. Such violence from such a non-violent soul—it saddened the killer.

I have to move fast, have to get rid of all the evidence. How? How do I make sure no one reads any of Judy's diaries or sees any of her old photographs? How do I silence her forever?

The answer was almost too simple.

Fire.

Highly flammable kerosene had already been strewn throughout the tiny study and over Judy's body. Loose papers were strategically laid about. Not too much kerosene and not too many papers. So far, so good, but there was no reason to get cocky.

After the killer had entered the house, everything had gone better than hoped. Judy had led them both down a thin corridor filled with poster prints by Chagall and Dali and even McKnight. When they reached the end of the hallway and stepped into the cluttered study, Judy made a key error.

She turned her back.

That was all the killer needed. The bust of Keats sat on its own podium by the study door. The bronze likeness was surprisingly heavy and a struggle to lift, but once the killer had it in the air, it swung down easily upon the back of Judy's head, landing with a sickening thud. Her body folded before crumbling to the ground.

The killer glanced around. The diaries were kept in this study, dangerous journals dating back more than thirty years ago. There was no need to check or read through them. Judy kept all her important papers in this study. Once they were destroyed, once they were consumed by the flames along with their author, no evidence would remain. Nothing would be able to tie the past with the present. They would all be safe again.

A cold gust of wind chilled the room, whispering a warning that something was being overlooked, that the past could not be so easily laid to rest.

The whisper mercifully faded away.

The killer's face twisted in thought. The fire marshals were sure to figure out eventually that this was no accident, that kerosene had played a key role in the spread of the fire, that this was indeed a case of arson. But by that time, the trail would have gone cold. The snow would have covered the tracks made by the kerosene containers. The rented car would be returned. The killer (now arsonist) would be long gone without so much as a trace left behind.

Perfect. Everything was so perfect.

So how come the tears were starting to flow again?

Why did it have to be this way? Even when the eyes were closed the image of Judy's bloodied body kept reappearing before the killer. And that meant there would be nightmares for a very long time after today. Poor Judy. Poor loving, sweet Judy. Why does she have to die? Judy could have simply left the past alone, forgotten about it and let it be. But instead she chose to prod it, to poke at it until it awoke and attacked with a torrid vengeance. Now there was only one way to satisfy its growing lust.

'Goodbye, Judy.'

A hand wiped away a stray tear, reached for the book of matches, lit one and . . .

. . . and heard a knock on the door.

The killer's heart rammed up into the throat, cutting off the air supply. Panic moved in with dizzying speed. Oh, God, what now? What now? The flame moved slowly down the matchstick.

Fire.

Another knock. Who? Why . . .? The match came close to the killer's fingers, too close. With a small yelp of pain, the match dropped on top of crumpled papers. They caught fire and began to consume the nearby journals, curling the pages inward as they turned black.

The die was cast. There was no turning back now.

Get out! a small voice said as the knocking came again, more urgently now. *Get out now!*

But suppose . . .?

The legs dismissed the doubt. They sprinted out of the study in a mad dash. The killer closed the study door, trapping Judy and the deadly blaze in the small area. The fire began to grow and fan out.

As the back door swung open, a voice from the

front porch called Judy's name, a familiar voice, a voice so frighteningly, terrifyingly familiar . . .

*   *   *

The front door swung open slowly.

Laura moved past the doorway and into the small foyer. The house was dark, the sun having disappeared completely during the past half-hour. A sole street light provided shadowy illumination. Laura's eyes moved from left to right, scanning the entire living-room area. There was no movement, no sounds.

'Aunt Judy?' she called out, but there was still no answer.

Laura took another step forward. Her nose twitched again from the strange, pungent odor that permeated the house. Gasoline or oil or something like that. It had to be coming from the garage. The smell was strong, nearly overwhelming. She took a deep sniff. Now that she really thought about it, it was not just a gassy or oily smell, not merely the smell of a gasoline station or some car-repair shop. No, now that she really analyzed it, the smell was more like . . .

. . . *like something burning* . . .

The odor suddenly made Laura ill. Her hand traced a path along the side of the wall until she located the light switch. She flicked it on. Fluorescent lights brightened the darkened room, startling her. She shaded her eyes from the surprising glare. When she was finally able to lower her hand and look toward the back of the house, she saw smoke pouring out from under the study door.

411

Oh God, no.

Laura ran toward the study. The smoke was getting thicker now, spiraling toward the ceiling in long, black gusts. She reached the door and placed her palm on the wooden panel. Her hand drew back.

The door felt warm.

Get out, Laura. Get out and call the fire department. Judy is not home. She went out and left an iron on or something. Get the hell out!

Laura could hear the crackle of the blaze behind the door.

Get out of here. Get out of here before the fire blows down the door.

The smoke crept closer. Laura covered her eyes with her hand and began to back out toward the exit.

Get out . . .

She was about to turn around and run when a sound tore through the door of the study. She froze. Her heart kicked hard against her chest. The terrible sound repeated itself, this time a little louder.

A cough.

Laura felt an icy coldness slide through her.

Then another cough.

Someone was behind that door. Someone was trapped in the study.

Without conscious thought, Laura took action. Her hand reached out toward the knob, turned it, and pushed open the door. Gusts of thick, black smoke rushed through the doorway. Laura fell and rolled to the side. She heard the cough again, the cough of a female, but this time it was more of a horrid choking sound.

412

Laura stood and moved back to the doorway. The smoke was everywhere, blinding her eyes and making them tear. Covering her mouth with her hand, Laura ducked into the study. On the ground below her, she found Judy.

Oh Christ . . .

Laura bent down. She opened her mouth to speak but the smoke poured down her throat and silenced her. Judy looked up with pleading eyes, still coughing uncontrollably. A stream of syrupy blood matted down her hair. Laura felt Judy reach up and put something into her hand, forcing Laura's fingers to form a fist around it.

'Take it,' Judy whispered hoarsely.

Laura transferred the items to her pocket and knelt beside Judy. She was unconscious now, her breathing sporadic. Laura grabbed hold of Judy's arm and began to pull. The fire remained mostly in the corner of the study, gaining strength at a slow but steady pace. Papers crinkled from the flames. A chair began to collapse.

Then the fire found the kerosene.

Without warning, the corner of the room burst into flames. The blaze began to gnaw its way onto the carpet. The fire danced across the floor, grasping and then consuming the curtains. And then Laura realized something else, something that made her pull ever harder.

Oh God, oh no . . .

Judy was covered with the kerosene. The flames were racing toward her.

Have to move. Have to get her out before . . .

The smoke made it nearly impossible to see, but Laura knew that the blaze would not rest until it claimed all its victims. The flames grabbed hold of the desk, the books, the chairs. Laura continued to drag Judy inch by inch, but they were not moving fast enough. The fire was gaining on them, circling closer and closer.

And then the flames reached Judy.

There was a short, hideous scream as the blaze crawled across Judy's torso and nestled in. Panic seized Laura in a crushing grip. She summoned some inner strength and renewed her pull on Judy's arm. They began to move faster.

They were only a foot away from the study's doorway when Laura tripped over the bronze bust of Keats. She lost her footing and began to topple forward. Her hands tried to move in front of her to cushion the fall, but they did not move fast enough. Her head caught the edge of door frame, sending shards of pain throughout her skull. Dizziness swam through her.

Have to get up, she thought through the murk. *Have to get up and drag Judy out of here.*

Laura's throat felt like it was being stomped on. Black smoke was everywhere now. She gasped for air and struggled to a sitting position, the flames licking at her feet. Her head reeled with pain. Her limbs felt like large blocks of lead.

Have to move. Have to do something . . .

She crawled slowly and reached out for Judy. The dull ache in her head consumed her. Breathing became impossible. Laura stopped moving. Her eyes rolled back. Her hand never made it to her aunt.

As Laura lost consciousness and collapsed to the floor, a powerful arm circled her waist and scooped her up.

414

CHAPTER TWENTY-FIVE

For the tourists, it was a unique photo opportunity. Here, in the lobby of the Pacific International Hotel, a mammoth local sheriff sprinted through the front door at breakneck speed, almost shattering the glass. Graham hurdled over suitcases, darted deftly between hotel guests, dashed across the tile floor. Without slowing, he made a left at the receptionist's desk, and traveled another twenty yards before finally pausing in front of a door that read General Manager. He grabbed the knob, not bothering to knock, and turned.

'Where are they?'

Gina Cassler looked up from her desk. 'Good Lord, Graham, you're all out of breath.'

He heaved in oxygen. 'Not important,' he managed. 'Where are the passport cards?'

She shook her head. 'They're in my file cabinet. Will you relax and sit down?'

Graham collapsed into the chair like a punctured lung. 'Hand them over, luv.'

She took out a key and unlocked the file cabinet behind her. 'I wanted to keep them safe for you.'

'I appreciate that.'

Her hand reached into the cabinet. 'Can I get you something to drink, Graham?'

'In a minute, thanks.'

She took hold of a large manila envelope and pulled it out of the file. 'Here they are,' she said.

'Have you looked through them yet?'

'Looked through them?' she repeated, tossing the envelope across her desk. 'For what? I don't even know what you're looking for.'

Graham nodded, satisfied. He took hold of the envelope and ripped it open. 'Was there any problem getting these?'

'None.'

'No one asked you why you needed them?'

'I told them I kept superlative records but one of my staff members had carelessly misplaced some data.'

Once again, Graham looked around the paper-cluttered room. 'They bought that?'

She nodded. 'Lucky for you they've never seen this office.'

He shrugged, slipped the cards out of the envelope, and began to sort through them. He piled the ones filled out by Americans on the side.

'What do you want to drink, Graham?'

Without looking up he said, 'Whiskey.'

Gina reached behind her into the same file cabinet and withdrew a bottle. She poured some into two shot glasses and passed one of them to Graham's side of the desk. He ignored it.

'Find anything yet?' she asked.

Graham shook his head and continued to flip through the cards. When he was finished, he picked up the pile of the ones he had sorted out. He skimmed through them. On the upper corner of each card, a receptionist had jotted down the room numbers. The name and address were underneath that, followed by the nationality (most Americans just wrote U.S.A.), the passport number, date of issue, place of issue. When he reached the passport card that had room 607 scribbled on the top, he checked out the address. Boston, Massachusetts. Then he read name. A hammer blow struck

Graham's heart. He read the name again.

'Sweet Jesus . . .'

'Graham, are you all right?'

The other cards slipped through his hands and onto the floor. Graham grabbed the shot glass in front of him and threw the liquid contents down his throat.

'Mary Ayars,' he said. 'Laura's mother.'

* * *

Dr Eric Clarich had lived in Hamilton, New York, since he was three years old. He had attended John Quincy Adams Elementary School, Heritage Junior High School, Hamilton High School, Colgate College. In fact, the only time he lived outside of freezing-cold Hamilton was during his days of medical school at Cornell. Even his residency and internship had been performed at the hospital nearest to the home of his childhood, adolescence and college years.

Eric was what prep-school students would call a townie. Many claimed that his devotion and indeed obsession with Hamilton was dangerous. Dr Eric Clarich's lack of exposure to the outside world, they claimed, would cause his outlook to be somewhat myopic. Perhaps that was true. But Eric did not worry about it very much. He had his life here. Delta, his high-school sweetheart-turned-wife, was pregnant with child number two. His new and growing practice was doing well. Life was good, solid. There was even talk of having Eric run for town council next year.

'Isn't she that famous model?' one of the nurses asked him. Eric nodded solemnly. Two women had

417

just been rushed into the emergency room. One he recognized; the other he knew very well. The two women were also related, he knew, the younger being the niece of the older. Eric had first met the older woman more than a decade ago. Professor Judy Simmons had brought Shakespeare to life for a sophomore Eric Clarich, offering insights and reflections that stunned and stimulated the lucky students who had been selected to take her class. She prided herself on being easily accessible to her students and Eric took full advantage of that fact. He would never forget the hours they had chatted over cups of herbal tea in both her faculty office and her home study. Now, from what he had been told, that study and indeed her entire home was little more than ashes.

Memories drifted gently across Eric's mind. Professor Judy Simmons had written a glowing recommendation to Cornell's medical school describing Eric as 'a true Renaissance man.' Describing someone as being truly renaissance, she explained, was the ultimate compliment. Many would-be doctors can claim a cold, impersonal knowledge of the sciences, but how many could combine that with a glowing love of literature and the arts? That, she surmised in her letter, was what made Eric Clarich, her student and friend, stand above the rest.

Eric took a deep breath and continued working. And what about the brilliant Professor Simmons herself? Would he describe her as a true Renaissance woman? Perhaps. But Judy had always been a bit of an enigma to Eric. He never understood why she never married nor even dated nor for that matter had any close friends. He had only broached the subject with her on one occasion, and she merely joked that her relationships with men read like a Dickens novel. Still, her whole attitude toward herself and the world was a little off-center. To the casual observer Judy Simmons was a pretty and cheerful woman, but beyond the facade, Eric saw her as some sort of sad-eyed, lonely character from a gothic novel Judy herself would undoubtedly cherish. Now, he could make that novel tragic.

Judy Simmons was dead.

He stared down at the charred and battered body of his friend. Eric hoped that she died quickly, that she had not survived long enough to feel her nerve endings being singed, that she had not known the agony of having her skin melted into thick clumps of waxy tallow. He prayed that fallen debris had mercifully knocked Judy unconscious before the blaze had a chance to swarm over her body and eat away at her flesh.

Dead. Another tragedy for a family that should have had everything. First, David Baskin. Now this. Two healthy bodies destroyed by two of Earth's purest elements. Water had claimed David Baskin. Fire had taken away Judy Simmons.

'More oxygen,' he barked to the nurse.

'Yes, Doctor.'

Eric turned his attention back toward his younger patient. Laura Ayars-Baskin, Judy's famous and beautiful niece, lay on the emergency-room stretcher. He checked her pulse again and spread ointment on a burn. With proper care and bed rest, Laura would be fine. Miraculous really. Just fifteen minutes ago, she had been lying unconscious in the middle of a blazing inferno.

419

By some bizarre twist of luck, someone had been walking past at the time, a very brave someone who rushed in and somehow managed to pull both women out of the burning wreck. This courageous fellow had then called the hospital. Paramedics were dispatched immediately, but by the time the ambulance arrived on the scene, the mystery hero was gone. Very strange. Most folks would be dialing up the local news stations to be interviewed on the eleven o'clock news. This hero decided to just take off.

'Do you have those emergency numbers yet?'

'Yes, Doctor. They were written in her telephone diary.'

'Let me have them.' The blonde nurse handed him the telephone numbers. 'Find me if anything happens.'

'Yes, Doctor.'

Eric Clarich walked over to the phone in the hallway. He pushed nine to get an outside line, waited for the tone, and dialed the number of Laura's parents. After four rings, the answering machine picked up and told him that he had reached the Ayars residence. Eric left a message and replaced the receiver.

Damn.

He checked his watch. Nearly seven thirty. Even if he did reach her parents, Boston was a good five hours from here—maybe more in this weather. He thumbed through Laura's book and found her father's office number. Bingo, he was a doctor. There was a decent chance that Dr James Ayars was still in his office at Boston Memorial Hospital. Worth a try anyway.

Eric dialed the number. On the second ring, a

420

receptionist picked up. 'Doctor's office.'

'May I speak with Dr James Ayars please?'

'Whom shall I say is calling?'

'My name is Dr Eric Clarich. This is something of an emergency.'

'Please hold.'

A minute later, the phone was picked up. 'James Ayars here. Can I help you?'

'Dr Ayars, this is Dr Clarich at St Catherine's in Hamilton, New York.'

'Yes?'

'I have some rather bad news.'

The voice remained steady, authoritative. 'I'm listening.'

'There has been a fire at your sister-in-law's home. Your daughter has been injured—'

'Injured?' he shouted. 'Is she all right?'

'She is going to be fine, Dr Ayars. She has a few burns and is being treated for smoke inhalation. Your sister-in-law was not so lucky. I'm sorry to tell you that Judy Simmons is dead.'

Thick, heavy silence. 'Dead?' he asked softly. 'Judy?'

'I'm afraid so.'

'I'll . . . I'll charter a plane. I'll call my wife at home and—'

'I just tried your home number, Doctor. There was no answer.'

Again, there was silence. When James spoke again, his voice was without tone. 'Are you sure?'

'The answering machine was on.'

'Sweet Jesus.'

'Dr Ayars?'

'I'll be up as soon as I can, Dr Clarich. Please let my daughter know that I'm on my way.'

James hung up the phone with a quivering hand. His leg was shaking up and down in the same manner that his daughter had inherited.

Laura was injured. Judy was dead.

He picked up the receiver and called home. The first ring blared through the receiver.

Please answer, Mary. Please be home.

But after the fourth ring, the answering machine once again picked up. James closed his eyes, waiting impatiently for the beep. When it came, he spoke in a calm, collected voice.

'Mary, there has been a fire at Judy's place. Laura has been hurt, but she is going to be fine. I'm flying up there right away. Do the same when you get in. She is at St Catherine's Hospital in Hamilton.'

No reason to tell her about Judy's death right now, he decided. It would just make her panic. James hung up the phone. Something was very wrong here. Mary was almost always home by this time, and on the rare occasions when she was going to be late she left him a message so he wouldn't worry. But not today. For the first time that James could remember, his wife had forgotten to leave him a message.

She could just be in the shower. She could have stepped out to buy a few groceries or pick up something at the pharmacy. That might be all there was to it.

James wanted to believe that, really wanted to convince himself that Mary was just around the corner or on her way from the store or at the

422

beauty parlor or in . . .

Hamilton, New York . . .

James felt his knees give way. Oh God, no. Please tell me no.

Maybe Mary paid her sister a little visit, had a friendly chat, yes a nice, friendly, cozy little chat . . .

Could Judy have been so foolish? Could she have said something to Mary? James was certain the answer was no. Judy would never tell Mary what she suspected, never tell anyone until she was certain it was true.

Then what was Laura doing up there, James? Just a casual visit to Colgate's campus? Seems like too much of a coincidence to me.

His face coiled in fear. Hamilton was a good five hours drive from Boston. By the time a plane was chartered and flew through this weather it would still be a few hours. But time was critical now. He had to get to the hospital as soon as possible, had to protect his daughter before the entire world fell around her.

If something bad happens to Laura, oh God if something bad happens to my baby girl . . .

James Ayars decided not to finish his thought.

*   *   *

Laura's eyelids felt like dead weights. She wrestled with them until they finally fluttered open. A light shone in her eyes, making it impossible to see anything but the bursting brightness of white. Mercifully, the light was pushed away and gradually, Laura's vision came into focus. She glanced around the clean room, the sterile smells chilling her. Almost immediately she realized where she was.

'Mrs Baskin?'

Her tongue seemed stuck to the bottom of her mouth. 'Yes?'

'My name is Dr Eric Clarich,' the man standing above her said. 'You are at St Catherine's Hospital in Hamilton, New York. Do you remember what happened to you?'

Laura's line of vision zeroed in on the young doctor's unshaven face. His bloodshot, brown eyes looked down at her with a concern and maturity beyond his years. 'Fire,' she managed.

'Yes, there was a fire,' Eric said. 'You suffered a few minor burns, but you are going to be fine.'

Laura uttered one word: 'Judy?'

As the doctor lowered his eyes, Laura felt her stomach drop. Dread rushed through her entire body.

'She died,' he said. 'I'm very sorry. I was very fond of your aunt. She and I were good friends.'

Laura's head collapsed back. She looked straight into the air, her eyes blinking spasmodically. Aunt Judy was dead, killed in the fire. Laura tried to recall her last moments with her aunt, the desperate look in Judy's eyes as the blaze crept closer and closer. She remembered tripping over something, banging her head, reaching out to Judy, and then . . . blackness.

'How was I rescued?' she asked.

The doctor half smiled. 'That is a bit of a mystery. A man pulled both of you out of the fire. For Professor Simmons, unfortunately, it was too late.'

'But who was the man?'

'We don't know,' Eric answered. 'He called the emergency room and then vanished.'

'Vanished?'

'I found it rather strange myself.'

Laura tried to concentrate through the grief. The fire was no accident, she was sure of it. Someone had set the fire. Someone had knocked poor Judy unconscious and doused her study with some sort of flammable liquid. Someone had set the fire with the intention of killing Laura's aunt. But who?

David's murderer.

Laura's head nodded at the thought. David's murderer had done this. Somehow, Judy had learned the truth behind David's demise and had paid for it with her life. But why a fire, especially when a simple investigation would prove it was arson? Why not simply use a gun or a knife? Why go to the trouble of burning down Judy's house if you just wanted to keep her silent . . .?

Not the house. The study.

Laura felt a coldness wrap itself around her spine. The study. The fire had taken place in the study.

'I spoke to your father,' Eric Glarich said, interrupting her thoughts. 'He is on his way. He should be here in a couple more hours.'

'Thank you, Doctor. When can I get out of here?'

Eric smiled and picked up a clipboard. 'We'll talk about that a little later, okay? Why don't you get some rest now?'

Laura closed her eyes though she knew sleep would not come. She felt scared and so very alone—a helpless amateur against ruthless killers and arsonists. What chance did she have? None really. And what was she supposed to do next? Judy was dead, silenced before she had the chance to tell

Laura what was going on. What had Judy learned that had cost her her life? What had Judy wanted to tell Laura that . . .?

'. . . *to show you, Laura. Show you . . .*'

Her eyes suddenly flew open.

'. . . *show you, Laura . . .*'

'Dr Clarich?'

'. . . *Take it . . .*'

Eric stopped scribbling and looked up. 'Yes, Mrs Baskin?'

Her mouth felt very dry. 'My personal possessions.'

'They're in a plastic bag in your closet.'

The blaze had almost been upon them. Laura could still feel Judy press something into her hand, forcing her to pocket the items while the fire moved in around them. 'May I have it, please?'

Eric sighed heavily. 'You really should get some rest. The fire chief is going to want to talk to you later.'

'I will,' Laura promised. 'I just need my things for a moment.'

Eric spotted the desperation in her voice. 'Okay,' he agreed. 'But then I want you to rest.'

Laura nodded eagerly. She watched Dr Clarich step toward the closet. Seconds dragged.

What did you hand me, Aunt Judy? What was so important that imminent death became merely a distraction?

Eric opened the closet, bent down, and came up holding a red plastic bag marked Emergency Room. Laura tried to sit up, each movement of her body rubbing a burn the wrong way. She thought for a moment of how close she had come to being burned alive and wondered once again about the

426

mystery man who had saved her life.

Dr Clarich walked back over to the bed. 'Here you go. I'll leave you alone now.'

'Thank you, Doctor.'

He smiled gently and left the room. When the door shut, when Laura had been left completely alone, she opened the plastic bag and began to sift through its contents.

A clue, Aunt Judy. Did you save a clue from the treacherous fire?

The first thing that caught her eye was the Svengali label on her ripped and slightly scorched blouse. Part of the sleeve and back were burnt black, the cotton and silk threads seared beyond repair. She found the rest of her clothes, her wallet, her pocketbook, her shoes, her car keys. Then she came upon one of the two things Judy had handed her.

A set of keys.

Disappointment shot down Laura's hopes. Why would Judy hand her a set of keys? What significance could that have? There were four keys on the chain. One she recognized as Judy's house key. Two others were for the car. Laura had no idea what the fourth opened.

So why did Judy hand her a set of keys?

Maybe her aunt's mind had been confused at that stage. Maybe she was trying to find her way to the car to make her escape.

You're reaching, Laura.

Any better ideas?

She put the keys down and reached back into the red plastic bag. This time her hand located a thick piece of paper or maybe a thin piece of cardboard. It felt wrinkled and old. She gently lifted the paper/

427

cardboard and brought it into view.

It was a photograph.

Laura's eyes narrowed in confusion. The photograph was an old black and white one. Her mother had a lot of these kind but this one had obviously been handled many times over. Brown spots dotted the photograph with age. But Laura was not interested in the technical aspects of the picture. She was interested in its content.

The picture showed a happy couple staring lovingly into each other's eyes. The man's arms were wrapped passionately around the woman's waist. The woman was Judy. She could not have been more than twenty years old. How happy she looked, Laura thought, how her face glowed in a way Laura had never seen before. It was more than just the simple glow of youth. There was love here, real love.

Laura turned her attention to the man in the photograph. Her throat constricted. It took but a few seconds for her brain to register the impossible truth. When she recognized the man's face, when she was absolutely sure who the man was, she wanted so very much to scream.

The man in the photograph smiled playfully at young, pretty Judy Simmons. His hair was tousled, his face strong and handsome like . . .

. . . like his youngest son's.

Her head began to swim. David's father. David's father who committed suicide thirty years ago. Sinclair Baskin and Judy were holding each other in a passionate embrace.

The picture dropped from Laura's hand. Judy's last clue. With death just moments away, this photograph had been her aunt's last desperate

428

effort to tell Laura the truth of what had happened to David, of why he was killed.

But what did it mean?

* * *

'Hurry, damn it.'

'Hey, buddy, I'm already going too fast. You want to end up in the hospital too?'

James sat back. 'Sorry. It's just that—'

'I know, I know,' the taxi driver interrupted. 'Your daughter is in the hospital in Hamilton. I got kids too, you know. I understand what you're feeling.'

James tried taking a few deep breaths. 'How much longer?'

'Five minutes. Considering the weather, I'd say we're making great time. Airport to Hamilton in a half-hour. That could be a record.'

'Could you go just a little faster please?'

'No need,' the driver replied. 'We're here.'

James tossed the driver a fifty-dollar bill. 'Thanks.'

'Thank you, buddy. Hope your daughter's feeling better.'

He stepped out of the car and sprinted into the hospital. His heart raced. The record-breaking, thirty-minute drive from the airport to St Catherine's had felt like weeks.

Laura is okay, he reminded himself. You heard the doctor. Just a few burns and some smoke inhalation. Nothing a little rest won't fix.

And James would make sure she rested. Oh yes, he would stand guard over her twenty-fours a day if necessary, but he would not let anyone ever hurt his baby again. No one. Not ever.

He stormed through the doors. Hospitals were familiar territory to him. He quickly found the on-duty receptionist and asked for his daughter's room.

'Down the hall and to the right,' the receptionist replied. 'Room 117. I believe Dr Clarich is in there now.'

James sped down the corridor. He circled right, his legs propelling him with surprising velocity—and then he stopped cold. His heart jerked to one side.

Oh no.

Down at the end of the hallway, just a few feet in front of Laura's hospital room, his wife sat crumpled into a plastic chair. Mary looked so small, so fragile. Her face was pale and harried.

'Mary?'

Her head swiveled slowly toward the familiar voice. 'Oh, James.'

How did you get here so fast, Mary? How . . .

She stood and ran toward her husband on wobbly legs, but James moved forward hesitantly, almost afraid to go near her.

She was here the whole time. She was at Colgate.

'I . . . I called the answering machine and heard your message,' she explained weakly. 'I got up here as soon as I could.'

In less than three hours? Talk about breaking speed records.

'Where is the doctor?' James asked, trying like hell to sound like his usual cool, controlled self.

'He's in with Laura. He said she's doing just fine.' Mary started to cry. 'Oh James, say it isn't true. Not Judy. She can't be dead. She just can't be.'

James took her in his arms and held her closely. His eyes closed and a transformation took place within him. This, after all, was what it was all about. He loved her. God forgive him, he loved her so damn much. She had sinned and done some horrible things, things most husbands would never forgive. But try as he might, James could not help but love her more every day. She was so seemingly innocent, so helpless and beautiful. He had to protect her . . .

. . . no matter what she may have done in the past.

'It's okay, my love,' James whispered, his eyes still tightly shut. 'I'm here now. Everything is going to be okay.'

The tender moment, perhaps the last Mary and James would ever share together, came to a sudden halt when the door of room 117 opened. James released his wife and automatically fixed his professional mask back onto his face. He turned toward Dr Eric Clarich.

'Dr Clarich?'

'Dr Ayars?' Eric asked. They shook hands. 'Glad you both are here.'

'Is she all right?' James asked. 'Can we see her?'

'She's doing just fine,' Dr Clarich assured him. 'She'll be out of here in no more than a day or two.'

'That's wonderful,' Mary said.

'She is a bit shaken up. It was quite a harrowing ordeal.'

'Can you tell us what happened, Doctor?'

Eric led them over to a waiting area where they all sat down. 'Apparently, your daughter walked in on a fire at Professor Simmons's home. According to Laura, she opened the study door and found

431

Professor Simmons on the floor. She tried to rescue her aunt and in doing so she nearly got herself killed. You see, Laura got trapped in the study. She tried to pull Professor Simmons out but the smoke was too much. Laura passed out.'

Mary looked at the doctor in horror. 'Passed out? Then how did she . . .?'

'Get out alive?' Eric finished for her. 'A bit of a mystery, I suppose. A man who has since chosen to remain anonymous pulled your daughter out of the fire. If not, she would undoubtedly have died in your sister's study.'

'Can we see her?' James asked again.

'She's napping right now. She should be awake in a few hours.'

'We'll wait,' James said, taking his wife's shaking hand into his own. 'Are you okay, Mary?'

She nodded.

'I contacted Gloria,' James continued. 'She and Stan are on their way up.'

Another nod.

James turned his attention back toward his fellow physician. 'Do they know what caused the fire?'

'Not for sure,' Eric replied, 'but they suspect arson.'

Dr Eric Clarich watched as whatever little color had been left in their faces vanished with his words.

*   *   *

Later that night, there was a soft knock on Laura's door.

'Come in.'

The door swung open and a head of blond hair

peeked around the corner. 'Hi.'

'Gloria!' Laura said as a smile jumped to her lips. 'I'm so glad you're here.'

Another female voice came from behind the door. 'What about little ol' me?'

'Serita,' Laura chuckled. 'How the hell did you two get here so fast?'

Gloria and Serita came in, the door closing behind them. They kissed Laura and sat on the corners of her bed. 'You will never guess in a million years,' Serita replied.

'Huh?'

'Stan drove us,' Gloria explained.

'And Laura, he was a perfect gentleman.'

'Where is he now?' Laura asked.

'Go on, Gloria. You tell her.'

'He left,' Gloria explained. 'He told us that he said some really stupid things to you the other night and that he couldn't face you yet.'

Laura looked puzzled. 'He told you that?'

Both women nodded.

'And now he's heading back to Boston?'

'That's right, honey. Can you believe it? The guy played chauffeur for the last six hours and now he's shlepping all the way back.'

'He was very drunk the other night, Laura,' Gloria added. 'He really feels terrible about it.'

Laura did not know what to say. 'Forget it.'

'So how you feeling, champ?' Serita asked.

'Not bad.'

Gloria wrung her hands. 'I can't believe this. Aunt Judy dead. It's so horrible. Mom and Dad are in shock.'

'I know,' Laura said. 'They were in here a little while ago.'

'Such a terrible accident,' Serita added.

'No accident.'

Laura's sister and best friend stared at her. 'What did you say?'

'It was no accident,' Laura repeated. 'Aunt Judy was murdered.'

'Are you sure?' Serita asked.

'Arson. The house was doused with kerosene and Judy had been knocked unconscious.'

'But who would do such a thing?'

Laura knew it was unsafe to involve anyone else in this, but her feelings of loneliness and despair made her reach out. She had to confide in someone. 'You have to promise me you won't say a word about this to anyone. Not one word. It could be a matter of life and death.'

'Not a word,' Serita replied while Gloria nodded her head in agreement.

'I don't know who killed Aunt Judy, but take a look at this.'

Laura reached into her bag and pulled out the old black-and-white photograph. She handed it to Gloria, who looked at it and then passed it on to Serita.

'I don't get it,' Gloria said. 'It's an old picture of Aunt Judy, but who's the guy?'

'Any guesses, Serita?'

'He looks familiar . . .'

'Like David . . . or maybe Stan?'

'A little, I guess.'

'What are you getting at?' Gloria asked.

'The man in the photograph is Sinclair Baskin. Stan and David's father.'

Gloria gasped. She remembered Stan's words about his father's death and she began to shake.

'I don't get it,' Serita said. 'What does this have to do with Judy's death?'

'I don't know yet. But take a look at them. This is no casual pose.'

'No,' Serita agreed, 'they definitely seem fond of one another.'

'And take a look at that banner in the background. Brinlen College 1960. That's where Sinclair Baskin taught. And 1960—that's the year he died.'

Serita continued to stare at the picture. 'I still don't get it. So your aunt might have had an affair with David's father before he died in 1960. What does that have to do with the fire today?'

'I haven't figured out the connection yet, but I know one exists. I have to go to Chicago and find it.'

'Chicago? Why Chicago?'

'Brinlen College is in Chicago. My mother and Aunt Judy were raised there.'

Gloria finally spoke, her words coming from a fog. 'We used to live there, Laura, before you were born.'

'I know. There has to be a connection somehow. There has to be a link between Judy's murder and Sinclair Baskin's suicide.'

Gloria nearly screamed. She put her hand in her mouth, her teeth biting down hard upon her tender skin. A small shriek made its way past her lips.

'What is it, Gloria? What's the matter?'

Gloria took her hand away. She remembered what Stan had told her just a few nights ago, just after she had woken from her nightmare. Her eyes bounced about the room as though looking for a place to hide. 'I . . . I can't say.'

Laura sat up and grabbed her sister's shoulders. 'This is important, Gloria. Whoever killed Judy may have killed David too.'

'Wha . . .? Killed David? But he drowned.'

'Maybe. Maybe not. Tell me what you know.'

'But I promised.'

'Promised who?'

'Stan. I promised him I wouldn't say anything.'

'You have to tell me, Gloria. You could be in danger. Stan could be in danger.'

'I don't know . . .'

Laura began to shake her. 'Tell me. Tell me.'

Serita stepped in and disengaged the two sisters. 'Just relax a second, Laura.'

Laura let go and lay back down. 'I can't relax. The killer is still out there.'

'You're not making any sense, girl. Pictures from thirty years ago. Murderers running around. A suicide that's thirty years old—'

'Not a suicide!' Gloria shouted.

Laura and Serita spun toward Gloria's voice. She was huddled in a corner, her whole body quivering and quaking as though she were caught in the grip of a fever. 'He didn't commit suicide,' Gloria said.

Laura could not believe what she was hearing. 'What are you talking about? Of course he committed suicide.'

Gloria shook her head violently. 'He was murdered. Sinclair Baskin was murdered.'

'What?'

'Stan was hiding behind the couch in his father's office. He was only ten years old but he saw the whole thing. Somebody murdered Sinclair Baskin.'

'But . . .?' Laura's mouth fell open. She stared dumbstruck. 'My God,' she finally managed. 'Does

Stan know who did it?'

'No. He didn't recognize the killer. But he remembers the face . . .'

Laura fell back on the bed. Another piece of the puzzle had been handed to her and, once again, that piece did not seem to fit. Murdered. Sinclair Baskin. David. Judy. Something had happened thirty years ago, something horrible and evil, something that did not end with the passing of a decade or two. Judy's haunting words came back to her, tearing at her heart with sharpened claws.

'. . . *There are things that you know nothing about. Things that happened many years ago . . . sometimes the past can overlap with the present. That was what happened with David . . .*'

'Serita?'

'Yeah?'

There was only one way to find the answer to what happened so many years ago, to what happened to David. 'Would you do me a favor?'

'Sure.'

'Don't tell my folks or the doctor.'

'I won't.'

'Can you get me a plane ticket to Chicago?'

CHAPTER TWENTY-SIX

Mark burst through the door. His breathing was uneven, his chest hitching from the mere effort.

'What the hell happened to you?' T.C. asked. 'You're a goddamn mess.'

'Get me something to drink. A vodka, anything.'

'You don't drink.'

437

He collapsed into a chair. 'I do now.'

T.C. grabbed two cans of Budweiser and tossed one to Mark. 'It's the best I can do. Jesus, Mark, your clothes are burned.'

Mark ripped open the can of beer and chugged half of it.

'You want to tell me what happened?'

Mark stood, the can of beer nearly crushed by his grip. His words came fast, his pitch unsteady. 'I got to Judy Simmons's house at seven o'clock just like she said. I parked my car someplace off campus and walked about a mile before I spotted Judy's house. Then . . .'

'Then?'

He swallowed. 'A taxi pulled up in front of the house. Laura got out of it.'

'Oh shit.'

'I ducked behind a tree. It didn't take a genius to figure out what Judy was up to. She must have figured—'

'—that if she put you and Laura together,' T.C. finished, 'the sparks would really fly.'

Mark chuckled sadly.

'What's so funny?' T.C. asked.

'Nothing is funny,' Mark answered. 'Just ironic.'

'Huh?'

'You'll see. Anyway, I'm hiding behind this tree, watching Laura . . .' He stopped talking, his mind drifting back to the memory. Laura. His eyes had crawled over every inch of her with a yearning so great he was sure he would die. Just seeing her again, staring at her lovely face turned red from the cold, watching her walk up the path, made his stomach ache with a sense of loss.

'Mark?'

'Sorry,' he said softly. He took a deep breath and continued. 'Laura knocked on the door and waited. No one answered. She called Judy's name. Still nothing. So she tried the lock and opened the door. She went into the house.'

'What did you do?'

Mark looked away. 'I just stood there frozen in place. I don't know why. I should have just turned and left. But I couldn't. I stared and stared—daydreaming, I guess—until I saw smoke.'

'Smoke?'

'A fire broke out.'

'What?'

Mark nodded as if to reconfirm his own words. 'The smoke started to billow out of the cracks in doors and windows. It couldn't have happened more than five minutes after Laura entered.'

'What did you do?'

'I ran into the house. What a goddamn mess. It was unbelievable. Flames were crawling up the walls.'

'Jesus.'

'All I could think about was Laura. Laura is trapped somewhere in here, my mind kept repeating like a parakeet, trapped in the middle of this deadly blaze. Nothing else mattered. It was weird. The fire became nothing more than a diversion to me. I scrambled around desperately, hoping against hope that Laura was still alive.'

'Don't tell me—'

Mark shook his head. 'I found her and pulled her out. The fire hadn't reached her yet. She was unconscious so I called 911 and stayed with her until I heard the sirens. I spoke to the hospital a little while later. She'll be okay.'

'Thank God.'

Mark swallowed hard. When he had lifted Laura, when he had taken her in his arms, he wanted so much to never let go, to protect her, to tell her everything was going to be okay. Tears found their way into his eyes before he forced them back down. 'The same,' Mark continued slowly, 'cannot be said about Judy. She's dead, T.C.'

T.C. shook his head. 'I'm sorry, Mark. I know she meant a lot to you.'

'Fires don't burn that fast, do they, T.C.? Somebody set that fire deliberately. Somebody murdered Judy Simmons.'

'You can't be sure of that.'

'I want to find that somebody, T.C. I want to nail that son of a bitch to the wall.'

'Or daughter of a bitch.'

'Huh?'

'Think about it a second. Who would want to silence Judy?'

'You're not suggesting . . .'

T.C. shrugged. 'Do you remember what Judy said to you on the phone?'

Mark thought for a moment. 'She wasn't making much sense. She said something about not knowing what I was doing, about not knowing the whole story.'

T.C. shrugged. 'Maybe,' he concluded, 'we don't.'

*   *   *

'Mrs Klenke will be with you in a moment.'

'Thank you,' Laura said. She readjusted herself in the seat. The pain from the burns was greater than she had anticipated. Every move felt like

440

sandpaper rubbing against a fresh wound. In the hospital they had given her painkillers. She had no idea how potent they were. Laura had managed to secure some codeine from a drugstore, but it was far from an adequate substitute.

Laura looked at her watch. It took her a good portion of the night convincing Serita and Gloria to help her get to Chicago. They agreed reluctantly in the end, probably because they were afraid she would try to get there no matter what they did.

They were probably right.

T.C., the crafty son of a bitch, would be proud of her in an odd sort of way. She had spent most of the morning in her hospital bed playing detective. She called Brinlen College, got in touch with various professors and staff members, and asked about Sinclair Baskin. No one knew very much about him. Very few professors were left from 1960.

But one call paid off.

'Have you spoken to Mrs Klenke?' an older professor had asked her.

'No. Who is she?'

'Well, back then she was Miss Engle. She was Sinclair Baskin's personal secretary and if rumor had it correctly, the word to be emphasized is personal. Get my meaning?'

The college office still had her name and phone number on file. Laura called up and persuaded Mrs Diana Klenke to see her. Now, just a few hours later, Laura was sitting in the woman's den.

'Mrs Baskin?'

Laura turned toward Mrs Klenke's voice. She had learned that Diana Klenke had been twenty-seven years old in 1960. That made her fifty-seven now, but she was still something to

441

behold. Her hair had gone gray but her bone structure and smile made her more than just dazzling. She was very tall and lithe, elegantly dressed in a black Svengali suit. Her every move was graceful and subdued.

'Call me Laura.'

'Only if you'll call me Diana.'

'Okay, Diana.'

Diana Klenke's smile turned gentle as she looked at the younger woman in front of her. 'My goodness, you're stunning. Pictures do not do you justice, Laura.'

'Thank you,' she replied. Laura wanted very much to return the compliment but whenever she had in the past, people thought she sounded phony and somewhat patronizing.

'Would you like something to drink?'

'No, thank you.'

'Anything at all?'

'Thank you, no.'

Diana Klenke sat on the plush chair next to Laura. The room was beautiful and immaculately kept by what had to be a large staff of servants. The Victorian mansion must have held twenty-five rooms, each done in a style that would have made the Palace of Versailles envious. 'How was your trip?'

'Fine,' Laura replied. 'You have a beautiful home, Diana.'

Diana Klenke smiled as she nodded. 'My husband loved this house. It was his pride and joy. He died ten years ago. Killed in a car crash on his way home from the airport. As you might have guessed, he was a very wealthy man and now,' she paused, laughing lightly, 'I am a very wealthy widow.'

'I'm sorry.'

'Don't be. We were never all that close. Besides, I have the older-man market cornered. They all want my money.'

'I'm sure that's not true.'

She shrugged. 'No matter. What can I do for you, Laura? You mentioned on the phone something about Sinclair?'

'Yes.'

'I read about your husband's tragic death. So damn sad. He was so young. Sometimes I think there must be a curse on the Baskin men.'

'It seems so,' Laura agreed.

'So what can I help you with?'

Laura's leg shook. It would do no good to try and stop it. The leg would only start up again. She leaned forward. Pain shot through the burns on her back as she reached into her purse. 'Will you take a look at this photograph?'

Diana Klenke took out a pair of reading glasses. Somehow, they added to her looks, making her appear even more stately and beautiful. Sinclair Baskin's former secretary took the photograph in her hand and studied it for nearly a minute without saying a word. 'That's Sinclair all right. The woman's name is Judy . . .'

'Judy Simmons?' Laura offered.

'Yes, that's the name. I remember that one very well.'

'That one?'

Diana nodded. 'Sinclair Baskin was a full-fledged womanizer, Laura.'

'He had affairs?'

She laughed. 'Dozens. Blondes, brunettes,

443

redheads—it made no difference as long as they were beautiful. He changed them in a blur. One day, this one. The next day, another. You see, Sinclair Baskin was a handsome, smooth-talking man. He fooled around with co-eds, with school colleagues, with married women. I remember when he slept with the department chairman's wife.' She stopped, smiled. 'He even fooled around with his own secretary.'

Laura was not exactly sure how to continue. 'You say there were dozens of other women?'

'At least.'

'Do you remember most of them?'

She shook her head. 'Hardly any.'

'But you said you remembered Judy Simmons.'

'Yes.'

'Why?'

'Because she was something special. For one thing, she was not his type.'

'Why not?'

'Just look at her photograph. Don't get me wrong. Judy was pretty. But Sinclair did not go after girls who were merely attractive. He wanted gorgeous. After all, he was looking for some extra-marital thrills. He already had a wife. Looks were all he cared about.'

'I see.'

'I mean, it would be normal for him to try to bed her once maybe, but not more than that.'

'And that's why you remember her?'

Diana Klenke shook her head. 'That's only part of it. The main reason I remember her so well is that she lasted. They were together for more than two months. It was the first time I had ever seen Sinclair care about a woman—myself included.

He was as close to helplessly in love as a man like Sinclair Baskin becomes. He even considered divorcing his wife so that he could marry Judy. Thoughts of other women disappeared from his mind. It was all highly irregular for him.'

'So what happened?'

'Happened?'

'What went wrong?'

Diana stood. She walked over to the window and drew back the curtain. The backyard was as magnificent as the house. There were statues, gardens and fountains. Laura could see a swimming pool, a tennis court and a gazebo. Diana stared out, inhaling deeply as if the sight alone would make the air fresher and better to breathe. 'Sinclair broke it off.'

'Just like that?' Laura asked. 'He was madly in love with her and he just let her go.'

Diana nodded, her eyes still looking out the window. Outside, a branch cast a thin shadow over her face. 'One day it was love. The next . . . it was over.'

'Was that normal? I mean, did Sinclair Baskin do that sort of thing a lot?'

'Like I said before, Judy Simmons was an unusual case. I was surprised . . . at first.'

'But why did he break it off? His family? His kids?'

She still did not face Laura. 'Not because of his family and not because of his kids.'

'Then what?'

A tight smile slowly came to Diana Klenke's lips. 'My husband loved this yard, Laura. When the weather was nice, he would come home from work early and just putter in the garden. Enjoying

445

the fruits of his labors, he would say. He found gardening to be very therapeutic. Me, I hate gardening. But I do love the results, don't you?'

Laura nodded. 'It's beautiful.'

'I'm sorry. You were asking me about Sinclair and Judy.'

'Yes,' Laura said. 'What ended their romance?'

Diana closed her eyes for a moment. When she opened them again, she slowly turned away from the window, her gray eyes locking on to Laura. 'His weakness. His weakness destroyed his relationship with Judy.'

'His weakness?'

'Beauty, Laura. Beauty came back and blinded him again.'

'You mean he found somebody else?'

Her smile chilled Laura. 'Not just somebody else. Like I said before, Judy Simmons was attractive enough, but his last girl . . .'

'Yes?'

'She was incredible to look at, a woman sculpted by the gods. Her kind of beauty could twist a man's mind, Laura. A man's soul. And this woman did just that. Her beauty tore at Sinclair until the pain became unbearable. My God, she was gorgeous, nearly as gorgeous as—'

Diana's words stopped so suddenly that Laura jumped. The color ebbed away from her face.

'What is it?' Laura cried. 'What's the matter? Diana?'

The older woman's whole body trembled, her eyes wide and out of focus. 'Mother of God.'

'What? What is it?'

'. . . as gorgeous,' Diana said slowly, 'as gorgeous as *you*.'

Laura's eyes narrowed into thin slits. 'I don't understand.'

'The woman who stole him away . . . she looked just like you, Laura. You're the spitting image of her.'

Laura's face froze in confusion. A stray thought, an awful, unforgivable thought, stabbed at her chest with a pointed edge. It couldn't be. It just couldn't be. 'She looked like me?'

Diana nodded.

Without thought Laura reached into her purse. Her mind and body were numb. She took out her wallet and thumbed through it. With trembling fingers she plucked out a photograph. 'I know it's been thirty years,' she began in a voice that had no tone, 'but could this be the woman?'

She passed the picture to Diana Klenke, who once again slipped her reading glasses onto her face. She stared at the picture for a very long time. 'Yes, that's the woman.'

'How can you be sure? It's been—'

'I'm sure,' Diana interrupted. 'You don't forget a woman like that.'

Laura snatched the picture back, almost defensive now. She held the picture against her chest as if it were more than just an image on paper. After a few moments, her hand pulled the picture back, her gaze studying the woman in the photograph as if for the first time.

Her mother.

'Mary,' Diana said suddenly. 'Her name was Mary.'

Laura felt drained, helpless, like a shaken prize fighter who was not sure where the next punch was coming from.

'And one other thing,' Diana added.

'Yes?' Laura managed.

'That woman was the last person to leave Sinclair's office before his suicide.'

*   *   *

Graham knew he would have to make the call. There was no real reason to put it off. Besides, he had no idea what had happened in room 607 when David went up there. Baskin may have just been on the receiving end of a chewing-out from his mother-in-law. Wouldn't be the first time a mother-in-law butted in to where she didn't belong. Graham's, for example, was a full-time nag. She probably wouldn't fly across the Pacific just to nag him, but Graham wouldn't put it past her either.

He picked up the phone and dialed Laura's number. Graham was a pure procrastinator, been that way since he was a kid. He liked to put things off, especially delivering bad news. He wasn't lazy, mind you, and yes he knew he would have to do it eventually, but if he put it off, maybe it would just disappear altogether or the world would blow up or reality would change. That was why Graham felt relieved when he heard the answering machine pick up.

He left a message asking Laura to call him and then took another swig of whiskey.

*   *   *

Richard Corsel loved to watch ice hockey. Players would gently glide across a floor of glacial grandeur, lost in the bliss of free-skating, only to be on the

448

receiving end of a bone-crunching wallop from some gargoyle with more facial scars than Michael Jackson in bright sunlight.

What a game.

Naomi was not so crazy about the sport, nor was she particularly happy about the way the twins had taken to their father's passion. 'You might as well have gotten them into professional wrestling,' she had scolded him.

'Come on, honey, it's not that bad.'

'I don't want my boys playing hockey, do you hear me?'

But Richard was not worried. After all, he had never played ice hockey. In fact he didn't even know how to ice-skate. But the game was the perfect spectator sport. Richard became so involved in the banging and hitting and, yes, the artistry of the battle that thoughts of the bank and the bills and his own mortgage disappeared.

TV 38 was his station. They carried the Boston Bruins games, though that expensive cable station was starting to eat up a lot of the hockey schedule. He would probably have to break down and order SportsChannel soon, but he hated the idea of paying to watch hockey on television. There was something blasphemous about it.

So Richard turned on the television and settled back in his old recliner. Roger and Peter were on the carpet in front of him, alternating between watching the game and imitating the action. The Bruins were leading the Oilers by a score of 7–5. It should have been a moment of pure diversion for Richard, a moment when his mind was completely at ease. Instead he was plagued by a small blurb he had read in the newspaper. He tried to clear his mind, tried to think of his wife and children.

His thoughts came drifting back to Laura—Laura and that fire at Colgate College.

Of course there was no evidence in the newspaper that the fire had anything to do with the missing money. There was nothing in the article to suggest that the psychopath who placed a knife against Richard's throat had decided to torch Laura and her aunt. None whatsoever. The article merely stated that the fire was being 'investigated'. That was hardly reason to start jumping to conclusions and pointing fingers.

'Goal!' the announcer yelled.

'Goal!' Peter and Roger mimicked in unison.

The Bruins had increased their lead to 8–5. Pete and Rog stood up and celebrated. 'Wasn't that an incredible shot, Dad?'

'Great shot, Pete.'

'Are you going to take us to a game again this year? How about when they play the Rangers?'

'I'll try my best.'

The children went back to their hooting and howling while Richard's mind remained anchored to Laura Baskin. Suppose for a second that the fire was not an accident. Suppose it was connected with David Baskin's missing money. The voice of Laura's father, who had visited him yesterday, floated across his mind:

'I suspect that there might be something more to this money transfer than meets the eye. There could be something else at stake here, something very dangerous, something that could hurt my daughter.'

He wished he could just turn his back on the whole thing, but that was no longer an option his conscience would allow. Why had he let Phillipe

Gaillaird at the Bank of Geneva tell him who had the money? And why had he listened to him?

Curiosity not only killed the cat, Richie, it kept him awake nights.

If Richard had never heard the damn name, then he would be free to sleep, eat and even watch the Bruins with a clear conscience. Now a decision had to be made. Should he keep his mouth quiet? Or should he tell Laura the name? When Phillipe first told Richard who had the money, the name meant nothing to him. A few weeks later, that changed. Boy, did that change. Now he knew the name too well. It had become a household word in Boston. And frankly, the whole situation had become more than just dangerous. It had become downright eerie.

Richard felt a frosty breeze slide through the room, as if it were he who was standing on the ice rather than the hockey players. What to do? What the hell to do? Should he keep his mouth shut, or should he tell Laura the shocking truth, a truth even Richard had trouble believing? Should he just mind his own business, or should he tell her that the man who had stolen David's money had also stolen his position, his scoring average and his nickname, that the man who had stolen David's money was none other than the Celtics' newest scoring sensation?

Mark Seidman.

*   *   *

Serita steered Laura into the elevator. Neither spoke. For that matter, Laura had barely opened her mouth since Serita picked her up at the airport.

Serita had seen Laura in every kind of mood—joyous, sad, wacky, conservative, serious, goofy, love-struck, angry—but never had she seen her friend like this. Laura's pupils were dilated, her eyes glassy and dull. She stared out dumbstruck at a world that had suddenly decided to ravage her mind, only asking one question the whole ride home:

'Has Estelle called you?'

'Your secretary?' Serita had replied. 'Why would she call me?'

'Before Judy died,' Laura explained with no emotion in her voice, 'she handed me that photograph I showed you and four keys. I know what three of them open. Estelle is up at Colgate right now trying to learn something about the fourth. I told her to call you if she hears anything.'

'Sorry. She didn't call.'

For the remainder of the ride, the only sound came from the car radio.

The elevator stopped at the eighteenth floor, depositing its two beautiful passengers in the corridor. Serita took Laura's key and guided her into the darkened apartment. The only illumination came from a small flashing red light indicating that a message had been left on Laura's answering machine. Serita flicked on a light switch while Laura collapsed onto the couch.

'Are you feeling okay?' Serita asked. 'You sure you don't want to go to a hospital?'

'I feel fine.'

'Yeah, I can see that. You grimaced the whole ride home. Every time I hit a bump I thought you were going to scream.'

'Never felt better.'

452

'Uh, huh. So do you want to stop bullshitting me and tell me what happened in Chicago?'

'It's too fantastic. You won't believe it.'

'I'm all ears. What did you learn? Did your aunt and David's father have the hots for one another?'

'Seems so.'

'While he was still married?'

'Yep.'

'Tsk, tsk.' Serita rubbed her hands. 'Go on, girl. You know I love good gossip.'

While Laura was well aware of Serita's love for gossip, she was also well aware that Serita would give up her life before she would ever betray Laura's trust. 'It gets worse,' Laura continued. 'They were serious—so serious that Sinclair Baskin considered divorcing his wife.'

'Juicy with a capital J,' Serita shot back. 'Do tell, Laura. What happened to this happy couple?'

'He dumped her for another woman.'

'Ah, damn him,' Serita said with a disappointed shake of her head. 'Men are such shits sometimes.'

'The other woman,' Laura continued, 'was my mother.'

Serita's mouth dropped to her knees. 'You're shitting me.'

'Nope.'

'Your mother stole a guy from her sister?'

'And cheated on my father at the same time. Nice, huh?'

'Holy shit,' Serita said. 'But what does it all mean, Laura? What does it have to do with the fire?'

Laura stood, her shoulders shrugging in helpless wonder. She walked over to her answering machine and pressed the rewind button. The tape sped backwards with a scratching noise that sounded like a Cuisinart. 'I still have no idea. The more I learn about the past the less I see the connection to the present.'

The tape came to a halt. 'So what do we do now, Laura?'

A loud beep interrupted their conversation. Graham's gruff voice blared through the speaker. 'This is Graham. When you have a chance, luv, give us a call, will ya? I may have found out who David visited at the Pacific International. I'll be at my home number all night.'

His voice . . . so sad, so defeated. Why? What had Graham learned? Laura checked her watch and lifted the phone. 'Now,' she answered Serita, 'we call Australia.'

*   *   *

Stan woke up from his nap with a jump. Another bad dream had plagued his sleep, another nightmare filled with wicked spirits that vanished from sight and memory once Stan opened his eyes and truly awoke. Then only the pounding of his heart, the shortness of his breath, and the frightening aftertaste in his mouth reminded Stan that once again his slumber had been beset by the evil demons of his past.

He threw on a robe and headed toward the kitchen. Tonight was the big meeting. Tonight Stan would see his father's killer for only the third time. The first time had been when he was ten years old. The second, when he was at the Boston Garden. And now the third, to receive his first payment. One hundred thousand dollars. It was a staggering amount of money and would go a long way to giving him . . .

Giving him what?

Stan stopped at the bottom of the stairs and looked at Gloria. She was unloading the dishwasher, just putting away some dishes, but Stan remained hushed and watched. The delicate curves of her body under the silk blouse, her soft gentle smile, the concentration in her eyes as she set about her simple task . . . it just made him stop and think. What did he need all that money for? He had stopped gambling. He was bright. He could get a job now, a real job, and stop running away for good. When Stan stopped and looked at Gloria, he thought he could do all those things.

But when she was not around him, when he was alone, he could still feel what B Man had called 'the itch.' He knew then that this talk about settling down was nothing but a pipe-dream, that he was never meant to live that kind of domestic life. And besides, who needed it? Who wanted it? Gloria was after all just a woman, another scheming, deceitful bitch who would disappoint him eventually. She may be a little more subtle than most, and her venom may be gentler, but make no mistake: Gloria was a woman like any other.

The one hundred grand was his protection money. When he finished feeding off Gloria he would have a nice little nest egg to carry him until he found his next mark. He would be on his way. He would be free.

But when Stan's eyes gazed upon Gloria, as they were doing right now, his suspicions broke apart and disintegrated before her warm beauty. He no longer merely lusted after her; he longed for her, to hold her, to comfort her, and yes to make mad, passionate love to her. Something about their relationship was . . . complete. Yes, complete. It was the only word that he could come up with to describe how he felt. What was this strange power Gloria held over him? And where would it lead?

She turned and saw him standing in the doorway. Her face lit up. God, he loved the way her face brightened whenever she saw him. 'Hi,' she said.

He returned the smile. 'Hi.'

'Have you been standing there long?'

'A couple of minutes. I just wanted to watch you.'

Her cheeks turned red. 'Did you have a nice nap?'

'Very nice.'

'You must be starving. Do you want some dinner?'

'No, thanks. Are you feeling any better now?'

'A little,' she said. 'I still can't believe Judy is dead.'

He took her in his arms. 'I know. It'll be a while before it sinks in.' His eyes found the clock behind her head. Seven thirty p.m. In one hour, he would meet his father's killer in an alleyway in south Boston. There, Stan Baskin would allow his fatherless childhood to be bought off for a few lousy dollars. One hundred thousand—Stan's going price on a father's memory.

She looked at him with great concern. 'Stan, are you okay?'

He held her tighter. 'I'm fine,' he said. 'I'm just fine.'

*　　　*　　　*

456

Serita studied Laura's face. Her skin was pulled tight around her high cheekbones, her eyes a mix of concentration and bewilderment. Laura was the most beautiful woman Serita had ever known. There was something positively hypnotic about it. There were times it unnerved and frightened Serita. Beauty like that could be dangerous. Beauty like that could be fatal. 'Do you want me to leave the room?'

Laura located Graham's number and began dialing. 'I'd prefer if you stay, but if you want to get out while you still have the chance I'll understand.'

Serita remained in her seat. 'I'm here for as long as you need me.'

Laura's shaking fingers were barely able to dial. 'You're a good friend.'

'The best,' Serita shot back with a smile. 'So tell me about this sheriff. Is he cute?'

Laura chuckled, appreciating the distraction. 'In a grizzly bear sort of way. He's a real mountain man.'

'I could use some of that, honey. Earl with all his smooth sophistication is starting to get to me.'

The call connected through. Laura heard the first ring. 'You love him, you know.'

Serita opened her mouth to protest. Then she closed it. 'Yeah, I know.'

Third ring. Laura's leg began to shake. Her hand gripped the receiver. 'About time you admitted it.'

Fourth ring. Serita smiled. 'I don't want to get corny on you, Laura, but whatever happens I want you to know that you're the best friend I ever had.'

Fifth ring. 'Same here.'

Finally, the ringing stopped. The receiver was lifted and a gruff voice barked, 'Hello?'

'Graham?'

'Laura, I'm glad you called.'

'I just got your message. I was away for a couple of days.'

'Anything wrong?' the big man asked.

'Plenty,' she replied. 'This thing keeps getting weirder and weirder.'

'Why? What happened?'

'My aunt called me the day before yesterday,' Laura began. 'She said she had to tell me something about David's death. The drowning had something to do with the past, she said. I don't know. She wasn't making complete sense. She wanted to tell me about it in person.'

'So did you see her? What did she say?'

'Nothing. When I arrived, someone had set fire to her house. My aunt died in the blaze.'

'Sweet Lord. That's awful.'

'I want to know what is going on before someone else gets hurt, Graham. Maybe I should just forget about it for the sake of everyone's safety, but I can't. David is dead and I want—I need—to know what happened to him.'

'I understand. He must have been a very special guy.'

Laura felt tears slide down her cheeks, tears for David and now for Judy as well. 'He was,' Laura said, 'very special.'

There was a moment of silence. 'Yeah, well, Gina Cassler finally got her hands on the passport cards.'

'And you've gone through them?'

Graham paused. 'Yes.'

'Was T.C. there?'

'No,' Graham replied slowly. 'Frankly, Laura,

none of this makes any sense.'

Laura nervously twisted the phone cord around her hand. 'Maybe David's mystery visit can clear this all up. Maybe the person who saw David at the Pacific International can explain what happened.'

'Maybe,' Graham muttered.

'Graham?'

He did not answer right away. 'Yes?'

'Who did David see at the hotel?'

'Your mother, Laura. Before he died, David visited your mother.'

The phone dropped from her hand.

Serita leaped out of her chair. 'Laura? Honey, what is it?'

Laura's eyes narrowed in concentration.

'What's the matter? What did he say?'

Now Laura knew that there was only one way to get to the bottom of this once and for all. Her line of vision swung toward Serita and locked onto her face.

'I have to talk to my mother,' she said. 'I have to talk to her right now.'

CHAPTER TWENTY-SEVEN

Time for Death Number Four.

The killer glanced at the clock on the car dashboard. There was still half an hour to kill before the meeting with Stan Baskin, the last meeting Stan would ever have with anyone. Stan was about to die. Stan was about to join his father, his sibling, Judy Simmons . . .

. . . and David? What about David?

I don't know anymore, the killer thought. *I just don't know.*

The gun sat in the glove compartment. It had been a long time since the killer had fired a gun, not since the barrel had been pressed against Sinclair Baskin's skull. The killer had watched while Sinclair's head exploded into small pieces. Blood splashed. Fragments of bone and tissue flew in every direction.

It had all been so simple. With one pull of the trigger Sinclair Baskin had been reduced from a human being with emotions and hopes and dreams to a worthless pile of decaying flesh.

So simple.

And it would not be too different with Stan Baskin. He was truly his father's son. Blackmailing a murderer. And not just any murderer but the murderer of his own father. Only a low-life would conjure up such an idea. Imagine: Stan Baskin wanted to turn his father's murder into a profit-making venture. What kind of depraved creature could do such a thing?

It boggled the mind.

The killer parked the car two blocks away from the alleyway. Time check: 8:10 p.m. Perfect. Twenty minutes to check out the surrounding area. What was the killer going to look for? No idea really. It just seemed the right thing to do; that is, to make oneself familiar with the murder scene before committing the foul deed. Just in case. This way, if something was wrong or had been overlooked, perhaps it would become obvious. Better safe than sorry.

The glove compartment fell open. A hand reached in and closed around the gun. It felt oddly comforting to handle such a powerful weapon—especially in this neighborhood. South Boston was the perfect place to commit a murder. The sound of a gunshot is more common to the inhabitants of this neighborhood than a school bell.

Would this be the last murder? Unfortunately not.

Not again. Please, not again . . .

After Stan was discarded, there was still one more person who had to die, one more weed to be pulled out by the root.

The car door opened. The killer stepped out and moved quickly through the cold toward the alleyway.

*   *   *

Stan pulled out of the parking space and onto the road. Finding a spot near Gloria's apartment was like finding a black man at a KKK rally. Not easy. This coveted space was claimed by another car before Stan had managed to unlock the door and get in. He would probably have to stick it in a garage when he got back. Twenty-five bucks to park. Highway robbery. But soon Stan would have one hundred thousand dollars. Soon he would have all the money he needed and there would be no need to circle the block four hundred times just to find a parking space.

Don't take the money . . .

The annoying voice in his head was babbling nonsense again. Of course he should take the money. Of course he should bleed the maggot for every cent he could get.

Don't go, Stan. Stay away . . .

461

He shook his head no. True, blackmail was a dangerous game. Very dangerous. But Stan had a switchblade with him and, more important, he was dealing with an amateur. This wasn't B Man or somebody like that. He wasn't screwing around with the big-time. His victim was a scared rabbit. Harmless.

That's right, Stan My Man. Harmless. Just ask your father . . .

Stan's mind journeyed back to May 29, 1960. The look on the killer's face as the gun went off, the hatred in the cold eyes . . . that face could kill again. That face may appear innocent and innocuous on the outside, but Stan had witnessed the rage behind the facade. Stan had seen what a normal, civilized citizen could become if pushed too far.

You don't want to do this, Stan. You don't want to take money from your father's murderer . . .

Then what was he supposed to do instead? Forget he had ever seen the killer? Seek vengeance? Tell the police? Walk away? What? What was he supposed to do?

Stan pushed the voices out of his head. Money. Lots of it. That's what he was heading for right now. To hell with studying the morality involved. What was he supposed to be anyway, a saint? Don't make me laugh. Stan Baskin did not let a good scam go by because of an irrational voice in his head. Stan Baskin did not let easy money just float on by him.

He turned left and headed into South Boston. He did not bother to look in his rearview mirror. If he had, he may have noticed a familiar red car following him.

*   *   *

462

Gloria stayed about fifty yards behind Stan's car. She was no detective and she had no idea of the mechanics involved in tailing a car, except for what she had seen on television and in the movies. This area of Boston was foreign to Gloria. She had no idea where Stan's final destination was, but she was sure there had to be a safer way of getting there than driving through this concrete jungle of muggings, crime and murder. What was Stan doing here?

Spying on a loved one was not something Gloria did often—never, to be more precise—and she was scared. But Stan was in trouble, big trouble. Every part of her knew it. Her body kept shaking as the familiar, unsettling cravings knocked on her door like an old friend.

Come on, Gloria, the cravings would say. *Just take a little snort and you'll be free. A little high never hurt anyone. You can control it now. Come on. Heck, you should have no trouble finding a little something to get you nice and high in this neighborhood. Just stop the car near that park over there.*

She could almost feel her hands listening to the cravings, turning the wheel toward the park. But she fought it off. Most people thought that drug addiction was a disease that could be cured. But that was wrong. Gloria had learned the painful truth: you are never fully cured. You may think everything is okay for a day or a week or even a month, but then something will happen. Something will go wrong with your life and you will feel all alone. That is when the addict in you strikes—not when you're strong and prepared to do battle, but when your defenses are down. Drugs, your addict reminds you, are your only real friends. They're there when you need them. They never disappoint or let you down. They make you feel good. They let you forget about the rest of the world.

The traffic light in front of her turned yellow. Gloria accelerated. She did not want to get caught at a red light and lose him now. The feeling that had swept over her all day, the feeling that Stan was in imminent danger, had grown stronger with each mile. She had to stay with him.

Her car sped through the intersection, still keeping a safe distance between itself and Stan Baskin. Why was she so worried? She could not say for sure. Stan had been acting strangely all day, more on edge than usual, more contemplative. Something was bothering him. More than that, something was terrifying him.

Oh Stan, what are you up to now?

He could be so foolish sometimes. In many ways, Stan was more insecure than she had ever been. He felt the only way he could get anywhere, the only way he could get people to like him or love him, was to use treachery and deceit. Everything was a scam to him, a con. Even emotions. Love was a tool to control or be controlled. But Stan was learning. He was beginning to trust, beginning to feel. Gloria could tell. They had come a long way since Stan had ripped off $100,000 from her at the Deerfield Inn.

She made a right turn. The sun had set, and even with the heaters on full blast Gloria felt a chill in the air. Yes, she knew all about Stan's little con game with B Man. Not at first, perhaps. At first she had been legitimately terrified and fooled by the whole charade, but when Stan developed no contusions or even minor injuries, she became suspicious. Later that evening, when Gloria was cleaning up the bathroom, she found the remnants of the blood capsules in a waste-paper basket. It did not take a genius to figure out the rest: Fake blood meant a fake beating.

Her first response was to strike back, to have it out with him, to throw him out of her life. But something held her back. Though probably deserving, Stan had been thrown out by everyone close to him all his life. Maybe she was being naive, but Gloria wondered if that was the reason Stan was so self-destructive, if that was why he chose to squander every chance at real happiness. She did not know for sure. She only knew he needed help.

And God help her, she loved him.

So Gloria decided to never say a word about the money. She would just love him the best she could. And it was working. Slowly, layer by layer, the Stan of phony charms fell away and the real Stan began to emerge. The phony Stan was still there, still strong, but its grip on his soul was weakening.

Up ahead, Stan turned down a one-way street and parked his car in front of an alley. Gloria stayed back. The whole area looked like the ruins of a futuristic battlefield. There were no lights, no other cars on the road except for abandoned wrecks. Broken cinder blocks and shards of glass were scattered everywhere. The window holes in the buildings were boarded up with rotted planks.

What was he doing here?

Gloria watched the door on his driver's side open. Stan got out and looked both ways, his eyes somehow missing her car. Then he disappeared down the narrow alleyway. Gloria's car crept down the street. She pulled in behind his car, made sure her doors were locked, and waited.

*   *   *

'You did what?' Mark shouted.

'Just calm down a second,' T.C. said. 'I was just trying to scare Laura off.'

'So you broke into her apartment?'

'Listen to me, Mark. She sneaked over to Australia. She was positive David had been murdered. She had stopped trusting me completely. I had to knock her off the track.'

'What the hell is wrong with you, T.C.? First you threaten Corsel and his kids and then you threaten Laura's family?'

'I did what I thought best.'

'You were wrong. Why didn't you tell me before?'

'You would have stopped me.'

'Damn straight I would have stopped you. I would have punched your goddamn lights out. So what exactly did you do to scare her off—besides leaving the VCR on?'

'I left a threatening note,' T.C. replied, 'and David's ring.'

'What ring?'

'The championship ring he was wearing when he drowned. I put it under her pillow.'

'Are you crazy?'

'Try to understand what I was trying to accomplish. I wanted to convince her that David's killers were men who played for keeps. Threatening her alone would do no good. But if I threatened her family, if I convinced her that these hoodlums who had David's ring were going to kill her sister

466

or her mother or her father, then she might back off. I used the ring for its shock value. It added authenticity to the threat. It dazed her long enough for me to win back her trust and—'

Rage overcame Mark. He grabbed T.C. by the lapels and threw him up against the wall. 'You son of a bitch.'

'Easy, Mark.'

'This is Laura we're talking about, not some drug dealer you can abuse with self-justification.'

'I was trying to protect her . . . and you.'

Mark held onto T.C.'s shirt for another moment. Then he let go, spun away, and grabbed his heavy overcoat.

'Where are you going?' T.C. called out.

Mark did not reply. He stormed out the door and into the cold winter night.

*   *   *

Stan looked at his watch, shivering in the bitter cold of the early morning. The killer was already five minutes late. The narrow ghetto alley worked as a wind tunnel making the weather unbearably raw. Stan paced nervously, trying to keep himself warm. Where the hell is the asshole? Stan wondered. And why the hell does the scumbag want to meet here of all places?

Stan's face twisted in disgust as the foul odors of garbage and urine reached his nostrils. Dirt. Filth. Scum. Behind him, a passed-out or possibly dead drunk lay buried under the heaps of refuse. This was not a place where Stan imagined the killer hanging out. No, the person who murdered his father was used to more plush decor, a more

467

controlled environment. Stan had been the one who'd spent most of his life in the gutter. He reached into his pocket and touched the switchblade. He would have the advantage on this turf.

He took another glance at his watch. Ten minutes late. Stan wished the killer would hurry up and get here so he could get the hell out of this shit-hole.

Stan stopped pacing, the night chill nibbling through his skin. No sense denying it, he was jittery, anxious. He wasn't sure why. The killer was only ten minutes late. Nothing to get excited about.

'Hello, Stan.'

He spun around. 'Hello.'

'Sorry I'm late.'

Stan shuffled his feet. 'That's okay.' Listen to this conversation, he thought. He was exchanging pleasantries with his father's murderer. 'Do you have the money?'

Don't take it, Stan. Run . . .

The killer held up an airline bag. 'It's all here.'

Stan could smell the fear coming off the killer. The eyes were darting all about the alley, the eyes of a frightened doe. 'Don't like it here, do you?' Stan sneered.

'Not particularly,' the killer confessed.

Stan smiled. His own fear was slipping away as he watched the killer's grow. 'It looks like you're actually sweating under that fancy coat. How come?'

'No reason.'

'Give me the money.'

The killer put down the bag and stepped back.

'I said give it to me,' Stan snapped.

'It's right there. Just pick it up.'

'Give it to me now!'

The killer's eyes continued to shift from side to side, trying to guard all angles. 'Okay.'

Slowly, the killer took hold of the bag and walked toward Stan. Stan's confidence grew. He was taking a bizarre satisfaction in barking out orders.

'Hand it to me.'

The killer did just that, stepping back quickly after Stan had the money in his hands.

'This is just your first payment,' Stan said.

'What? You said on the phone—'

'Don't worry about what I said on the phone. I want another ten thousand next week. Do you understand me?'

'I just can't keep giving you cash. When will it end?'

'When I say so,' Stan said coolly.

'But—'

Rage had now fully replaced Stan's fear. 'You killed my father.'

'It was an accident.'

'An accident? I was there, remember? You shot my father right through his forehead. You took my childhood away from me.'

'I didn't mean to.'

'Bullshit!' Without thinking Stan stepped toward the killer. 'You called him a bastard before you fired.'

'You don't know what he did to me.'

'And I don't care.' Stan moved closer.

The killer's face was completely white now. Frightened eyes searched for an easy exit. 'You have your money. I'd like to go now.'

'I don't want your goddamn money,' Stan

shouted.

The killer's back was flat against the wall. 'What . . .?'

Stan took another step forward. 'There's no place to run,' he said. 'No one will hear you scream.'

'Please, just leave me alone. I'll pay you anything you want. Anything.'

Stan closed the gap between them to less than a yard. 'No good. Money can't bring back my father. Money can't give me back my childhood.'

'You don't understand—'

'Save it,' Stan said, his fury forcing the tears out of his eyes and onto his cheeks. When was the last time he cried? He did not remember. But it felt right, oh so right. For the first time in his life, everything felt right. Gloria, Boston, no booze, no gambling. Everything just felt so right. 'Someone has to avenge my father's death,' he said. 'And someone has to pay for what happened to him. And to me.'

'No, listen—'

'I bet he thought that he could just toss you to the side,' Stan continued, reaching into his pocket. 'I bet my old man thought you were completely harmless.'

As Stan moved in, the killer's hand came out from underneath the long overcoat. 'And he paid for it, Stan. Just like you.'

The gun fired. A bullet tore through the night air.

*   *   *

Richard explained the whole situation to Naomi.

She sat at the kitchen table, drinking coffee from the mug Peter had made her in school. 'World's Best Mom' was crookedly hand-painted on the side. Rog had made a 'World's Best Dad' mug for Richard the same year. She did not say one word while he spoke, did not interrupt even once as Richard recounted every detail. He told her about David Baskin's first phone call from Australia, about Laura's visits, even about the crazed psycho with the knife who had threatened the twins. He left out nothing.

Naomi's expression did not change. She was a short woman, cute and tiny with curly dark hair and a bright, friendly smile she used to disarm any potential hostility. She sat calmly now, sipping at her coffee. Surprisingly, the twins had gone to bed a half-hour ago without the usual kicking and clawing. In fact, they had actually gone to bed an hour earlier than their standard bedtime. Miraculous really. They had a soccer game tomorrow, the twins explained, and Coach Duckson had said that sleep would enhance their performance. So Roger and Peter strolled past their stunned-speechless parents and headed up to bed. Now, like most nights after Roger and Peter had been tucked away, the house was strangely quiet. Each sound was amplified, echoing throughout the still environment.

'So what do you think I should do?' Richard asked when he had finished. 'Should I tell Laura what she's up against or keep my mouth shut?'

Naomi stood and walked over to the Mr Coffee. She poured herself a second cup. Second cup after dinner—no good. Too much caffeine. But Naomi had a feeling she would be up most of the night no matter what she did or did not drink. 'So this is why you've been acting so weird lately?'

Richard nodded.

'Why didn't you tell me about this before?'

'I don't know,' he said. 'I sort of hoped the problem would just go away.'

'Just go away? How?'

He shrugged. 'I didn't say it was a realistic hope, Naomi, just a hope. What do you think I should do?'

'You're a good man, Richard.'

'Huh?'

'You're a good father, good husband, good provider, good son to your parents, good friend.'

'I don't see what you're getting at.'

Naomi took another sip of coffee. 'I married a good man, that's all. Most people can't be bothered with somebody else's problems. Most people would have forgotten the whole thing a long time ago. But not you, Richard. This whole thing has really been tearing you apart, hasn't it?'

He hesitated and then nodded. 'Yeah,' he said, 'it has.'

'The way I see it then,' Naomi continued, 'you have no choice.'

'You mean . . .?'

'Sure I'd love to forget the whole thing,' she said. 'I probably could too. But you can't, Richard. You're not built that way. You'll drive yourself crazy and I don't want a good *crazy* man for a husband. So this is what we'll do. Until this thing is settled, you'll have to drive the twins to school in the morning. I'll pick them up in the afternoon. Their activities will have to be curtailed a bit. We won't live in pure fear, but we'll have to be more

472

careful for a while.'

Richard said nothing. He lowered his eyes and slid his hand across the table. Naomi grasped it. On the outside she may have been composed, but Richard knew that an earthquake of pain was erupting inside of her. Her hand gripped tighter. He looked up and saw that she was crying.

*   *   *

Gloria adjusted the car mirrors to cover all possible routes that could be used to sneak up on her. Then she tried to settle back, her eyes rotating between the three mirrors and the front windshield. No one had approached her. No one had even ventured onto this street.

Gloria felt like she was being watched.

She knew it was just her imagination, that there was no eye staring out between the cracks in one of the decaying boards. She reached down to turn up the heater. No good. It was already set on full blast. There were no sounds, except for the occasional car horn or screeching of brakes on a nearby road.

What was Stan doing here? What kind of trouble had he gotten himself into this time? Trouble followed a man like Stan. It lagged behind him, tapping him on the shoulder whenever he tried to pick up speed and outrun it.

Be careful, Stan. For God's sake, be care—

A gunshot shattered the silence of the still night.

Oh God, no. Please . . .

All concerns for her own safety and welfare fled. Gloria grabbed the door handle, pulled, and rushed out of the car. Her legs flailed wildly as she ran for the alley entrance, her body almost tripping and spilling onto the hard concrete. But she ignored that. She ignored the cold.

Stan. Oh Stan, please be all right . . .

But something in the wind seemed to laugh at her prayer. She turned the corner. One of her shoes fell off but Gloria did not miss a stride. She kept moving forward, kept running down the narrow alley until . . .

. . . until she found him.

'Stan!'

Footsteps echoed as somebody disappeared around the corner, but Gloria's conscious mind did not register the noise, did not register any sound at all. Her ears pounded. Her eyes were wide with horror.

When Gloria reached where Stan lay, she knelt down quickly. The bullet had hit his chest, his blood spreading and staining everything in its path. Stan's hand tried feebly to hold back the blood and stop the flow, but it was not working. He was still breathing, still conscious, but the life was spilling out of him and onto the pavement.

Helplessness overwhelmed her. There was no phone nearby, no way to move Stan toward the car and safety. She took off her coat and pressed it against the wound, tears streaming down her face.

'I'll be right back,' she said. 'I'm going to get help.'

Stan looked up at her through his dying eyes. Delirium was beginning to set in. He was going to die, goddamn it. He was finished, through. There was no pain now but he could feel his soul slowly being torn away from his body. Something was tugging at him, dragging him away from this cold alley.

Stan could make out Gloria's concerned eyes. Another woman looking down at him with pity. Women had been the bane of Stan's short, miserable existence on this planet. They had punched him, abused him, hated him. They had ripped deep into his soul, leaving scars and wounds maybe death would finally heal. But Stan still craved vengeance on them, on the whole vile gender. As Gloria looked down upon him, he had one last chance before he died. He had one last opportunity to crush a woman like an insect. He would tell her that he had never cared for her, that he only used her, that she was nothing but a worthless whore like all the others.

She rose to leave but his hand reached out and grabbed her. Now she would know pain, he thought. Now she would know what it was like to have your insides shredded.

'Gloria?'

'I'm right here.'

Death crawled toward him. His eyes began to roll back and close. 'I love you.'

CHAPTER TWENTY-EIGHT

They were only one block away now. The time had arrived. In a few moments, Laura would see her mother.

Serita drove the car slowly. She resisted the temptation to gun the engine, to speed her white BMW down the road and past the driveway up ahead. In many ways, she wished that the ride would last longer, that they would never get out

475

of this car, that they would never find out the truth about David's death. She felt like they were sitting alone in a doctor's office waiting to hear the results of some life-and-death test, trying to distract themselves by reading the diplomas on the wall and the useless health pamphlets.

'Laura?'

Laura's breathing came in short gasps. Serita could almost feel her friend's mind pulling in different directions, stretching to the point where it would not snap back. 'What?'

'You sure you don't want me to go in with you?'

'No,' Laura said firmly.

'What time do you want me to come back for you?'

'I'll make my own way home.'

'Humor me, Laura. I'll come back in a half-hour and wait out here until you're ready, okay?'

'Okay,' Laura replied.

Serita flipped up the blinker. There was no way to put it off any longer. She swung the car into the driveway, her headlights dancing across the bushes as though searching for an intruder. She drove the BMW up to the front door of the house. No lights shone through any of the windows. No lights illuminated the outside of the familiar home. Laura opened the door and stepped out.

'Looks like nobody's home,' Serita said.

'Not yet,' Laura answered. 'My father is working late tonight. My mother should be home in a few minutes.'

'Are you going to wait out here?'

'I have a key.'

'Right,' Serita said. 'Well, good luck, Laura. Keep your cool.'

476

'I will.'

Laura turned away from the car and made her way to the door. She fumbled through her purse, found her key, placed it in the lock. The door opened easily. She moved into the house and closed the door behind her.

Her hand located the light switch from rote memory. She had been flicking that switch since she was a fat infant who had had to stand on her tippy-toes to reach it. She glanced about the surroundings of her youth as though they were all new to her. The familiar house seemed different today, like a book she had only skimmed through but never bothered to read from cover to cover.

Laura climbed the steps to the upper level of the house. She knew exactly where she was heading. At the very least, her mother was an organized person. Everything had its place. Mary Ayars lost nothing. It was a characteristic her youngest daughter had not inherited. Whenever Mary had visited Laura's office, she invariably asked, 'How can you work in this mess? How can you find anything?'

The truth was that half the time Laura could not find what she was looking for, but then again that was why she had Estelle. Estelle, who was up at Colgate with Judy's mystery key, kept great files, freeing Laura to create mass disarray in peace. Laura's mind worked fast, too fast sometimes. Ideas flew in and then details would slip out. Not so with her mother. Her mother was a plodder. She did one thing at a time and she did not take on a new task until the prior one had been completed.

My mother would never hurt me, never hurt our family. She loves us . . .

Laura's head pounded. Her mother. Her

beautiful, loving, often smothering mother. Mary Ayars had taken care of her daughters when they were sick, had held them when they were scared of the dark. She had read them stories before bed and tucked them in with a kiss before sleep. Could it have all been a lie? Did Laura ever really know her mother? Questions like these ate away at Laura's brain, ate away at her ability to be rational. So few things in life were consistent. Her mother had always loved her unequivocally and unselfishly, but now Laura was forced to wonder about the very foundation of her life. Mary Ayars's ravishing facade was being slowly peeled away, and Laura no longer wanted to see what was underneath it.

There has to be a mistake. There just has to be . . .

But her mind knew that her mother held the key to David's death. How, why, she could not say. Her mother had hated David from the beginning, had begged Laura not to see him. Why? She had never even met him, had never even sat in the same room with him. Why was she so against their relationship? Couldn't she see how happy he made her, that for the first time she was truly in love? Had a thirty-year-old love affair blinded Mary so? Had the past forced her to fly to Australia, meet with David and . . .

And what?

A chill passed through the corridor. Laura did not know the answer to that question but it would come soon enough. Right now, there was something else that Laura had to do. She entered her parents' bedroom and made her way straight to the night-table on her mother's side of the bed. She pulled open the second drawer and spotted the blue cover almost immediately. She took it out, opened it, quickly glanced through the pages. In a matter of seconds, her fears were confirmed. She had known it was coming, had prepared herself for it, but the confirmation still wrenched her heart painfully.

It's true. My God, it's true . . .

A door opened downstairs. 'Hello?'

Her mother's voice. Even the sweet voice now seemed tainted. 'I'm up here, Mother.'

'Laura?' Mary called back surprised. 'What are you doing here?'

She placed the blue item from the drawer into her pocket. 'I came to talk to you,' she yelled down.

'At eight o'clock at night? Why didn't you call, darling?'

'I . . . I don't know.'

'You should get to a hospital. Dr Clarich says—'

'I feel fine.'

'And how did you get here anyhow? Your car isn't in the driveway.'

Though the voice was only coming from downstairs, it seemed to echo from so far away. 'Serita drove me.'

'Then you'll be staying the night?'

Laura could hear the hope in her mother's voice. 'I don't think so. She'll be back for me in a little while.'

Mary moved into the kitchen. 'Why don't you come downstairs, Laura? All of this yelling is giving me a headache.'

A headache? Laura thought as she crossed the room. *Did you ever see David get one of his headaches, Mother? No? Then you have no idea what a headache is. You think that slight prick of discomfort in your head is truly painful? What a laugh, but then again you have always had it soft,*

479

haven't you, Mother? You've always been shielded from life's hardships. You let your beauty twist and mold everything to suit your needs. You never worked a day in your life. You spent your life pretending to crave independence when all you wanted to do was make excuses. Dad always took care of you, kept you fed and clothed and happy like some overgrown child. And how did you repay him, dearest Mother? By betraying him. By sleeping with David's father and who knows how many others.

With each step Laura let the rage build and fester until her mind was ready to explode. Gone were thoughts of prudence, thoughts that maybe there was a logical explanation for all of this, thoughts that maybe her mother had nothing to do with David's death. Seething anger had crept into Laura and taken over reason. She strode into the kitchen and faced her mother.

Mary spun around and stared at her daughter's face worriedly. 'Laura,' she said, 'are you okay?'

Laura did not respond. She reached into her pocket and withdrew the item she had taken out of the night-table. When Mary saw what was in her daughter's hand, her eyes widened with fear. 'What are you doing with that?'

'I just got it out of your drawer,' Laura said.

'You have no right to go through my things.'

'And you had no right to kill my husband.'

The silence was staggering, suffocating. Mary took one step back, her hand fluttering to her throat. 'What did you say?'

'You heard me.' She flipped the passport toward her mother. Mary jumped back as if it were a chunk of hot coal. 'You were in Australia during our honeymoon. Don't deny it, Mother. Passports don't lie.'

Mary said nothing. She moved farther and farther back until she nearly crouched in a corner.

'How did you find out we were there, Mother? Did Dad tell you? Or Gloria?'

Mary closed her eyes and shook her head hard.

'Did they tell you or—?' Laura stopped speaking. Her mind jerked back to the break-in at their new house, the open calendar on the desk, the shredded photograph . . . 'It was you.'

'What?'

'You were the one who broke into our house while we were away, weren't you, Mother? That explains why there was no forced entry. You got the key to the house from my apartment, and I told you the alarm code when we first had it installed. You were the one who went through our calendar. That's how you knew where we were. And it was you who tore up the picture of David's father, wasn't it, Mother?'

Mary still said nothing, her body quaking in the corner.

Laura's shout vibrated through the room. 'Wasn't it, Mother?'

Mary's shoulders sagged. Finally, she nodded.

'But why?'

Mary began to speak in a voice that quivered on every word. 'Because I could tell something important was going on between you two,' she said. 'Your office had no idea where you were. Your father and sister said that you were probably on a business trip, but whenever you had traveled in the past you let me know. You never just took off without calling me. So I became scared. I went to your apartment to look for some clue, but there

481

was nothing there. Then I saw the key to the new house you bought with David. I drove there and rummaged through the desk until I found David's calendar. It told me all about your secret elopement to Australia.'

'And what about the photograph? Why did you rip it up?'

Mary turned away, nervously repositioning the rings on her fingers. 'I didn't plan on ripping up any photographs,' she said. 'The photo album was just sitting on the desk so I started to look through it. I was so upset . . . I guess I just lashed out at a photograph.'

'Not just any photograph,' Laura replied carefully, 'but a photograph of Sinclair Baskin. Do you remember him?'

'No, Of course not—'

'Let me refresh your memory then,' Laura interrupted, fighting desperately to keep her temper in check. 'You stole Sinclair Baskin away from Aunt Judy thirty years ago.'

Mary's face went white. 'How . . .?'

'You had an affair with him,' Laura continued, 'or have you had so many affairs over the years that a few have slipped your mind?'

Mary clasped her hands over her ears. Her eyes squeezed shut. 'No, no . . .'

'And now that I think of it, wasn't Aunt Judy dating Dad before you met him? Didn't you steal Dad away from her too?'

'No, no . . .'

'And Sinclair Baskin broke it off with you, didn't he? When he was finished having his fun and using you, he tossed you away.'

'That's not it at all . . .'

482

'How could you do that to Dad? How could you sneak behind his back like that?'

Mary's head fell into her hands. For the first time, her voice was above a whisper. 'Don't you think I ask myself that every day? I love your father very much. I never, *never*, had another affair after that.'

'How big of you,' Laura shot back sarcastically.

'Back then,' Mary continued, 'your father was working at the hospital day and night. I never saw him. I took care of Gloria and sat at home all day watching soap operas. Sinclair came along. He was a handsome, charismatic, worldly man and I was young and naive. I fell for him. You of all people should understand the attraction. Your David probably possessed similar charms.'

'Don't compare what I had with David to your sleazy affair.'

'I'm not,' Mary replied. 'I'm just saying that I was lonely and young. I made a mistake. I don't expect you to understand, and I don't want your sympathy.'

'Good, because you're not going to get it. But I have another question. Why did you kill Sinclair Baskin?'

Her mother stopped. 'Kill Sinclair? He committed suicide like . . .'

'Like who, Mother?'

'No . . . Nobody. Sinclair Baskin committed suicide. He shot himself in the head.'

'Another lie, Mother.'

'No, it's the truth—'

'It's a lie!' Laura shouted. 'Sinclair Baskin broke it off with you. You were crushed, destroyed. After all, nobody breaks up with the gorgeous Mary

483

Ayars, right? And according to his secretary, you were the last person to see him alive.'

'He committed suicide, Laura. Everybody knows that.'

'Wrong, Mother. Stan Baskin was there. He was hiding behind a couch. He saw his father being murdered.'

Mary's body swayed. Her head kept shaking, denying her daughter's words. 'I never harmed Sinclair, I swear it. Yes, we had an affair thirty years ago, but I had nothing to do with his death. You have to believe me. For thirty years, I've had to pay for what I did back then. We have all had to pay in ways I could have never imagined.'

'Including David?'

'It was never supposed to happen that way.'

'What way?'

'David was never supposed to die.'

Laura stopped in mid-breath. 'You killed him,' she said in a hushed voice.

'I didn't mean to,' Mary cried. 'I thought it would all end differently. I thought I was doing what was best for everyone.'

'You killed David!'

Mary shook her head. 'You don't understand. It was unplanned, an accident. I thought he'd react differently.'

'React differently? Did you really think that you could just talk him into leaving me?'

'Something like that . . .'

'You thought he would dump me just like Sinclair Baskin dumped you thirty years ago?'

'It was a chance I had to take.'

'And when he refused, you had him killed.'

Mary's head snapped up. 'No! That's not it at

all.'

'You hated him because of what his father did to you thirty years ago.'

'No!'

'And you didn't want your daughter to make the same mistake you made. After all, like father, like son, right? You decided he was no good.'

'That's not it,' Mary said. 'You don't understand.'

'How could you be so blind to David, Mother? He was nothing like his father. David was warm, sweet, considerate, caring—'

'I know!' Mary interrupted loudly. 'I know he was a wonderful young man. I know he was nothing like his father. Don't you see? I never wanted him to die.'

Laura stopped. Her puzzled eyes locked onto her mother. 'Then why, Mother? If you thought he was such a wonderful man, why did you have him killed?'

'I didn't have him killed. I never killed anyone.'

'But you just said—'

'I caused his death,' Mary explained, 'but I didn't kill him.'

Laura's mind spun. 'You're not making sense. You wanted to destroy a relationship between your daughter and a man you just described as wonderful. You wanted to break us up so badly that you flew to Australia, met with him, and begged him to stop seeing me, right?'

'Yes.'

'Then when he refused to leave me—'

'He didn't refuse,' Mary said. 'David promised me he would never see you again.'

Laura could not believe what she was hearing. 'What are you saying?' she snapped. 'You talked

485

David into leaving me?'

'I guess I did. But I didn't realize the cost. You were the one who said, like father, like son.'

'So?'

'So David loved you. He couldn't stand to be away from you. After we talked, I thought he was just going to leave you, disappear from your life. That's what he promised. And I knew you would be devastated. I knew how much you loved him. But you were strong and young. You'd be able to snap back from the heartbreak. Your family would help you. Don't you see, Laura? I just wanted David to leave you. I never wanted him to commit suicide . . . like his father.'

Laura felt her knees buckle. 'What?'

'Right after I convinced David to leave you he drowned. Doesn't that seem like a strange coincidence to you? I never imagined that my words would make him kill himself.'

Laura felt blows landing on her head. She tried to fend them off but there were too many and they were coming too fast. She felt dizzy, sick. 'Are you trying to tell me that David was so upset about his father's indiscretions that he committed suicide?'

'No. That's not it at all.'

'Why couldn't you have just left us alone?' Laura ranted, tears flowing freely now. 'We were happy and in love. Why should your disgusting affair have anything to do with us?'

'Unfortunately,' Mary said sadly, 'it had everything to do with you.'

'But why?' Laura demanded. She was on the verge of striking out physically at her mother, of punching and kicking until she dropped from exhaustion. 'David was an infant when Sinclair

Baskin died. He was nothing like his father—you yourself said that. Why was it so important for you to destroy my marriage?'

Mary swallowed. She stood upright, her spine rigid. She turned to face Laura as if she were preparing to receive a terrible blow. Her body trembled. 'Because,' she said slowly, 'you were married to your brother.'

CHAPTER TWENTY-NINE

'This way, Miss.'

Estelle followed the president of First National of Hamilton into the bank. It was late, well past closing, but Estelle had managed to get him to come down and open the bank for her. How? Trade secrets. Estelle knew how to network better than anyone. She had taken the simple ritual of talking on the phone and transformed it into an art form. Give her a telephone and a local directory and Estelle could locate anybody or anything—like the truth behind Judy's mystery key.

'Please have a seat. May I have the key please?'

Estelle handed him the key.

'And the notarized letter?'

She passed him the notarized letter Laura's attorney had drawn up giving Estelle full access to whatever the key might open.

The banker headed down the hallway. He returned a minute later with the box under his arm.

'Here it is.'

He handed her the box. Estelle opened it and skimmed through the contents. A lot of old bonds.

An employment contract from Colgate College. Insurance claims.

On the bottom, Estelle found a diary from 1960. Laura's words came back to her.

'What exactly do you expect me to find, Laura?'

'I don't really know. Something to do with the past.'

'The past?'

'1960 to be more precise. Something happened to my aunt that year and I need to find out what.'

'I don't understand what you mean.'

'Neither do I. Don't worry about it. Just keep your eyes open for anything involving 1960.'

Without further delay, Estelle poured everything from the box into a small bag with the other items. She thanked the banker and hurried to the taxi. The chartered jet was fueled and waiting for her at the airport. Estelle looked at her watch. With a little luck, she could be back at Laura's apartment with the diary in just over two hours.

*   *   *

For more than a full minute, the kitchen remained silent. Only the sounds of Mary's sobs penetrated the stillness that surrounded the two women. Laura was too stunned to move, too stunned to allow the truth to go any deeper than the periphery of her mind.

'My brother?' she was finally able to utter. 'David was my brother?'

Mary nodded. 'Sinclair Baskin is your real father.'

'No,' Laura said with a dull voice. 'That can't be.'

'It's true. God, I wish it wasn't, but it's true.'

'But how . . .'

'Because I was stupid and careless. During my affair with Sinclair, I became pregnant.'

'Maybe Dad was the one. Maybe Dad got you preg—'

Mary shook her head. 'Your father and I had not slept together for nearly two months.'

'You became pregnant?'

She nodded.

'Did you tell Sinclair?'

'Of course I told him. Like I said before, I was young and confused. I thought we were in love. I was prepared to leave your father and start life anew as Mrs Sinclair Baskin.'

'So what happened?'

'When Sinclair found out that I was pregnant, he threw me out.'

'Just like that?'

Mary nodded. 'Sinclair said that he didn't care what I did with the baby as long as I just got out of his life right away. I was so scared, Laura. Terrified. I never felt so alone in all my life. I had nobody to turn to. I never had many girlfriends except on a superficial level. They thought I was pretty and popular but no one ever wanted to know me. I mean, there was no flesh and blood and feelings in pretty Mary. I was just a beautiful painting or landscape for people to stare at and admire. Nothing more. You must know the feeling.'

Laura did. 'So what did you do?'

Mary went over to the sink, turned on the faucet, and filled a glass. 'I cried a lot. And then I sat down and tried to think it through. What was I going to do? Abortion was not a real option back then. I mean, you could get one if you had the money but James handled all of our finances. He would know

489

in a second.

'I considered telling James the truth, but can you imagine what would have happened? He is very possessive. If he had ever learned what had happened, well, I don't know what he would have done to me.'

'Probably divorced you.'

'Probably,' Mary agreed.

'So what did you decide to do?'

'Isn't it obvious?' she asked. 'I pretended the child was his.'

'How? You just said that you hadn't slept together in months.'

'The night after Sinclair threw me out, I started seducing James. Almost every night for months we made love.'

Laura felt sick to her stomach. 'Seduction was always the answer for you, wasn't it, Mother?'

'I wish there had been another solution, but what else could I do? I had to make him think you were his child. It was not easy. You were a very difficult pregnancy. For weeks I was sick as a dog and delirious. I vomited every morning. I was bleeding profusely. I thought I was going to miscarry and, God forgive me, I wanted to so badly. Days went by that I spent in the grips of a fever and could barely remember anything.'

'But you still managed to seduce him.'

'I had to, Laura. I had to make him think the baby was his. There were two big obstacles standing in the way of my deception: timing and family resemblance. You see, if everything kept on schedule, you were going to be born nine months after I became pregnant by Sinclair, which would be a month or two too soon if you were really James's baby.'

'How did you get around that?'

'I figured that in the basking light of parenthood, I could gloss it over as an early arrival. But luckily, you were a very late baby anyway. I didn't need to lie.'

'And family resemblance?'

'You ended up looking just like me. No one noticed if there was a similarity between you and James. We moved to Boston a year later. My secret was safe. With Sinclair dead, the only other person who knew the truth was my sister.'

'You told Judy?' Laura asked in disbelief.

'I needed to trust someone, Laura. I couldn't do this by myself. So I confided in the one person I could always depend on.'

'Wasn't she still furious at you for stealing Sinclair from her?'

'We were sisters, Laura. Just like you and Gloria. Judy could no more turn her back on me in a time of crisis than you could turn yours on Gloria. Without her help, I don't know what I would have done.'

'So Aunt Judy knew everything?'

'Yes.'

'And she was going to tell me, wasn't she? That was why she called me the other day.'

'Yes,' Mary said slowly. 'I think she planned on doing just that.'

'So you killed her too.'

'What?'

'You set the fire.'

'She was my sister . . .'

'The same sister you stole men from?'

'That's different. I loved Judy, you know that.

491

And she loved me.'

'So tell me why Judy chose to betray your trust all of a sudden.'

'I don't know, Laura. I wondered that myself. I know how it must look, but I did not set that fire. I swear. Try to understand. I was only trying to do what was best. And if you look at it from a distance, wasn't it working out, Laura? Until you fell in love with David, everything was wonderful. James loves you more than anything in the world.'

'No, Mother. He loves a lie.'

'Don't say that. He loves you. Biology doesn't mean a damn thing. If we had adopted you, he'd still love you just as much, right?'

'But you didn't adopt me. You created a lie.'

'A lie that was working just fine until you stopped listening to me.'

'Stopped listening to you?'

'Once I realized that David was Sinclair's son, I begged and pleaded with you not to see him. Why didn't you listen to me, Laura? Why didn't you stay away from him? I tried to stop you. I was sure I could. But then you ran off to Australia and got married. So I followed you. I had no choice.'

'Why couldn't you just tell me the truth?'

Mary's eyes never left her daughter's. 'My deception was thirty years old by then, Laura. The lies were snugly wrapped around this family. I was afraid of what would happen if they were suddenly removed. So I went to Australia to talk with David, to tell him the truth. I told no one I was going—not even Judy. When I arrived, I called David at your hotel. He was surprised, of course, but he agreed to meet me in my room at the Pacific International Hotel. We talked for a very long time. Oh Laura, it was the most awful thing. David was so confused. One minute he was furious and storming about the room. The next he was crying. Every word I said tore him apart. He was so devastated. Remember, you're hearing it after the fact. But David had to decide what to do. He loved you. He couldn't live without you. But he also knew how badly you wanted children and how dangerous it would be to ignore the truth. Suddenly, his whole world was anchored to ice. And my words were pulling up that anchor. When I spoke to your father a few days later and he told me David had drowned, I knew that my words had been the cause of it. I just wanted him to leave you, Laura. You have to believe me. I wish there had been another way but there wasn't. I couldn't just sit back and let you marry your brother. You see I had no choice, don't you?'

Laura fell back. She let the tears spill down her face. Oh David, I don't care what the world thought. We could have made it work. We could have adopted kids for chrissake. Or you could have just left me. Anything but what you did.

A new voice chased away her thoughts.

'Hello?' James called out. 'Anybody home?'

Laura and Mary both spun. James stood in the doorway, his medical bag in one hand, his briefcase on the floor by his foot. His eyes widened in surprise and concern as he looked at both his wife and daughter.

'What is going on here?' he asked.

'Nothing, honey,' Mary answered quickly.

James turned toward his daughter and studied her face. 'Laura,' he began, 'is there anything wrong?'

Love and sadness rushed through her. Laura wanted so much to hug him, to put her arms around him and tell him how much he meant to her. How many times had he comforted her when she needed it? How many times had he sacrificed his own wants for hers? Countless. She glanced briefly at her mother and wondered if she should tell him the truth, if she should tell him just what kind of a woman he had married. But what good would it do? It would only hurt him. He had lived with her and loved her for more than thirty years. If he was still blind to her faults, it was because he chose to be.

'Nothing, Dad.'

'You look upset. You both look upset.'

'We were just having a heart-to-heart,' Laura said. 'It got a little emotional, that's all.'

Mary looked at her daughter gratefully, but Laura did not give her the satisfaction of being acknowledged.

'I see,' James said, but his tone said otherwise. 'Serita's car is outside. Do you want to invite her in?'

'No, I have to go.' Ignoring her mother completely, Laura picked up her coat, put it on, and kissed her father goodbye.

'I love you, Dad,' she said to him.

His smile seemed sad. 'I love you too, sweetheart.'

'I better go now.' Without another word, Laura walked down the corridor. When she reached the door, she turned one last time and looked back at her parents, both staring at her worriedly. They seemed so small, so vulnerable, and yet it was a familiar, comforting picture to Laura. James and

Mary Ayars. Her mother and father.

Laura opened the door and stepped out into cold night air. She had no way of knowing that she would never see them together again.

*   *   *

The wind swirled its blades of cold through the Boston night. T.C. wrapped his arms around himself in a futile attempt to keep warm. This was not an evening to be outside. This was an evening to curl up in bed, throw an extra comforter or two over you, and just watch something mindless on T.V.

He blew air into his fists and then dug his hands into his pockets. Like a true idiot, he had left his gloves at home. His hands and feet were beginning to feel numb. And damn, he needed a cigar, but those too were sitting at home with his gloves, all warm and cozy.

Damn. Damn it all to hell.

T.C. continued to stroll along the Charles River. He quickened his pace now, the cold really starting to get to him. A minute later, he found what he was looking for:

Mark.

T.C. shook his head. The wind-chill factor had already dropped the temperature well into the minus range, and Mark still chose to stand alone along the river's frozen edge. There were no other people in the park. The young couples that normally strolled here had opted for cozy indoor fireplaces—even the homeless had decided that the shelters were less of a risk than this arctic cold.

'Mark?' T.C. cried out, the wind grabbing his

words and spreading them aimlessly.

Mark slowly turned toward T.C. He waved to acknowledge that he had heard him and then turned back around toward the water.

'What the hell are you doing down here?' T.C. shouted.

Raising his hand and cupping his ear, Mark signaled that he could not understand what T.C. was saying. T.C. jogged down alongside his friend. 'What the hell are you doing here?'

'Just taking a walk.'

'Kind of a cold night for it.'

Mark shrugged but said nothing.

T.C. hesitated. 'Look, Mark, I'm sorry. I never meant to hurt Laura.'

Mark nodded slowly. 'I know.'

'I guess I have a tendency to go too far,' T.C. continued. 'I lose perspective, become tunnel-visioned. I was just trying to protect her.'

'Forget it.'

A blast of freezing-cold air sliced through T.C.'s skin until it reached the bone. He had never been the sympathetic-ear type, but the tortured look on Mark's face was nearly unbearable to watch. 'You wanna talk about it?'

'About what?'

'About whatever's bothering you.'

'You a psychiatrist now?' Mark asked.

'No,' T.C. replied. 'I'm just a guy who's trying to help you out.'

'You've done too much already,' Mark said. 'I can never repay you.'

'I don't want to be repaid. Look, I'm your friend, right? Friends are supposed to help each other out. Would you have done the same for me?'

'No chance.'

T.C. laughed. 'You're still an asshole. I remember—'

'Careful,' Mark interrupted. 'The past is over. You're the one who told me that.'

'Yeah, I know. Sorry. You want to be alone?'

Mark did not respond right away. T.C. watched him. Yeah, he decided, he wants to be alone. He glanced at his watch. Have to go anyway, I have to be—

'What am I doing?' Mark asked out loud. 'I mean, am I doing the right thing?'

'Hell of a time to ask,' T.C. said.

'Would you have done the same?'

'Nope. But it's easy for me to say that. I wasn't in your shoes.'

'Why didn't you stop me?'

'Truth? I couldn't think of a better solution at the time.'

'And now?'

T.C. shrugged. 'Like you, I wonder what if. Maybe it didn't have to go this far. Maybe we panicked.'

'What else could I have done?'

'I don't know. I just don't know if I would have the courage to do what you did.'

'Courage?' Mark repeated. 'What a load of bullshit. What I did didn't take any courage.'

'You're wrong, my friend. You gave up the only thing you cared about. That takes courage.'

Mark waved him off. 'I had no choice. You know that. But what do I do now?'

'Go on. Survive. It could be worse. You could be dead.'

Mark smiled sadly. 'Like David Baskin?'

497

'Sort of.'

'Once you're dead, the pain is over. Isn't that what they say?'

'Some.'

'Then he's pretty well off, isn't he?'

'Maybe he is,' T.C. said. 'Who knows?'

'Oh cut the crap. You can be as bad as your friends at the FBI.'

'Meaning?'

'All of this Mark shit when we're alone. It's not necessary.'

'Don't you remember what I told you in June?'

'Yeah, yeah, I remember,' Mark began. 'You said that if we went through with this whacko idea we would have to do it right. That means that we have to make David Baskin dead, really dead, even in our minds.'

'And even in private,' T.C. added. 'David Baskin is dead.'

'But he's not dead,' Mark said. 'We've given him a new name, changed his face, his voice, his eye color. But we haven't killed him. He still lives. He still wants to play basketball. He's still your best friend. And most of all, he still . . .'

'. . . loves Laura?' T.C. finished.

Mark nodded. 'So let me hang on to David when we're alone. You'll be the only one who knows he's still alive. I don't want him to die, T.C. I don't want to be just Mark Seidman. Mark Seidman is some fictional character that I still don't understand. He barely even knows Laura.'

T.C. shook his head. 'You have to accept him. You have to let go of your past.'

'I'm not Mark Seidman, T.C. There is no such person. You can perform all the cosmetic surgery you want, but you can't change me into a man who does not love Laura.'

'As a brother?'

Mark chuckled sadly. 'Touché.'

'David Baskin was a hell of a guy,' T.C. continued. 'He loved Laura like no man has ever loved a woman. But David Baskin also learned the unpleasant truth. And accepted it.'

'We could have made it work. It would have been difficult but we loved each other.'

'You want to give it a try?' T.C. asked. 'You want to tell her the truth now?'

Mark thought for a moment and then shook his head. 'No.'

'I didn't think so.'

'So what now?'

T.C. shrugged. 'Let's get out of here. I'm freezing.'

'You go ahead. I'll be home in a little while.'

'You sure?'

He nodded.

Without another word, T.C. turned and left.

Mark did not take his eyes off the fog floating above the river like a bad special effect from an old horror movie. Thoughts of what might have been, of what should have been, scurried across his mind. The present and the past merged into one obscure reality. Only one thought remained clear and in focus:

Laura.

*   *   *

Serita dropped Laura off in front of her apartment building. 'Do you want me to come in?'

'Thanks anyway. Why don't you head home and get some sleep?'

'Are you sure?'

Laura nodded. 'I need time to just sit and sift through this.'

'You'll call me if you need anything? Even if you just want to shoot the shit at four in the morning?'

'You'll be the first to know. You're a good friend, Serita.'

Serita gunned the engine. 'The best.'

Laura moved past the security guard. The elevator was already on the ground level. She stepped in, pushed the button, and watched the door close. A minute later, she was on the eighteenth floor. Her key unlocked the door. She pushed it open and entered her apartment. The room was dark, except for the lamp in the corner. The lamp shone on a sight that made Laura inhale sharply.

'Laura?'

Laura ran across the room. Gloria's lips were thin, her eyes hollow and wide. 'What's the matter? What happened?'

'Oh God, oh please . . .'

Laura wrapped her arms around her sister in much the same way she had when Gloria's sleep had been plagued by those terrible nightmares during their childhood. For a moment she understood what her mother had meant when she discussed the bond between sisters. They might fight or disagree or be from completely different worlds, but they were eternally linked in a way that they could never hope to understand.

'What's wrong?' Laura asked gently. 'Did Stan do something?'

Gloria looked up. Her bleak eyes were swollen and red. 'He's dead.'

Laura thought she had misunderstood. 'Dead?'

Her sister nodded. 'He was shot in South Boston tonight. I just got back from the police station. They say they're going to investigate but nobody cares, Laura. They think Stan was just a punk and a gambler who played games with the wrong people and got a bullet in the chest for his troubles. They're not even interested in finding out who murdered him.'

Laura said nothing. There was indeed a curse on the Baskin men. Three of them were dead now, all tragically killed in their youth. But what about the curse on the women they left behind? What about the broken hearts and shattered dreams they left scattered about?

'He stopped gambling, Laura. I know you don't believe me. I know he did some terrible things to a lot of people . . . including you. But he had stopped. He was getting better. A few days ago, one of his old bookies called because he had not placed a bet in such a long time.'

Holding her sister, Laura started to cry.

Gloria snuggled closer. 'You never got to know him, Laura. I barely got to know him. He was the most unhappy person I have ever met. But Stan was changing. You could see it, feel it. And I'm not just talking like some blindly optimistic girlfriend. Stan was finally getting his chance, his one last shot to lead a normal, happy life. Someone took that away from him.' She fought back more tears. 'And someone took that away from me.'

'I'm so sorry.'

Gloria closed her eyes as though she were

summoning up some hidden strength. 'His death has something to do with what's going on lately, doesn't it?'

'I don't understand.'

'Neither do I but I've had a little while to think this through and here's what I know: Aunt Judy wanted to speak to you about the drowning. Before she died, she handed you a thirty-year-old picture of Sinclair Baskin. Only one person witnessed Sinclair's murder and could identify the killer. Stan. Now he too has been murdered. It's all tied together, Laura, isn't it? All the deaths are connected—Sinclair, Judy, Stan . . . and even David.'

Laura lowered her head. 'I think so.'

Gloria's eyes did not waver. 'Then we have to find out what happened to them.'

The doorman's intercom buzzed. Laura moved over to the squawk box and pressed the talk button. 'Yes?'

'There is a woman named Estelle here to see you,' the doorman said. 'She says she has an important package for you. This may sound weird but she said to tell you it has something to do with 1960.'

Laura turned back to her sister.

'Does Estelle's package have anything to do with this?' Gloria asked.

'Probably.'

'A clue?'

Laura nodded. 'She may have found something that solves this whole puzzle.'

'Then I want to see it.'

'Are you sure?'

'Yes.'

Laura pressed the talk button again. 'Send her up.'

When Laura turned back, Gloria stood on shaky legs and said, 'Tell me what's going on, Laura. Please.'

Laura moved across the room, her fingers rubbing against her palms. 'Sit down,' she said. 'I'll tell you everything I know.'

CHAPTER THIRTY

The bitter cold slit through the night like a sharpened razor, but Mark did not really notice. He stood in the present yet his mind was somewhere in the past, untouched by the icy surroundings and frosty blasts. He flashed back to June 17, to their honeymoon in Australia. He smiled sadly. How perfect life had been on that day.

And how quickly it had changed.

He could still hear the phone ringing in their suite, could still remember picking it up, could still remember the panic in Mary's voice.

'I have to see you, David. I have to speak to you right away.'

'Where are you?'

'I'm in Cairns. The Pacific International Hotel. Room 607. Come right away.'

More confused than frightened he agreed to go. He left a fun note for Laura with the receptionist, walked down the dirt path to the main road, hailed a cab (the only car on the road) and headed into the city of Cairns.

He stood by the Charles River now, half a globe

and a full lifetime away from the warmth and joy of his honeymoon bliss. Had he known back then what was about to happen to him? Had Mary given him any clue? No, not really. There was just a slight trembling in his heart, a faint stab of fear in his chest. But David had no way of knowing that the taxi was taking him from Heaven to Hades, that he was heading into an emotional ambush without a single weapon of defense. The familiar pain rushed through him as he remembered hearing the awful truth.

'I don't care if it's a sin. I love your daughter.'

'You can't mean that. Laura is not just my daughter, David. She's your sister. Think about her for a moment. She's always wanted to have children, a family. You can't give her those things.'

Because of his father. Damn him, that callous son of a bitch. David had been an infant when Sinclair Baskin killed himself. He did not remember his father at all, not even a blurry image of what he might have been like. He had spent much of his childhood wondering what sort of man his father had been, what had driven him to kill himself, what kind of a man could pull a trigger and leave his wife and two small children to fend for themselves. Now maybe he knew.

Sinclair Baskin. His father. He had been dead for as long as Mark could remember and yet he had managed to reach from beyond the grave and crush everything that mattered to his youngest son. His father had created Laura, and he had taken her away from him. Life's cruel ironies.

'Then I'll tell her the truth.'

'No! Please, David, I beg you. If you say something, Laura will lose a father she loves dearly and never

504

forgive me for what I've done. In the end, she may be left with none of us. You have to think of what's best for her.'

'Then what am I supposed to do?'

'Break it off. End it. If you love her, let her go. She will be hurt at first. Devastated even. But you'll be surprised how resilient the heart is.'

But even then, David had known that he could not just hurt her and walk away. He would never be able to tell Laura that he no longer loved her, that his love for her had died. His heart wanted so much to ignore the frightening reality of his situation, to deafen his ears to everything he had heard. But he also knew that Mary's words were true. What choice did he have? All their dreams of a family and life together had been trampled to death by the heavy boot of past sins. They could no longer stay together. Telling Laura the truth would not change that fact. It would only hurt her father and tear her away from her family. He would have to leave her. He would have to turn his back on the only thing in life that truly meant anything to him.

But how could he do it? How could he tell Laura that his love for her had withered away and died? How could he say that the love they shared had been a lie after Laura had risked everything and given him all that she had?

Better, he decided then, to have love ripped away from you than to think it had never been more than a deception. Better to have lost love in a tragedy than to be told it had never really been.

A plan began to form in his mind.

Completely numb, David walked out of room 607, took an elevator to the lobby, and called T.C.

505

'She'll call you first.'

'What about her father?' T.C. asked. 'Or her sister?'

'She won't want to worry them yet. She'll figure you'll know what to do.'

'Okay. Now call your bank as soon as we hang up. Then stay hidden till I get there. I'll take care of the rest.'

David Baskin died that day. And Mark Seidman was born.

Back in the present, Mark turned away from the Charles River and headed up the embankment. His face was red from the cold, his breath coming in frigid gusts.

It was time to go home.

* * *

Estelle stepped through the door. She had moved the contents of the safety deposit box into a large manila envelope during the flight home and now she handed them to Laura.

'The key opened your aunt's safety deposit box at the First National Bank in Hamilton,' she told her.

'Thanks, Estelle.'

'No problem, boss. You need me for anything else?'

Laura shook her head. 'I'll see you on Monday. Thanks again.'

'Bye.'

Laura closed the door and moved back toward the couch.

'So what are we looking for?' Gloria asked.

'I don't know exactly,' Laura admitted. 'I guess it will have something to do with Sinclair Baskin. It may be nothing but more old photographs.'

'Let's get to it.'

'Are you sure you're up to it?'

'Positive.'

Laura took hold of the letter opener and slit the envelope at the belly. The contents fell to the cushions of the couch. She put down the opener and started to shuffle through the items.

'What are all these things?' Gloria asked.

'Savings bonds. Mom has some too. Grandma left them to her.'

'Laura, you don't really think that Mom could have killed anybody, do you?'

'I don't know. I hope not. But then again, I never thought she would have an affair and deceive all of us.'

'It's all so crazy. What is going on? Why is everybody being killed?'

The diary was face down, but Laura knew what it was even before she turned it over. 'That's it.'

'What?'

Laura picked it up.

Diary 1960.

Gloria inhaled sharply. '1960. Isn't that the year they had the affair?'

Laura nodded. 'This is what the murderer was trying to destroy in the fire. Judy kept all her diaries behind her desk in the study. The blaze destroyed them all.'

'Except this one.'

'Right.'

Laura held the old volume in her hands. She opened it up and recognized Judy's handwriting. It had not changed much in thirty years. Some of the letters looped a little higher back then. The pen had a lighter touch against the paper. But there was no mistaking the penmanship.

Gloria moved closer. 'Start reading, Laura.'

*   *   *

James grabbed an apple from the refrigerator. His wife was upstairs in bed, the lights out, her eyes open. None of them were going to get any sleep tonight, he thought. Words had been uttered that were best left unsaid. Secrets had been stirred that were best left to sleep.

He took a bite out of the apple. James was compulsive when it came to health. He allowed no cookies in his house, no cakes, no ice cream. Sherbet was okay because he felt it improved digestion. Snacks consisted of raisins, nuts, rice cakes and a variety of fresh fruits. Apples were his favorite. McIntosh.

He sat alone in the kitchen with the light off. The lamp from the hallway provided enough illumination, casting giant shadows across the spacious white kitchen. James felt cold in his pajamas and robe, cold and alone. He had worked so hard to keep his family together, to provide for them and care for them. When had it all gone wrong? When had everything that mattered to him been leveled by deceit and lies?

He took another bite. He almost felt tears but quickly pushed them away. James Ayars did not cry. He was strong. He would remain strong and somehow save his family from the past. Thirty years ago, his wife had tried to deceive him. She had packed her lies into a snowball and let it roll down the slope, growing bigger and bigger with the years. Nothing had changed. Lies still ruled their lives.

Tonight was a perfect example.

Mary. His achingly beautiful wife could charm him, seduce him, convince him to ignore or forget things that she had done. But when she lied to him, James always knew. He could always tell when she was trying to deceive him. Deep in his heart, he had known about Mary's affair thirty years ago—even before he received oral confirmation. He had not known with whom or when or even how. But he knew.

He stood, tossed the apple core into the canister, and headed down the corridor to his study. Tonight, Mary had lied again. So had Laura. He had not interrupted a casual mother-and-daughter chat. No, their conversation went well beyond that. Laura learned something during her excursion to Chicago. When she arrived back in Boston, she immediately came here. She pressured her mother until Mary cracked.

How much had Mary told Laura?

James did not know. As little as possible, he was sure. But Mary had undoubtedly opened her mouth and let the past rush out. She had told Laura enough to threaten the very fabric of the family he so cherished.

Everything was going wrong now. The deceptions that held their lives together were coming unglued in front of his eyes. He had to do something to hold the pieces together before they blew away like tiny grains of sand.

But what? What could he do to save his family?

Whatever it takes, he thought. He reached his study and flicked on the light. His long overcoat hung on the tall brass rack Mary had given him on their anniversary last year. He loved that rack. It fit in perfectly with the polished oak bookshelves of medical textbooks, the antique globe, the Persian carpet. The study had always been the most important room in the house for James. This was where he did all his serious thinking, where he planned for life's blows and the strategies he would use to fend them off.

He reached into the pocket of the overcoat. His hand withdrew a gun. He stared at the weapon for a moment, almost hypnotized by its power. He crossed the study, flicked off the light, and moved out the front door without looking behind him.

If he had, he may have noticed his wife standing in the shadows.

*   *   *

Hours passed. How many? Laura and Gloria could not say. The clock seemed to speed around like some cartoon prop. The sun started to rise. Laura kept on reading. Her eyes filled with tears. These words had been written by a Judy Simmons that Laura had never known. The author of this diary had been filled with such hope, such dreams, such youthful optimism. In many sections, Judy rambled randomly about a budding flower or a blue sky or her burning desire to be a novelist. She dreamed of living in Paris, of having a family, of spending summers in Cannes, of writing bestsellers.

Regret echoed through Laura's heart. Judy had ended up doing none of those things. Somewhere along the way, her dreams were derailed and lost forever. When Laura reached February 16th, she learned how the derailment had begun:

510

February 16, 1960
I met the most handsome and charming man in the world today. He is a professor at Brinlen College and his name is Sinclair Baskin. Now I understand what books mean when they speak of unbridled passion, of heroines who would do anything to stay with their man . . .

Laura read parts out loud, skimmed through others. The relationship between Judy Simmons and Sinclair Baskin progressed rapidly. Judy soon learned that Sinclair Baskin was married with two children, but by then it was too late. As Judy herself admitted, love can make you more than blind; it can make you cruel and selfish. It could make you do things you never imagined:

February 24, 1960
I love him. I cannot help my feelings. Emotions are not water faucets that can be turned on and off or made warm and cold as I please. I know about his past. I know that I am not his first. But still I know that I am special to him. Most would dismiss me as terribly naive but I know the truth. I can see it in the way he looks at me . . .

Laura felt ensnared by Judy's words. She was trapped in 1960 with no possible escape but to read on. Laura wanted to go back and warn Judy to stay away from Sinclair Baskin. She wanted to reach right through the pages and shake Judy to her senses.

March 18, 1960
I have never been so happy, never knew such happiness existed. Losing James has ended up being a blessing in disguise. Mary and James are happy and now I'm ecstatic! Could life be better? I doubt it. I am so filled with feelings of love that I am sure I will burst. I want to shout from the top of tall buildings, 'I love you, Sinclair!' He has started talking about divorce even though the idea of hurting his two sons is tearing him apart. Stan is only ten years old. David just a few months. But we are meant to be together and soon we will be. I must have patience . . .

More love notes followed. Pages and pages of sonnets that brought tears to Laura's eyes. She read about the softball game where the photograph had been taken, about walks in the day and lovemaking in the night. The diary was like some bizarre novel whose characters were all too real. Laura watched Judy merrily skip down a path filled with hidden mines. She called out a warning, but Judy would not hear her. Right now it was March of 1960. Young Judy cared not for what was to come. The world was bright and sunny and no one could tell her otherwise. Laura wanted to lock her in, to somehow suspend her aunt's memory in March of 1960. But the diary had to move on. When Laura turned the page, it was April. March of 1960 was gone forever.

April 3, 1960
We're going to visit my family today. I don't expect them to be thrilled for me. I doubt they will understand. But how can they deny the glow in my

face? How can they be upset when they see how happy we are? They will have to accept us. They will want to accept us. Of course, my parents are going to be upset about his being married, but love conquers all, right? I'll let you know how it goes when we get back.

Later. Something changed today, I don't know what. Everything went well with my family—as well as could be expected. My parents were upset but managed to remain fairly polite. Mary got along very nicely with Sinclair as did James. In truth, my family reacted just as I suspected they would. So why this dark feeling inside? It's Sinclair. He was different today. Oh, he still looked at me with love. He still kissed me good night and told me that he loved me. But something was . . . off. He was distracted, not completely there. Of course that's understandable. Today was a stressful day for him too. But still, there was something wrong. Something in the air . . .

'Listen to that something,' Laura said out loud, calling through time itself to patch wounds that still bled. 'Get away from him.'

'She was young,' Gloria said. 'She was in love.'

'He was a married man, Gloria.'

She smiled sadly. 'If you had learned David was married, would it have changed anything?'

'Of course it would—'

'Really? Be honest with yourself, Laura.'

Laura tried to push the allegation to the side and read on, but it remained there, swaying occasionally but never fully leaving.

April 17, 1960

My life is coming to an end. The sun no longer rises. The flowers no longer bloom. Something has taken away my Sinclair. More than that, something has begun to destroy him. I approached him today in the hopes he would confide in me. He has been acting strangely for two weeks now, ever since our visit to my parents' house. I asked him what was wrong.

'Nothing,' he said quietly. 'There are problems.'

'Problems?' I asked.

He nodded. 'I think we have to end this.'

My heart disintegrated then, right in his stuffy, book-congested office, right in front of the works of Keats and Browning and Shakespeare and Dante.

I think we have to end this.

Seven words. Seven words destroyed my life. I of all people should not be amazed by that. Words, I know, can be all-powerful tools. That is all well and good on an analytical front, but the heart is an object that knows merely emotion and feeling. First James was taken away from me and now I am losing Sinclair.

'What do you mean?' I asked stupidly.

Sinclair was very upset. He was chain-smoking. His hair was all over the place. He had not shaved in a week. His eyes were bloodshot. 'It's over,' he said matter-of-factly. 'I don't want you to come around here anymore. I have a wife, kids.'

'That bastard,' Laura said.

'Keep reading.'

For the next month or so Judy delved into her depression. Nothing she tried could make her forget Sinclair Baskin. What could have changed him? Judy wondered. Could she have been so wrong about his feelings for her? Could Sinclair

514

have been lying to her this whole time? She thought not. Young Judy kept blaming something else. Something 'alien,' she said, had twisted his perception. Eventually, Sinclair would see the light. She would just have to wait. Sinclair would come back to her if she remained patient. Judy settled into a comfortable unhappiness, secure in the knowledge that one day she and Sinclair would be together for all eternity. Love would, in the end, conquer all.

Then something happened in late May that altered her outlook, something that made Judy react in a way that changed their lives forever:

May 27, 1960
My whole body is still numb. Even picking up this pen to write to you is an arduous, unfeeling task. I cannot comment on what happened today. I can only replay the events as they happened.

This morning, Mary called me in a panic. 'Can I come over? I really need to talk to you.'

'Of course.'

'I'll be there in an hour.'

I spent the hour straightening up my closet of a dorm room and taking some notes for my new short story. At exactly ten a.m., Mary knocked on the door. When she entered, I was struck anew by her beauty. I had lived with her all my life but her stunning looks still held me in awe. I knew that her beauty was a dangerous weapon. I just had no idea that it could also be lethal.

'I think I'm pregnant,' she said, her eyes tainted with fear.

'That's wonderful,' I naively replied. 'Gloria will have a little baby brother or sister.'

'You don't understand. The baby . . .'

'Yes?'

'It's not James's.'

I gasped. 'What? How can that be?'

She began to cry. Oh what a devastating weapon even her tears were. 'I'm having an affair.'

'You?'

Mary nodded. 'I never meant for it to happen. I was alone all the time with Gloria. James works so hard and he's never home. Along came this charming man . . .'

She went on and on, making excuses for her carelessness and putting the blame on everything but herself.

'Have you told this man?' I asked.

'He wants me to get a test to make sure.'

'Sounds like good advice to me.'

Mary shook her head. 'I'll take the stupid test, Judy, but I know the truth. I know I'm pregnant. I can feel it.'

I poured us both a cup of tea and asked a casual question that came more from being nosy than concerned. 'Do I know the man?'

Mary's head shot up. 'My God, I forgot. You don't know . . .'

'Of course not,' I said with my smile still on my face. 'How should I know?'

'I thought maybe he told you.'

'Who?'

'Sinclair.'

I don't remember what else was said. My mind froze from that moment until the present. Everything around me collapsed when she said Sinclair's name and yet everything around me became clear. Mary's beauty. That was the alien force that had taken away

516

first James and now my Sinclair. Why didn't I stop her long ago? Why didn't I destroy her ravishing beauty in its infancy? I slept beside it as a child, befriended it, and watched it grow. Now it was destroying me . . .

Laura read about the next day. Then she read it again and again, hoping that the words would eventually change. They did not.

'Laura?' Gloria called out.

'Yes.'

'What's it say? Read it to me.'

But Laura did not have the strength. She handed the book to her sister.

*   *   *

There were some habits of David Baskin's that Mark Seidman could not get out of his system. Early morning basketball was one of them. David had loved to go to the Boston Garden first thing in the morning, enter through a side entrance, and shoot baskets by himself for a few hours. It relaxed him, made him forget, let him remember.

No one else was around this early. Joe, the Garden's head custodian for twenty-some-odd years, did not come in until eight-thirty, so David was truly left alone with his thoughts and the legends that surrounded him. He took the basketball out of his bag and began to dribble on the parquet floor. The sound echoed throughout the arena, from the court to the rafters where the championship flags hung. Fifteen thousand empty seats watched him move up court, the ball dancing between his legs and around his back.

He stopped and jumped. His fingers gently lofted

the ball into the air. It went through the hoop with a swish. His jumpshot. Having a unique jumpshot may be effective on the court, but it was a severe handicap in maintaining a new identity. According to Mike Logan of the *Boston Globe*, only one man had truly been able to duplicate David's jumpshot:

Mark Seidman.

David shook his head. If Logan only knew the truth. If they all only knew the truth. But the fact remained that they would never guess because there was no reason to suspect that David Baskin might still be alive. Only someone who understood his situation would have any chance of figuring out the truth. For that person, David's unique jumpshot had led not only to danger but death.

Judy's death.

Like other sports fans, Judy had seen the similarity between David Baskin's shooting style and Mark Seidman's. Unlike everyone else, she knew enough about the past to realize that they were one and the same, that David had not really drowned in Australia, that he had faked his own death and taken on a new identity. From the beginning, David had recognized that there was a chance that she would figure out his secret. He had accepted that risk. After all, Judy knew that David and Laura were brother and sister. She would realize why he had pretended to die. She would not interfere.

'You don't understand anything, do you?'

'What do you mean?'

'I mean that you think you know what you're doing, but you don't. There are things about this whole situation that have been kept from you.'

Judy had been murdered, he was sure of it.

But why? Was someone trying to prevent her from telling the truth, from exposing what had happened? Had Mary been afraid she might tell Laura the truth? Perhaps. But murder? Could Mary murder her own sister?

David did not think so.

He took some lay-ups and wondered what he should do next. He could not just pretend that Judy's death had been a coincidence, that the fire was unrelated to his disappearance six months ago. The whole situation was still one great big mystery. Nothing made any sense. Why had Judy called him in the first place? Why had she tried to bring them back together? Come to think of it, Judy had always encouraged their relationship—even in the beginning. While Mary fretted and tried anything to separate brother from sister, Judy had been supportive of their love affair. Why? Why had she never tried to break them up?

A whole heap of questions. Absolutely no answers. David circled toward the basket, leaped high in the air, and dunked the ball hard through the cylinder. The whole backboard shook.

'There are things about this whole situation that have been kept from you.'

But what are those things, Judy? What are they?

*   *   *

Gloria took the diary from Laura. 'Are you okay?' she asked.

Laura shook her head. 'I don't know what to do.'

'About what?'

She turned away, her features sagging. 'You'll see. Read.'

May 28, 1960

Revenge. Is that what I was after tonight? If so, I should have remembered that revenge can be a double-edged sword. I fear I have done something wrong. But alas, dear diary, you do not want my opinions. You want the facts. So here they are:

When I woke up this morning (woke up? I never fell asleep) I knew what I had to do: exact my revenge. Mary had stolen two men away from me. It was time to start returning the favor. I visited James at the hospital today . . .

Gloria looked up. 'Oh Christ, she didn't. Tell me she didn't.'

'Keep reading.'

James met me in his new private office. It was all done up in typical, immaculate doctor decor with diplomas and medical journals. He was very proud of it. He boasted that he was the only resident who had his own office. No surprise really. I always knew James would be successful. I loved him at one time. I loved him from the moment we first started dating all the way through his marriage to Mary. I was crushed when he left me for her. I thought my heart would never recover. But it has. It started to heal the day I met Sinclair. He released James's hold on me, and now James seemed to me no more than a fine man, a very good catch for a husband.

Am I saying that I feel nothing for James anymore? Not exactly. But the truth is that I wanted to take him away from Mary more than I wanted him for myself.

We began by chatting about this and that, but with James casual conversation does not last very long, especially when he has patients waiting. He quickly turned on his cool, calm exterior. His voice became as brisk and professional as his well-groomed appearance.

'You said you had to see me about something urgent?'

'Yes,' I said. 'I'm just not sure how to tell you.'

'How to tell me what?'

I took a deep breath then and feigned looking confused. 'I just feel so bad.'

'About what?'

'I hate to see you play the chump, James.' I reached across the desk and took his hands. 'There was a time when you meant a great deal to me. Do you remember?'

'Yes of course,' he said impatiently. 'Now what is it?'

That was when I did it. I told James everything. I told him his wife was having an affair. I told him that Mary was sleeping with Sinclair Baskin. I told him that she was carrying his baby.

At first James did not react. He merely played with the pencil between his fingers. Then his jaw set. His face turned red. His hands clenched, snapping the pencil in half. Suddenly books were flying, then chairs, then furniture. He was a man out of control, completely crazy. I tried to calm him down, tried to warn him that someone would hear him, but he did not pay heed. He tore apart the office he so loved until his rage finally gave way to exhaustion. He crumpled back into his chair (it was the only thing still standing except me) and dropped his head into his hands.

I circled around the desk. 'Don't worry, James. I love you. I'll take care of you.' I reached his seat and put my hands on his shoulders. He winced in repulsion. My hands flew back to my sides as if his shoulders were on fire. Slowly his head rose. He glared at me with a twisted look, a look of intense hatred.

'I don't want you,' he said. 'I want Mary.'

Gloria looked up. 'Dad knew?'

Laura nodded.

'And he never said anything? He just raised you as his own?'

'I don't know but I think we should read on.'

'Why?'

'This was written on May 28.'

'So?'

'Sinclair Baskin died the next day.'

May 29, 1960

Help me. God, what have I done? The whole situation has become too much for me to handle. It's completely out of control now. It's taking on a life all its own, and I don't know where it will lead. I fear the worst, but what else could possibly happen?

Mary just called me. The pregnancy test came back positive. Though James has kept up a good facade up till now, jealousy has already nibbled away at his ability to reason. What is he going to do now that speculation has become fact?

Mary is on her way to Sinclair's office to tell him the news. Sinclair, my beloved, what have you done? I understand the power of Mary's beauty, the sensuous spell she can cast over a man. But wasn't our love strong enough to fight it off? Wasn't our love powerful enough to deflect her physical charms harmlessly into space? Will you grow tired of her and come back to me eventually? Yes, I am sure you will. I must wait.

Later:

My life is over. The moment I saw the blood on James's shirt I knew what had happened. I said nothing. My face showed no emotion. But inside someone was screaming until the vibrations wore through me.

'I didn't mean to,' he said to me, his voice bordering on hysterical. 'I just meant to confront him, to confront them both.' His hands were shaking. 'It just happened.'

'Just happened,' a voice echoed. I guessed it was mine.

'I was listening in at the door of his office, my ear pressed against the wooden frame. I could not believe what I heard. Mary wanted to leave me. She wanted to run away with that son of a bitch.'

I still said nothing.

'But the bastard wouldn't listen to her. He threw her out. He was so cold to her, so heartless. He knew he had impregnated a married woman and the son of a bitch reacted by tossing her out of his office like yesterday's garbage.'

'What did Mary do?' I asked.

'She was in shock. She could not believe he was just going to abandon her like this. She called him a bastard and ran out. I ducked in an empty doorway down the hall as she sprinted past. The next thing I remember the gun was out of my pocket and in my hand.'

'No,' I cried, while my mind kept shouting, 'Sinclair is dead, Judy, James may have pulled the trigger but your jealousy killed him.'

James was in a trance now, his eyes wide and dreamy. 'I stepped out of my hiding spot,' he began, 'and moved slowly down the hall. When I reached his door, I peeked into his office. He was just sitting in his chair looking out the window. His back was to me. I crept closer. My hand gripped the gun. I had not held a weapon since I was in the service, but it felt so right in my palm. As he began to swivel his chair toward the door, I placed the gun against his forehead. He froze for a split second. His eyes, so full of fear, locked onto mine, and I think he knew then that he was about to die. I called him a bastard and then I pulled the trigger . . .

'Dad?' Gloria asked, though she knew the answer. 'Dad killed Sinclair Baskin?'

Laura felt herself slowly slipping into a shock. 'And Judy,' she managed, 'and even Stan . . .'

'NO! Not Dad! He couldn't!'

'Who else? Didn't you say Stan saw the murder take place, that he remembered the killer's face? He must have recognized Dad when he saw him at the game.'

'It can't be.'

'And Judy,' Laura went on, 'was going to tell me everything.'

'But I don't understand. Why did Judy wait so long to say something, Laura? Why didn't she tell someone years ago?'

'I'm not sure,' Laura said, 'but she was probably scared out of her mind. She blames herself for what happened to Sinclair. If she had not betrayed her sister's trust, he would still be alive. She might have seen herself as an accomplice. And what would have been the point of saying something anyway? It was over. Telling people would not bring Sinclair back.'

'So what made her change her mind after all these years? Why did she finally say something?'

Laura thought for a moment. 'David's drowning,' she concluded. 'When David died, she must have realized that the past could not just be wished away.'

Gloria shook her head. 'It still makes no sense. David drowned six months ago. Why did she wait all that time to tell you? And there are other questions. What happened to David's money? And how did someone get hold of his ring and put it in your apartment?'

Laura stopped. 'I don't know. But there may be a way of finding out.'

'How?'

Laura went to the closet and got her coat. It was six thirty in the morning. They had been reading the book all night. 'You stay here and finish going through that diary. See if there's any more about what happened.'

'Where are you going?'

She grabbed her keys and headed to the door. 'To talk to Dad.'

Gloria turned the page. The next day was May 30th.

*   *   *

James drove very fast. He had never been afraid of being stopped by the police for speeding. After all, he was a senior staff member at Boston Memorial. He would just tell them that there was an emergency at the hospital. A matter of life and death. How that phrase grabbed people: a matter of life and death. People stopped and listened when you said it. For a fleeting moment, they considered their own mortality.

He reached the apartment building on the outskirts of the city. It was a run-down neighborhood, but then again cops were not the highest-paid people in the work force. He glanced at the clock on the dashboard. Six thirty in the morning. T.C. would probably still be asleep. James would have to wake him. After all, this was an emergency. This was a matter of life and death— for all of them.

James stepped out of the car. He had known from the moment Laura first called him from Australia six months ago that Mary had once again lied to him, that she had gone to Australia instead of California, that she had been responsible for David's sudden disappearance. The dread that coursed through him at that moment was black and cold. Why had he been so foolish? Why hadn't he seen it coming? Why hadn't he found a way to stop Mary before she had the chance to say something to David?

If only he could have stopped her. If only David had not listened to her. If only David had ignored Mary's every word and run back to Laura. If only. Those two words stretched back thirty years to the moment when it all began: if only Mary had been a faithful wife instead of a cheap whore.

But alas, none of that had happened. Thinking of what might have been cannot change what has already occurred. James had to go on. He had to make the best of the situation. He had to salvage what he could from the tiny fragments that were still left. There was no time to cry over the past anymore. Too much time had passed. Too many

526

people had already died.

He knocked on the door. The gun was in his pocket just in case T.C. did not cooperate. He hoped that he would not have to use it quite yet. All he wanted from T.C. was one small piece of information:

Where was Mark Seidman?

When he found Mark Seidman, then the gun would be put to use.

James knocked again. Why hadn't David drowned in Australia? If he had, this whole episode would be unnecessary. But David was alive and, as a result, he was still a threat to James's family. James had come too far to lose everything now. Just one more little pull of the trigger. Just one more bullet searing through a skull. Then it would all be over.

T.C. came to the door. It was obvious from his appearance that he had been asleep. He pushed open the screen door and squinted through sleepy eyes.

'Dr Ayars?'

'Can I speak to you a moment?' James asked. 'It's very important.'

T.C. stepped back. 'Come on in.'

'No, this will only take a second.'

'Okay,' T.C. said. 'What can I do for you?'

James licked his lips. 'I need to speak to David.'

'Huh?'

'Please don't play dumb with me. I know that David and Mark Seidman are one and the same. I've known for quite some time.'

'I don't know what the hell—'

'Listen to me. I know David's drowning was a fake. And I know why he did it. I don't want to cause any trouble. I just want you to tell me where I can find him.'

T.C. said nothing.

'It's a matter of life and death,' James urged. 'Laura's life is in danger. I have no interest in revealing his secret. I only want to talk to him.'

T.C. shrugged. 'David is dead, Dr Ayars—'

'Damn it! Judy has already been murdered. Stop playing games—'

'—but,' T.C. continued evenly, 'if you just want to speak with Mark Seidman, he shoots baskets at the Boston Garden every morning from now until about eight a.m. He's alone in there, if you need to talk to him.'

'Does he use the same side entrance David used to use?'

T.C. nodded.

'Thank you,' James said and turned to leave. Perfect. No one would be in the Garden this early. James could sneak up on David, put the gun against his head (just like he had done with David's father), and fire.

And at long last it would be over.

James jogged back to his car. His hands were in his pockets—one touching his car keys, the other touching the weapon he would use in his next (and last) murder.

*   *   *

Gloria chose not to read about May 30, 1960 right away. Judy's journal was like a bad-tasting medicine that could only be swallowed in moderate doses— and May 29, 1960 had given her more than a mouthful.

528

She put down the diary, walked into the kitchen, and poured herself a cup of coffee. She glanced out the window. Laura too had a view of the Charles River. Gloria remembered how much Stan had loved to look at that river, how he cherished the time he spent just staring out from the balcony. He was such a simple man really, a simple man who had turned down a few wrong paths and could never find his way out of the thicket. Gloria had found him there. She had begun to lead Stan into the clearing when someone killed him.

Someone, nothing. Her father had done it.

How? she wondered. How could a man full of love be such a monster underneath? She did not know the answer. She was not sure she wanted to know. She sipped her coffee, sat back on the couch, picked up the diary and read about—

May 30, 1960.

Gloria's eyes widened.

Blood . . .

Soon the words began to swim in front of her eyes. Her stomach contracted painfully. Images, horrible, terrible images—

Blood, there was so much blood . . .

—jerked her mind back and forth. Gloria's darkest nightmare was coming to life, chasing after her with—

blood . . .

with a lust for destruction. She had been so young at the time, just a little girl, and mercifully she had never remembered what had happened.

'Mommy! Mommy!'

'Get out of here, Gloria. Get out of here now!'

But that was about to change. Visions jolted her, stinging her nerves. All of a sudden, Gloria was a five-year-old child moving down that darkened hallway again, except this time she knew where she was heading: her parents' bedroom. She was thirsty and wanted a drink of water. So she took Floppy Rabbit with her and began to trek down the hallway toward her mommy and daddy's bedroom.

Gloria wanted to turn away from the diary, to close the book and never open it again. But her eyes were locked to the pages, moving over the words at a brisk, even pace. The words were opening a door that had been closed in her mind since childhood. Suddenly, little Gloria was in front of her parents' bedroom door again. She stood up on her tippy-toes and stretched for the door knob. Floppy Rabbit was cocked under her elbow.

'Get out of here, Gloria, Get out of here now!'

The knob turned in her hands. Soon, Gloria would see what was behind that door. She had spent her whole life forgetting this moment, but now the image was being forced upon her. Even when she closed her eyes she could still see the door swinging open.

She looked inside the room. And remembered. And screamed.

Gloria put down the diary. She was shaking. The words Judy had written about May 30 1960 revealed everything. It was all true. Every last word was true. Her father had killed Sinclair and Judy and Stan and . . .

. . . and what about David?

The doorman's intercom buzzed again. Gloria walked over to the squawk box. She noticed on the kitchen clock that it was nearly seven in the morning. Who would be visiting them now?

'Yes?'

'There is a Richard Corsel down here to see Laura,' the security guard said. 'He says it's urgent.'

Laura had just mentioned his name. He was the man at the Heritage of Boston Bank who'd transferred David's money. 'Send him up.'

As Gloria sat and waited, the reality of what she had just read sank into her brain like a concrete brick in quicksand. Her heart hammered away in her chest. The truth became apparent, and even more tragic than she could have ever dared imagine. She grabbed the diary off the couch, flipped forward in time, and read onward. Soon, her eyes found what she had already known to be true. The words on the page merely reconfirmed her darkest fear:

Her mother had been wrong. David and Laura were not brother and sister.

CHAPTER THIRTY-ONE

Laura pulled into the driveway and leaped out of the car. There were still so many holes that needed to be plugged up: David's ring under her pillow, his missing money, and maybe most of all, the reason Judy had waited so long to try and say something. Laura did not know why but she was sure that was the crux, that once that was answered the rest would fall into place.

She did not bother to ring the bell and warn her parents of her early morning arrival. She simply unlocked the door and stepped into the front foyer.

'Laura?'

She turned toward the voice. Her mother was

sitting on the couch, wearing a robe.

'Where is Dad?'

Mary's face clouded over. 'He's not here.'

'Where did he go?'

'I don't know. He stayed in his study all night. Oh Laura, you're not going to tell him, are you? Please—'

'He already knows,' Laura said evenly. 'He's known for thirty years.'

Mary's head fell to the side, 'What?'

'Judy told him the day after you told her. I have Judy's diary from 1960. It's all in there.'

Mary's face twisted in puzzlement. 'But that's not possible. He never said one word to me.'

Laura's words spilled forward in wild gasps. 'Judy was furious at you for stealing Sinclair from her. Telling Dad was her way of getting revenge. But she never expected him to lose control. He murdered Sinclair Baskin right after you left the office.'

Mary's mouth dropped open. 'It can't be.'

'It's true.'

'But James never said a word. He never threw me out. He loved you and raised you like his own. Why?'

'I don't know, Mother. I suspect it has something to do with his love for you.'

Mary's whole face emanated bleakness. She shook her head. 'Not James,' she said weakly. 'He's a doctor. He would never hurt anyone.'

She knelt beside her mother. 'We have to find him, Mother. We have to confront him and find out what really happened.'

The roar of a blasting engine made them both turn. Laura opened the front door and peered out. Gloria's car raced up the road at what had to be a hundred miles an hour. As she turned into the driveway, one of the tires swung up onto the grass but Gloria did not pause or even hesitate until she came to a stop near the front door. She jumped out of the car.

'Gloria, what the hell—' Laura saw her sister's face and stopped. Gloria's eyes were wide and frenzied and out of control. Her right hand grasped the diary and a white envelope.

'Richard Corsel came to see you,' Gloria called back.

'What?'

'He told me to give you this envelope. He said it would answer all your questions.'

Laura's heart got caught in her throat. The missing money. Richard had traced down the missing money.

'And May 30,' Gloria shouted, holding up the diary. 'Something terrible happened on May 30.'

*　　　*　　　*

James was back in his car and on the road in a matter of minutes. He had to give David credit. Creating Mark Seidman had been a stroke of genius. James realized that Judy was right, that David had not committed suicide. With the help of his cop friend (he could never have pulled it off by himself) David had faked his own death and taken on a new identity: Mark Seidman. Genius and yet so simple.

James imagined the scene in Australia six months earlier. After David had met up with Mary at the Pacific International Hotel, David realized that he would have to give up Laura, that he would have to leave her for her own good. At the same time, he could not tell her why—lest he hurt her further.

So what was the logical solution?

Disappear off the face of the Earth, of course.

And how do you do that without giving up everything you have?

You transfer your money around via Switzerland, fake an accidental drowning, go in for a little cosmetic surgery, take on a new identity.

Who would suspect such a thing from a wealthy, successful basketball star who had just married the world's most beautiful woman? From a man who seemed to have everything?

No one—not even Mary, James or Judy.

There was only one potential flaw in the plan but it could be worked around: David's unusual jumpshot. Somebody was sure to recognize it. But so what? If Mark Seidman's style of play was similar to David Baskin's, what would that prove? It would take a wild stretch of imagination to leap from a resemblance in shooting form to a fraudulent death.

Only someone who knew about the past could possibly suspect the truth. That, David must have thought, involved two people: Mary and Judy. Sinclair was dead. James, he thought incorrectly, knew nothing of what had taken place.

Mary, of course, was no threat at all. In the first place, she knew nothing about basketball. And even if she did by some odd coincidence figure it out, she would never say anything. She would just be thankful that David was out of Laura's life.

Judy, however, was another story. She was both intelligent and a big basketball fan. She might just be able to figure it out. But where was the threat in that? If Judy figured out what David had done, she would certainly not tell anyone. After all, David and Laura were brother and sister. David had done this to protect Laura from the truth. Why would Judy do something to rehash what had happened when it would only bring more pain and misery to her niece?

James smiled. Why indeed.

Only James knew why Judy chose to expose Mark Seidman's true identity. You see, Mary did not tell David the whole story during their meeting in Australia—not because she was trying to hide something. No, in fairness to Mary she told David everything she knew. Unfortunately for them, that was not enough. She did not know about . . .

. . . *May 30, 1960.*

That was the day after Sinclair Baskin died. Mary had never learned what happened on the evening of May 30, 1960. Only two people knew. Only two people had borne witness to the event that had taken place on May 30, 1960. One had recently burned to death. The other was about to commit one last murder.

May 30, 1960.

When Judy had first realized that David was still alive, she snapped into action. His strange survival was her last chance at redemption, her last chance to save Laura from the clutches of the past. James, on the other hand, had seen David's survival as the path to his family's destruction. He knew that Judy was going to tell Laura and Mary everything. He knew that she was going to reveal secrets that she had promised to take with her to the grave. So James did the only thing he could: He helped Judy

535

keep her promise.

He escorted her to the grave.

He set the house on fire with her and all her damn diaries in it. The secret of the past had burned into nothing but worthless smoke and ashes. There had however been a serious miscalculation in Judy's death: Laura got caught in the blaze. But that was not his fault. Mary started it. She should have never slept with Sinclair. And Judy was at fault too. She should have kept her mouth shut. Lucky for both of them that the mystery man had saved Laura. James now had a pretty good idea who that mystery man was.

It was a pity that he had to die.

James drove through the Fenway and turned onto Storrow Drive. David Baskin and the Boston Garden were only five minutes away.

*   *   *

Gloria moved up the front porch and into the house. The three women stared at each other, each noticing the horrifying pallor of the other two and wondering if they too looked like they were wearing death masks.

Laura spoke first. 'What happened on May 30?'

Gloria wanted to tell her sister and yet she wanted to put it off for even a few more moments. 'The diary will explain everything,' she said, 'but you better read Mr Corsel's note first. He said it was urgent.'

Laura could feel beads of sweat on her forehead despite the cold. The envelope was plain and white, the kind you could buy in any stationery or card store. She took it from Gloria's hand and ripped the seal. She withdrew a small note card, also on unmarked white paper. Richard Corsel had a marvelous economy of words but Laura understood why. The less said, the better:

Please destroy this note as soon as you have read it. The name of the person who now controls the missing money is Mark Seidman.

Her legs almost gave way.

Gloria and Mary moved in. They led Laura to the couch in the den. All three sat down.

'What does it say?' Gloria asked.

Laura's head swirled but somewhere in the gyrations she saw a faint light. At first she swore it was just her imagination, a case of desire turning a hope into a reality. It was all so crazy. It was a mirage, it had to be. And yet, the more it ran through her mind the more she understood everything: why T.C. had lied to her, why David had called the bank, why she had felt so strange around Mark Seidman, why he had been afraid to go near her, why his jumpshot was so familiar, why T.C. had helped him sneak out during the cocktail party when he had one of his . . .

'It's okay. I got you.'

A muffled cry.

'Hang in there, old buddy. Just lean on me. I'll have you home soon.'

'I didn't want to see her, T.C. I didn't want to go near her.'

Tears ran down Laura's face. Her mind tried to accept that she was finally face to face with the truth. 'He's still alive.'

'Who?' Gloria asked. 'What are you talking

about?'

She held up the piece of paper. 'This proves it. Mark Seidman is really David.'

'What?' Mary shouted.

The pieces began to come together in her mind even as she spoke. 'David never drowned. He never committed suicide. He just wanted us all to think he was dead. He wanted you to think he was out of the way and he wanted to protect me from the truth. It all makes sense now. And T.C. was in on it.'

'But what about his ring showing up under your pillow?' Gloria asked.

'That had to be T.C.'s doing. He was trying to scare me off. He was afraid I would learn the truth.'

Laura ran for the phone.

'What are you doing?' Mary asked.

'I'm calling Clip Arnstein. I want to find out where Mark Seidman lives.'

'No!' Mary screamed. 'Don't you see? This doesn't change anything. You can't be with him. David is still your brother.'

Laura spun back toward her mother as if the words she had spoken had wrapped themselves around her throat and pulled. 'But—?'

It was Gloria who raised her hand to silence her. Her tear-streaked face mourned her own loss, but Gloria now realized that there was hope for Laura.

'No, he's not,' she said.

Mary looked at her. 'What are you talking about?'

'David is not your brother,' Gloria repeated, handing Laura the diary. 'May 30th. Read May 30th.'

*   *   *

538

Only a few blocks to go. Nothing could save David now.

James felt his sweat stick his shirt to his body. He hated perspiration. He kept extra dress shirts in his office so that he could always change into something fresh. But he would be able to change soon enough, as soon as he took care of this problem.

He was no professional killer, that was for sure, but he had managed to leave no clues behind and provide himself with good alibis. Take Judy's murder, for example. If anybody wanted to know where James had been at the time of the fire, Dr Eric Clarich would gladly confirm that James was five hours away in Boston. Dr Clarich would testify that he had called Boston Memorial Hospital half an hour after the fire had been set and reached James.

Conclusion: James could not possibly be involved. No sense in digging any deeper.

How had James pulled that one off? If he had been up at Colgate committing a murder, how could he have miraculously returned to Boston in time for the expected emergency call? Simple. He didn't. He merely set his office extension to transfer automatically all of his calls to a pay phone not five minutes from St Catherine's Hospital in Hamilton, New York. Brilliant, no? Then all he had to do was make his way to the airport, wait a few hours, and show up at the hospital all harried as if he just rushed all the way from Boston.

That part had gone very smoothly.

His real moment of fear came when he finally did arrive at the hospital and saw Mary was already there. Panic washed through him. There was only one way she could have gotten from Boston to Hamilton so fast. She had to have been on her way up to Colgate to talk to Judy. Did Mary reach her in time? Did Judy have a chance to tell her anything before she died? Luckily, the answer was no. One look at Mary told him that she still knew nothing of what had occurred on May 30, 1960. Besides, Laura was the one Judy wanted to tell, not Mary.

BEEP, BEEP, BEEP, BEEP, BEE—

James reached for his belt and turned off his stupid beeper. Damn. He would have to call in. If not, the hospital would start making calls and James did not want that.

In the distance, James saw his target: The Boston Garden. It could wait another couple of minutes. He pulled over to the side of the road, got out of the car, and trotted over to the phone booth.

*   *   *

Gloria's words jolted Laura like an electric shock. 'What do you mean David is not my brother?'

'May 30,' Gloria repeated. 'Read it.'

Laura took the diary from her sister and moved down toward the couch. Mary sat next to her in order to read over her shoulder.

'I don't understand any of this,' Mary said.

Gloria swallowed. 'Just read.'

Laura opened the book. Her fingers fumbled the pages back and forth until at last she arrived on the right day:

May 30, 1960
This nightmare will never end. I spun the web and now

540

I am caught in it. James's plan is completely insane and completely ingenious. He has turned Mary's own charms of seduction to his favor and me into his unwilling accomplice.

'You're involved in this too,' James told me in a cruel voice. 'I will tell everyone that you helped me kill Sinclair Baskin.'

'I'll deny it. It will be your word against mine.'

His smile was so diabolical, so evil. 'You are so stupid sometimes,' he spit out. 'Who do you think a jury is going to believe—a jealous harlot who slept with a married man and then betrayed her own sister or a wronged doctor who is a pillar of the community?'

I said nothing. I was too scared to speak.

'You are going to help me with this because once you do, our secret and our fates will be eternally sealed together. Neither one of us will be able to reveal the other's sin without condemning themselves as well. After today, we will go on as if nothing has changed. We will never speak of this again.'

'But can't you see that this is all wrong?'

His face clouded over. 'I know it's wrong. Murdering Sinclair Baskin, well, that was justice. This time, it is not so cut and dried.'

'Then don't do it,' I urged. 'Forget this whole crazy scheme. Forget about everything. I'll never tell anyone, I swear.'

'No,' he said firmly. 'I can't just forget and go on. I have to make things right—even if it means the death of an innocent soul. Don't you see? Mary will unwittingly go along with this. Sinclair has abandoned her and she is certainly not going to tell me the truth. What other option does she have?'

'None,' I admitted. 'She'll have to pretend that the

541

child is yours.'

James smiled. 'Exactly. So let's make her wish come true, shall we?'

The house was pitch dark. In the den I could hear the radio playing a familiar tune but I couldn't place the name. James and I crept down the hallway past little Gloria's room. My niece is such a sweet, pretty child. I wonder what her young mind will remember of this night. I pray she will recall nothing.

We were a few feet from their bedroom door when I whispered, 'Are you sure Mary is unconscious?'

'I gave her enough drugs to knock out a horse. She'll feel nothing until morning. Then I'll give her a fresh batch.'

We reached the door. He swung it open, the dim light from the hall fell onto Mary's sleeping body. She did not move.

'Come on,' he said. 'Let's go.'

'Please, James, think about this.'

He grabbed my arm. 'Let's go.'

He pulled me in with him and shut the door. He flicked on the overhead light, illuminating the room. Mary still did not stir.

He smiled. 'You see what I mean? Out like a light, the no-good whore.'

'Then why do you stay with her?'

He looked at me as though I had asked a priest why he believed in God if there was so much cruelty in the world. 'Because I love her,' he said, and I think I understood.

He took out his medical bag and opened it. His hand reached in and grabbed a metallic instrument. 'I took this from the hospital. Menacing-looking, isn't it?'

I nodded. My body felt so damn cold. I stepped

back and back again until I ran into the wall and could go back no further. James's face changed as if he had put on a mask. He was now the cool doctor again. He took the device and went to work. At the first sight of blood, I nearly vomited. I closed my eyes but my ears could still hear the scraping sounds. I wished he would hurry. I wished it was over.

Time passed, and finally the sounds stopped. Another life had been terminated. 'Clean this mess up,' he said to me. 'Make it fast.'

'Do I have to?'

'Yes. Now hurry.'

Before I could move more than a few steps, the door flew open. I turned in time to see little Gloria standing in the doorway. Her eyes were wide with fear.

'Mommy! Mommy!' she shouted, her eyes staring at the puddle of blood between her mother's legs.

'Get out of here, Gloria!' James shouted. 'Get out of here now!'

The child did not move. She was frozen in some kind of trance. I grabbed her and hurried her out of the room, away from the blood . . .

Laura could not stop shaking. Neither could Mary.

'It's true,' Gloria said, 'Every word. The nightmare I could never remember . . . this is it. It all came back to me as soon as I read Judy's words. I could see the blood. I could see Mom's body sprawled out on the bed. I could see the twisted look on Dad's face. I even remember seeing Judy huddled in the corner.'

'He aborted the fetus,' Laura uttered.

Gloria nodded.

Laura stared at her mother who was quivering

as if she were in the grip of a fever. Everything began to click together. 'He turned all your tricks against you, Mother,' Laura said. 'You ended up being the one who was fooled about the identity of the real father, not him. You ended up being the one tricked into seducing him so that he could impregnate you for real. You were the one who got so caught up in the bliss of fooling James that you dismissed my "late arrival" as your good fortune.'

'And my difficult pregnancy?' she asked.

Laura nodded. 'He caused that too. He kept you drugged out so you wouldn't be able to guess what was going on. You told me you were feeling sick but were afraid to go to a doctor, right? It would have been too dangerous, you said, because Dad might find out. That gave him the time he needed. You continuously slept with him because you wanted to fool him into thinking he was the father when all along he was trying to get you pregnant for real.'

Gloria moved toward them. 'And that answers the question about why Judy waited so long to say something, Laura. When David died, there was no reason to tell you the truth. David was already dead. But when she saw Mark Seidman at the Boston Garden, she must have realized that David was still alive. She knew then that it was not too late to bring you two back together.'

'My God,' Mary managed, 'then David is not your brother?'

Laura shook her head.

'Then that gun . . .'

'What gun? Mom, what are you talking about?'

'I thought nothing of it at the time. I figured there had been some trouble at the hospital and he needed it for protection . . .'

544

'Needed what?' Laura shouted. 'Tell me.'

Her eyes fixed onto Laura's. 'I saw your father leave earlier. He had a gun.'

Laura sprinted to the phone. The house remained silent, everyone lost in their troubled thoughts. Laura quickly dialed. The phone was picked up on the first ring.

'Hello?' the voice said.

'Clip?'

'Oh hello, Laura,' the old Celtics president said. 'How are you?'

'Fine thanks.'

'Sorry to hear about your aunt. Terrible tragedy. This whole year—'

'I'm in a bit of a hurry,' she cut in. 'I need to speak to Mark Seidman right away. Do you have his phone number?'

'Seidman? Why do you want to speak to him?'

'Please,' Laura begged, 'it's very important.'

'Well, if you really need to reach him quickly, you can head over to the Garden. He's usually shooting there by himself in the mornings . . . just like David—'

Laura did not hear the rest of his words. She was already sprinting toward the car.

*　　　*　　　*

'Discontinue his IV and monitor his vital signs,' James barked in his familiar authoritative voice.

'Yes, Doctor.'

'Tell Dr Kingfield to look in on him. I'll be in in a few hours.'

'Yes, Doctor.'

James glanced out the booth and into the streets.

545

The Boston Garden was so close now. He only had to drive another hundred yards at the most. 'Is there anything else?'

'No, Doctor.'

'Good,' he replied. 'I'll call back in a little while.'

He did not wait for her 'Yes, Doctor.' He hung up the phone and strolled as casually as he could back to his car. It was not easy. He was anxious now.

The car started right away. He checked the traffic behind him and moved the car into the flow. A minute later, he turned into the lot at the Boston Garden. The timeworn arena needed so much construction that it was nearly impossible to figure out what should be worked on first. Still, the Garden had a certain majesty to it. He felt an undeniable awe when he gazed upon it. Whether his awe emanated from the building's history or from the thought of the atrocity he was about to commit within its sacred hall James could not say.

He parked not too far from the side entrance David had always used in the past. One peek out the windows told him that there was no one around this early in the morning. The area was completely abandoned.

Perfect.

James took his gun out of his pocket. He opened the chamber. All loaded and ready to go. The gun he had used last night to kill Stan was sitting in the bottom of the river. This was a new gun—entirely unrelated to the one that ended Stan Baskin's life. Also untraceable. He put it back in his pocket and got out of the car.

He walked over to the heavy exit door and took one more look around. Nope. Nobody in sight.

He opened the door slowly. There was no creak. He stepped inside. Behind him, the door began to swing closed. James turned around and realized that the door was going to slam shut. He put out his hand to slow the accelerating movement of the weighty portal. It worked to some degree. The door did not slam, but it did not close silently either.

James was in the dark cavern on the bottom level of the Garden. He turned around. Down the hall was the famous parquet court. In the distance, he could make out the distinct echo of someone dribbling a basketball.

CHAPTER THIRTY-TWO

David worked on his foul shots. He rarely missed foul shots in a game, shooting a career ninety-two percent—the highest in the league. Missing foul shots was something he had always considered unforgivable. It was a free shot, free points. There were no hands in your face, no players bumping you or trying to swat the ball into the seats. And there was only one thing you needed to do to be a good foul-shooter: practice. So many games came down to them. So many games were won or lost on the charity stripe.

He had made twelve foul shots in a row when he heard a faint noise. Someone had just come in via his side entrance. David grabbed the ball and speed-dribbled down to the other end of the court. Sweat trickled down his body. His hair, now curly blonde instead of wavy brown, was matted against his forehead.

His ears did not detect footsteps. Strange. The sound of the door closing was fairly unmistakable. Very few people knew that he kept that particular door unlocked when he was working out in the mornings. There were his teammates of course. Clip and the coaching staff. T.C., Laura, Gloria and James. And that was about it.

So who was here now?

He drove hard to the basket and took a reverse lay-up, always a favorite move of his when he was up against a taller player. He would leap in the air, use the rim for protection against the long arm of the defender, and drop the ball against the backboard on the other side. Two points. Three, if he could draw the foul.

Since becoming Mark Seidman, he had worked out with Nautilus weight machines four times a week. The exercise regimen had an immediate impact on his athletic body. It made Mark Seidman's physique somewhat thinner and more toned than David Baskin's. David found this also increased his foot speed and leaping ability to some degree.

Still no sounds from the entrance ramp.

He shrugged. Maybe it had been the wind against the metal door. Maybe it was just one of the towel boys doing some early laundry in the locker room. Whatever.

After another few seconds, David forgot all about the slamming door. He tried to concentrate on his long-distance jumpshot, but other images jumped in the way.

*   *   *

548

Gloria's car swerved off Interstate 93 and onto the exit ramp. Her eyes stared out the windshield, seeing nothing but the road in front of her. Her foot pressed down harder against the accelerator. The car lurched forward.

In the passenger seat, Laura sat with the diary laid open on her lap. She read and read but still one thought kept going through her head, one thought that pushed away the mounting horror of the past.

David. David was still alive.

She looked over at Gloria. 'Are you okay?'

'Dad murdered Stan,' she answered. 'He killed the man I loved.'

'I know,' Laura said softly.

'How? How could he do that?'

Laura's voice was barely a whisper. 'You read the diary. He's a sick man. He's out of control.'

'Did you get through the month of June yet?' Gloria asked.

'Just about.'

'Then you see the full scope of what he did. Dad kept drugging Mom so she wouldn't figure out what he had done. Then he kept sleeping with her until she was pregnant again—except now the baby was his, not Sinclair's.'

'And Judy said nothing,' Laura added. 'She was terrified of what would happen if the truth came out.'

The car turned right. They were not very far away now. 'They lived with that secret for all those years. They just pretended nothing had ever happened.'

'I don't think it was all that simple,' Laura said. 'I doubt a day went by that they didn't think of what happened in May of 1960.'

Gloria's grip on the steering wheel tightened. 'I just can't believe it. I mean, what could have twisted Dad's mind like that?'

'I don't know,' Laura said. 'His blind obsession with Mom maybe, with the whole idea of family.'

'How can he act like he loves us so much and still be a killer?'

'It's no act,' Laura replied. 'At least I don't think it is. He loves us—maybe too strongly. He has always been the one to take on responsibility without help, protecting his girls from harm. Whenever there was a problem, Mom never raised a hand to help him. She just sat back and relied on Dad. Somewhere in his mind, he believes he has done all of this to protect his family.'

'All this time . . . and we never knew.'

Laura nodded. She tried to look down and continue reading the diary, hoping to block her thoughts from what was about to occur. But it was senseless. Anticipation rubbed against her raw nerves. David. After all this time, David was still alive. She was going to see him soon, hold him, tell him that they were never meant to be apart.

Just a few more minutes.

*   *   *

James crept down the darkened hallway. He moved past a media room, past an empty water cooler, past the visiting team's locker room. On his left, he saw a large garbage canister stuffed full with paper cups and programs. He checked the other end of the corridor. Nobody in sight.

Everything had been going so well until Mary realized that David Baskin was Sinclair's son. Then

550

she panicked. She flailed around until she awoke the sleeping past. The mask that hid all of his deceptions—his useful deceptions—began to crack and fall away. He tried to keep Mary still, but how could he protect Laura and David's relationship without telling his wife what she had made him do all those years ago? The whole foundation that supported his family would crumble into worthless ruins. Families, like lives, are fragile things. They are held together with flimsy tissue. Stretch that tissue too far . . .

He moved forward. Up ahead, he could see the entrance ramp. The players jogged down this very hall and out that ramp to the sound of swelling applause or boos. Light cascaded in from the playing area. The sound of dribbling became louder.

James had been in this building just a few days ago for the opening game of the Celtics' new season. He had come with high hopes, with the genuine belief that the worst was behind them. But he was so wrong. That visit to the Garden, that damn opening game, had unraveled the spool of lies like no other occasion ever had. Judy had been only one loose thread that needed immediate attention.

The other had been Stan Baskin.

Stan had recognized James at the basketball game. He knew that James had killed his father. But instead of seeking vengeance, Stan Baskin had decided to turn a profit by playing a little game of blackmail. Disgusting. What kind of sense of family did a man like that have? James quickly realized that a pay-off would do no good. Any man who could be bought off by his father's murderer could

551

not be trusted to remain silent. Furthermore, this scum was seriously involved with his oldest daughter. James would not allow Gloria to fall in love with such a man. So once again, what choice did James have? Only one, really.

He silenced Stan for good.

The entrance way was only a few yards away. The time had come. No more mere clipping away at the weeds to improve the appearance. He needed to dig deep and rip up the evil by the roots, to destroy it in one bold stroke. Then they would all be safe.

Drastic situations called for drastic measures. And in this case, that meant murder. He would not shy away from the unpleasantness of what must be done. Personal feeling had to be put aside.

One last murder.

He pressed his back up against the wall. He leaned forward and peered out. David was performing dribbling drills near center court. He was stationary, the ball moving in a figure eight between his legs.

'It's good for the hand-eye coordination, Dr Ayars.'
'Please. Call me James.'

He closed his eyes and pushed the memory away. Then he dared another peek. David's back was to him. Silently, James moved out from the entrance way and ducked behind a row of courtside seats. David had not heard a thing. He just continued dribbling in figure eights, now using two balls, each traveling in a different direction. James slowly raised his head and glanced out like a soldier in a foxhole. David stared straight toward the basket at the opposite end of the court. He did not watch the basketballs as they moved in a blur beneath him. The orange spheres were like well-trained animals who obeyed his every command.

'How do you do that, David? How can you dribble so fast without looking down?'

'I practice.'

'You never watch the ball when you're dribbling?'

'Never. There are too many other things to watch.'

James was close enough now, only ten yards away. He would not miss from here. He reached into his pocket and gently slid the gun into his hand. Once again, the weapon felt so right.

The time had come. Tears welled in his eyes. Not now. He had to save his daughter, his family. He had to end this thing once and for all.

He took aim.

*　　　*　　　*

Gloria pulled the car into the abandoned North Station Garden parking lot. They circled around to Area B where the side entrance was. When they reached that lot, Laura nearly screamed. Her chest tightened to the point where she could barely breathe.

'No,' she whispered. 'NO!'

Laura jumped out of the car before it came to a complete stop. She sprinted toward the side door, passing the one car in the lot, a familiar car.

Her father's car.

*　　　*　　　*

James's hand shook, but it no longer mattered. The target was within range. All he had to do was pull the trigger. It would all be over. Once again, peace would descend over his family. The past would be foiled before it could destroy any more lives. It would rise no more.

His thumb pulled back the hammer.

That was when he heard the door swing open.

The heavy metal door banged hard against the wall, the sound echoing all the way down the hall and into the arena. David turned around quickly. He froze when he saw James.

'Daddy!' a voice screamed from the distance. It was Laura's voice. He could hear her footsteps as she ran toward them both.

Time was running out. There was no time to dawdle. He had a job to do, and whether his daughter was here or not, he would do it. This was, after all, for her benefit. Once again, he aimed the gun.

David's eyes met James's. He said just one word: 'Don't.'

James chose to ignore the request. His finger squeezed the trigger. The gun fired.

*   *   *

Laura heard the gunshot.

'NO!' she shouted.

She raced down the hall, turned right, and sprinted with everything she had toward the entrance ramp. In the distance, she could hear somebody running away.

Oh please, oh please, oh please . . . not again. Don't let me lose him twice.

But when she reached the playing area, when she crossed the portal that David had happily jogged through so many times, her heart fell into the pit of her stomach.

'No . . .'

Blood. Blood on the floor.

She ran toward the dark red substance that flowed freely over the parquet floor. Her world, already unglued, began to melt away into nothing. When Laura finally looked down, she saw the still body. His head lay in a murky puddle of blood.

Laura screamed.

EPILOGUE

Laura drove herself. Gloria and Serita had volunteered to go with her and wait in the car, but Laura had decided to go alone. She wanted no help.

Her heart swelled in her chest as she made the right turn into the familiar parking lot. She was dressed conservatively in a dark Svengali business suit. Her hair was pulled back away from her face, highlighting her high cheekbones. As always, she wore very little makeup. As always, she was breathtaking.

Laura circled the car around the decrepit edifice. The parking lot was completely empty, the sun just beginning to form dull streaks across the pavement. She checked the time on her watch and saw it was nearly seven in the morning. The ride had only taken her fifteen minutes but in Laura's world, fifteen minutes was suddenly a very long time.

She parked the car not too far from where her father had parked a scant two days earlier. Two days and a lifetime ago.

A moment later, Laura opened the car door and stepped out. Yes, she thought, it was finally time. The past had claimed its vengeance. It had punished the guilty and struck down the innocent. But now it was over. At long last, the past would succumb to the present and future.

She strode toward the side entrance door. Her hand pulled the door back and she stepped inside. Like two days ago, the hall was dark. Like two days ago, there was a ball being dribbled in the distance.

Laura walked neither very fast nor very slowly

toward the court. Her legs felt numb but her pulse raced. Her heart beat so hard she was sure it was visible to the naked eye.

When she reached the entrance ramp, she stopped and took a deep breath. Her body quivered. She stepped out.

The player continued to dribble and shoot. He had not yet seen her.

It took her a few moments to find her voice. Finally she called out to him.

'Hello.'

Mark Seidman's body went rigid when he heard the voice. The ball rolled away. He turned toward her slowly, hesitantly, as though he were afraid to reconfirm with his eyes what his ears already knew to be true. When he finally did see her standing by the entrance ramp, his eyes darted away. He spun back toward the basket and retrieved the ball.

'Hello,' he managed.

She stepped in and sat down in one of the box seats. 'Do you mind if I watch for a few minutes?' she asked.

He shrugged. 'No one is supposed to be in here.'

'I won't stay long.'

He glanced at the clock on the scoreboard, his eyes never swerving in her direction. 'I really have to be going.'

'Wait,' she said. 'Don't go. I'd like to watch you shoot. Please.'

Mark broke his own rule: he chose to stare at the dribbling basketball rather than look up. 'Okay,' he said after a few moments had passed, 'but I can't stay very long.'

He began to shoot, missing more shots than he could remember missing since he was eight years old. His arm shook. His fingers were no longer nimble. Dare he speak to her? Dare he even look in her direction? After some time had passed, he said, 'I'm sorry about your father.'

'Thank you,' she said. 'My father was a troubled man who in the end thought the only way to protect his family was to kill himself.' She swallowed away the lump in her throat. 'Nothing can hurt him anymore. I think he is finally at peace.'

He said nothing.

'Mark, can I ask you a question?'

He dribbled the ball away from her voice. 'Yes.'

'What do you know about my husband's death?'

Shrug. 'Just what I read in the paper. He got caught up in some rough tides and drowned.'

She leaned forward in her chair. Tears were beginning to form in her eyes. 'Not exactly. That's just what David wanted everyone to think.'

Mark continued to dribble, his eyes never leaving the floor.

'We were in Australia on our honeymoon when it happened,' she continued, her eyes staring off with the memory. 'We were so in love, so goddamn happy. It was like the whole world had been created just for us. He could make me laugh. He could make me cry.' She stopped. 'He could make me *feel*, you know what I mean?'

Mark turned his back toward her. 'I don't understand why you're telling me this.'

She ignored his statement. 'Before he died, David visited my mother at a hotel near the one where we were staying.'

With her words, Mark's body spasmed. He still would not turn around.

'She told him some things he found very

upsetting.'

'Why are you telling—?'

'But she was wrong.'

He hunched over as though in pain. His hand reached up toward his face and wiped his eyes, but he still refused to show her anything but his back. He began to dribble mindlessly. 'Wrong about what?'

Laura's leg began to shake. Waves of emotion kept crashing over her. Her breathing hitched. Her words came quickly. 'She had an affair with your father, that part was true, and she did get pregnant—'

'I don't know what you're talking—'

'—but the baby was aborted.'

He stopped dribbling. His hand flew up to his mouth as though he were stifling a scream. 'What?'

Laura moved toward him, his back still facing her. 'We are not brother and sister.'

He spun around. His eyes flew open wide. His face crumpled into a mask of confusion. 'But . . . ?' After all this time, after all this suffering . . . 'Not brother and sister?'

'No, David,' she said. 'That baby was aborted. I'm not your sister.'

He stared at her. His eyes filled with tears. 'How . . . ?' He stopped. His mind felt like it was being torn apart. Reality spun out of control. He tried to steady himself, tried to comprehend what she was saying.

'Please,' he began in a soft voice, 'please tell me it's not a dream.'

She shook her head, her tears flowing freely. 'It's not, David. I swear it's not.'

He looked at her. His bleak eyes suddenly

flickered with hope. She ran toward him and threw her arms around his body, clinging to him tightly. David held her, his eyes squeezed shut. So many torturous days, so many tears, so many times he dreamed about holding her again . . .

'Don't you ever leave me again,' she whispered.

'Never,' he uttered. 'I promise.'

They hugged fiercely, not letting go, not daring to even loosen their grip for fear that one of them would slip away and be gone forever. They stayed that way for a very long time, letting the past dissolve away and the healing begin.

David smiled through his tears. 'Do you still want to have children?' he asked.

She laughed. 'What about having rabbits?'

'Rabbits? Okay we'll have both. Rabbits and children.'

She nodded. 'But first things first. Where did you get that awful curly blond hair?'

'You don't like it?'

'You look like a character from *Godspell*. It has to go.'

'I'm kinda used to it.'

'T.C. must have picked it out. He has no taste. And your new face. You know how I hate pretty boys—'

He stopped her with a kiss. 'That's still the only way to keep you quiet, huh?'

'Then don't just stand there, Baskin. Shut me up.'

KE 213